Ethereal Secrets

Shadows of Otherside Book 3

Whitney Hill

Benu Media
6409 Fayetteville Rd
Ste 120 #155
Durham, NC 27713
(984) 244-0250
benumedia.com

To receive special offers, release updates, and bonus content, sign up for our newsletter: go.benumedia.com/newsletter

ISBN (ebook): 978-1-7344227-5-7
ISBN (pbook): 978-1-7344227-6-4

Library of Congress Control Number: 2020925491

Cover Designer: Pintado (99Designs)
Editor: Jeni Chappelle (Jeni Chappelle Editorial)

For those who have reached turning points, and those who are picking up the pieces of stories that began long before their time.

Part I

Chapter 1

The part of my thigh left bare by my denim shorts stuck a little as I bounced my leg. I caught myself and stopped. The slick plastic chairs at Raleigh's police department were more than a little gross if you had just come in from an unusually hot, muggy, North Carolina spring day, but I tried to get my nerves in check. I was here as an independent private investigator wrapping up a job, not a perp. Acting like the latter wouldn't score me any points when I was trying to close a case, get paid, and keep Otherside safe.

For the last few weeks, a lich lord had terrorized the Triangle. Not that anybody in Raleigh, Durham, or Chapel Hill had had any idea that an undead sorcerer was what had caused them all to feel like they wanted to kill everyone else and then themselves. Nah. That was an Otherside secret, one that I, as the arbiter of a new alliance, was trying to keep on the down low. The first few months of this new job had been rough.

I wasn't used to being in a position of authority or power. Quite the opposite. Yet I was now the voice of Otherside in the Triangle, at least as far as my allies were concerned, and they were some of the most powerful folks around. Torsten's vampire coterie, the varied weres of the Southeast United States, the elven House Monteague and their allies House Luna, the Djinn Council, and my own little group of fellow elementals—everyone was counting on me to sell this so that we could all go back to planning the Reveal. The coming out of the local supernatural community to the humans.

Catch number one: my former legal guardian and Otherside's mob boss leader, Callista, was planning a Reveal of her own.

Catch number two: I'd only just come out to Otherside myself a few months ago, being a sylph and therefore under an elven death threat which was, for the moment, suspended.

Catch number three: My powers had recently expanded, and I could manipulate not only Air but also—to a lesser extent—Fire. It was unheard of, and it made some people nervous.

None of that would matter if the humans figured out a corrupted sorcerer was responsible for stealing all the bodies from the Raleigh city morgue and raising them as zombies, so here I was, trying to buy us all some more breathing room.

"The detective's ready for you, Ms. Finch."

I recognized the heavyset Black officer. "Davis, right? From the callout to Mason Farm?"

He smiled. "That's me."

"Did your K-9 officer have any more trouble with her dog?" I rose and gathered the leather backpack that doubled as both purse and camera bag.

"No, ma'am." He led me back to the space where Detective Rice, my Raleigh PD contact, had his desk. "Parton says things have been feeling better lately, although she's ready to snap Johnson's nose off if he doesn't quit messing with her about it."

That just redoubled my suspicion that the dog handler they'd had on the callout was a sensitive of some description. Normally it was the sort of thing I'd have reported to Callista in my role as a Watcher, but demanding my semi-independence had strained our relationship. And when I say "strained," I mean she was furious that I'd stood up to her, withheld information to do so, and was forming my own power base.

It had been an interesting few months. Not in a good way.

"Hope you've got something good for him," Davis said in a quiet drawl as we approached the desk. "He's got a bug up his ass about this one."

"Thanks." I hoped I had something good as well. More importantly, that it was believable enough to close the case.

Detective Clayton Rice unfolded from his chair as he spotted us. I don't know how such a buff man fit into such a small chair, but I figured that was half the reason he was in a mood. The other half might be how tight his dress shirt fit him or the fact that he felt obliged to iron a crease into his pants. He was bald, and his skin was the same dark umber shade as Duke's.

I pushed aside a momentary pang for my now-estranged guardian. Making the alliance hadn't come without a cost. Sometimes it felt like I'd paid more than most.

When we shook hands, Detective Rice's grip was firm, but he didn't play that nonsense of trying to crush my hand. It was the first time we'd met in person. I decided I liked him, even if his scowl sent Davis packing.

"So you're the PI Chan keeps raving about," he said in a bass rumble.

"I've helped Detective Chan with a few things from time to time, sure." Chapel Hill was the first police department I'd worked with. Tom Chan had sent my name to a few of his fellows, probably in the hopes I'd finally agree to that coffee date he kept asking for if he got me more work.

"Talk to me."

I took the seat he indicated. "My working theory is that the bodies were taken by a medical experimentation ring."

I wished I had elven powers of Aether to make the lie go down a little easier. My elven captor-turned-ally Troy Monteague would have done this, but I was the one with the case. Besides, a little lie was less suspicious than the heavy-handed tactics the

Darkwatch were prone to using when they needed to do an Otherside cover-up.

"A medical experimentation ring." Detective Rice's voice couldn't be any flatter. "Really."

I shrugged. "A few discarded medical-grade implements, some nasty-looking cages, imprints where generators might have sat...that's the only thing that makes sense to me."

"Where are they now?"

"Who knows? They cleaned up their operation before I could move in for more details. Torched the bodies and the hole they were in and skipped town. Tire treads in the mud match heavy vehicles, likely the stolen vans." Definitely not Troy's SUV, of course, or my Honda hatchback, both of which had been there. "Some sick shit out there too. Pieces of animals and I don't even know what scattered around. A real mess."

Detective Rice steepled his fingers and studied me over them. His focused quiet was a sharp contrast to Detective Chan's studied idleness with doodles and chattering, and I wondered how well they got on.

Focus. Sell this, or Troy will step in. I pulled a manilla folder out of my backpack and slid it onto the desk. "Photos and an address for the scene. There were also some personal effects. I left them in place in case your team needed to maintain chain of custody, rather than have me screw with the scene." Personal effects that had been carefully planted in the piles of ash that were all that remained of the corpses after the local witch coven sanitized the lich's lair. Maria had recovered the effects from the zombies that had been sent to attack Claret and test how difficult it would be to overthrow the Raleigh vampire coterie operating out of the wine bar's basement. A little realism and truth to tighten the lie. "That was all that was left of them."

Rice leaned back in his chair, arms bulging as he crossed them. "Why wouldn't they sell the effects?"

I mirrored his body language and kept my breathing even, willing him to believe me so that we didn't have to get the elven Darkwatch in. I was supposed to be handling this. "You're breaking into morgues with advanced tech and selling body parts. You really gonna risk getting caught on a small-time fence for a gold-plated ring and a Tiffany bracelet when you've already made bank with organs?"

A small crack in Rice's façade gave me hope. "Fair." His eyes fell on the folder. "I almost wish you'd just collected the effects and saved me the trouble."

"Not much trouble saved if someone asked why the civilian PI is playing CSI, though, is there?"

The crack widened to a small smile. "Also fair. Fine. I find the whole story outrageous, but since this wasn't a violent crime, I need to close it. If there are no bodies to recover, the effects will have to do for closure." He tapped a finger on the desk, his dark eyes distant. "One thing doesn't line up. Why did they go to Mason Farm?"

Shit. I'd been hoping he wouldn't bring that up. The lich had gone for an artifact, one we didn't know about because we had yet to track down the accomplice we thought had stolen the vans and acted as chauffeur. It was top of the agenda for the alliance, at least until the vampires kicked off the Reveal.

"Beats me," I said. "I bet they didn't count on crashing the van though." When Detective Rice kept studying me, I slouched in my chair and offered a Cheshire Cat's grin. "Happy to look into it for you. On a new contract."

He frowned at the reminder that finding vans was not what I'd been hired to do. I had—as far as he was concerned— tracked down the morgue's missing bodies, which *was* what I'd been hired to do. My friend the medical examiner, Doctor Michael Miller, had sent over a statement that Rice didn't know

I knew about, confirming that the effects matched photos of those on the missing bodies.

Doc Mike was a latent necromancer who'd only just discovered he had powers, thanks to this case and my bending Otherside rules to give us space to work it out. I'd also rescued him from the lich, with help from Troy. Doc was feeling pretty grateful and also pretty keen to put this to bed before scrutiny fell on him. Not only was he a public servant, but his powers didn't fit in his view of what a good Christian should be able to do. I wasn't sure whether he was more worried that the state or his church would find out about him. Either way, I sympathized. I'd lived in fear that someone would find out what I was up until earlier this year. Still did, if to a lesser extent.

With another glance at the manilla folder, Rice extended his hand. "I think we have everything we need to close this one up. Hell, with all the violence going on lately, I'll be glad to have one less case to worry about."

I shook his hand and decided to take that as thanks. "My pleasure, Detective. You know where to find me if you need any more assistance."

As soon as I was in my car, I let out a heavy sigh of relief and tilted my head back to look out the sunroof. My shielding slipped for a second, and the hot air slipping out of my cracked windows gusted a little before I regained my grasp on Air.

Maybe I could do this, after all. Most of the others in the alliance disdained mundanes, or thought of them as food, but I had a soft spot for them. I'd played human most of my life, keeping my elemental powers under wraps and refusing to develop them until an elven terrorist had walked into my office and hired me. Shit got real weird after that.

I called Maria as I pulled out of the parking lot. Raleigh was vampire territory, and I needed to check in on the Reveal. "It's done," I said when she answered. "Raleigh PD will close the case."

"Nice job, sugarplum," she said, practically purring in a way that was beginning to affect me more than it used to. Whether that was Maria's growing power or the recent breakup with my boyfriend, I didn't know. Roman had opted to return to his estranged and toxic werewolf pack and family in Asheville. He hadn't wasted any time putting Durham—and me—in his rear view. That was fair, I guess, but I'd let myself fall for him. He'd said he'd always put me first, until he didn't.

"You're thinking about the wolf again," Maria said when I took too long to say anything else.

"I'm going through my to-do list." I ran my free hand over my curls, irritated that she'd busted me. "Not that it's your business either way. How's planning going?"

"Come to Claret. I can fill you in and—bonus!—I'm excellent with to-do lists. Just ask Torsten."

I should have said no. Maria was an inveterate flirt, though it was really just a cover for how fucking clever she was. She'd also chosen me for her next long hunt. Going to see her would probably send all of the wrong kinds of signals, to literally everyone.

Fuck it. I was tired of being forced to be separate from everyone else. Not only that, but I was kind of starting to care about the other members of the alliance in a weird way that I was more than a little uncomfortable with. Kind of like they were family.

Family hadn't turned out so well for me. My parents had died shortly after my birth. Callista and the djinn who had raised me had saved me only to use me. Most recently, Troy killed my big-sister-slash-cousin when she came at me with a bronze knife. I'd let myself start thinking about a future with Roman, and he'd left. Most of my own people, the other elementals in the Triangle

I'd only recently discovered, shunned me because of my associations with the elves. It all left my heart more than a little bruised and raw. I hadn't heard from Val, my dea friend, in a week; I assumed she was still recovering from having been kidnapped and a captive of the lich lord. That, and a guilty part of me was afraid that she blamed me for bringing elementals to everyone's attention. Including the lich.

I pushed aside my discomfort. "I'll be there in fifteen."

"Looking forward to it, poppet."

Chapter 2

I'd never been to Claret in the day. The vampiric staff might be sleeping but not because they had to. Contrary to popular legend, vampires could be out in daylight, although the effects of direct exposure worsened as they got older. Anything that damaged cellular growth, other than aging, did a number on them: fire, UV light—hell, even the glucose from refined carbs. Vamps were the original health nuts. The virus kept them alive after their first death, but they had to feed it plenty of animal-based iron and protein. Blood was the easiest way for them to do that, although most of them just enjoyed it and preferred to indulge their heightened hunting instincts over alternatives.

The psychic presence of the coterie's master, Torsten, weighed on me as I ignored the closed sign and knocked on the front door of the bar. Something about the power signature felt different, but I couldn't put my finger on it. Probably just that it was daylight.

The door swung open seemingly by itself, and I stepped in quickly, trying to be sensitive to the fact that whoever had opened it was trying to avoid daylight by staying on the side protected by the bar's heavy window shading.

"Don't you have underlings to open doors for you?" I teased as Maria shut and locked the door behind me.

"Noah is too valuable to waste on that medieval shit," she said. "These days, anyway. And you, baby doll, smell too good to trust to anyone else. Especially now that you've been practicing regularly. Got the hang of Fire yet?"

"No," I said, annoyed both with the reminder that I was a worthy hunt and that I wasn't making better progress with my new element. It had only been a week, but Air came so naturally that all I had to learn there was control. Fire danced away like a will-o-the-wisp. I wanted to ask Val about it but…yeah.

"Hm. Could have fooled me. You smell like thunderstorms with a hint of wildfire now." Maria grinned wide enough to show fangs. "Spicy. I like it."

I gave her a flat look to cover the flutter in my stomach. "Like it in your head, or I'm heading right back out."

She only smiled wider before heading behind the bar. Her peplum dress in a rose quartz pink would have looked ridiculous on me. On her, it just played up the soft-looking waves of her long emerald hair and the grace of her movements. "Drink?"

"No, thanks. I'm driving."

"I don't believe that stopped you the first time you were here."

She was right; it hadn't. But I'd been trying to fit in then and not concerned with how my growing elemental powers might also be triggering a growth in the Chaotic results of my drinking alcohol. Being fully half elf and half djinni, the two sides of Aether were perfectly balanced in me—and so was the potential for Chaos magic, including an embarrassing propensity to rouse the passions of those already attracted to me when I was drunk. Val called it being a maenad. I called it fucking annoying.

"Not today, thanks, Maria."

"Work, work, work, always working."

"Somebody has to." I allowed a small, teasing smile to curl my lips. I liked Maria, even when I wanted to be annoyed by her or keep my distance. Raleigh's number two vampire might be hunting me, but she hadn't crossed any lines.

She cracked open a can of lemon sparkling water and slid it over to me. "So. Otherside is safe from mundane attention once more, thanks to our dashing leader."

I winced. "Don't let Callista hear you say that."

Maria shrugged. "You've done more for us in a few months than she has in decades. Centuries, maybe. She's gotten too bloody comfortable."

"Don't let her hear you say that either. I like not being a pain pretzel in her basement." I shuddered as I remembered Callista's threat to me. Nails of bronze inserted under my skin, a slow poison that would cut off and prevent my connection to Air, and a session in her dungeon. Not the fun, sexy kind either. "Please tell me this means we can move forward with plans for the Reveal though."

"It sure does, sugarplum. If the humans aren't thinking of zombies and the icky undead, we're free to be the sexy rock stars they believe us to be." She skimmed her hands up her body and shimmied.

I sipped my drink, pretending to be unimpressed by her lithe movements. "Awesome. Torsten's on board?"

"He thinks it's less than wise. But he knows how close we came to disaster with the Modernists," she said, referring to the internal battle the weres had helped her with to solidify our new alliance. "Those idiots have agreed that a Reveal will do as a compromise. It saves Torsten from having to slaughter too many more of his coterie. The sorcerous necromancer is still an issue though." She wrinkled her nose in disgusted annoyance.

Torsten being on board was a relief, at least. Groups of Othersiders occasionally had wars, whether within or between factions, but the modern era of cell phones and YouTube made it virtually impossible to cover up that much blood in the streets. The elves had hackers, good ones, but not enough of them to catch everything. Especially not with the new genetic test developed by a healthcare startup right here in the Triangle. Too many data points were converging, and we had to out ourselves in a managed Reveal before we were dragged from the shadows by some crisis. Doing it our way might allow us to control the narrative.

At least, we hoped it would. If it didn't, the gods hounding my dreams with whispers of remaking the world would be the least of my worries. The memory of Neith and Mixcoatl stalking me made my stomach clench.

"Walk me through the plan." I shook off thoughts of the gods.

Maria's nostrils flared, and she narrowed her eyes at me. "Something on your mind, poppet?"

"Nothing you need to worry about. The plan?"

She pouted but launched into the latest. "Torsten's agreed that I should be the one to do the interviews. If this goes badly, we won't have exposed our true leadership. I'm strong enough now that I should survive anything except beheading, being set on fire, or being staked out in the desert."

Ew. I hoped it wouldn't come to that.

"Plus you're just more...palatable," I said, thinking of the thousand-year-old Viking. His presence alone was off-putting, he wasn't nearly as attractive or contemporary as Maria, and he'd spent less time actively navigating the modern world.

"Well, aren't you sweet," Maria said with what might have been genuine pleasure. I flushed, and she laughed before continuing. "But speaking of all the grisly ways for me to die, we'll need to work out security."

"Of course," I said. As a private investigator, security wasn't my gig. But I'd been doing well in hapkido, I'd gotten my concealed weapons permit, and I could probably sort out some kind of detail of more qualified people for Maria from the weres or the elves. "I'll figure something out."

She preened. "Now I really feel like a rock star."

I smiled in spite of myself. "So. You, on TV. Local stations, national…"

"Local for in-person, with call-ins to a few morning shows showing to key demographics."

"Morning shows. Nice touch." With the coming of summer pushing dawn earlier, that would demonstrate that some of the human legends, like daylight restrictions, were untrue, thus opening the door that others—like bloodlust—might be as well. "You think people will go along with it?"

She shrugged, face hardening. "We have preparations ready for those who react badly. Noah is fortifying the nest and a few outlying properties. We've also scheduled a…what's it called when the police do it? A ride-along?"

I nodded.

"One of those, with a local station. A day in the life of an average vampire."

"Noah?"

Maria winked. "Of course. He's charming."

"And yours, and breaks the mold of the old white vampire?" Noah had been either Black or biracial in life. Melanin still graced him in undeath, leaving him looking like a golden god with rich brown eyes.

"Precisely." For all her played-up amusement, a hard, calculating look had come into her eyes. "There's a danger to it. Americans, in particular, are funny about race. Bad enough that he would be Black *or* gay *or* a vampire, for some of them. To be all three, plus attractive and successful besides…" She pursed her lips. "I worry he's putting a target on his back. I didn't ask him to do it though. He saw the opportunity and the optics and volunteered. Far be it from me to deny him a chance to rise in the coterie."

I reached out to squeeze her hand, not having realized how deeply she thought about her people's needs as fully actualized beings or how much she cared for Noah's development in particular. "We'll protect him."

Fire sparked in her eyes. "We'd better. He's the best of my fledglings. In five hundred years, I've never found base material so good as him." She frowned and hugged herself. "Besides, I'll need a second."

"That sounds ominous." My investigative sense tingled.

With a wince, Maria busied herself with tidying the already immaculate bar. "Nothing to worry about, poppet."

The tingle strengthened. She was lying, though whether it was something to do with Torsten or entrepreneurial plans of her own was not something she'd share with me just now. I let it go, knowing better than to push a vampire on her own turf. "TV and interviews. Anything else?"

That perked her up. She spun back to me with a wide smile. "A ball."

"A what?"

"A *ball*, Arden. Guests. Dancing. Bubbly." She waggled her eyebrows, excited by the possibilities.

"I don't—why a ball?" Sweat broke out on my brow despite the cool air of the bar. The only time I really danced was when I got shitfaced in the woods behind my house and indulged in a little fun under the moonlight, where there was no risk of anyone being affected by any Chaos magic that might rise from my dancing. I *could* dance. I just didn't do it with other people.

Maria cocked her head, amused by my reticence. "Because it's fun and glamorous and lets a few carefully selected humans get close to the 'exotic' vampires."

My mind raced along the likely angles for that. "Carefully selected as in, politicians and the donors who own them."

She clapped, delighted. "Oh, Arden. You would make the perfect solidaire. Skilled, sharp, attractive, and powerful. Shame you're so afraid of your own potential."

I frowned and started to deny that then stopped. She'd hit a nerve, one that stung me deeply, all the more because it was how Callista had kept me under her heel for so many years. That it still bothered me meant I needed to go home and sit with it a spell.

"Introspective as well," Maria mused. Then her smile turned wicked. "No wonder our dear Prince of Monteague is as taken with you as I am."

That snapped me out of my thoughts. My lip twisted. "Fuck off. He can't stand me. He *drowned* me, Maria."

"He can't stand you." She tapped her lips. "Which is why he risked pissing Torsten off to hang around in the shadows when the zombies attacked the basement? That's a very good trick, by the way. I haven't seen an elf able to fully draw shadow and mask his presence like that since…the Marquis de Sade?"

I shook off the part about the Marquis de Sade being an elf and addressed the important bit. "He was protecting his House's interests. Or the Darkwatch. Like he always does. I'm sure it's a mission, nothing to do with me personally."

A furious roar echoed up from the basement, cutting off her response.

I was off my stool and reaching for the elf-killer in my backpack before I realized what I was doing. The enchanted lead knife wouldn't do anything at all against even the lowliest of vampires. I reached for Air instead.

Maria had frozen into the impossible stillness of the undead, her eyes glazing over. Then she hissed in pain and cringed. "You need to go." Her words shaved out through a grater of pain. "Now."

"Are you—"

"Now, Arden!"

If whatever was happening downstairs was not something she thought I could help with, I was more than happy to get the fuck out. I fled for the warm sunshine as she headed for the back stairs almost faster than I could see.

Chapter 3

I'd hoped to take the rest of the evening off, but a text from Roman scuttled that plan. It was written with his usual inattention to capitalization or punctuation, consisting of just one line: *vikki arriving at my place 10pm wants to see you asap.* A string of numbers that I assumed was her phone number followed.

"Thanks for the heads-up, Roman," I muttered, wondering why he'd left it so late.

The leopards and the jaguars had ceded territory to the wolves, but as far as I knew, the transfer hadn't been completed. Vikki's arrival seemed like it should involve some kind of ceremony, knowing weres, but I had no idea what the protocol was for introducing a visiting were to the locals. Neutral ground would be best, I was sure. Roman had welcomed Sergei with a ceremony involving meat and mead, but I didn't know if that was a werewolf thing or a general courtesy.

After stewing over it for a good five minutes, I scoffed at myself.

"Ask. Just ask." The whole point of having all these allies was not having to stumble from one incident to the next until they conjoined and became a clusterfuck.

Terrence picked up after a few rings, sounding distracted. "What can I do you for, Miss Arden?"

The wereleopard's low, easy drawl held a hint of annoyance. Fair, given that I only ever called when something happened.

Reminding myself that that was literally my job as arbiter, I loosed some of my tension in a small breeze and said, "Hey, Obong Little. I—"

"Uh oh, she's coming with respect and titles. Must be a big one." A hint of a tease had slid in alongside the annoyance in his tone, a cat swatting at an irritating cub when it really wanted to just lay in the sun and nap.

"I'll let you be the judge." I kept my voice even. "The Volkovs are sending a representative to prep for the Reveal and, I imagine, claim their new territory. I thought you might want to know before she arrived in town."

An interested rumble made the hairs on my neck stand up. "She? Not little Vikki, by chance?"

"That's who I've been advised to look for. Arriving in Durham about 10 P.M."

"Interesting choice." Terrence mulled that over. "I don't expect you're up on were politics?"

I winced, wondering how bad it would be for me to admit my ignorance and going for it anyway. "I'm not, actually. That's the other half of why I'm calling—I was hoping you might advise how I can avoid offending Acacia Thorn, Jade Tooth, or Blood Moon."

"Asking for help from folks who know better? How refreshing. You might actually be a leader and not just a boss, Miss Arden."

"I meant what I said when we set this all up," I said as neutrally as I could manage despite the flush in my cheeks. "I'm not trying to be another Callista, and I promised you a seat and a voice."

"Words are just words, until they're not." When I didn't respond, Terrence added, "I'll arrange the ceremonial items. But we'll need neutral ground. Not one of the state parks. Somewhere more private, in case it goes south."

"Is that likely?" I asked, my stomach sinking. I had to keep shit from boiling over until we could pull off a managed Reveal—and get it done before Callista.

He sighed. "I like Vikki, but she's not coming just as herself this time and after that mess with the boys, I dunno what nonsense old man Volkov is filling his whelps with these days. Better safe than sorry."

"Yeah." I thought fast, not liking the solution I arrived at but telling myself it was for the greater good. "Y'all can use my place. The yard is fenced, and the property backs straight onto Eno."

Silence met me.

"I'm sorry," I said, my wince blowing into a full-on grimace. "I know you said no state parks, but I'm in—"

"You'd offer us your land? For a pan-were council?"

Words stuck in my throat. What the hell had I just done? "Yes? Is that bad?"

"That you'd extend that much trust and risk predators on your land? It's a powerful statement of your certainty in yourself, but more importantly, it's an honor. One that Callista hasn't extended, not in generations."

The warmth in his voice made me flush. "Oh. Well, my kobold friend will expect tribute, but I mean, whatever we have to do to keep the peace and our words, right?"

"Right. A moment, Miss Arden." Terrence muffled the phone, but not before I heard him shout for Ximena, the jefa of the werejaguar prowl allied with his leap. They spent enough time together that I wondered if they were really just allies or a little more. I caught an exchange in a disbelieving tone before the phone crackled.

"Arden?" Ximena said. "Is this true? You invite Jade Tooth and Acacia Thorn to meet with Blood Moon on your lands?"

I bit back my first response—that they were starting to make me reconsider with this to-do about it. "It seems like the solution that best serves all our needs at this time," I said carefully. "I know my land. A kobold will help keep the peace. Y'all might not be revealing yourselves anytime soon, but that doesn't mean you're any less deserving of a say."

"You just made the three dominance battles I fought this week worth it. We'll be there," Ximena said, a blend of relief and pride in her voice.

I tried to stop myself from squirming in discomfort. It was weird being not only seen but respected.

"Sundown, three days from now?" That should give Zanna time to finish the work on my bedroom, trashed in a demon attack last week.

"That'll do, yes. Will Vikki have a second?"

"I don't know." I thought quickly. Sergei had come alone, but from the way he and Roman had spoken about Ana and their mother, there might be different rules for werewolf women. "You can each bring a second. If Vikki's alone, they stay in my house as guests while we talk."

"Agreed. We'll bring tribute for the kobold. Text us the address, and we'll see you soon." Ximena hung up before I could say anything else.

I slumped in my chair, scrubbing my hands over my face before looking around wide-eyed at my house. It wasn't the perpetual state of organized mess that bothered me. My back and shoulders were tight, and I rolled them and my neck, not liking what I'd just done. This was my home, my refuge, my sanctuary. Yet I'd just invited representatives from two wereclans to meet a third here.

Duke and Grimm used to pop by, sometimes, but they were my kin, dysfunctional as that family bond was. They'd raised me, and they'd helped me buy the land, build the place, and set stones with minor protection wardings at the boundaries. I hid from the world here, Otherside and mundane alike. Roman had been the first person other than Zanna that I'd invited inside. Then Troy had broken past the wards and into the house to save me from the rabisu and kept dropping by. I'd sent my three elemental friends and Doc Mike here to lay low after the fight with the lich. After years of being solitary, secret, hidden, not only I but also my home were becoming publicly known.

It scared the bejeezus outta me. I didn't have multiple safehouses like Troy or the safety of a pack, clan, coterie, or House behind me. It was just me and the good graces of those few people who had the foresight and courage to imagine a different future. Sergei had already demonstrated how that could go wrong, allowing Callista to tempt him and, temporarily, the Volkovs, away from supporting me. I was growing stronger, but I was still just one woman. Maria might help, but I didn't like leaning on other people's power.

I gave myself one more minute to be worried and anxious then shoved it all inside a mental box and shut the lid. In Otherside, fear made you prey. I was nobody's prey, and I had work to do before the meeting.

* * *

Something told me it would be better to go see Vikki in person. The little nudges of intuition usually came when I was on a case, but whatever the circumstance, I always listened. Duke had the Sight, and while I wasn't djinn enough to see the future, I did seem to get hints about it sometimes. I waited until eleven, then headed over to Roman's aging manufactured home across from the Cabe Lands Trail at another section of Eno River State Park, not far from me.

Roman's old Ford F-150 was parked out front. A pang hit me at the sight of it, despite my determination to let my ex go. A woman I took to be Vikki lounged in a tatty lawn chair when I arrived. She ignored the bugs swarming in the porch light as she sipped from a can of beer and watched me do a U-turn so I'd be facing the right way to leave. A massive wolf lay beside her, a studded collar around its neck. It lifted its head when I rolled onto the patchy lawn and parked then rose and bared its teeth in a soundless snarl when I got out of the car.

"Down, Sergei," the woman muttered, keeping her eyes on me as she chugged her beer and crumpled the finished can.

I froze, eyes darting to the wolf as he thumped to the ground with poor grace and fixed me with silver eyes I thought I might recognize. *Sergei? What's he doing back here? And as a wolf?*

Tossing the can in the general direction of the door, the woman stood. She was a little shorter than me and built like a gymnast—muscled, heavy in the shoulder, and somehow graceful with it. She had the same pale skin, light eyes, and dark hair as her brothers. She wore her hair long, pulled into a ponytail set at the crown of her head, and she didn't wear any makeup. Cut-off shorts, purple flip-flops, and a worn white T-shirt gave her a down-to-earth look that matched Roman's, a far cry from Sergei's peacockery.

"You must be Arden," she said in a musical voice with a light mountain accent, flicking her eyes over me as she inhaled deeply. "Huh. Roman wasn't exaggerating."

I stopped a good ten feet back, eyeing them both as adrenaline surged. "Vikki?"

"That's me."

"And..." I glanced at the wolf and lifted my eyebrows, wanting to be certain, because why the fuck would she bring him back to the Triangle?

"You remember Sergei, don't you?" A shit-eating grin showed a gap in her front teeth as she patted the wolf on the head like he was just a big dog. Whether the grin was for me or her brother playing wolfdog, I didn't know, and I didn't like it.

"'Fraid so," I said. "Can we talk? Inside?"

"Sure," she drawled, casually giving me her back as she took a few steps to the door and opened it. I flashed back to Sergei's reluctance to do the same thing and wondered if it was confidence or arrogance on Vikki's part.

When I hesitated, darting a glance at Sergei, she snapped her fingers at him. "Git, you. Be a good dog."

With a silvery glare, Sergei slunk inside. I followed without further hesitation, knowing that Vikki was testing me. She wasn't what I'd expected. Where the baby Volkov had come in designer suits and a top-of-the-line Range Rover, Vikki would fit right in with this neighborhood and with Terrence and Ximena. An equal, not someone trying to be better than everyone else. Clever. Roman had been right about her having more political savvy than Sergei.

I felt Vikki's gaze on me and pretended to be unbothered as I made myself at home and flopped onto the couch. The flicker of irritation on her brow was so like Roman's that it almost hurt, but I allowed myself to be soothed by the knowledge that I'd scored a point in whatever game she was playing.

"Beer?" she offered as she shut the door behind us and headed for the fridge.

"No, thanks."

"That's right. Roman said you don't drink in public but not why." The casual tone was a little too casual, like she knew I wasn't going to answer but couldn't help being nosy.

If we were playing games, I'd play.

"I reckon that's my business," I said, using one of my passive abilities as a sylph to mimic Roman's voice perfectly.

Sergei's panting mouth snapped shut, and he snarled again.

Vikki just lifted her eyebrows. "Neat trick. You sound just like him."

"Just one of many talents," I said, reverting back to my own voice and keeping it light. "I hope I don't have to show you the others. Sergei here had to learn the hard way."

Cracking open her beer, Vikki lounged against the counter and studied me before taking a sip. "Understood."

"In that case, welcome to the Triangle. I'm sure Roman filled you in on all the pertinent political considerations?"

"He did, although I look forward to making my own judgments. And claiming our new territory, of course." Her eyes were bluer than those of her brothers, and they danced with amusement for reasons I couldn't see.

"That's why I'm here. You're invited to meet with the Acacia Thorn leopards and the Jade Tooth jaguars at sundown, three days from now. My place. He—" I pointed at Sergei "—is certainly *not* welcome, not after the shit he pulled the last time he was in town."

The amused look slipped from Vikki's face, and she straightened. "You offer your home to broker a deal? As arbiter of this alliance?"

"I do. As long as Sergei stays here. I mean no harm, but I take no shit."

She flapped her hand at her brother as he looked at her and whined. "He'll stay here. He's only here like this as a punishment. Pops is mad that he fucked everything up so badly, and Roman's mad that he got played." Vikki glanced to the side, and I followed her gaze to a bowl full of kibble. "He'll be my faithful hound for now, seeing as a little woman like me can't possibly make it in the big world alone. But now that I'm here, he can stay chained in the yard."

The muscles in her arms and the way she batted her lashes made me laugh. She was probably more capable than either Sergei or Roman, both intellectually and in a fight. Some of the tension in me eased. Maybe that was her intention, but I couldn't help liking her, especially when Sergei yipped and she bared her teeth at him in return.

"Keep that up and you'll stay a dog forever," she said in a low, threatening voice. "And wouldn't it be a damn shame if we had to go and get you fixed?"

Sergei dropped to the floor and showed his belly with alacrity, whining.

"That's what I thought." Vikki nudged him with a toe. "Now, shoo."

Tail low, Sergei gave me one last glare before slinking to the door and letting himself out with a single big paw on the door handle.

"Brothers," Vikki scoffed when the door had swung shut behind him. "Broke my heart to lose Roman. Now getting him back means we might lose Sergei. Fucking mess, but it's on Pops and Sergei. Ma told them not to play it that way."

I kept my eyes on her, not staring her down but not showing weakness as I breathed past the twist in my guts. "So how would you and your mom have played it?"

"Like this," she replied with a shrug, taking a swig from her beer. "Woman to woman. Everything we've heard suggests that you're looking for allies. We get that—no wolf wants to be without a pack. Ma and I said that all we had to do was offer support to secure yours in turn, but the men wanted to make a big play for more. Were we wrong?"

Meeting her direct look with one of my own, I said, "No. You weren't."

She grinned. "Then I'm pleased to say that the Blood Moon clan and the Volkov pack extend our best wishes for the success of this alliance. You're already keeping up your end of the deal by arranging an honorable meeting with the local clans, so I'm all right with setting aside my Plan B for now."

I was suddenly glad that I'd swallowed my pride and called Terrence earlier, rather than trying to fumble my way through this. Was I learning at last?

"I do have one favor to ask," Vikki said, her expression suddenly tight.

Leaning forward on the couch, I asked, "What's that?"

"I need to introduce myself to Torsten's coterie and the Monteagues. Or re-introduce myself, I guess, as a beta female and not a pup. The sooner the better. They've always been a mite touchy about new predators in the vicinity."

With a sigh, I pushed up from the couch.

"This should be fun," I muttered as I pulled out my phone.

Chapter 4

There weren't many places open at midnight that would offer enough privacy for our needs. I refused to go to House Monteague. Getting me to Raleigh or Maria up to Durham would take all night, and I wasn't keen on having Vikki at my place before the other weres—or anyone at all. In the end, we settled on The Umstead. Somehow, the coterie owning the luxury hotel and spa had taken me by surprise, but maybe it shouldn't have. It was the only five-star hotel in the state, with its own acclaimed restaurant, also rated five stars, on a peaceful tract of woodland surrounding a small private lake.

Under any other circumstances, I think Troy and Maria would have told me to go fly a kite. A last-minute meeting involving the three top Otherside species on vampire territory was highly unusual. But a new were in town, combined with the urgency of getting all the little pieces in place for a harmonic Reveal, had everyone far more cooperative than I would otherwise have expected given how much trouble it had been to get them all in an alliance in the first place.

Maria had gotten us a private conference room, the kind big business-types would use to hash out some kind of intimate arrangement. A bottle of amber liquid and a platter of carpaccio, cheeses, olives, and mini toasts waited in the middle when Vikki and I arrived. Maria and Troy shifted to face us with the pinched features of people who had just been bickering. Troy's hair was getting long, and black locks fell over eyes the color of sandstone and moss. He must've been getting some time outside, because his tawny skin had taken on a richer golden tone.

"Well, look who's all grown up." Maria's expression morphed to a warm smile as she rose to greet Vikki with cheek kisses. "I bet you give your brothers a good thrashing."

"When they've earned it," Vikki said, equally as warm. "It's good to see you again, Maria." She bowed and extended her wrist. "I offer myself in gratitude for this irregular meeting."

I frowned, wondering what this was all about.

Maria's eyebrows lifted as she pressed two fingers to the pulse point after a brief hesitation. "Your offer is gracious and unnecessary. Roman was of great assistance in our time of need."

With a grin, Vikki straightened. "I thought so, but Lupa knows I'm not trying to make Sergei's mistakes."

Troy rose, crossing his arms to make muscles bunch under a plain black T-shirt. "Speaking of, I'm surprised you don't have a second." He darted a glance at me. "Or are you claiming Finch?"

"Prince Troy," Vikki said, inclining her head. "I'm here as little ol' me. Sergei was a bad dog, so we left him at Eno."

Maria and Troy exchanged glances. I moved into the room, happy to be ignored by the rest of them, and propped myself up against the wall halfway between everyone else.

Maria cracked open the bottle, and the rich, sweet scent of mead blossomed as she poured into three glasses. She glanced at me as she reached for a fourth, and I shook my head. I was here to observe and facilitate, not take part.

When Vikki had joined her and Troy at the table, Maria lifted her glass. "With meat and mead, we greet our guest."

"With meat and mead, we keep the peace," Vikki and Troy echoed solemnly. They all took a swallow of their drink then ate a slice of carpaccio. I hadn't really thought about vampires consuming anything other than blood, and I frowned until I caught Maria watching me with a knowing look.

"Well." Vikki set her glass back on the table and cocked her head as she took in everyone in the room, me included. "It's not every day that a vampire second and an elven prince greet you in your own fashion. I have to say, I like this new world we're building." She sounded much more serious and sly than she had up until now.

A considering look settled on Maria's face, so different from her usual flirtatiousness that I couldn't help but stare. "It's not every day that weres support vampires, as Roman and our local cats did, or show enough honor to request a cordial meeting immediately upon arriving in town. I have to say, I like your style much better than Sergei's."

Vikki inclined her head politely then turned to Troy. "And you? This might be the first I've seen or heard of elves condescending to ally with anyone or meet on disadvantageous territory."

He didn't react, answering calmly after glancing at me. "Roman's agreeing to assist the vampires freed me to assist Finch with the lich. Working together saved the Triangle—and all of our territories."

"That's right." Vikki narrowed her eyes shrewdly. "The lich. Destroyed by elemental magic but only because an elf set aside a species grudge of several thousand years to let said elemental keep her head. Or had you already tried and failed to kill her?"

Troy's blank expression made Vikki inhale to scent the room then nod. "Not quite tried and failed then. But there's a complication between the Monteagues and the Arbiter."

The elf prince leveled a look at me, but I was not about to jump in when Vikki was demonstrating exactly why Roman had thought she should have been the one sent here in the first place. The idea of Callista turning Vikki against me rather than Sergei gave me a sickening combination of chills and nausea. The middle Volkov was frighteningly adept. Wariness settled in me as I saw deeper beneath the lighthearted country girl exterior she wore as effectively as Maria wore flirtation.

"So," Vikki said, pouring herself another serving of mead after Maria nodded at her questioning glance. "My outcast and packless brother showed better judgment than the one sent under our father's auspices. The elves have an obligation to one they'd normally see dead before allowing to live within a hundred miles of their territory. The vampires reap the benefits. I appreciate the insights."

Maria casually flicked a hand, though the pinch of her eyes betrayed her annoyance. "Times change."

"You're exceptionally well-informed," Troy added grimly.

Twisting in her chair, Vikki fixed me with a sharper gaze than I'd seen up to now. "Which begs a question, Arden. Why aren't you taking your place at the table?"

I blinked, not having intended to be a part of whatever the three parties were hashing out tonight. "I'm just the facilitator."

"Just the facilitator," Vikki mused. "An elemental who can handle more than one element. Who can bring elves, vampires, and weres together. Who Callista fears enough to risk the wrath of the strongest were clan on the East Coast by enticing its only eligible heir to look to her rather than the rising power."

Blood drained from my head, leaving me dizzy as I realized that even in the mountains out west, they were speaking of me as a power that could rival Callista. I didn't know if Callista had Watchers in the Asheville area, but I knew I had to be marked. The knowledge added another reason to secure my power base among those present and another level of urgency to the Reveal.

Which meant sitting my ass down at the table and taking some responsibility.

Reluctantly, I pushed off from the wall and pulled out the empty fourth chair. As they watched, I poured a splash of mead into the fourth glass and took a piece of slivered raw beef from the plate. "With meat and mead, I keep the peace," I said grimly. This was not how I'd planned on participating this evening.

I washed the hoarseness from my voice with mead, ate the carpaccio, and washed it down with another swallow of mead. The alcohol curled through me, warm and inviting, and I slapped down the Chaos that crested to meet it, noting the twitch in Troy's cheek as I did. Two sips weren't enough to free it, but all my practice with the elements had made Chaos even more chaotic lately.

Vikki leaned back in her chair and looked around the table, swirling her own drink. "That's better. A clearer picture of the power structure on this side of the state."

When nobody contradicted her, something that might have been fear, but might also have been vindication, stabbed through me. I'd spent the last three and a half months trying to gather enough strength to stand alone. Was I finally getting somewhere?

If the predators at the table scented my emotions, they were polite enough to ignore me.

Troy reached for another piece of carpaccio, looking like he ate raw meat on a regular basis. Then again, with the second set of teeth elves had, maybe he did. "Why don't you tell us the real reason you insisted on a midnight meeting and used Finch to get it?"

I found myself wishing for a moment that he hadn't closed off our bond because the line of his shoulders suggested that his internal state was nowhere near as calm as what he showed externally.

Maria smiled broadly enough to flash her fangs. "Yes, Viktoria. Do tell."

Vikki ran a finger around the rim of her glass, her sudden hesitation making me sit up and frown. "If I was here on a mission of my own, could I be heard without judgment or fear of exposure?"

Maria locked eyes with me as Troy shifted to lean forward on the table. I nodded, not particularly caring what Vikki wanted as long as it didn't do anything to fuck with my chances of standing against Callista. Better that we heard her out here and now than shut her down and send her sniffing after the same trail Sergei had.

After a long look at Troy that carried the weight of decades of carefully managed deals, Maria said, "We will hear you, but you know how this works."

Vikki glanced at all of us, her gaze resting longest on me before she nodded. "I want to form a new clan."

Apparently I missed the significance of the statement because both the elf and the vampire stiffened.

"Here?" Troy said in a tone that was just shy of a snarl. "In the Triangle. You want to start a new wolf clan on the territory ceded by Acacia Thorn and Jade Tooth, in the shadow of Blood Moon, which controls the tri-state area tooth and nail and most of the Eastern seaboard through pack alliance. Do I have that right?"

Vikki nodded, resolute. "You do."

"Why, by Hekate, would we agree to that?" Maria asked in a velvet tone simmering with delayed violence.

"Because my father is weakening," Vikki said bluntly. "My mother runs the Volkov pack in all but name and, through it, the Blood Moon clan. The clan will splinter with his death, and I want to lead the wolves into the future. One where women have an equal say."

Maria pursed her lips. "You want to learn from the elves and our cat prides while you're here. Gather information and allies. Then strike when your father falls."

Vikki inclined her head. "I'm not fixing to start anything. But should an opportunity arise…"

I sighed. "Vikki, I didn't sign up for this."

"You don't ask, you don't get," she snapped, quoting something Roman had once said. "I'm not asking for favors. I'm just extending a courtesy. We're all here, in the unlikeliest place in the world for a shift in the balance of power. A *shattering* of the balance of power. Who the fuck would look to North Carolina to usher in the next chapter in Otherside history? In *world* history? Shouldn't it be New York? London? Johannesburg? Mumbai? Tokyo? Somewhere bigger, with more of us."

She looked around the table, meeting our eyes solidly. "But it's not. It's here. And why should either of my brothers inherit leadership of the most powerful clan in this part of the country, just for being male, when I'm more qualified?"

Nobody answered her.

"I won't upset anything. But I won't stand aside if power falls to me either. And I trust that those of us here can see their way to a new future, seeing as we're all daring so much already."

My heart thundered, and I tried to keep my breathing steady. *It doesn't rain, but it pours.*

Chapter 5

Troy and Maria seemed to have come to the same conclusion.

"So be it," Maria said with a tight expression. "Call me a hypocrite, but I won't commit vampire lives to fighting for your cause. Not yet. But so long as you don't seek trouble, I will do what I can to keep the Raleigh coterie out of your business."

"I can't give such a unilateral declaration," Troy said. "House Monteague is one of three high Houses in the area, and I'm only a prince. My queen and the heir apparent would have final say. But so long as balance is maintained..." He glanced at me.

I shrugged, not knowing what he wanted from me.

"I will advance your cause, should it come to it. On the condition that you don't take any of this, or anything at all, to Callista." He said the last to Vikki, but his eyes were on me.

I managed to keep my face straight, but if I didn't know any better, I'd think Troy was spending political capital to keep me safe from Callista. He'd pushed for us to be allies, but I hadn't really thought he'd act on it until now. Maria was giving me a serious look, like Troy had done exactly what I thought he'd done. I didn't know how to feel about that.

Turning to me, the werewolf asked, "And you, Arden?"

I slouched into my chair to think then sat up when I remembered that I was a leader now, not just me. "I won't have harm come to the rest of the alliance. But I also won't stand in the way of progress."

Vikki squared her shoulders. "That's all I ask. A fair shot. The rest is on me to handle."

Maria filled everyone's glasses with the last of the mead. "To new beginnings."

We all echoed her then drank. The alcohol sat poorly in my stomach, roiling as badly as my thoughts. We weren't going to get one big change with this. Vikki was right. It was going to be a complete and utter shattering of Otherside as we knew it—just as the gods wanted to do the same with the world.

As that pleasant thought circulated in my brain, Maria said, "While you're all here, we'll need security for the Reveal. We'll be hosting a ball here at The Umstead and inviting a number of powerful mundanes. I need my people focused on managing the humans and looking glamorous. Can I count on the alliance?"

"Sure," Vikki drawled, smiling slyly. "If you call it a sweetener for my request."

Maria pursed her lips, pensive, then inclined her head. "Fair."

"I'll be there." I spun my glass on the table. "Not sure how much good I can do as security, but I can help coordinate."

"I'll talk to my people," Troy said. "But the Captain will need to approve using the Darkwatch, not just the queens."

"I will await his response with bated breath," Maria said. "Remind him that we're doing this for all of Otherside, hmm? The old man does live and die for the matriarchy."

Troy sighed and rose, looking tired. "You're not wrong."

"Well. Sounds like we're all caught up." Vikki stood and saluted everyone with a little wave. "Thank you all for your time. Arden, see you tomorrow."

I nodded, praying that the werewolf didn't have any more bombs she wanted to drop in the midst of a meeting with leopards and jaguars while on my property.

As I stood to follow Vikki and Troy out, Maria cleared her throat delicately. "A word, Arden?"

I hesitated, frowning. Vikki had driven separately, so I didn't have an excuse not to stay.

When the room was empty, she said, "I'm surprised at you. For someone who wants to stand against Callista, you're oddly reluctant to take your place at a table of equals. Why?"

Half a dozen answers flared through me as I ran hot then cold. I thought about lying then spoke the truth that burned in my heart. "Because I'm tired of this political shit. I didn't want to be special or in charge or anything other than alive and left the fuck alone. I wanted normal, Maria. I wanted honest friendship or at least partnership. That's not an option anymore, and I don't know how to feel about it." I thought back to Troy's long look as he took a step to protect all of us, but maybe especially me, from Callista.

Maria shifted. "Honesty works for you?"

"Yes."

"Not power? Not sex? Not money?"

"For crying—no. Power is what started all this trouble to begin with, and I'm not Callista. If I want sex, I've got a perfectly functional Rabbit at home. I need money, but it's not why I'm doing any of this."

"You're strange. You must want something of value."

I scrubbed my hands over my face. "Why am I still here, Maria? I know you're nocturnal, but it's well past my bedtime. I want to go home. Alone."

"What if I was honest with you?"

"I'm too tired for this."

"Hear me out."

I was pretty sure she'd make me hear her if I tried to leave, so I crossed my arms and nodded. "Fine. But then I'm going."

"I intend to use you."

"You and everyone else." I scoffed, covering my hurt by rolling my eyes as I turned to go.

She caught my arm. "Wait." When I didn't turn back around, she came around to face me again. "Arden, whether you like it or not, you are power. Not just powerful, which you are in your own right, as an elemental. You are *power*. The Triangle is balanced on your decisions, your ability to navigate the political currents. Vikki is right. It should have been New York or Miami or LA that was brought to a reveal first, but it was here."

"Get to the point."

"That is the point. This simple desire to be nobody? To vanish back into obscurity once the Reveal is done? It's not going to happen. That went out the window the day Leith Sequoyah drew you into his conspiracy against the queens. So get over it. Step up. And lead. Use us in turn."

I jerked back, startled and a little offended by her bluntness. "Who the hell do you think you are?"

"I'm the number two vampire in the state and in the top five for the Eastern seaboard. I'm trying to solidify my position before Giuliano comes down from New York or Luz comes up from Miami to take this situation in hand. Torsten won't last much longer." Before I could ask what she meant about Torsten, she said again, more softly, "You can't be nobody. And I can't afford weakness. So, yes. I want your blood. The boost I got from draining a Sequoyah prince was enough to see me through the spring fights with the Modernists and the lich, but if— *when*—Torsten dies, numbers will beat strength if nothing changes. That's assuming Giuliano or Luz or both don't make a play."

"You're saying, more trouble's coming and better the devil I know."

A hint of her usual charming smile flickered. "I'm happy to be your devil, if that's what it takes. But honestly, Arden? I'm tired. I'm beyond fucking tired of waiting for Torsten to take me seriously. I'm tired of fighting off those who want to usurp my place. I want to take what should be mine. Spain is far away and almost five hundred years ago. This is my home now, and here you are, born and bred to this land with power not seen since Atlantis running through your veins. The gods are watching you, for Hekate's sake. And you think you can be normal?" She scoffed, fixing me with dark eyes and lifted brows. "Why be normal when you could be more? Claim more?"

A lump caught in my throat as a tingle ran down my back. Why indeed? I looked to the side, uncomfortable with her little speech. She reached out and turned my face back toward her with strong fingers. My breath caught.

"Relax," Maria said. "I would never bite you without your consent. But I need you to understand this."

"I get it."

"Do you?"

Jerking my head free, I glared at her until she backed up a step. "I said, I get it."

"And?"

I tried pushing away the spark of attraction I'd always felt for her, ever since she'd sidled up next to me at Claret's bar and asked what my type was. I reminded myself that losing myself to attraction was what had left me wide open to Roman's betrayal. "I don't see what I get out of it. You're already bound to help me because of the alliance. If the whole East Coast is looking at Raleigh, it seems like I'd just be painting another target on my back."

Maria stared at me, unblinking.

I lost the battle not to fidget and snapped, "What?"

She closed her eyes. Inhaled. Exhaled. A shiver ran over her before she opened her eyes again.

It was as though someone had removed the filter from an Instagram photo, stripping the soft glowy overlay. She looked thirty-five or forty, not twenty, with tiny crow's feet at the corners of her eyes and faint lines across her forehead. Less polished and more human. The sheen on her emerald hair faded a little, and a frightening knowledge sprang from the depths of her dark brown eyes. She no longer looked too perfect to be true. She just looked real.

My heart pounded.

"This is me." She tilted her head, and her nostrils flared as she tried to gauge my reaction. "Yes, I would use you. Yes, I want to drink from you. It's what I am, what the virus made me, and I won't apologize for it. Goddess, I embrace it, wholeheartedly. But Arden, five hundred years ago, Torsten convinced me to damn my soul to escape being burnt at the stake. You make me want to live again. Enough that I offer a partnership. My blood for yours, my strength for yours. My body even, if you'll have me. I could give as much as I take."

I inhaled sharply as she reached out and ran a single finger along my jaw.

"Come to me," she said.

They were only words, devoid of the pressure of glamour, but I wavered on my feet as though it was Torsten issuing the command with the full force of his power behind it.

She dropped her hand and stepped back. "I won't force you into this, Arden. No tricks, no games, no glamour." A rueful smile flashed as she said, "Of all my hunts, you're the only one I think would break free of me."

I closed my eyes, not wanting to see the earnestness in her gaze. Or more accurately, not wanting to believe it. Roman's politically driven departure had been unexpected and painful. I didn't want to tumble into someone else's arms and risk catching feelings again.

She didn't say anything else, and I opened my eyes again, struck—as I had been at our first meeting—by the exquisite delicateness of her features and the strength behind them. She played the flirt, charming and saucy, bossy and bold, but when she stopped trying so damn hard to seduce me, the fortitude she hid behind layers of artifice shone through, a beacon. Before I realized it, I'd taken a step closer.

Maria held perfectly still, an utter lack of movement that only the undead could manage. It should have been off-putting, a warning that I was stepping into danger. I couldn't even tell if she breathed as she waited for me to decide.

Another step. Still, she didn't move, though I was well within her personal space. This close, I could pick up not only the faint scent of woodsmoke and iron that clung to all vampires but also a hint of amber that had to be all her.

What am I doing? part of my brain asked.

Letting go of Roman, the other side responded.

I trembled, wanting her but so afraid of what it would mean.

When our lips touched, I don't know who was more surprised. She stood perfectly still, not reaching for me, not trying to control me, letting me decide. I paused, and she didn't move away. I leaned in again, tentatively resting my hand on her waist. Her approving noise made me pull her closer. As our kiss deepened, she slid her hands slowly up my arms. When I didn't pull away, she clasped them around my neck.

It felt good, but it didn't feel *right*. Heart pounding, I pulled away.

She let me go, sighing.

"Maria, I can't. Not right now." Shaking, I did my best to wall away my confusion, though whether it was to protect her or myself, I didn't know.

She nodded, her face carefully blank. "I understand. The wolf did a number on you."

That was part of it but not all of it. I couldn't find a good way to articulate what it was though, so all I said was, "Yeah."

Something else flickered in the back of my mind. It might have been a dagger of what remained of my affection for Roman. It might have been my fear of giving of myself again so soon after losing him. Or it might have been something else entirely. All I knew was that as much as I wanted to follow the thread of attraction I'd always had for Maria, I couldn't. Not now. Not yet. "I'm sorry."

"Don't be. It makes things more interesting." She was back to being flip, which meant that I'd hurt her without meaning to.

"Seriously, Maria. I am sorry."

"Nothing happened, so there's nothing to be sorry for. I'll see you at the next planning session," she said lightly. "Be a dear and do what you can to convince Troy to work security even if the Captain says no to using the Darkwatch. The Raleigh coterie has worked with House Monteague for the last quarter century. One of them needs to attend for appearance's sake, and Evangeline's a bitch. When he agrees, bring him to Claret. Torsten will want to feel like he had a say in all this."

I nodded, offered a tight smile, and fled to my car before I died of awkwardness.

"Fuck," I said when I was safely ensconced inside, resting my head on the steering wheel. I had an elven prince lodged in the back of my skull, intertwined with my aura so deeply that we didn't know how to disentangle ourselves. My ex's sister saw me as the key to independent power. And one of the most powerful vampires on this side of the country had just made a play for me. My personal and professional relationships were a shitshow of epic proportions, and I hadn't even dealt with Callista yet.

Chapter 6

The next morning came too early, given how late I'd been up and how tired I was.

I indulged myself and lazed on my temporary bed on the sofa when I woke. My bedroom was only partly repaired from when the thrice-damned lich lord sent a rabisu—an Akkadian demon—to my home as a goad to get me to join him when I was moving a little too slowly for his liking. The demon had shredded my bed, and fighting it alongside Troy had destroyed my bedroom.

I couldn't claim a demon attack on insurance, so that'd meant heading to Lowe's and paying in cash for new windows and door frames then doing the same again at Rooms To Go for a mattress and Target for sheets and curtains. Zanna, the kobold who'd appointed herself my landlord, was more than handy enough to fix everything, but she'd needed materials to start the work.

The only good news was that Maria had paid me under the table, and I was sure as shit not paying taxes on vampire cash. Roman being gone meant I'd need to find a new way to launder payments from Otherside, so for now, it was home improvements.

Not wanting to give Roman more space in my brain brought me back to the other interpersonal thing I'd been avoiding: I needed to call Val. I hadn't spoken to my one friend among the local elementals in a week, not since sending her out of the lich's lair with her sister, Doc Mike, and an oread who'd been locked up with us. Once I'd gotten up and put some clothes on, I pulled out my phone and stared at it, considering my options and weighing my guilt. She'd been taken because I'd drawn attention to us. She probably blamed me.

I'd been a little hurt when it became apparent that the rest of the elementals in the area didn't want anything to do with me. Now, I just thought they were smart. My association with the elves was bad enough for any elemental's health. Adding in the gods and their obsession with their Wild Hunt would only make it worse. I had suspicions that their plans weren't too different from the lich's. That meant they'd need elementals too.

It was almost enough to make me skip calling Val. I stabbed my thumb at the dial button before I could chicken out.

"I wondered when I'd be hearing from you," Val said in lieu of hello. Her tone didn't give me any hints as to her feelings on the matter.

"Is now a bad time?" That sick feeling that I'd screwed up a friendship sat heavy in my stomach.

"No worse than any other. What's up?"

I grimaced and tried to assemble the words I'd been searching for over the past week. "Look, I'm so sorry about the—you know."

"Hang on. Are you beating yourself up over the kidnapping?"

"Yes?" The sweat oozing from me had gone cold.

"Goddess, Arden, you are a piece of work. That asshole used soul magic to track us down, not any association with you. If it was elves who came for us, I'd be pissed. It wasn't, and you got us out. I've been waiting to thank you. On behalf of my sister and Laurel too. I was going to text, but 'Thanks for saving my and my sister's lives' felt like something to say in a phone call."

"What?" My brain couldn't compute that. Val's sister, an undine named Sofia, had lost a finger after being taken by the lich lord. The bastard had assembled one of each type of elemental plus Doc Mike, plotting to use our conjoined powers to wash the earth clean of polluting humans. The two of them and Laurel, the oread, had been exposed to Troy. He'd surprised me by politely ignoring them while breaking me out then agreed to overlook their existence on pain of death. But they had to be feeling marked.

"You free for our usual drinks? If you're recovered, I gotta catch you up on what the rest of us have decided about the Reveal."

"Sure," I spluttered, still trying to catch up with the complete one-eighty of what I'd been expecting from this call. "I need the distraction."

"From what?"

I winced. "I, uh, need to bring Troy Monteague in on Maria's plans for the Reveal. The guy who came for us."

"The Darkwatch agent? Jeez, Arden. Play stupid games, win stupid prizes?"

"I know. I've already had a few of those." I shivered as the memory of an icy lake tried to intrude. "But we have to get this done."

"I hear ya. Okay. Anything else?"

"You know how I called that lightning bolt to destroy the amulet? I can call Fire now. By itself," I said, blurting out the words without any of the preparatory talk I'd rehearsed.

"Excuse me?" Val said after a long pause.

"Well, not really, because it burns the fuck outta my hands. Lightning is a lot less painful. The first time, I thought it was just because I had you and Laurel with me, but I can do it by myself now. Is that normal? Please tell me that's normal." I clamped my jaw shut to stop the verbal gale blowing out of me.

"Um. Shit."

I managed not to say anything into the long silence that followed, but the air plants hanging in their bulbs overhead swayed as I channeled the effort into releasing a gust of Air.

"Have you by any chance been having strange dreams, maybe?"

My stomach twisted. I didn't know if it was relief, fear, or both.

"If you're talking about the Crossroads, I am fucking sick of that place and everyone in it." The empty white nothingness, where time was both too fast and too slow and nothing existed but for what the gods and the djinn created, was the only place I hated being more than Keithia's Chapel Hill mansion.

"What the hell, Arden? How many times?"

"Enough." I kicked a toe at the kitchen floor. "They visit. Sometimes." I was afraid to mention the part about those visits being on this plane. I might be an Othersider, but until a few months ago, it had been in name only. Embracing and using my powers had meant opening doors I hadn't even known existed. I was beginning to feel like Pandora had nothing on me.

"We need to meet. Even trueborns are just supposed to be stronger, not have multiple elements to call on. I didn't even know that was possible. If you've been to the Crossroads on top of it, the fucking humans are the least of our worries."

"Great." I drew the word out in sarcasm and squeezed my temples with one hand. "I can do any time Sunday or later, but I have to go have a chat with the elves at some point today."

"I do not envy your life. Can we meet at your place, Sunday morning? Ten? We can't have this discussion in public. Can't afford to talk in metaphors. I'll bring breakfast."

That didn't bode well. "Sure. Fair warning, my landlord is a kobold, in case you didn't meet her before."

"I'll bring a little something extra then."

"Thanks, Val. See you then. I'm glad we're okay." I slumped when the call ended, resting my forehead on the kitchen counter.

Fuck, fuck, fuck. I should have been overjoyed. My one real friend didn't hate my guts or blame me for her and her sister's kidnappings. But there'd never been anything so momentous that we couldn't tiptoe around it in public.

I clutched my pendant, wondering for the millionth time what had driven my parents to break every djinn and elven law to be together. Not just be together but to have me. They'd known what they were doing. Everyone—even sheltered, ignorant me—knew what happened when beings with the two halves of Aether mated. Contraception would have been easy on either side had they wanted to use it, whether magically or physically implemented.

My birth had been a choice. Duke had hinted that my mother had sought out my father and that there were things known to him but forced into secrecy by a geas. Or several geasa. Speaking the truth would result in a nasty death as the curse was activated.

Why their choices, and why all the secrecy?

"Callista knows," I muttered. "She has to."

I hadn't decided what to do about that yet. Callista had been a power in the Triangle for centuries and still had a strong backing among pretty much everyone who wasn't with me.

With one of my friendship worries soothed and no new ammo to use against Callista, my thoughts returned to Roman. I scrubbed my hands over my face, wishing I could set the feelings aside and focus.

Deciding that I'd just have to feel my feels for a bit, I indulged in a little bit of petty anger as I tidied my house ahead of the coming meeting with the weres. I wondered what Roman was doing and how things were going in Asheville, even as I told myself I didn't care and it didn't matter. He was gone, patching things up with his family and the werewolf woman he'd gone home to marry so he could solidify his place in the pack. We might both feel like shit about where that left me, but at the end of the day it changed nothing.

He was gone. I was here, alone.

My thoughts wandered to Maria's flirtations then to her odd comments about Troy being attracted to me. It didn't matter. It meant as much as my finding Troy physically attractive—he was damn fine to ogle, but there was too much dislike for it to go anywhere.

Which brought me back to Maria. Was that why she'd mentioned Troy? Not for any attraction on his part but because she thought casting him as the other option would make me more likely to choose her?

Joke was on her. I found her almost as attractive as I found Troy, but neither of them were realistic options. Nobody was, not now and not for a while. I didn't need more baggage or distraction. Definitely didn't need to be involved with either of Otherside's big players in the Triangle. I needed a break and time to heal. I needed focus and rest that I wasn't likely to get for a while yet.

Being lost in my thoughts got my cleaning sorted out in record time. I'd given in to the rising sense of burnout and dropped my mundane caseload for my PI firm, which had me anxious about my financial situation but meant I had the rest of the morning free. Free time meant practice.

I hesitated at the sliding door to the deck out back, clenching my fists. Now that I knew Val wasn't mad at me, I should probably wait until I saw her again before practicing with Fire.

If you keep waiting for someone to teach you, you'll be back where you were in January. Unprepared when a shitstorm blows through. I scowled and grabbed the first aid kit from the shelf as I went out, leaping down the stairs and hopping my back fence to follow the path down to the river. I'd be careful, but no way was I waiting around for someone to tell me what to do. Never again. I didn't even know if elemental powers could be taught. Air came to me as naturally as breathing. How could I teach someone to breathe? If it was the same for Val, there was no use waiting to find out.

I gathered fallen sticks and branches on my way down to the spot that was increasingly my little haven. The massive rock I'd overturned into the river with Air had become a small island as part of the Eno diverted around it. I'd cleared a space alongside, rolling a couple of logs around the fire pit I'd blown out with compressed Air. I'd needed hand tools to level the convenient stump into a table, but now I had the perfect space to practice and, when needed, to catch a break from the rest of the world. The river was shallow enough here that I'd only ever seen one kayaker, so it was safe enough.

The wood went into the pit, ready for my next attempt. The first aid kit went on the stump table, within easy reach for when I burnt my hands like I did almost every time I practiced; I'd had to go to Costco and buy Neosporin in bulk to keep the first aid kit stocked. I left a bucket down here in case my efforts with Fire got out of control, and I filled that from the river before getting started. Safety first.

I fingered the knotted scar on my right shoulder and looked inside for the remembered feeling of Mixcoatl's arrow of obsidian and lightning. I always had to draw deeply on Air to find Fire, like my inborn power was a channel for the new one. I remembered tracing the chords of Air and Fire as I withdrew the arrow, thinking of the volcanic lightning that made it easier to sympathize with my new element.

As always, lightning came first, sparking over my fingertips. Lightning was the child of Air and Fire, easier for me to manage than Fire alone. Calling on Fire in its full strength burned my hands to hell and back, but I could do little crackles of lightning after a few fumbling days of practice.

I scowled. That would be great if I wanted lightning, but I wanted fire, like the balls of flame Mixcoatl danced from finger to finger.

You're mortal. Not a god.

After trying a little longer I let the sparks go with a frustrated snarl and indulged in sending a gust of wind through the clearing. Maybe I was pushing too hard. Or my lightning shortcut wasn't really all that short. Having two elements might be cool one day, but for now working with raw Fire just meant ending every day like I'd put my hand on a hot stove, which sucked big time. My healing was fast enough that I'd recover by the next morning, but after a while, my body started dreading being forced.

Not in the mood to end on a low note, I switched to Air.

Strength, I had in plenty. Control was another story. Managing multiple chords, or managing a single chord to a fine purpose, needed work. I didn't get much time off lately, so every spare moment went to practice. I was daily given reason to wonder how the hell anyone had functioned before now. *Callista's fingers in all the pies, probably.*

Either way, I was running out of time to strengthen myself. I had to work harder.

Chapter 7

When I was satisfied with my practice, there was plenty else to do. The vampire Reveal was item number two on my to-do list. Handling the rogue sorcerer-turned-vampire who'd become the lich's accomplice was a thin first, but we had to find him before we could do anything else. That took witch magic, not elemental. Without a mundane case on my docket, I figured getting Troy on board with Maria's plans was my next most important task.

I could have just called Troy and relayed Maria's request, but that would have been too easy. And let's be honest, a bit too much of a sting to my pride. Besides, I had to prove to myself that Maria was wrong about the jerkoff elven prince having a thing for me. He didn't. He was an ass, regardless of his backwards apologies and claims that we needed to be allies.

Aside from last night's meeting, Troy and I had had a little game going since we'd come to our understanding the morning after the alliance was finalized. With the bond between us muted until he could figure out a way to remove it, we were back to relying on skill rather than magic to locate each other. I knew two of his hidey-holes, and he knew that I knew of one of them because I'd been there. That meant he'd be avoiding it, which was why I was parked in a middling neighborhood I'd once tailed him to in Carrboro, hoping he'd be avoiding any other safehouses he might have so as not to lead me to those too.

Fortunately, there was a home for sale down the block. On a Saturday afternoon, that meant an open house and a lot of unusual cars in the neighborhood. He might miss mine. If he even turned up. For all I knew, he was home, and his Acura was just in the garage. Or he was somewhere else entirely, on some super-secret mission for the Darkwatch.

Just call him. I sighed and fiddled with my phone, keeping my eyes on the house as I debated. I might be between cases at the moment, but maybe I should be figuring out a way to help the witches locate the lich's accomplice, not playing silly games with an elf in a misguided effort to prove that he didn't scare me anymore. I was running on fumes these days. My judgment might be off.

A knock on my window startled me. A subtly pretty woman with honey-colored eyes, chest-length locs pulled back into a ponytail, and skin a shade lighter than my sienna-brown stood on the sidewalk. She looked trim and capable in expensive running clothes.

"Excuse me?" she said, the words muffled by my shut window. "Can I help you? Are you lost?"

I kicked myself for being snuck up on like that and rolled down the window. "Hey, hi. Do you live in the neighborhood? I'm looking at that house for sale and would love to hear more about the area."

The woman inhaled as though scenting the air then smiled as the smell of meringue and herbs rose.

I forgot to breathe as I locked down my shields. I had amnesty from House Monteague, but she didn't look like one.

"I don't think you are looking to buy a house," she said, her suburban cheerfulness replaced by silky danger. "I think we're both familiar with the other side. Turn off the car, get out, and come with me."

Her mentioning "the other side" told me she knew I wasn't human, even if she couldn't place my scent and didn't quite know what I was yet.

Shit. I broke out in a cold sweat as flashbacks of Leith Sequoyah intruded. The scent of burnt marshmallow intensified as I hesitated.

"Get. Out." She tensed, ready either to draw a weapon or try something with Aether.

I forced down my panic and turned off the car. If I could survive Leith, I could get out of this. *I should have just called Troy.* Elves usually moved in multiples of three, but I'd assumed he was still on his own since the other two of his Darkwatch triad had died on the Redcap mission and he always turned up alone. I'd also assumed that this was his house, when it could very well be one owned by the Darkwatch, or House Monteague. Looked like I'd been wrong in at least one of those assumptions. *Fuck.*

As soon as I got out, the elfess's smile was back. "I'd be happy to tell you about the neighborhood! Come on with me, I've got some sweet tea in the fridge."

"You're too kind." I forced a smile to match hers. If I played along, maybe I could buy time to get away.

She chattered about the recent improvements to the area as we approached the house I'd thought was Troy's. As soon as the door shut behind us though, she hit me effortlessly with the kind of mental Aether sting I'd come to associate with the Monteagues.

"Chill," she snapped.

I'd had enough practice with this shit to resist the command, for the most part. I allowed my body to drop bonelessly to the floor but fought off the mental maze that should have rendered me unconscious, closing my eyes to make it look like it had worked fully. Immediately, I started looking for all the little hooks of Aether that were forcing my muscles to "chill" and ripping them free.

A dial tone told me she was calling someone.

"Get back here. Some Othersider was watching the house. No, I don't know what the fuck she is. Gunmetal grey Honda Civic hatchback, souped-up model from the look of the wheels. I got her inside and downed her."

I let my body flop when a toe nudged me.

"Yeah, she's out. She is! Why the hell wouldn't she be? You know her or something? Fine."

The sound of a phone being shoved in a pocket accompanied a grumbled, "Aether-resistant my Black ass."

I scrambled against the Aether net as we waited. The elfess didn't harass me, which meant I was free to find the edges of her entrapment and start working at them like I had the first time Troy had put me in a maze. Then, it had taken me too long to break out and I'd nearly died for it. Now, I might have a chance.

No joy. The front door whooshed open and slammed shut before I could do more than unravel the first layer.

"That was fast," my captor said.

"I was already on my way."

It was Troy, and it took every ounce of control not to smile. Maybe I wasn't totally fucked after all. Maybe.

The next time he spoke, it was close enough that he must have knelt. "Finch, stop messing around."

I opened my eyes to find him on one knee beside me, and the elfess frowning in consternation.

"It's not entirely an act," I said, my words coming out like I'd had a Novocaine injection.

"What the hell?" Lady Elf said.

Troy looked at his watch. "How long ago did you hit her?"

"About four minutes ago? Five? Troy—"

53

He held up a hand then fiddled with his watch and lifted his eyebrows at me.

Challenge accepted. My hand twitched when I tested to see how far I had left to go. I found more hooks and went after them one by one. I couldn't handle Aether—only elves and djinn could— but I'd learned that being half of each meant I could see the shape of it when cast by elves and use Chaos to snap its hold when it was freshly settled on me.

Maybe I can use that to break the bond with Troy? It hadn't occurred to me before, but when I turned my attention there, the magic was buried deep, with bigger, nastier hooks tinged by pulses of Chaos. I left it and grunted as I opened my eyes, slowly pushing myself up to lean against the wall.

"Seven minutes, give or take." Troy almost sounded impressed. "Faster than Jordan Lake. Much faster."

I started to say that I hadn't had to break free of a mental maze this time but decided to keep that to myself. I didn't know who the other elf was, and I didn't need to let Troy know I could do it.

"You wanna tell me what the hell is going on?" the elfess said. "How can she resist an enchantment enough to break it? What the hell is she? She should have been out for thirty minutes!"

Troy smirked. "Alli, meet Arden Finch, private investigator and arbiter of the new alliance. Finch, meet my sister, Allegra Monteague."

"*This* is the arbiter? Burn you, Troy, you could have told me she was swinging by instead of letting me spell her. Goddess!"

"Your sister?" I blinked as I looked between them. Troy and Evangeline looked Mediterranean or West Asian, if you discounted the lilac eyes Evangeline got from their grandmother. Allegra looked Black.

Allegra rolled her eyes as she said, "Cousin, technically. Our mothers were sisters, so we were raised as full-blood sibs. I'm *so* sorry about this." She glared daggers at Troy, who looked far too amused for either of our liking. Then her look landed back on me. "I've never smelled anything like you, so when I spotted you lurking I had to assume you were a threat."

"Uh..." I used the wall to press to my feet, not knowing how well my being an elemental would go over and not wanting to be sat on my ass for the revelation.

"She's a sylph," Troy said in as neutral a tone as I'd ever heard from him as he rose along with me. "But you didn't hear it from me. Grandmother and the Captain want it kept quiet."

Allegra went deathly still. "A sylph."

My smile was more of a grimace. "Nice to meet you."

Burnt marshmallow smell rose so fast and hard that I gagged and pulled on Air out of reflex.

"Hey!" Troy slid between us. His fingertips brushed my shoulder.

A spark of magic jumped between us. The bond flared to life. He looked in control, but somewhere in the back of his mind, he was panicking.

I didn't understand why, so I stumbled backward, trying to get space as I looked around, seeking an exit.

"Allegra, don't!" Troy said. "Finch, take it easy!"

"You take it easy!" I snapped, blood surging, more pissed off than scared now. "For fuck's sake, do you have to tell *everyone* we meet what I am or what I can do?"

"Troy," Allegra said before he could answer me, her eyes darting between us. Her voice was way too calm for what she said next. "Have you made an Aetheric bond to an elemental?"

The little lump of Troy in my head froze like a rabbit when a hawk's shadow passes overhead. "Damn it," he muttered. "Alli..."

"Troy."

They looked at each other.

"Let go of Aether, and I'll tell you everything," Troy said when she didn't budge.

The scent of burning meringue eased. I exhaled and let go of the chord of Air I held ready to throw in a punch but kept myself ready to grab it again in a heartbeat.

"Why would she think you'd made a bond?" I asked, careful to avoid confirming that he actually had.

"Because she has the rare talent of being able to read Aetheric residue, even after it's settled," Troy said tiredly. "That information doesn't leave this room."

I nodded. "Sure."

"You too, Alli," Troy said.

Allegra's eyebrows shot up. "Oooh, brother. Evie doesn't know? Keithia?"

"No."

"How'd that happen then?"

"Finch is my assignment."

That was news to Allegra and me both, apparently.

"Excuse me?" we said in unison.

Troy scrubbed his hands over his face as the bond roiled. "This was not how I wanted to do this."

"I'll get that tea," Allegra said gravely. "If Arden will excuse my reaction. I thought the elementals were all dead. Not every day you meet the boogeyman in person and find out it's just a girl like you."

"I—of course," I said, unsure of what was going on. If she didn't want to kill me, I could work with that. More allies among the elves couldn't hurt anything except my already tenuous relationship with the few elementals who would speak to me.

She gave Troy a hard look before heading for the kitchen.

"Finch—" he started.

"Your *assignment*? The Darkwatch is still keeping tabs on me? Or Keithia is?"

He gave me the expressionless look that said, *I'm not going to answer that.*

"I guess I'm not surprised. You keep turning up."

"Trust me, there are a dozen other things I'd rather be doing than keeping tabs on you," he said before stalking after Allegra. He was upset enough that I could hear his footsteps, for once.

Three glasses of iced tea were beading with condensation on the table when we got there. Troy dropped into a chair next to Allegra at the small, round four-seater, looking far more comfortable than he ever had with Evangeline, even if Allegra was mad at him.

I grabbed a glass and leaned against the fridge. I knew how fast elves were, and I didn't want to be in their reach.

Allegra smirked at me then turned to Troy. "Spill. Now."

As Troy recounted the story of how we'd come to be bonded, her face hardened.

"So you tried a tracking tag on an Othersider of unknown species that ultimately resulted in bonding her without her consent." Disgust twisted her features. "Troy!"

The slap she dealt him snapped his head round. He squared his shoulders and faced her again as that cheek darkened and the bond raged with a blend of anger and deep shame. "I had a mission, Alli. You know what the Captain—"

She slapped his other cheek then studied him as he sat there, grinding his teeth. "Of all the dumbass moves, Troy. You really didn't know what you were doing?"

"No," he admitted. "Not that it makes the result any better."

"At least you acknowledge that." She turned to me, looking grim. "He owes you."

"I know," I said after my first attempt to speak looked like a goldfish drowning on air. I had *not* expected this when Allegra had knocked on my window. I quashed the vindictive thrill rising in me, striving to stay professional until I figured out what this all meant. "We've come to terms."

"Good." She sipped her tea then shook her head. "Fucking idiot. Prince of the highest House in the fucking country, and you go around pulling this shit. Fucking disgraceful."

I blinked. The Monteagues were that powerful?

Troy kept his eyes on the table. "I'm *trying* to *fix* it."

"You can't," Allegra said after glancing between us a few times, eyes narrowed. "Maybe right after it was made but not now. There's enough Chaos in her that the net has twisted." She tilted her head and squinted some more. "It goes both ways, now, right? She can read you? Find you, if she tries hard enough?"

"Yes," I admitted in a whisper.

Troy shut the bond down at the reminder, and my stomach eased a little as his emotions faded.

"So to complete one mission, you made yourself a security risk for every subsequent one." Allegra shook her head. "What were you planning to do when Evangeline found out? Or the Conclave or the Captain?"

Troy just looked at her.

"I can't with you right now." Allegra flipped her hand at him and looked at me. "Asking if you're okay with this is wrong, but…"

"You need to know if I've got a target on him," I said.

She nodded, grim-faced, and I sipped my tea to give me a minute to think.

"No, I don't." My chest eased as the word left me. I didn't have to like him, but it felt like a turning point. One less thing to worry about. "I mean yeah, it's a fucked up situation, and I think we both wish it hadn't happened. Seems like he's at least as much harmed by it as I am though, so an eye for an eye. I can be satisfied with that and with what he's agreed he owes."

I grinned, letting out a little of the savage glee I felt at seeing him taken down a notch. I wouldn't admit it, but it was also nice knowing where the bastard was and getting a read on him. Doubly so if I was his damn "assignment."

"Thank you," Allegra said. "That's exceedingly generous of you. Callista would have demanded much more."

"You don't know the terms," Troy muttered. He pressed his lips into a thin line when Allegra gave him a look that said she didn't care, he was paying up.

"I'm not Callista." I let my voice go harsh. I would *never* be Callista. "I haven't necessarily forgiven him, but it is what it is."

I refused to add that it seemed like he was beating himself up more than either Allegra or I were and was genuine in both his shame at what he'd done and his desire to make amends. He'd needed a bit of bullying to get there, but there was no resentment toward me in the bundle of emotion I'd gotten from him. He wasn't holding onto the idea that he deserved to be let off the hook. "We've got bigger issues."

"Yeah. This Reveal." Allegra drew a spiral in the ring of condensation her glass left on the table. "That's actually why I'm back in town. I want to help."

Chapter 8

"Help how?" I asked. *This could be handy.*

Allegra shrugged. "However I can. Troy told me about the alliance y'all were building and Maria's request for event security. I completed my assignment and needed another one." She held up three fingers. "I volunteer."

"Why? I mean, I don't exactly see the rest of Otherside—or even the rest of House Monteague—falling in alongside us. Besides, I'm an elemental."

Her eyebrows rose, and she gave me a look like I was being a little dense. "As far as any humans are concerned, you're a Black girl that makes the sensitives feel a little off. With the Reveal, you're a Black girl with freaky powers." She saluted. "Just like me. I spent enough time in the public school system and at UNC to know how that will shake out. Being Black in those spaces was hard enough. Adding high-blood elf with powers most elves don't even have? There's being young, gifted, and Black, and then there's being us. I'll take solidarity where I can find it. As long as you don't hurt my brother, anyway."

I glanced at Troy, wondering how he'd take all of this—and for the first time, how he was perceived by the humans. Frustration and a hint of pain tightened his features, until he caught me evaluating him. Then he washed them clear and looked back at me with his usual tense neutrality.

Clearing my throat, I said, "As it happens, Maria made another request after you left last night."

Troy scowled. "An actual request or more button-pushing and games?"

"You tell me." I finished my iced tea and decided to dare a seat at the table. Allegra's encouraging smile seemed genuine, and I reminded myself that my shoulders shouldn't live up around my ears. "Your particular presence has been commanded at the Reveal ball. Something about your House and Torsten's coterie have been allies for decades and needing to keep up appearances."

"Has she turned rakshasa? Vampires don't command elven royalty."

I sighed and shrugged. Sometimes, being the arbiter felt like being the team mom. "I know, all right? But you don't get to pick and choose how to satisfy your oaths. You swore to the alliance. Keep your word."

Allegra laughed. "Oh, I like her. You'd best not do anything foolish to her, T. I know your damn honor is stinging you over the elemental laws."

Troy's eyes cut to me, and I barely stopped myself from recounting the story of Jordan Lake.

"I'm sure he wouldn't dream of crossing me," I said in tones bland enough to suggest that he'd gone beyond dreaming and into doing.

The prince's shoulders eased all the same when the expected blow of the recounting of his past transgressions didn't come. I filed that away for later as the saying about catching flies came to mind. If he could make an effort to be better, maybe I could—should—stop hassling him. He hadn't been wrong when he'd said we needed to be allies.

"I'm surprised at you, Arden." Allegra leaned back in her chair. "You're powerful enough that I can feel the air currents shifting and the air itself even tastes cleaner after, what, twenty minutes with you in the house? I wouldn't have noticed it if I didn't know what you were, but now that I do, such a powerful sylph should either be waging war on us or hiding under a rock as far away as she could get. But you're sat here drinking tea with two Monteagues?"

I fought the wince that wanted to crack my face when she mentioned passive sylph abilities, not having realized that I'd become strong enough that they just kind of spilled out. We did tend to purify the air and shift currents around us, among other gifts like echolocation and vocal mimicry. Most people didn't notice. That Allegra had said she was at least as powerful as Troy.

Or that I was. Maybe both. That was an interesting idea.

The pendant that had belonged to my elven father burned where it hung between my breasts, beneath my shirt. Not from any power within it but from my knowledge of it and what it might mean. Leith Sequoyah, the elven terrorist I'd killed this past winter, had had a similar one. I hadn't worked up the courage to ask Troy what that meant.

I kept my hands on my glass and my eyes on her as I said, "Times are changing, and I'm a survivor. We're on the verge of something big, and I'm not trying to die when I've made it this long."

"Which brings us back to this ball," Troy said flatly.

Allegra elbowed him. "Oh, fuck off, T. It'll be fun."

"No," Troy said as I tried to figure out why he was suddenly being so stubborn. "Regardless of what Maria thinks, she doesn't command me. Besides, the Captain hasn't approved the request yet."

"You're being an idiot. *Think*. The Prince of Monteague alongside the Arbiter? As guests of honor at a vampire ball, surrounded by influential humans? *Please* tell me you see the opportunities. Besides, I can convince the Captain, and you know it."

Troy scowled and crossed his arms.

"You're being stubborn." Allegra rolled her eyes and scoffed then turned to me. "I have no right to ask this of you. I'm sure my people have been assholes to you and that everyone and their mother is asking you for favors right now. But could you get me in? Please? I'm sorry about spelling you earlier, for real, and I meant it when I said I want to help. I'll talk to the Captain."

She wants a piece of those opportunities for herself. I wasn't completely naive. I didn't get the sense that she thought I was either, more that she assumed that if I'd managed to become "The Arbiter" that I had a reasonable level of savvy and could read between the lines. It was strange to be assumed competent, after so many years of Callista and the djinn treating me like I was a fool. That the respect came from an elf, one of the people I'd been raised to automatically fear? It was heady stuff.

"You're in," I said. She might be using this as an opportunity for herself, but I'd promised Maria security. Allegra was powerful, perceptive, and insightful. If she wanted to be my ally, fuck it, I'd take her.

"Good." Troy slouched a little, a small smile curling the corners of his lips. "You've got a Monteague knight. You don't need a prince. Royalty is royalty."

I narrowed my eyes at him, irritated by his thinking he'd foist this shit on Allegra and me and get away with skulking in the shadows like he usually did. Maria was taking on a danger for all of Otherside, and he wanted to be an ass about making an appearance to help? Was it about being seen with me in public? Or the leverage he'd needed for whatever reason, which had driven him to help me with the lich?

Either way, nah, he wasn't getting out of this. If I didn't take Troy in hand, he'd be a pain in the ass for however long the alliance lasted. I had to bring him to heel. Right now. If he wouldn't respect a request from Maria, I'd use something else to remind him that he might be a prince but I was the goddamn Arbiter.

He sat bolt upright in his chair as something in my face telegraphed my next action. "Don't do it, Finch."

"Do what?" Allegra glanced between us like the world's secrets were in our unspoken thoughts.

"Troy Monteague, Prince of that House and agent of the Darkwatch," I started.

"Goddess damn you, *don't!*" He rose so quickly the chair toppled over.

Allegra's pupils dilated, and she grinned as she sensed something about to happen, not knowing what it was but excited anyway.

"I call in the first of the debts owed," I intoned.

Troy slammed his fist on the table in the greatest display of emotion I'd ever seen from him.

"You will come to this fucking ball, as requested by your allies. You will assist me in fulfilling any further requests Maria might make in relation to the Reveal. And you will put a fucking smile on your face as you do it. So it is, and so the debt begins to be paid."

Allegra threw back her head and cackled, clapping and stomping as Troy bowed his head.

"Classic! Oh, my Goddess, I love it. It's been *years* since— Wait." She sobered as suddenly as she'd laughed. "*Begins* to be paid? Troy, what the fuck did you do to have *multiple* debts owed to an elemental? You did more than bind her?"

"That's between Arbiter and Prince." I decided to play my new role to the fullest. Start as you meant to go on, as far as I was concerned. Besides, I'd already boxed him in with the promise.

A lock of black hair fell across Troy's eyes as he glared at me. "This doesn't count. We agreed on a measurement for the debts."

Lives. We'd agreed on lives. Maybe it was unwise to waste one of my three lives on forcing him to attend this ball, but if I had leverage, I'd use it. Troy would be an ally, but clearly there were limits to what he considered worthy of allyship. Fighting a lich? Sure. Political wrangling? Not so much, apparently. But I wasn't keen on having Troy kill for me, not yet, so I stared right back, embracing Air to make my eyes flash gold and remind him of a few things.

"Shit, she is the real deal," Allegra muttered, scooting her chair back.

Troy was still trying to stare me down, so I propped an elbow on the table, leaned toward him, and willed Fire to join Air. Sparks of electricity danced over my fingers.

Allegra's jaw dropped in my peripheral vision, but I kept my focus on Troy. "You're going," I said. "Accept that this is one less mark on my ledger and be grateful."

Troy tried challenging me a few seconds more then gave up, righting his chair and dropping back into it. A mocking smile curled his lips. "Careful, Finch. We wouldn't want another Callista on our hands, not when we're trying so hard to get rid of the one we have."

I covered the pain that comment caused me with a hiss of anger. "Don't you dare. She raised me. I know *exactly* what she's capable of and how far she's willing to go, and this isn't anywhere close. If paying a debt is so onerous, you'd best think more carefully about your actions in future."

He started to say something then swallowed it. He glanced at Allegra, who watched raptly as this all played out, then back at me. His hazel gaze searched my face. Whatever he saw prompted him to take a breath and say, "So the debt is called, so it shall be paid. And so it is."

We shook on it, and I swear, he pushed magic at me this time because the usual little spark burned like Fire. Petty little shit.

I ignored it and rose. "Fantastic. Then we need to go to Raleigh tomorrow evening to sort shit out with Maria, Troy. I'll see you at Claret at sunset. Call ahead so we can avoid another incident. Allegra, good to meet you." I stomped my way to the door then paused, turned, and inclined my head. "Thank you for your hospitality. No offense is taken for the circumstances of our meeting."

It was a standard form for acknowledging and excusing the little accidents that happened sometimes between unknown Othersiders. Couldn't hurt to be polite to someone who didn't want to kill me or make my life harder.

"The honor of hospitality was mine to give. May we meet again in peace," Allegra replied, equally formal.

With a nod to her and a last hard look at Troy, I left. At this point, hunting a witch-born vampire was more palatable than spending a second longer in the prince's company.

Chapter 9

I debated between going home and going to my office for the rest of the afternoon. The office won despite it being the weekend. The twenty grand I'd earned from Maria for helping her track down the Modernist splinter of Torsten's coterie was largely going toward repairing the damage done to my house in the rabisu attack, which meant the break I'd taken to give myself space to deal with burnout was over. I needed to sort out my next job.

The whole money thing had me in a bad enough mood that I forgot my hoodie in the car when I arrived. The coworking space in which I rented an office was human-owned, which meant that as spring edged toward summer and the heat increased, so did the blast of air conditioning. As a sylph, my presence would gradually balance the air temperature to whatever made me comfortable, but that took time and ran the risk that someone would start to wonder why the thermostat always seemed off around me.

Not having my hoodie irked me. My inbox pushed me into full-on vexation. All mundane cases, just as I liked it. Or rather, just as I *had* liked it. After handling a few cases for Otherside, cases that pushed me to be stronger and better, queries about cheating spouses and deadbeat parents just seemed so...well, mundane. Boring. Beneath my skill level. I'd spent my whole life trying to avoid Otherside's notice, but now that I had it and hadn't died, a new aspiration had quietly started flickering.

What if I was Otherside's private investigator?

I was already doing some of the work for free as arbiter of the alliance. I tapped my fingers on the desk as I tried to figure out how Callista produced income. She had the bar, of course, but that by itself wouldn't cover everything. Information had its prices, as I well knew, having leveraged some to get out from under her immediate influence.

Protection money? I didn't want to be that bitch. Callista was a mob boss. I wasn't sure what I was yet. All I knew was that my life was at an inflexion point. Things were changing whether I wanted them to or not.

I was a survivor. Survival meant adaptation. Becoming. But becoming what?

I slouched in my chair, playing mental Tetris with the pieces that were my obligations to the alliance, my business and financial needs, the relative risks of a pissed-off master vampire versus a vengeful, masterless rogue sorcerer dabbling in necromancy and demonology, and the resources available to deal with all of that. Another round went to trying to figure out what Duke had been doing in the time since he'd disowned me, what Callista might be planning, and when they might come for me. That both of them had their own plans and deals running went without saying. The question was how they'd work out with my little group. I was playing political chess with beings thousands of years my senior, and all I could count on was that they'd be petty, vindictive, or both.

Sighing, I buried my face in my hands. Deep down, I was afraid that adapting to all these new considerations meant letting Hawkeye Investigations go, not just shifting to accepting Otherside clientele. I wasn't ready for that yet. Dealing with so much Otherside business had me craving normality, which for me was humans and their smaller, non-world-ending problems. Not only that; I'd built my PI firm from scratch, determined to have something that was mine when Callista's influence was at its heaviest. This business was my baby.

"If it's your baby, push through and make it work," I muttered. I looked for the most unusual case I could find in my incoming leads box and started to dial.

As I did, a familiar haziness shimmered in the far corner. The overwhelming wash of power that accompanied it stole my breath and told me this wasn't an errant djinni.

I rose, drawing on Air. I couldn't fight a god, but even a cat bristled at a threat. I could do at least as much.

The figure that materialized wasn't any of the gods I was familiar with. Usually it was Neith who visited me, in her ancient Egyptian garb and twirling a *was* staff, or Mixcoatl, who danced balls of fire on his fingers and had the Milky Way spinning in his eyes.

This goddess stood as tall as a modern man and was muscled like one. A bow and a quiver of arrows were racked on her back. She wore a long tunic belted in leather tooled with a pattern of conifer branches alternating with leaping stags and hunting dogs. A blood moon shone from her eyes, and shaggy hair the color of a red deer was knotted atop her head.

Given that the only gods who seemed interested in me were those of the hunt, one name popped to mind. "Artemis?"

She stopped her sneering perusal of my office, and I wavered when those moon-tinted eyes landed on me. "I am not certain whether to be amused at your disrespect or impressed by your fighting spirit. Best not make me decide."

I released Air and averted my eyes, sweating bullets and trying to remember to breathe.

"Better," the goddess said. Sandaled feet moved as lightly as a dance as she circled me. Having her behind me made my skin crawl, but it wasn't like she was any less dangerous in front of me. "You're not what I expected."

"I'm not sure what to say to that, um, my lady."

Artemis's fingers burned on my skin when she completed her circle and tilted my chin up. My breath froze in my lungs when my eyes met hers. A million full moons spun behind them, calling the kernel of Chaos that had started cresting in me at that time of the lunar cycle. My bones ached as she seemed to dive into my soul, deeper, deeper, until she ran up against the knot that was my bond with Troy.

"That's interesting," she murmured, prodding it. "Odin said you would likely need a Hunter to reach fulfillment as Mistress, although I think that declaration was premature given the recent development of your gifts. Still, good of you to be proactive in seeking one out. That pleases me."

I couldn't answer because I still couldn't breathe. My vision was going white at the edges. My phone buzzed on my desk, but it sounded like it was on the other side of the world.

"Oh. Of course."

Artemis dropped her fingers, and me. I caught myself on my hands and knees, dragging a breath in and shaking my head to clear it.

"I have a task for you, little mortal. One of my nymphs escaped my wrath many years ago. She broke free from her starry prison and has been hidden from me since. Imagine my surprise to find her here, a stone's throw from my new Huntress. A curious convergence of fate, no?"

I stared at the carpet, trying to organize my thoughts. "Your nymph, lady?"

"Yes. We would have our Wild Hunt and wash this world clean, but she represents an issue. Therefore, you shall be my tool." Amusement tinged her voice. "Consider it a test. If you can best this quarry, you are fit to be our Mistress of the Hunt here on Earth and shall be favored as such. She's not a celestial anymore, so it can't be that difficult. Even for one so new to her power as you."

"My lady, do you know where she is?"

"No. Only that the energy is here. I was told you were a seeker. Go seek. Don't disappoint me."

A ring hit the floor in front of me with a clang that sounded too loud for such a small trinket. "When it's done, put that on and call for me."

I couldn't find words as I reached for the ring with a shaking hand. My fingers writhed and cramped at the power leaking from it. It was etched in the same conifer pattern as her belt. What the hell did it mean to be Mistress of the Hunt? What fucking nymph? How the hell was I supposed to recognize one? I had no idea what they smelled like or the shape of their magic.

Before I could ask, the pressure vanished in a psychic thunderclap. I sat back on my heels and found myself alone in my office, head spinning and half a heave away from vomiting. When I could breathe normally again, I grabbed a Kleenex from the desk to wipe the sweat from my face since my shirt was damp with it.

What the hell had just happened? Neith and Mixcoatl usually pulled me into the Crossroads for a chat or invaded my dreams. Neith had started manifesting on this plane in the last few weeks, and her slap in the Crossroads had made me bleed in the real but...

A realization hit me like Neith's metal-edged blow had. They had my blood. Janae had worried about that when Neith had half-manifested at one of the alliance negotiation meetings. The ancient Egyptians had been able to do all kinds of magic with blood. Hell, even a modern vodoun or santero could do some powerful spells with a little of it. That the gods could use a few drops of mine to find me and cross the planes shouldn't have surprised me. I just hoped it wasn't more than that.

"Fuck," I muttered, repeating it louder when saying it softly didn't quite encompass the extent of my feelings. It looked like I had my unusual case, not to mention a lesson in being careful what you wished for. I reviewed my updated to-do list.

One: find and eliminate a rogue vampire sorcerer who was probably a necromancer, along with any possibility that the rabisu summoned by the lich could return.

Two: get the vampire Reveal out of the way before Callista could thwart it.

Three: figure out which of Artemis's nymphs were in the Triangle, and four, what the hell to do about it. I wasn't fixing to kill some poor girl just because an arrogant goddess said so, but I also wasn't keen on dying for the same reason.

The buzz of my phone pulled me out of the merry-go-round of my thoughts. From my spot on the floor, I reached up and patted around until I found it, bringing it back down so I could lean against the desk. My voice rasped as I said, "Hello?"

"What the hell were you doing with the bond?" Troy snapped.

"It wasn't me." I needed some water. Wine would be better.

An irritated sigh rippled down the line and I could practically see him gathering self-control. "Do tell."

"Artemis."

Silence. Then, "Excuse me?"

"The goddess. Artemis. She paid me a visit. She thinks you're my Hunter. That *I* bonded *you*. She's pleased." My stomach rebelled, and I swallowed, focusing on breathing to keep it from emptying.

"*What?*" The receiver crackled, as though he'd covered the mouthpiece, then again when he came back. "Where are you?"

I laughed, tasting bitterness in the back of my throat. "You're asking?"

"Don't give me that," he snarled. "We have an agreement. I keep my word. Now, where are you?"

"Doesn't matter. I suggest you focus on getting ready for the Reveal. Or go help the witches find the sorcerer."

"Are you serious? If you want me to—"

A headache bloomed, throbbing across my forehead. "Yes," I said, cutting him off. "I'm serious. In the meantime, I'm going to be working on all the other problems that have been dropped into my lap—none of which pay, by the way, and we don't all come from royalty and wealth. Figure. It. Out."

I hung up and dropped my head between my knees, trying to find the presence of mind to have a panic attack. Nothing came. I was so overwhelmed that it was all beyond processing.

Chapter 10

After another ten minutes of trying to decide on a human case, I called it a day and went home. Goddess knew I needed the money from a mundane job—bills and car loans didn't pay themselves, and I couldn't conjure up money like the djinn had to buy the land we'd built my house on. My brain was still scrambled from my brush with the divine though. On the drive home, I cursed myself as six different kinds of fool for not negotiating income into the agreement for the alliance.

When I pulled into my driveway, I cursed for a different reason.

"Seriously?" I said before I'd even slammed my car door.

Troy straightened from his slouch against his black Acura MDX, giving me a flashback to his insisting I take him with me to fight the lich. A black duffel bag hung from his shoulder, and I shuddered, remembering Leith Sequoyah having a similar one.

The elf was unbothered by my mood. "We weren't done talking, and you turned your phone off."

"For a fucking reason! You need to quit turning up at my house." I needed to have someone out to check the boundary stones. Unless they were working, and he really didn't mean me harm. That possibility made me frown as I brushed past him, jumping at the usual spark then fisting my hands and rounding on him in a fury. "And stop doing that too!"

"It's not me! It's whatever your Chaos magic has done to the bond. You think I like being around someone who radiates static electricity?" He narrowed his eyes at me. "How far back is your elven ancestor for Chaos to be that strong in you, anyway? I did some research, and it should be things like standing coins on their edges, not warping tracking spells."

That was interesting, but I wasn't ready to answer his question.

"Why are you here and how many policemen did you have to mindmaze, speeding like that?" If he'd been in Monteague territory in Chapel Hill or Carrboro, that was twice the distance I'd had to drive.

"Seriously?" He mimicked my pitch and tone to send my blood pressure rocketing higher. "You name drop a goddess, suggest that she *wants* us to be bound together, hang up on me, and think I'm not going to come looking for you? I need answers, Finch. Not tomorrow, not whenever you feel like it, but now."

"Go away, Monteague," I said in an icy whisper. "You're not getting them." I turned my back on him and stomped toward my house.

"Then I guess you're not getting this," he called.

I didn't want to turn around and look, but everything Troy did served his own interests. As long as he was bound to fulfill debts to me, that interest might well run parallel to mine. With a growl of frustration, I stopped on the top step of my porch and spun around.

Troy was standing with dark eyebrows lifted, slapping a large stack of cash against one palm.

"What's that for?" I asked grudgingly, unable to help myself from watching it. Even if it was all ones, that was a decent amount of money.

He shrugged. "Call it expenses. I don't need you distracted with a silly mundane case right now."

Like I said. Always serving his own interests and lucky they paralleled mine. I wanted to tell him to keep the money.

"How much?" I asked instead.

"A thousand, small bills. It's all I had on me."

I kept my face blank as I wondered who the hell went around with that much cash. "I guess that'll do. For now."

"Does that mean I can come in?"

"Nope." I marched back down the stairs and extended my hand for the money.

"Finch—"

"This is not a discussion we are going to have."

Troy frowned. "This isn't the first time I've heard you talk about the gods. Or seen one with you."

Another question I didn't want to answer, but since it concerned the bond between us—and I'd already babbled about it—I might as well. "Odin seems to think I'm not strong enough to end the world by myself and is apparently a gossipy little shit, so he told Artemis I needed a Hunter. I don't know if it's good or bad that Neith and Mixcoatl haven't popped in this week, but I'll count my blessings."

He blanched. "You talk about them like they're people."

I threw my hands out. "What the hell else am I supposed to do, sit down and cry? As far as I can tell they're like djinn with scarier powers and bigger grudges. Which means, at the end of the day, they're petty as fuck and just as self-absorbed. Have I answered all your questions now?"

"You can't join the Wild Hunt."

"You think I want to?"

"I think they'll find a way to tempt you."

"The lich lord tried that as well. Where's he again?"

Troy's lips twisted. "Be careful, Finch. You're drawing the wrong kind of attention."

As I stood there trying to figure out whether or not that was a threat, he tossed the stack of bills into the air, reaching into his truck as I caught it.

"One of these days, we need to start seeing less of each other," I said, deciding that he was just jerking my chain.

"Don't spend all that in one place," Troy shot back as he pulled out case after case of craft beer, blazoned with logos from what had to be every brewery in the Triangle. "Make sure the kobold gets this. I don't need a fae curse on top of everything else."

I started to clap back when he held up a hand, pulled out his phone, and frowned.

Something dark and angry flickered across his features as he swiped a response and put it away. "As fun as this has been, I need to be somewhere."

I fumed and wondered what the hell that text message had been about as he turned the SUV around and rolled down my gravel drive. At least he hadn't tried doing anything fancy. That would have sent gravel shooting all over my overgrown excuse for a yard and pissed off Zanna something good. I didn't quite understand the kobold's landscaping requirements, but they were strict.

"Zanna?" I called as I hopped back up to the porch, shifted the block of Air I left in place to trip up unexpected visitors, and entered. "You home?"

"Working!" she hollered from the direction of my bedroom. I paused to pull a few bills from the stack and shove them in my pocket then put the rest in the fireproof safe hidden behind one of the river stones flanking the fireplace. My bedroom smelled like freshly cut wood and wet paint, and the sense of evil that had clung to it like sap to a tree had finally faded, replaced by the lingering scent of juniper smoke and Janae's aura signature.

Zanna was atop my tallest step ladder, armed with a caulk gun as she finished sealing the new window in place. "Done soon," she said. "The elf?"

"Yeah, that was him." I scowled.

"Shows up lots."

"Tell me about it." I almost told her to go ahead and hex him the next time but held my tongue. My turbulent feelings about Troy shouldn't be a reason to set a kobold on him. Finding a balance was my problem, not anyone else's. Like it or not, he'd been right when he said our antagonism was the weakest link in the alliance's chain. I got along with everyone else just fine, or reasonably so.

Big girl boots, I reminded myself as I closed my eyes, inhaled, and held it. When I let it whoosh out, I relaxed my hold on Air and enjoyed the flow of eddies around the room. It almost felt like it used to.

"He brought your beer," I said. "Ten cases. Where do you want it?"

Her face lit up under its mane of curls. "Room inside?"

"Sure." I'd make space in the pantry or something. It'd spoil if we left it outside in the heat.

Zanna grinned to show pointy teeth. She might well be the richest kobold in Durham if things kept up like this.

"This is good work." I peered more closely at the room. In the week since the attack, she'd swept up all the broken glass, repaired the shattered window and door frame, filled in the deep grooves in the ceiling where the rabisu had slithered in, and assembled the Ikea nightstand I'd bought to replace the one that had been demolished. It looked like I'd be able to sleep in my own bed soon. The couch wasn't bad, but I wanted to stretch out more than it would allow.

"Good to be busy again," she said.

"Let me know if you need anything else. I'm gonna go fetch the beer inside."

Sweat dripped in a damp line down my back and chest by the time I got the pantry rearranged and all the cases in. My gold-wrapped onyx pendant stuck to my chest, and I tugged my shirt, trying to get some air circulation. Flipping on the fans helped. They set the little glass bulbs stuffed with air plants to swaying and the fronds of my parlor palm to dancing, which made me smile. *Getting there.*

Having my house back in order brought to mind some of the smaller cares I'd had before it had been torn to shit. I toyed with the pendant as I surveyed the room. I'd figure out my heritage eventually, but everything else had to come first for now. Speaking of, I hadn't had an update on the hunt for the lich's accomplice in a while.

Janae answered almost as soon as I'd dialed. She did that sometimes, like Spirit told her when someone would be calling. "Blessings upon you, child. We haven't found anything yet."

"Blessings upon you as well. I'm sorry to hear that."

"So am I." She sounded annoyed, probably nothing to do with me, but I chose my words carefully anyway. "Ms. Janae, we need to make every effort to find the lich's accomplice. Whatever it takes. We can't do the Reveal with enemies like that around, and we're running out of time."

"I know, but he's gone to ground. I don't like it, Arden. There aren't many places that could hide a sorcerer-turned-vampire, not and allow space for demon summoning."

"I don't like it either. Keep me posted?"

"Of course, child." She paused, and I started to wish her blessings and hang up when she said, "Am I getting old and addled, or did I sense a planar disturbance downtown earlier?"

I shivered. "Artemis paid me a visit."

Janae knew about the gods visiting me, though not what to do about it. She whistled, low and long. "That can't mean anything good. I suppose we do need to hurry with this business, before it doesn't matter for all the wrong reasons."

"Agreed." Relief tingled that she hadn't asked what Artemis had wanted. Maybe Janae would have been able to help me track down this nymph, maybe not. Either way, I needed that rogue sorcerer handled and one less variable to worry about with the Reveal. When she didn't say anything else, I wished her well and hung up, burying my face in my hands.

"Work in the bedroom's done. Do your own sheets," Zanna said from behind me.

I jumped, having been too busy ruminating to pay attention to the shift in air currents.

"Bless you, Zanna. Best landlord ever. Beer's in the pantry." Never thank the fae. Weird shit happened when you did, and I had enough of that in my life just now.

She beamed and strutted to the pantry to grab a few bottles while I tried to figure out how to find an enemy who didn't want to be found. A lightbulb went off: go back to the scene of the crime—the lich's lair—and see what I could dig up. It had been daytime before. In the chaos of killing the lich and his zombies, and the urgency of our departure afterward, I might have missed something that would lead us to the accomplice. Or maybe something would be obvious in the wee hours of the night that hadn't been at sunset. Raleigh PD might have gathered all the mundane evidence, but they wouldn't be able to do anything about magical residue.

Grimly, I shouted to Zanna that I'd be back in a bit and headed for the car. I couldn't fix everything, but I could at least try harder to do something about the lich's accomplice before Callista outmaneuvered me.

Chapter 11

The abandoned cemetery was the same as it had been the last time I was here. Only the crawling sense of dread and death was lighter. The new moon made it almost impossible to see, since I didn't have wereanimal, elf, or vampire night vision to navigate by starlight alone and there was no other light to see by this far out in the countryside.

I stood by my car, taking in the clearing until the headlights shut off, shivering with the night's chill and remembered fear. Troy had been waiting down the road last time, but it was just me here now. I didn't know what the hell I'd been thinking coming here, other than the fact that we had to get something fucking moving or I was going to be crushed under the weight of everything that was being asked of me just now.

Get your ass in gear. Gritting my teeth, I strapped my enchanted lead-and-steel knife to my thigh then turned on my phone's flashlight and shone it around the clearing for another look. Nothing moved. No sound or breath jostled the air molecules around me. The clearing was as still as it had been on my first visit. I didn't want to go underground at all, let alone at night, but someone had to look.

"There's nothing to worry about," I told myself. I'd burned the lich and his zombies with newly found Fire. The witches had come in after me and cleansed the lair spiritually so that the rabisu that'd attacked my home couldn't find a way back on its own via the evil permeating this place. The mundane cops had been here next, collecting evidence, and all they'd done was bitch about not catching the sick son of a bitch who'd steal and defile a morgue's worth of bodies.

So with all the rounds of cleansing and investigation that had gone on here, why did the Sight still scream of danger?

Without the full djinn ability to see the future in visions, I was forced to rely on my own senses. I paused, digging deep for the cause. Scented the breeze again. Held my breath and listened for as long as I could. Reached with Air to sense any disturbances. Nothing made itself known to me.

It has to be residual evil. My intuition hadn't steered me wrong yet, but this place had been so completely corrupted that I couldn't be sure that that wasn't what I was sensing. *One quick look. Just to be sure nothing got missed.* I'd never tried using Chaos intentionally before, but given that I was probably the only being in the Triangle who could, I had to at least give it a shot.

I breathed deep. Exhaled hard. Drew on my power. Steeled myself. And entered the lair once more.

As before, a long, dark tunnel sloped downward. The human skulls that had studded the walls on my last visit were missing, leaving divots in the wall like missing teeth in a jawbone. I concentrated on my breathing. In. Out. In. Out. Slow and steady, like my paces as I descended. I hated being underground. The air always felt stifled. There was nowhere to move. It was hard to breathe, and I couldn't sense my element moving around me.

Here it was worse—I'd fought for my life and my friends' lives desperately enough that I'd developed a new power.

I kept my fear tightly leashed as I revisited the room where my friends and I had been held captive. Then I explored the other tunnels. There was no hint whatsoever that the lich had had any help in his work. If I hadn't caught the witch-born vamp trying to turn Doc Mike or if the lich himself hadn't spoken of his accomplice, I wouldn't have known he existed.

After a few tries, I managed a burst of Chaos. I didn't know what the hell it would do, but no magic sparked off of it. That much raw power should have triggered something if there was something to trigger, but nothing happened.

I wasn't sure whether to be relieved or disappointed.

Adrenaline coursed through me as I made my way back to the main room and the tunnel to the surface. I didn't know if it was relief or the pounding fear pushing itself to the fore, but I couldn't take much more of being stuck underground.

The scuff of a foot in the dirt ahead of me brought me to a halt, breath held as I tried to press myself into the wall. Had we missed a zombie before?

"There's no use hiding, sylph," a contemptuous masculine voice spat.

My heart pounded so hard I thought it'd burst from my chest. I recognized the voice. For some reason, I hadn't thought I'd ever hear it again. Callum had been one of my captors at Leith's boathouse at Jordan Lake. He'd leered at me after beating the hell outta me, suggesting with his eyes and his words that I could expect the worst if he ever got me alone.

The Redcaps hadn't been eliminated by the Darkwatch after Leith's death, as I'd assumed. They'd gone underground—and they'd found me.

Callum stepped into the beam of my phone's flashlight.

"Good to see you again. Hello." He grinned, making space for more elves to spill into the chamber as he kept coming toward me. "And goodbye."

Most of the newcomers had the light coloration of Sequoyahs. Those faces held an extra measure of hatred. I hadn't just ended their little conspiracy when I'd killed Leith. House Sequoyah had been decimated, ancient Rome-style, by Callista afterward. As they spread out, blocking my way forward, puffs of ash rose from where zombies had burned. The light of their lanterns made their shadows climb the walls and arc over me like one of my nightmares.

I swapped my phone for my knife, Chaos for Air, and bared my teeth at them in a snarl. They all knew what I was, and if I was about to fight to the death, I wasn't about to hamstring myself as I had before.

Troy slipping out of the shadows to close the circle hit me like a fist in the gut, and my grasp on Air stuttered. I drew on it even harder as I counted them. There were nine, including Troy.

Of course he betrayed you. Bile roiled in my stomach, blending with self-contempt and the weight of something I couldn't identify as it broke in my chest. Not my heart but some sense of rightness. I'd actually believed him. Thought he, among all other elves, might have my back after all his grand words and gestures. Believed him strongly enough that I'd spared him the last time we were here.

But there he was, grim-faced as he drew his longknife.

"Monteague, you were late. That means you soften her up on your own. Take her," Callum ordered.

Every elf in the room smiled to show sharp fangs as Troy squared up and rushed me. If they were showing off their secondary teeth, then they were confident that I wasn't going to survive this encounter. Nine elves was probably more than I could handle, but I'd go down fighting and take as many of them with me as I could.

The thunder of my blood faded into the background. I gripped both Air and Fire, knowing my eyes flashed an even brighter gold as I held my strike until Troy was close enough that I could follow up with a killing blow from my enchanted knife.

I'd seen him fight. He was too fast for me to afford making a mistake.

As I prepared to throw enough lightning to stop his heart, he stopped muting the bond between us. I got a whisper of intent that made me hesitate, something that felt protective rather than murderous. My heart skipped as I held the bolt a half second too long. Then he whirled under my raised knife, slipping behind me and jarring me as his back pressed to mine.

Gasping in shock, I released the elemental buildup in a crackle of lightning at the blond elf now directly in front of me.

The Sequoyah danced aside with an outraged shout as Troy snarled, "None of them can live."

"Are they all down here?" Still shaken, brain scrambling, I prepared a wall of Air.

"Yes." The scent of burnt meringue choked me as Troy drew deeply on Aether.

Hatred painted Callum's face, and he nodded as though a suspicion had been confirmed. "We all wondered how the hell the elemental had survived. I guess that means you're both responsible for House Sequoyah's fall too."

Angry mutters and curses agreed with him. Troy didn't answer.

At a hand signal from Callum, the Redcaps attacked en masse. I set the wall of Air at the entrance to the tunnel and tied off the chord of magic, praying that it would hold long enough to finish the fight. That done, I spun a whirlwind through the room to stagger half the group. Realistically, I would play crowd control while Troy killed them, but I wasn't about to rely on him to do all the work.

Callum came straight for me. He'd taken me down easily at the boathouse, mocking my beginner-level hapkido skills as he smashed through my blocks. I was better this time—and I wasn't trying to hide what I was. He bellowed in pain as I stabbed an arrow of Air at him, staggering as it caught him in the upper left chest. Another elf slipped in front of him, and I lifted him with Air to throw him into the recovering Callum.

Behind me, Troy muttered spells in elvish as the sound of clashing blades rang dully in the enclosed space. The knot of our bond was heavy with focus in the back of my head. Having a sense of where he was both helped and distracted me as I did my best to keep our opponents from coming at us more than two or three at a time.

The shadows cast by LED lanterns ringing the room gave the elves something to twist and hide in, making it hard to trust my eyes. I had to read the air molecules to make sure I was sending strikes where they would actually land and not at a false shadow.

My knife sparked as I caught a Sequoyah with a glancing slash. I bit back a scream as I took a shallow gash from someone on my other side.

A Redcap was trying to flank us. I looped a coil of Air around his ankle and pulled. He went down with a surprised shout, and Troy ducked under a sword slash to pivot toward the fallen elf and slice his throat. Blood spurted, and the other seven Redcaps fell back, evaluating the situation.

"Separate them. Kill the bitch and get her head this time," Callum said. "Take Monteague alive. He'll die slow."

If they rushed us again, we were fucked. Troy was good, but we were up against a crowd almost as good as he was. My grasp on Air was weak this far underground, with nothing fresh coming through, so pulling on this much of it was tiring me faster than it should. The psychological weights of the earth overhead and remembered terror of the Redcaps pounded at me as well, blending with the memory of the lich and Grimm's death. And as Maria had pointed out, numbers beat strength.

I panted, my back pressed against Troy's.

Aether rose as six of the Redcaps linked, first three and three then all together, and started chanting. Callum grinned, fisting the hand not holding a damn machete on his hip as he waited. They could have used magic from the start, but as I remembered from the boathouse, these assholes liked hurting people with their hands. I supposed it was a compliment that they'd take the easier route now.

Troy drew hard on Aether. "Don't let them finish that spell!"

He threw something that I couldn't read the shape of, which Callum deflected with a shouted word of elvish.

An idea struck me.

"Hold your breath," I whispered.

Troy inhaled deeply without question, and I did the same. The Redcap chant started to crescendo, and I sent an explosion of Air outward, knocking them back and cutting it off. As they all exhaled with the force of the blow, I thinned the air in the room.

Not realizing what had happened, they stood, mouths open to continue their spell...then stumbled, gasping for breath. Troy started a lunge toward the closest, and I grabbed him to keep him close to me as I unleashed a crackle of chain lightning with my other hand. My hair rose as it zapped through the room, striking its targets now that they were too slow and addled to dodge and leaping from one to the next.

Blood trickled over my lips as pushing too hard triggered yet another damn nosebleed. This had to work because I didn't have much more in me.

Chapter 12

The remaining seven elves tried to cry out as they fell, but all they managed were sickly rattles. My stomach twisted at what I was doing, but it was me or them. When they were all down, writhing with oxygen deprivation and electric shock, I rebalanced the air and let go of Troy.

As one, we finished our enemies. Troy cut throats, starting with Callum. I let my enchanted blade drink heart's blood as my own heart raged. The same green flame that had consumed Leith's corpse sparked from each of the three I killed. Their life energy flowed into me as they died, revitalizing me a little too much. I imagined it was like sticking a fork into an electrical socket, a sudden, overwhelming jolt that threatened to fry my synapses. One or two lives, or lives with less magical strength behind them, might have been manageable. I didn't know what tomtar enchantment Nils had put in the blade. What I was discovering was that three lives powered by active, high-blood elven magic was far too much.

The extra energy raged within me, threatening to split me into pieces. "Fuck," was all I had time to mutter before I did the only thing I could think of: send it into the ground.

Earth responded. Not just *the* earth, but *Earth*, elemental power that I hadn't been able to touch since the last time I was here, with Laurel guiding my magic through a lattice to destroy the lich lord's amulet. A rumble sounded. Then another. The ground quaked, and a clod of dirt thudded to the floor, followed by another. The wall of Air shattered with a discordant twang only I could hear, adding a jolt to what was pouring into the chamber walls.

Troy looked up at the dirt ceiling then launched himself at me as I tried to ride the wave of power and do something to control it. I staggered, lost between the physical world and the power I could see shining in the veins of the earth with my third eye, as he tried to pull me in his wake.

"Damn it, Finch, move! Before the ceiling comes down!"

When I couldn't, too lost in the unending depths of Earth and the terror that accompanied it deep within me, he growled and tossed me over his shoulder before running for the tunnel. I bounced against his back, trying first to stop the energy pouring out of me, then to call it back. Nothing worked, and being upside down was making me lightheaded.

We made it halfway out before the cavern behind us collapsed, sending a shudder through the tunnel. Troy swore and dropped me before gathering me under him, against the wall. I clung to him, unable to do anything else as the tunnel went the way of the cavern.

Soil covered us. Among my many nightmares, this was a big one—being unable to move or breathe or touch Air through the solid weight of earth. Suddenly, I couldn't fill my lungs. Every breath was small, too shallow and smelling of a sickening blend of the grave and elves. I thought my heart would thunder out of my chest.

Troy grunted as I struggled beneath him.

"Be still!" he snapped. Without the push of Aether behind it, his words did absolutely nothing.

"I have to get out. Have to get out. Can't—I need air!" With the dregs of the stolen energy, I grabbed for the last of my connection to Earth and pushed as hard as I could.

The ground above us exploded upward. Troy let me go with a growled exclamation to the Goddess as I scrambled to follow it, clawing my way up from the pit to haul myself out. When I was aboveground, I lay in the grass and looked up at the sky, hyperventilating and shaking so hard my teeth rattled, convincing myself that I wasn't buried alive. I was free, in the fresh, open air, and I could breathe.

I reached for my magic, filling myself to bursting with it just to prove to myself that I could.

"I need to stop being present when you discover new powers." Troy breathed heavily as he flopped to the ground beside me. When I didn't answer, he propped himself on an elbow and frowned as he peered down at me. "Are you okay?"

I pushed him out of my line of sight so that I could see the stars. A spark jumped between us, as usual, and deep concern echoed through the bond. "I need the sky," I said hoarsely. "I can't—underground is—I need air."

He didn't respond, just rolled onto his back and lay next to me as I found all the constellations I knew then counted all the stars I could see through the ring of trees overhead. When my heart rate had returned to normal and I no longer shook with fear and adrenaline, I said, "I'll count that as one of the lives."

"I was hoping you'd say that," he said blandly.

We lay in silence a little longer as guilt nibbled at my heart.

"Actually, I guess it's two," I finally said. "One for siding with me against the Redcaps. One for protecting me when the roof came down on us, since that was my fault."

Grass whispered as he tilted his head toward me. "With the marker you called in for the vampire ball, that would make us even."

Wariness radiated from both his tone and the bond.

I grimaced, not liking to admit that I'd liked having him owe me but unable to talk my way out of doing what I knew was right. "Yeah. I guess it does." With a sigh, I added the formal words. "Debt was owed, and debt is paid. Three times offered, and three times taken. And so it is."

"And so it is," Troy echoed. Relief surged through the bond, heavy enough to wash the last of the tension still in me.

"What's all that?" I asked.

"All what?"

"The relief."

With a flash of embarrassment, he muted the bond again, locking it down so tightly that all I got was a vague sense of him being alive. "Maybe you'll believe me now."

I frowned. "About what?"

"Being an ally." He sat up and picked at a blade of grass. "I saw your face when I entered the cavern. You didn't trust that I'd fight for you."

I refused to feel guilty about that or to apologize for it. "You play a lot of shit close to the chest, Monteague, and if there's one thing I can be sure of, it's that you'll do anything to keep your word. I just never know which oath will be most important to you in a given situation. The one to the alliance? To the Darkwatch? I assume there's one to your House, and your queen, and your sister. Too many loyalties, and it's not like anyone is ever—"

I stopped talking, pressing my lips together before I could turn what was actually an okay moment into a bitchfest that he wouldn't care about.

Yeah. Roman's leaving had hit me way harder than I'd thought. Tears welled, and I turned my face away, blinking until they were gone.

Troy glanced down at me, then into the trees. "You need to feel like someone's on your side. For your sake. But we're all supporting you for reasons of our own. Is that it?"

"Finally!" The word exploded from me, and I threw my hands in the air then pushed myself to a seated position. "Someone gets it. I don't know why it's you of all people, but yeah, that's about it."

Why was it easier to talk to someone who'd been a deadly enemy a few months ago than it ever had been to talk to Roman?

"Trust me, Finch. I know the feeling."

"Doubt it. Nobody wants you dead," I muttered, annoyed for some reason about how quickly our moment of understanding had become about him. What else had I expected?

"Is that so?" He rubbed his chest over his heart, where I remembered there being a long, wide scar, sounding contemplative rather than defensive. "I'll be sure to tell Alli. She'll be relieved not to have to look out for any more assassins."

He wasn't saying it in a poor-me kind of way. It felt more like an offering. Showing me a little more of what was behind the mask of neutrality or uncaring hostility he usually wore. Maybe it was his way of saying thanks for acknowledging the debt as paid and freeing him from one of his oaths, promises, and vows.

I didn't know what to say to that or how to feel about it. Leaning to nudge his shoulder with mine, I said, "Not sure what to do with you when you're not being an asshole."

"You mean when I'm not throwing you into lakes or making you see my grandmother? Or when we're not killing people together?" he said dryly.

I snorted a laugh then froze at the fact that I'd done so, which made his lips curl in a small hint of what might be the first smile I'd seen on the man.

All he said though was, "Let's see what the hell you did and get out of here before I have to explain something I'd rather not to people I'm not sure I can trust."

I wasn't keen to return to the collapsed mound, which now looked like a sinkhole getting ready to drop, but I wasn't about to admit fear to Troy. He might have seen me deep in its throes not too long ago, but pride wouldn't let me bow to it again.

Hugging myself, I followed him to the edge of the round disturbance and forced myself to prod it with a toe.

"What did you mean when you said you're not sure if you can trust people?" I asked.

He glanced back from where he'd crouched a few steps into the disturbed area, shading his eyes from my phone's flashlight until I pointed it away. "Those were the last of the Redcaps that the Darkwatch was sure of. A few were killed when Callista punished the Sequoyahs. The rest went to ground after Leith's death was confirmed."

"You're saying someone sheltered them."

"That, and called them together again." He rose and dusted his hands off, not that it did any good, given the rest of him was covered in dirt. "Someone who didn't know I was in deep cover with them."

My blood chilled by degrees. "Someone sent them after me?"

"I think so."

"But you aren't sure, which is why you've been following me around the Triangle since the end of January. You were hoping to catch them."

Troy shrugged, his expression closing. "Partly."

And partly because I'm your "assignment"—whatever that means. We might have reached a new level of understanding, but there would always be layers with him.

"Who's on the list?" I asked instead.

"Very few people," he said, sounding grim. "All of whom will be problematic to deal with. Can you sense any magic left here? I've dispelled the Aetheric residue and muddled my signature as best I can."

The change of subject bugged me—I wanted to know who needed to be at the top of my shitlist. But I let it pass, telling myself it was delegation. Troy was clearly inclined to figure it out, and I needed to focus on finding another angle in the hunt for the vampire sorcerer now that I'd thoroughly destroyed anything that might have been missed here.

Forcing myself to breathe evenly, I reached first for Air then, carefully, for Earth. I hissed as the ground tried to swallow me again and pulled back. "Echoes of Earth. But I'm the only elemental I know of who'd be able to handle that much of it, and as far as everyone else knows, all I have is Air and Fire." I leveled a look at him. "This time, I'd like to keep it that way."

"As far as I'm concerned, tonight never happened," he said flatly.

I eyed his dirty, blood-spattered clothes and disheveled appearance. "Right."

"Alli will cover for me."

"If you say so."

We stood there on the grave of our enemies, looking at each other until a wave of tiredness made me sway on my feet.

"I'm gonna get going," I said.

Before I did, I gave him a last, long look. We weren't friends, but I thought we might be coming to an understanding at least. He was respecting boundaries and had kept his word to me. Tonight could have been much, much worse.

"Glad we're allies, Monteague." I couldn't quite keep the grudging tone out of my words, but I did mean it.

"Likewise."

I couldn't read the soft note in his voice, and I wasn't going to work myself into knots trying.

Chapter 13

The drive home seemed to take twice as long because of how fucking tired I was. I slumped when I pulled into my driveway, resting my forehead on the steering wheel and thinking I had to stop using myself so hard. The echo of the position I'd been in at The Umstead brought back the memory of kissing Maria, and I warmed.

I'd liked it. A lot. Too much maybe.

But being trapped in the earth, my panic and the overwhelming feeling of being crushed, never to feel the brush of a breeze on my face again…

I shuddered and got out of the car, which suddenly felt far too confining.

Being with a vampire would mean spending a hell of a lot more time underground. Just the thought of it made my heart race, and I had to take deep breaths as I embraced Air to calm down. *I can't. If only because of the lifestyle.* I needed the sun and the trees, the wind and the fog rising over the Eno on chilly mornings. More than anything, I needed more fresh air than I'd ever get if I was a vampire's partner. As much as I liked Maria, I'd have to find a way to gently let her down. I didn't look forward to that conversation.

Maybe there's a compromise. I trudged up the stairs of my front porch, unraveling and shifting the block of Air more out of habit than attention. That led me to the idea of people tripping over it, which reminded me that I was going to have a bunch of strangers here tomorrow evening. This evening? Soon. My chest and jaw tightened.

"Zanna?" I called as I opened the door and went in, dropping my knife on the kitchen table and my backpack on the floor alongside it. "You around? I'm gonna take a quick shower and then make a snack."

If she was, she'd make her way in from the crawlspace. I went around and opened all the windows, needing the reassurance that just because I was indoors didn't mean I was underground or trapped. Cool evening air slipped in, and I let it soothe me as I scrubbed my hands and arms then cracked open a bottle of Sangiovese to let it breathe. If I didn't want to have a power hangover for tomorrow's big wereanimal gathering, I'd need to see about balancing the elements with Chaos.

I wanted to luxuriate in the hot shower, but the night wasn't over yet. The tub was filthy when I finally managed to scrub all the dirt and blood from my curls and body. The cut I'd taken was already healing, and I decided to let it be. I dressed quickly in boxer shorts and a T-shirt, throwing a light robe over it before heading back to the kitchen.

A shift in the currents announced Zanna.

"Hey," I greeted her without pulling my head out of the fridge. Food would help stave off the hangover as well. "Drink? Snack?"

"Always welcome." She climbed onto one of the chairs around my dining table.

Maybe it won't be so bad having other folks here. I'd adjusted to Zanna easily enough. It had been strange to come home from killing Leith to find that a kobold had claimed my property, but the fae had become a friend. Or at least a friendly face. I relaxed into the feeling as I prepared a plate of Muscadine grapes, nuts, charcuterie, and sharp cheese. I had no idea what beer matched the food I'd pulled out, so I just grabbed one and set it in front of her along with the plate.

"What are you eating?" She snagged the whole cluster of grapes.

I blinked then went back to prepare a second, smaller plate. The amount of food a kobold could eat always surprised me.

"Are you around tomorrow?" I asked when I'd gotten everything together and settled into the chair across from her. "I'm expecting guests."

"Around." She eyed me, noshing on a wedge of cheese. "The elf is courting?"

"Uh, no. Definitely not." That that had been her first assumption unsettled me. First Maria, now Zanna. I frowned. Maria's comments I had written off as teasing the obvious antagonism between Troy and me. What the hell did they see that I didn't? Or was this just that nonsense of people thinking boys bother girls when they like them? Shaking it off, I said, "Roman's sister is in town. Vikki. She needs to meet with Terrence and Ximena, and we need space and privacy. They're all based in Durham, so..." I shrugged.

"Should be interesting," Zanna said cautiously. "As long as they're courteous."

"I'm sure they will be. They're aware that this land is protected by one of the fae."

As intended, that comment made her puff up with pride and take a satisfied sip of her beer. "I won't tolerate rudeness."

"Ximena promised to bring proper tribute." I nibbled a slice of ham, relaxing a little as Zanna nodded in satisfaction. "Can I give them the address then?"

"Oh. You waited to speak to me first?"

"Of course. We both live here." Even if she hadn't been invited, Zanna more than pulled her weight. Besides, I didn't want to find all my eggs suddenly gone off or my belongings cursed.

"A model tenant. Yes. They may come." The platter that should have served two full-grown adults was empty, and she finished the rest of her beer before collecting the crumbs on her fingertip. She rose and left the can and platter for me to clean up. "See you tomorrow."

For once, she managed not to trip over the block of Air on the way out. I wondered if that made me predictable.

Sighing, I topped up my wine and picked at the rest of the food on my plate, deciding to wait until the morning to text the weres my address so that I'd have one less thing to lose sleep over. I hadn't just called Zanna in for a friendly snack and an update. I'd been trying to avoid the thoughts I knew would be waiting as soon as I was alone.

Leering, sharp-toothed elves.

The press of earth all around me.

The ongoing weight of feeling like I wasn't good enough at any of this to pull it off, sitting heavy in my belly and keeping me up at night with worry. Callista had had centuries to secure her power base. I was trying to dismantle it and set up my own in months. With a Reveal involved, failure wasn't an option.

A sick feeling curled up from my gut to my throat, closing it as too many gross emotions warred. I washed them down with more wine, trying to focus my attention on freeing Chaos enough to even out the extra power draw earlier. Glancing at my knife, I wondered if the energy of the lives I'd taken would balance it. The thought that Janae wouldn't approve of using life to fuel magic made me even more conflicted. The older witch was becoming something of a mentor to me, and I hated the idea of disappointing her. At the same time, I refused to feel bad about what had happened. They'd come for me, and I was done taking shit. Her morals were good for what she needed them to guide. Mine had to be a little different.

Still didn't make me feel any better. Conflict tilted back and forth in my mind and heart. I knew I'd only done what I had to, but that still felt like a slippery slope. Had Callista started out only doing what she had to?

A ripping tug at my core was all the warning I had of an interplanar shift. I froze as Neith stepped through nothingness, looking around my house with interest before leaning on the half-wall that separated the dining area from the front door. She was in battle garb again today, strip-leather armor on top, a red kilt wrapping her hips, and a strip of red cloth holding thin locs away from her face. For once, she'd left her staff on whatever plane the gods held, but she still whirled a hand-sized ankh on a leather thong.

"Stop worrying about it, girl," the goddess said while I gaped.

Her voice was a little too much for my ears, and I winced as the adrenaline crash from earlier was reversed. A headache ratcheted to the fore, and I clenched my fists to stop them from trembling as I averted my eyes. From what I'd read, respect would do as well as fear with the gods. Neith, in particular, seemed to favor me.

She caught sight of my almost-full wine glass. "You offer tribute. How clever to anticipate my arrival."

Heart pounding, I slid the glass across the table. *What the everloving fuck does she want and why is she here?* I needed to get a stronger warding for my house. Fast.

"A Roman grape," she said, her eyes on me as she sipped. "Fine tribute. I don't know what Artemis was bitching about. You're perfectly well-behaved."

"I am glad my lady is pleased," I managed to say. My mouth was dry, and I looked at the table, watching her in my peripheral vision. "To what do I owe the honor of this visit?"

"I think you know." Her voice echoed with the lonely wildness of wind skirling across the red desert.

Other than Artemis's side quest, the only thing that the gods were interested in—as far as it concerned me, anyway—was my usefulness to them as Mistress of the Wild Hunt.

"I used Earth," I said, barely audibly.

"So you did. Foolish of you to come so close to entombing yourself, but I suppose that is what your Hunter is for. We are pleased that he serves so ably. You may keep him."

Troy would be overjoyed to know that the gods didn't require him to become an offering of bone and blood as part of whatever they were planning. I swallowed, hard, and didn't answer. If the gods could not only find and see me but were watching, shit was a lot more serious than I'd thought.

"Nothing to say?"

"I...no, my lady." I didn't know if I could do it again, but she'd probably be expecting it.

"That is well. You will continue to develop your powers." Neith reached out and tipped my chin up. My head spun at the backwash of power that casually ebbed from her, and I fell into eyes so dark they were black. Ages echoed in them, the weaving and sundering of lives so immense that I couldn't breathe. "I do not see Water in you yet, but if you have Air, Fire, and Earth, then you are a primordial elemental. Water is there. You will do whatever it takes to break through to it. Our primordial powers were spent creating this world. You're all we have to reshape it."

I shuddered, wavering, and she freed me. All I could do was focus on remembering who the fuck I was.

"We will have our hunt. It will be led by a primordial, as is proper. How fortunate that we did not kill you in the disappointment of our first meeting." Neith smiled then grew stern as her voice hardened, hitting me like a gale. "Do not think to defy us or play the fool. The time is coming, and you will serve. Until then, a gift."

I gasped as she released me from her attention and reached into empty air to draw a dagger from the ether of another plane, stabbing it into my wood dining table alongside my tomtar-crafted blade. Neith's gift was smaller, deceptively simple in styling, with a serpent carved into a hilt of ivory and a scarab carved from black stone making up the pommel. The blade was the same grey-black as the one Troy carried. Meteoric iron?

"To match your little toy there." She eyed my elf-killer dismissively. "Be careful. It will not do for you to die before you can use it on our behalf." Before I could answer, she shimmered, shifted planes, and was gone.

The door banged open, bringing me to my feet as I drew on Air and readied a strike. I had to look down to see the intruder: Zanna, teeth bared and hazed with power.

"Interplanar visitor." I winced an apology.

Shaking her head, she eased off whatever fae magic she had prepped and crossed her arms. A dangerously furious expression crossed her face. "The gods *never* show proper respect. Rudest of all guests."

Shaking her head, Zanna let the door slam behind her as she headed back to the woods, muttering about troublesome tenants and arrogant gods, leaving me with a single thought.

Neith had called me a primordial elemental.

Chapter 14

Val took one look at my hands the next morning and swore. She was a firefighter; she knew what burns looked like in all their stages. "Are you kidding me? Arden!"

I shrugged, annoyed and pained at having burnt myself worse than usual in a pre-dawn practice session, driven by the sleeplessness brought on by nightmares of elves and gods. Had I been human, I'd have needed hospitalization. As it was, the dregs of djinn healing ability in me would have the last of the damage healed well before I had to meet Troy in Raleigh to get Torsten's approval on security for the Reveal. Good thing too. I wasn't about to explain anything to him.

"Come on in." I swept one hand, shiny with ointment, inward.

With a frustrated noise, Val surged to the house with her paper bag of breakfast. "You've been forcing it, haven't you?" The kitchen filled with the scent of eggy burritos and fresh biscuits as she made herself at home and unpacked it. "You have to *embrace* Fire, not wrestle with it! It's a *dance*, not a, a—whatever you've been doing!"

Her passionate exhortations cut through the gloom that had carried over from yesterday, and I cracked a smile. "So, I shouldn't just grab at it?"

"No! You have to—" She looked up, tossing short bangs out of her face, and rolled her eyes when she caught sight of my expression. "Fine. You learn the hard way."

"I think I have been," I said with a grimace. "It's not usually this bad. I just…some shit went down with the elves, and I dunno. I guess I needed to let it out." I didn't know if we were that close of friends yet, to complain like this. I was definitely still feeling funny about the whole kidnapping thing. But I was tired and lonely and needed a friend, dammit.

"Why didn't you say so?" She abandoned breakfast to launch herself at me.

I grunted as her small but bulky form hugged me. Between burned hands and my own awkwardness, I just kind of stood there until she was satisfied that I was comforted.

"Let's eat," she said, pulling away. "Then we talk about how in Hades you can even *do* this. Then we talk about the Reveal. Okay?"

"Sounds good. And thanks. I really, you know, thought you'd be mad at me."

She shrugged, settling in at my small dining table and biting off an unbelievably huge chunk of her breakfast burrito. It was only half-chewed when she said, "I think I'm more pissed that you let the lich talk you into showing up. Without all four elements, he was a little screwed for the whole, 'We're going to take over the world!' part of his plan."

I snagged a biscuit to be polite—breakfast wasn't really my thing—and picked at it with my fingertips. "How're the other two?"

"Sofi will mend. I wasn't excited that she revealed herself to Nazneen, but it actually made things easier. Naz would do anything for her." Sadness flickered in her eyes, and she paused in her aggression toward her breakfast. "I just hope she doesn't have to. Laurel is…Laurel. She was always a bit of an oddball. Hard to tell."

"Am I still persona non grata?"

Val winced. She'd been the messenger for the news that the other elementals really didn't want anything to do with me. I drew too much attention to myself and had too much interaction with elves. "Pretty much. Laurel might talk to you, but she's got a farm between here and Hillsborough that keeps her pretty busy."

"Fair enough." I set aside my biscuit and tried not to sound as disappointed as I felt.

"Cheer up." Val stuffed the last bite of her burrito into her mouth. "At least this way, nobody else has to have their minds blown by a sylph who can handle Fire. Talk to me."

I frowned, trying to sort out what was important. "Mixcoatl shot me with a lightning arrow back when I was dealing with the Sequoyah case. To pull it out without electrocuting myself, I had to touch Fire. You'd said Fire and Air were sympathetic, so…" I shrugged. "Anyway, the lich's amulet was formed of Earth, but Fire lived in it."

"Ignoring that you're talking about the *gods*, Laurel said the stone felt like it had been labradorite once. Igneous—formed from lava."

"Dunno. But could feel Earth and Fire in its structure." I squirmed and reached for my pendant before I could stop myself. I didn't like remembering that. "So, with her creating a structure of Earth and you to provide a shortcut for Fire, I reached and made lightning. Like in the arrow."

Val sat back and crossed her arms, looking dumbfounded. "You just…reached."

"Yeah."

"And that's what you do now."

"Yep. Lightning isn't *easy* but it's manageable. I can make flames but..." I held up my hands, palms out.

She shook her head. "I guess that's to be expected. I'm naturally fire-resistant, but you weren't born with Fire. That might happen no matter what you do or how much practice you get."

"No free passes in magic." I sighed. "I'll try being less grabby with it next time."

"I'd almost advise just sticking to adding a dash of it for lightning if you have to do something active. Fire's the least predictable element and the fastest to twist. The dea of legend could cause spontaneous combustion, screw up people's nervous systems, melt shit. It's not just pure flame. As strong as you are with Air, it wouldn't surprise me if one of the higher active powers manifested for you by accident."

I grimaced, not having realized those were all possibilities. "Noted."

"Good. I'll check the lore, now that I have a better idea of what you're dealing with." She eyed the other burritos on the counter. "You having one?"

"Take mine. Zanna might pop in later for the other one."

Val didn't need to be invited twice. Before digging in, she asked, "What's the latest on the Reveal?"

I updated her with everything I knew, adding, "Elementals are still excused from everything, but you'll have to be careful. The mundanes are going to lose their shit. If you go out on an alarm and aren't burnt when they think you should be—"

"Got it." She scowled. "It's annoying, but it could be worse. We could be the vampires." Her expression cleared, and she lifted her eyebrows. "Speaking of, Maria's cute."

"She is." I had no problem agreeing with that and kept my hands under the table to stop myself from running a finger over my lips, remembering the kiss.

"But you're still hung up on the wolf."

"I—it's not that. He's not coming back."

Val's expression turned wry.

"He's not," I insisted. "Even if he did, why would I go back to someone who set me aside to run back to his abusive family the first chance he got?"

She pulled a not-bad-Obama face, the corners of her lips pulling down as her brows lifted. "Fair. So what's stopping you? Just not into her?"

"I don't know." I folded my arms on the table and rested my forehead on them. "I've got enough to worry about. Maybe if it was just figuring out her hunting me, but then there's the gods and handling Troy fucking Monteague, finding the vampire sorcerer while hoping the rabisu doesn't have a way back to this plane, managing the Reveal...it's too much, Val. I'm tired. I don't have the energy to take a new case, let alone dating."

"I'm not even sure I want to ask about half that shit. Just promise me you'll find some time for play soon."

"Sure," I said, not believing it.

"Seriously, Arden. Don't burn yourself out. We need you. The elementals, not just Otherside. The old-timers are still bickering, but some of us want to join the rest of the community, like you have. Fuck elven law. We want to exist openly. You're managing. It gives the rest of us hope." She squeezed my shoulder.

I know she meant it as support, but it just felt like another burden. Everyone needed me. Everyone wanted a piece of me or my power. Everyone wanted me to solve problems that had been part of the fabric of Otherside for hundreds or thousands of years, at a time when we were trying to pivot toward the humans.

"I'll do what I can," I said. Having the elven death sentence lifted, even from just one House, had been life changing. I'd been strong enough, and desperate enough, to go toe-to-toe with an elven terrorist and the most powerful queen in the Triangle. I didn't owe anyone anything, but how could I deny others like me the chance to enjoy the freedoms I now did, such as they were?

"I know it's a big ask."

I lifted my head and summoned a smile. "It is. But it's important. We'll get it done."

I just prayed that it would cost me less than the alliance had. Grimm's life and Duke's goodwill, lost in exchange for an ever-growing heap of shit that shouldn't have been my problem and now was. But hey, I was the one who'd wanted enough power to stand alone. I just hadn't reckoned on the strings attached.

After Val left, I spent the rest of the day in research to help the witches narrow down possible locations for the rogue sorcerer then cleaned myself up and got ready to go to Raleigh. Vamps appreciated style, so I put on my nicest pair of black jeans and a slinky cowl-neck sleeveless top in a gold that would match my eyes if I was pulling on Air. Sensible black flats won out over heels. No way was I getting caught in Torsten's nest in impractical footwear again. I left my curls to their natural abundance, figuring I could use the extra presence. I applied a damn good smoky eye and a tinted lip gloss to round out the look.

After too much debate with myself, I left my pendant in the drawer of my nightstand. I missed its weight as soon as it was gone but there'd be no hiding it in this top, and I wasn't ready to ask Troy about it. Or more accurately, I wasn't comfortable letting him any further into my life than the bond already forced.

Between the usual accidents and perpetual roadwork, I was almost late. The Triangle was growing faster than city infrastructure could accommodate, especially around Raleigh. The flipped pick-up truck that traffic crawled past on I-40 was unfortunately not even the worst accident I'd seen. Too many transplants from too many different areas meant an overload of cars and a clash of driving cultures. A concert at the PNC Arena caused another slowdown at the Wade Avenue exit, and I thumped the heel of my now-healed palm against the steering wheel until I was clear.

Parking took another chunk of time, and I was on the edge of frazzled as I arrived at Claret just past sunset.

"About time." Troy straightened from his lean against the wall and flicked his eyes over me as though surprised that I'd bothered to dress up a little. He'd cleaned up as well, opting for a fern-green shirt with a slight gold sheen that picked out those colors in his eyes, untucked over black slacks with black leather shoes that looked like they'd cost as much as my monthly car payment. The sleeves of his shirt were rolled up to his elbows in the heat and the first two buttons of his shirt undone, showing a silver chain with green stone pendant. He frowned when he caught me staring at it.

It looked just like mine. And just like Leith's.

To cover how much that bothered me, I dug in my purse for my membership card, not deigning to grace his comment with a reply. What the hell did the pendants mean?

"Where's Allegra?" I asked.

"On other business."

"Fine. Did you call ahead?"

He nodded.

"And?"

"And it would have been a hell of a lot easier to negotiate this if you hadn't blabbed about my being here before."

Good of him to admit it. I'd belatedly realized that Troy had been present when Roman and I had investigated the zombie attack on Claret. He'd kept himself cloaked in shadows, gathering information for the Darkwatch and probably breaking several treaties between House Monteague and the coterie. Maria had been pissed when I'd blurted it out at the meeting that solidified the alliance. Apparently, she'd gotten over it in the name of having Darkwatch agents as security for the Reveal, but it wouldn't surprise me if they were both still sore about the whole thing.

Troy kept pace with me as I skipped the line and flashed my membership card.

"Maria's expecting me," I said over disgruntled comments from the people we'd passed.

The bouncer lifted his eyebrows. "Go on in. You with her?"

I glanced back to see Troy nod.

"Where's your card?" the bouncer asked, to Troy's obvious consternation.

Rolling my eyes, I reopened my clutch and dug out a few bills. It wasn't like Troy would carry anything smaller than a twenty, and this early, they wouldn't have much change. Claret, like many of North Carolina's bars, got around state liquor laws by being a "private" club. That meant paying a few bucks and signing your name on a list. I was willing to bet that Troy had only ever been to Claret in his capacity as a Darkwatch agent— in other words, as a literal shadow sneaking in. Vamps didn't take kindly to elves in their territory, which was why I was all a-tingle about how this evening would go.

"ID," the bouncer demanded.

Troy dug his wallet out, giving the impression that he was above all this and bemused at being asked.

"Sign," I prompted Troy when he hesitated as the satisfied bouncer extended a clipboard with a table of names and signatures.

He scribbled something illegible and accepted the business card he received in return.

"How old does your ID say you are?" I asked teasingly as we stepped inside.

"Old enough."

"Your real age?" Elves lived longer than humans. Troy could be thirty or a young-looking fifty. At some point they started ageing slower.

"Yes. Not that it's your business."

Seemed like we were back to our usual dynamic. I held back a sigh of frustration as I led him through the crowd to the end of the bar, reminding myself that we were allies and that was it. I hopped onto a stool and pretended to look at a menu while Troy leaned back against the bar, looking like a bodyguard. The mundanes instinctively gave us a bubble of space the room couldn't really afford. Tension crackled between us, and my mood soured by another lemon.

"I think I owe you another apology," he said, startling the hell outta me.

I glanced at him, chest tightening at his grim expression. "What went wrong this time?"

Hazel eyes darted to me and away, picking up gold flecks in the low light as he scanned the packed room. "I said we'd be allies, but I don't always like it." His lips thinned, and he frowned before he smoothed his features. "I'm sorry."

I leaned away, surprised by this hint of decency. "Is this because you know you were being an ass about helping with the event?"

Troy nodded, still not looking at me. "I'll do better. About balancing my personal situation with our agreement."

"Well, shit." I waved off the approaching bartender and held up the menu as though I was still deciding, at a loss for words. "Thanks, I guess. But what's in it for you?"

His shoulders eased. "Options. Maybe I'm also hoping you'll stop sizing up my car. And me." This time when he glanced at me, he held my gaze. "I've got enough to deal with without having my car totaled. Or being struck by lightning."

The laugh that escaped me was tinged with equal parts amusement and satisfaction. After I'd held my own fighting off the Redcaps, he was finally as scared of me as I'd been of him. The taut wariness that always snarled up inside me at his presence eased.

His face softened a little when it did. We still weren't friends, but maybe we could be in the same room together without putting everyone else on edge. I wondered how much of this discussion was him and how much was Allegra. I wasn't sure it mattered. Troy was a "say what you mean and mean what you say" kind of guy as far as I'd seen.

"Don't you two look good enough to eat?"

I spun on my stool to find Maria behind us. She was in a dress, as usual, a deceptively simple A-line in a rich russet color that brought out the depths of her eyes.

A small smile curled one corner of her lips when she saw me noticing her outfit, and she gave me one of those silly air kisses. She kept her eyes on Troy the whole time, seeming disappointed when he didn't react. "So glad you agreed to come, princeling."

Troy didn't react other than saying, "Finch made a convincing argument."

Maria smiled as though we were all old friends, but I saw the curiosity in her eyes. "Sounds like an oath was involved. Remember what I told you when you reached your majority?"

That pinged my juicy-meter. How long had they known each other? What had Maria told him? Troy didn't answer, but a muscle in his cheek jumped and the tension from earlier was back.

Maria winked and headed for the back stairs before I could do more than look interested. I knew better than to ask Troy, so I followed the vampire.

Chapter 15

The stench of zombie blood and rot was gone when we got downstairs, a hell of a feat given the state of the place when I'd been here last. The feeling of being underground still weighed heavy on me though. I didn't like being cut off from fresh air.

Noah, Maria's fledgling, nodded a salute from where he stood stiffly at the door to Torsten's chambers. "He's waiting."

A grimace flickered across Maria's face before it smoothed.

"Hang on." I halted and crossed my arms. "Anything I—*we* should know before we go in?"

Noah looked at Maria. Her mouth tightened.

"Maria?" I prompted.

"Torsten has objections. He's making threats."

My blood went cold. "What kind of threats?"

Maria tensed, and her pupils widened. "The kind that make him kill fledglings who remind him of what's coming."

"Fantastic." I hoped they caught the sarcasm. "Any tips?"

The vampires stared at each other before Maria shrugged and flicked a hand.

Noah leaned closer. "The Master has been impatient lately, and short-tempered." He looked Troy up and down, not quite a sneer, but definitely not as neutral as he should have been, given that we were supposedly all on the same side. "The prince should probably not do the talking."

I expected Troy to bristle after his exchange with Maria upstairs, but he just nodded and took a step that placed him in a bodyguard position behind my right shoulder.

"Better." Noah's posture eased as he cast an eye over me. "And good that you both dressed up a little. That should help."

I hadn't expected all this prep talk. Reminding myself that they could smell fear, I took a breath and looked for my inner bad bitch, letting it ooze out into my stance.

Noah nodded. "Much better."

I glanced at Maria. Her tight smile confirmed Noah's appraisal. The flicker of sadness as she glanced at Troy confused me. The heat as she looked at me did not.

"Let's go," she said. No hint of her thoughts came through in her voice.

I stopped myself from glancing at Troy before following her into Torsten's chambers.

The fire was going, despite it being late April and quickly approaching summer-level heat and humidity above-ground. Torsten sat glowering on his throne this time, rather than on the sofa now edged against the wall as he had the last time I'd visited. Waiting, indeed. I split my attention between the master vampire, Maria, and the handful of other vampires whispering in the corner.

Maria curtsied as she reached the bottom step. "Master, Arbiter Arden Finch and Troy, Prince of House Monteague, are here to discuss security for our upcoming event."

She held her curtsy, so I kept my head bowed and assumed Troy was doing something similar behind me, given that Torsten didn't react. Good to know that our princeling could play along when necessary. I wasn't sure if Troy was here as a Monteague, a Darkwatch agent, or as himself, and I didn't care as long as he didn't fuck up everything else with ego.

"Rise, my scion. Rise, Arbiter, and be welcome." Green eyes that were a little too close to pupil-black darted between the three of us. "You, elf." Torsten stood. His hand drifted to the arm of his throne, where the hilt of an honest-to-Goddess sword rested. "What is one of your kind doing here?"

Shit. "I requested his presence," I said when Maria stood pale and tongue-tied. "The prince is a key member of the alliance we have all sworn to and would be honored to support your coterie in the Reveal."

"I asked him, sylph. I smell something, and it isn't honor." Glamour seeped from him, not the steady thunder of power it usually was but more prickly and painful.

Something was very wrong.

I bowed my head again to hide both my eyes and my wince, having gone from "Arbiter" to "sylph" in a few sentences.

Troy's voice was tight. "It is as the Arbiter says. In these times of—"

Torsten's sword sang as it cleared its scabbard. The master vampire was down the stairs with the blade to Troy's throat before I saw him move. He was smaller than everyone present except Maria, but he was the most dangerous person in the room. Normally I'd pick an elf or a djinni over a vampire in a fight because Aether is loads more effective in battle than glamour. But normally, we weren't dealing with a master vampire who'd been born a Viking and was wielding a broadsword. He had age, power, speed, and fighting skill on his side, and none of his fledglings or adopted members of his coterie were likely to stand up to him.

Madness glinted in Torsten's gaze as he held Troy at sword point. "We banned your kind from this place." The vampire's pupils were so wide that only a thin ring of green edged them. "Something about a terrorist? No, Maria?"

"Yes, Master," she said hesitantly. "But that one was of a different House. This one is a Monteague. They have been our allies for many years now."

"No matter." Torsten cocked his head. "This House, that House, they'll all burn when the gods ride. Why not send this one on early?"

Troy kept his hands out to the sides. "I'm here at your fledgling's invitation." He spoke through his teeth, not moving his jaw, keeping his eyes on Torsten's chin rather than meeting his gaze. "I have guest right, both by invitation and by alliance."

"Master, it's true," Maria said with deferent urgency. "Just as the Arbiter has said. We agreed to ally with Monteague, and we invited him and the elemental both, remember? For our Grand Reveal to the humans? It will keep us safe and fed in the new era."

It was like Torsten hadn't heard a thing anyone had said, including himself. His head snapped to me so fast I thought he'd broken his neck.

"The sylph," he said. "Yes. Your hunt. We liked her. Her power sings of aeons and ages, blood and bounty. Chaos ripples around her, enough to call the gods to *their* hunt."

Troy tensed at that, which drew Torsten's attention back to the elf.

I made a mental note to ask Troy what he knew about the Wild Hunt and tried not to be creeped out as I slowly edged to put myself between Troy and Torsten.

Troy hissed as a spark jumped between us. At my back, he was so rigid he felt like oak.

Torsten watched me with sudden interest. "Aha! The very sylph in question. You're going to end the world, you know."

"I'll try very hard not to." I slid the blade away from Troy's throat, wondering what the hell was going on. With my other hand, I pushed at Troy behind me, trying to force him back.

115

Protecting the Prince of House Monteague from an unstable master vampire was not how I'd wanted to spend my evening, but we didn't always get what we wanted. Me less than others, it seemed.

Torsten allowed it out of amusement, if the confused grin quirking his lips was any indication. "I could end you now, and then you wouldn't have to worry about Ragnarok," he said. "It's a terrible burden. I'd be doing you a favor."

I hissed as my fingers slipped along the edge of the sword. The metallic scent of blood blossomed, and the room itself seemed to breathe as a desperate inhale sounded from every vampire present. *Fuck.*

The point of the trip down here had been to get Torsten on board with elven security for the Reveal. I still had an option, but there was a big chance of it going sideways with a vampire as powerful as Torsten. I could resist glamour if it was just eye contact, but I had no idea what would happen if my blood was in a vamp's mouth.

Hand shaking, I held it up and decided to make the most of the situation. "Forgive the trespass, in exchange for a forfeit? I offer a taste if this elf and one other can have safe passage, now and forever, so long as they keep peace."

I'm not sure what scared me more, the clang of the sword as it hit the floor or the vampire's roar of laughter.

"An elemental offering blood tribute for an elf?" Torsten doubled over, gasping as tears rolled down his face. "Girl, you always offer amusement beyond measure. Very well. For this and a taste, yon Prince of Monteague and one more of his ilk may have safe passage now and always."

"Done!" I extended my oozing fingers before anyone could say anything.

Maria flinched as Torsten grabbed my wrist so hard the bones ground together.

I winced, swallowing my protest and pain, looking anywhere but into his eyes as he licked the trail that had reached my palm and sucked on the two cut fingers.

Tingles rippled over me, and warmth spread sensual fingers through my belly. I didn't realize that I'd knelt until my knees hurt. Pressure beat at my mind, looking for a way in. I resisted it, but my shields blocked Aether, not glamour. Something else walled the glamour out. Troy? The bond with him? I pulled on it and built a secondary wall. More energy flooded into me as the pressure crested, holding it at bay.

"Master!" Maria's voice had none of its usual liquidity, and its harshness scared me as much as finding myself curling forward, the nails of my free hand scrabbling against the concrete as though that would keep me conscious.

Torsten released me. My knuckles thudded to the floor at the end of my numbed arm, and I stared at healed fingertips with wavering vision. Bile rose in my throat. What had he done? Worse, what had he tried to do?

"Truly, a worthy offer. We like her. Bring her back sometime, Maria. That's an order. You, elf. I remit you to my fledgling's supervision. Don't waste the sylph's gift, hmm? And don't let your people kill her. I want to see if she ends the world first. This one has become dull. I always wondered if Ragnarok would be more interesting, and it looks like I may yet find out."

Torsten's boots left my field of vision, the sound of his footsteps fading as he left the room. I shook my head to clear the thunder of blood as my heart raced, overcompensating for the adrenaline.

Russet skirts brushed me as Maria went to a knee beside me, hands hovering as she started to touch me and then pulled back. "I'm so sorry, Arden. But what were you thinking?" Frustration warred with guilt in her voice. "And for *Monteague?*"

"Trust me, I wouldn't have asked for it either," Troy said in an undertone as he knelt to my other side. "She's too valuable to the alliance. Talk to us, Finch."

"I never want to do that again." My words slurred. "I don't even know what that was."

Maria's face tightened. "It's just his glamour. It'll pass."

I let myself sit all the way on my ass, lifted my knees, and hung my head between them, not giving a fuck if the remaining vampires in the room thought that was weak. I'd just wrangled their master when none of them had the balls for it.

"Breathe, Arden," Maria said. "It looked like he tried to roll you."

"He did," Troy said.

"How would you know?" Maria snapped.

"He did," I echoed as Troy's energy got spiky and cross in the back of my head, prickly as ever. He must have had to undo whatever he'd done to block the bond. If it meant Torsten couldn't force his glamour on me, I'd thank Troy rather than getting pissy.

Someone in the room said, "Bullshit. Nobody resists the Master."

I lifted my head and looked in that general direction, fighting dizziness to embrace Air and crack an uncontrolled whip of it toward that side of the room. Three vampires cried out in pain and surprise, and the perpetual fire in the fireplace sparked and roared higher at the extra oxygen. My voice was harsh and nasty as I said, "I'll bullshit you three times over if you even think of trying me."

"Get out. All of you," Maria said in her scary, number-two-vampire voice. "Before I drain you myself."

The room emptied in a flurry of too-fast, clockwork movement, and Troy took his hand away from whatever weapon he had hidden at his ankle. Worry still bled through the bond though.

"What the hell was that?" I asked. "We're on the same fucking side! I didn't bully Evangeline down just to have Torsten decide his rules matter most. This was supposed to be a formality for the alliance, not a test or a donation."

"This can't leave the three of us," Maria said after a stretch of silence long enough for my head to stop spinning. She smoothed her skirts.

Troy and I nodded, eerily in sync, but she didn't comment on it, telling me how shaken she was.

"Torsten's lineage is prone to madness. He's evaded it longer than most." She shrugged. "But even he isn't immune."

I blinked, processing that as I remembered Torsten's previous number two. Aron had been a rakshasa—a vampire with incurable mental decay brought on by age and cellular damage—when he'd broken free of wherever they'd been keeping him and attacked me on my first visit to Claret.

"Are you telling me the Triangle's master vampire is becoming a rakshasa?" I hissed. "Right as y'all are about to reveal yourselves in a series of public events?"

Maria winced. "Yes."

"This can't—"

"I know." Her words were tight and clipped. Bitterness and a little pain lay beneath them, so I pressed my lips together to stop from clapping back. "The only way to unseat him *permanently* is to kill him. I need it to be me who wins, or the Modernists might take their chances with whoever rises in his place."

"Okay? Is this why you had us come in person? I feel like there's something you're not saying."

Her coffee-dark eyes weighed heavy on me. "I'm not strong enough yet. Close, but only because I feasted on that elven prince earlier this year." Her eyelids fluttered at the memory of draining Leith, and she inhaled before refocusing. "I'll need help. Especially now that he's had a taste of you. The power in your blood will keep him stable a little longer but not forever."

I knew where she was going with this. She'd been after my blood for months, although up to now I'd thought it was more of a sexual thing. Looking for a partner rather than, or at least as much as, a donor. Now I saw it was that and more. She needed my blood because the Master of Raleigh was going mad and without it, she wasn't sure if she could hold the territory. "How long do we have?"

"With your blood in him? Maybe another few weeks of clarity before he starts slipping again."

The little knot in my head that was Troy solidified, growing heavy and watchful. A hunter looking for options. I elbowed him, not liking where I sensed his thoughts going. "Then that's a few weeks to figure something out."

Maria huffed and rolled her eyes. "Fine. Let's all just pray that a few sips of elemental blood are enough to keep a thousand-year-old vampire in his right mind for a month."

"Then we move it up," Troy said.

I stared at him. "Move what up? The whole Reveal?"

"I don't like it either. But if we only have a few weeks of sanity and need Raleigh's master vampire at full capacity?" He lifted his brows. "Unless you're volunteering to play blood donor for either him or Maria, Finch."

I shuddered before I could get a hold of myself. "No offense, Maria, but I'm not super excited about repeating that experience."

The expressionless look she gave me spoke volumes about the fact that she'd be patient, but she wasn't giving up.

Instead of pushing the issue in front of Troy, I deflected. "We need to find the lich's accomplice. Right fucking now. We can't rush the Reveal with a witch-born vampire necromancer and Callista's meddling setting it up to be a clusterfuck."

Troy's brows lowered.

"So you want to rush a hunt instead? Not just any hunt but one that might involve a demon?" His tone suggested that he was less than impressed.

I pushed to my feet. Troy's hand hovered when I wavered, but I found my balance as they stood alongside me. The lack of options weighed on my shoulders, hemming me in and making me feel trapped. I didn't like being underground as it was. This just made it worse. "Time was always running out," I snapped. "For both events. Especially when you consider that the gods are going to get involved again at some point."

Troy winced. "You don't know that."

"Enough," Maria broke in. "Arden's right. We'll deal with Callista when we have to. We've outmaneuvered her so far. But I won't risk the coterie being exposed with a necromantic traitor and possibly a demon on the loose."

Nodding, I took a deep breath and blew it out.

"Great. I'll call you when I know more." I headed for the door.

Troy trailed behind me, deep in thought.

I barely resisted the urge to run as we passed Noah on our way out and headed back upstairs. My shoulders didn't come down from around my ears until I was back out in the open air. Relief brought clearer thinking and questions.

"Was that you? Blocking him?" I didn't look at Troy. Something had helped me shore up defenses against the master vampire. I shouldn't have been able to stand against a city master with a thousand years behind him, not with my blood on his lips. My power was growing, but I didn't have that much yet.

"Yes," Troy said. He closed the bond between us again so all I was getting was a distant sense that he was alive somewhere, not the roil of emotion seeping from him and the tautness of his shoulders as he walked beside me.

"Thanks." I didn't want to be bonded to an elf, but I wanted to be a vampire's plaything even less.

"Thanks for the safe passage. That'll come in handy." Troy shoved his hands in his pockets, as close to an outer acknowledgement of his inner turmoil as I was likely to get.

We didn't say anything else as we reached the door and went our separate ways.

Chapter 16

After another restless night I rose early, full of tingly anticipation. The weres were coming. To take my mind off the coming disruption that guests represented for me, I researched various creation and destruction myths, the Wild Hunt, and the many gods of the hunt. Every time I'd gained in power, so had they. At first, I'd had to be pulled bodily into the Crossroads. Then they used my dreams. Neith and Mixcoatl had only managed to cross over when they had my blood and in Mixcoatl's case, only after I'd gained Fire. Artemis had followed. With Earth, Neith—one of the oldest faces of the goddess— had manifested fully on this plane, bearing the strange and dangerous gift I wasn't sure I wanted to use.

Goosebumps rippled over me as I remembered Neith calling me a primordial elemental.

Had this been what the book I'd found in Torsten's library meant by "wielding the primordial forces of creation"? Was that why I'd been able to break the lich's amulet? Wouldn't Val have mentioned that when I picked up Fire—or didn't she know it was possible?

I needed to get the other elementals together. Wincing, I tried to figure out whether forestalling the Wild Hunt went above or below the Reveal and the hunt for the lich's accomplice in terms of priority.

But since I had guests tonight, I needed to make a run to the grocery store. It had only ever been me at home until recently, so I didn't keep much extra food on hand. Definitely not enough to feed five weres if they ate like Roman.

That task done, I texted my guests my address then did all the prep I could think of to welcome Terrence, Ximena, their seconds, and Vikki. I washed the windows, cleared all the spiderwebs from the porch, prepared a few nice plates of nibbles and marinated some steaks in case talks ran late. I even dragged my deck furniture down to my spot by the river and arranged it in a cozy grouping, along with a cooler full of non-alcoholic beverages, mead, and a salami tray, hoping to create a feeling of magnanimity even as I kept it within the bounds of what I could realistically manage by myself. If Callista had never offered them this honor, I wanted to outdo even the offer. Creating my own power base—and using it to keep myself safe—depended on binding these three wereclans to me. That meant demonstrating, without a doubt, that I was a better option than Callista. That I cared more.

A little part of me whispered that this looked desperate.

"It's service leadership," I muttered to myself as I wiped my dusty hands on my shorts. "Not dictatorship. I'm a leader, not a boss."

Yeah, I was doing all this for my own sake, but that meant I'd also do it on my terms. And making an effort didn't necessarily mean I was bending over for the wereclans or anyone else. Right?

I scowled as I made my way back up the slope to my house. I'd come a long way since Leith Sequoyah had walked into my office, but I was still fumbling for authority and power and still felt like a doormat sometimes. Part of me felt like that was the way it should be. I'd met royals from Houses Monteague and Sequoyah, and all of them—even Troy—suffered from a terminal case of entitlement and self-importance. They'd never had to work for what they had. At least, not like I'd had to, standing up to a death sentence just for being born an elemental. Hell, I'd had it not just from Otherside, but from the humans as well, for presenting as a Black human woman. Allegra had been right about that.

Focus. Winding myself into a tizzy over elven privilege and human racism was neither here nor there. The weres would be here soon.

I had just gotten cleaned up and dressed when a knock on the door announced both sunset and the first of my guests.

"Welcome," I said to Terrence and Ximena, repeating it to the man and woman standing behind them as I opened the door wide. "As soon as Vikki gets here, we'll move down to the river for space and privacy."

"You honor us," Ximena said. She was a little more dressed up than I'd seen her before. Still in comfortable clothes, but the black shorts were probably a linen-cotton blend and the pink top was more blousy. Terrence had opted for black jeans so new I could still smell the dye and a grey collared t-shirt.

The weres' interest in my home was obvious. They used all their senses to inspect it while trying to appear as though they weren't, and I forced down a spike of annoyance that they could probably smell and ignored.

Terrence refocused on me, sliding aside a little to allow me to see the other two people better.

"This is Joachin, Ximena's second." He indicated the lithe, dark-haired man at her shoulder, carrying two cases of beer with a paper-wrapped parcel atop them. "And this is Lola, my second." He nodded toward the woman with him. Her skin was just dark enough to call brown, and her eyes were so dark as to be black. Both were dressed similarly to the clan leaders.

"You're all welcome to take refreshment until our last guest arrives." I waved them to my dining table. I'd removed the knife and stuck it with Mixcoatl's lightning arrow and Leith's pendant in my closet, but all of them shuddered and paused as they drew nearer.

"What happened here?" Ximena asked a little too lightly, fingering the gouge the godblade had left and licking her finger. Her face twisted like she wanted to spit, but she didn't.

"An unexpected visitor," I said flatly, opening the window wide so that she could spit while my back was turned. I definitely wouldn't want that taste in my mouth.

The weres exchanged worried looks as I went to the fridge but settled themselves around my table, holding themselves tensely as I poured lemonade, dropped in a few sprigs of mint, and grabbed the first platter of food. Joachin set the beer by the fridge, and I smiled in thanks, assuming that was the tribute they'd promised for Zanna and not something for right now.

"Your visitors are unusually powerful," Terrence said. Wariness tightened his voice.

"Some of them are," I agreed.

Silence stretched as I set the refreshments in front of them. That was fine by me. I wasn't going to start explaining the gods popping in whenever they damn well pleased. Not yet, not when I didn't quite know what to explain. Bad enough that Troy knew.

"Be welcome in my home," I said instead, using formality to move the conversation along. "My table is yours, my hearth is yours, and my roof is yours, while you are here."

"We honor our hostess. While your home is ours, our strength is yours," they responded as one, agreeing to defend my home so long as they were guests here.

Inclining my head, I busied myself in the kitchen while they talked about mundane things—the coming Durham Bulls season, whether the clans should spring on tickets for *Hamilton* at DPAC for their winter solstice shindig, the annoying increase in unleashed dogs running loose in state parks. The more they talked, the more I calmed down about having strangers in my house. Maybe that was their intention—I'm certain they could smell my nerves—or maybe they were just doing what they'd do anywhere else. Either way, I appreciated it.

Just as I was about to join them at the table, a knock on the door signaled Vikki's arrival. The tension in the room crept back up as jaguars exchanged tight looks with leopards.

"Excuse me." I moved around the half wall and checked out the window before opening the door.

"Hey there." Vikki knocked some dirt from her cowboy boots as she scented the air. "Seems like I'm the last one?"

"Everyone's here." I scowled as I glanced over her shoulder and caught sight of a big canine form in the bed of Roman's truck. Narrowing my eyes and holding the door where she couldn't pass, I lowered my voice. "We had an agreement, Vikki."

"We did," she agreed easily. "And I was fixing to stick to it, until Callista summoned me to the bar."

A blend of frustration and anger pricked over me as the weres at my kitchen table muttered.

"And...?" I asked.

"I played the game, of course. Told her I'd give her request due consideration as soon as I was settled. But it didn't seem prudent to leave my baby brother all on his lonesome where someone could, oh, I dunno, call animal control, for example."

"I see." She was right, of course. Callista had made a play for Sergei once. I imagined the spoilt brat would be more than happy to take her side again, if it meant getting out of playing wolfdog and eating kibble from a metal dish.

I went back to the kitchen, breezing past the frowning werecats, and dug around in the cabinets for a heavy Pyrex bowl.

Once I'd filled it with water, I stomped out and set it in the grass. "I'll see if Joachin and Lola won't mind keeping an eye on him. But he stays in the yard. In fact…"

My long driveway and the thick vegetation and trees surrounding my house gave me enough privacy to shield a quick burst of magic from anyone who might drive by. Without warning, I pulled on Air, lifting the werewolf from the truck bed and dropping him to the ground before he'd finished a startled yelp. With another thought, I built a wall of Air around him and the bowl, making it three times higher than I thought it needed to be before tying off the chord of magic.

"There," I said, satisfied.

Sergei shook himself then lifted his lip to show me his teeth. When I just smirked at him, he tried to lunge forward—and crumpled like an accordion with a yip as he hit the boundary of my wall.

I couldn't help snickering. "Stay," I said. "And consider yourself lucky I gave you water and shade."

In response, Sergei lifted his leg and marked the wall before giving us his back.

"Sergei!" Vikki snapped after shaking off an awed look. It shifted to ire as she focused on her brother. "You earned every bit of this, and you'll earn more if you don't start showing some respect."

"Don't worry about it," I said. "If he wants to be stuck in a cage he can't see the boundaries of with the smell of his own piss, that's on him."

The four werecats were looking at me with wide eyes shifted to peridot and citrine when I led Vikki inside, holding themselves very still. I frowned, confused as to what'd spooked them, until I realized that they'd never actually seen me use my power. Nobody had, except for the other elementals, Doc Mike, Troy, and Allegra. Another piece of me exposed.

"Sergei won't be joining us," I said firmly, keeping my breathing steady. We weren't about to have weres shifting in my house in a repeat of the incident at Roman's when I'd first met Sergei. "He made the mistake of deciding that Callista was the better bet after pretending he came here for the alliance. I won't tolerate that shit, not against me and not against my allies."

Terrence glanced at Vikki then out at Sergei, sulking in the yard. "That's understandable, Miss Arden. Your steps toward our safety are appreciated."

"Glad to hear it. Might I ask Lola and Joachin to stay here and keep an eye on him?"

Ximena and Terrence exchanged a long look before turning to me and nodding. Terrence straightened his collar—not that it needed it—and said something sternly in Spanish. The two seconds tensed but nodded.

"Thank you," I said when it seemed they were done. "Please, make yourselves at home and help yourself to whatever's in the fridge. Oh—and if Zanna pops in—"

"No worries, Miss Arden." Lola tugged one of the gold stud earrings that lined her left ear. "We know how to show proper respect to one of the fae."

My brows shot up. "Sounds like there's a story behind that."

"The fae have always been friends to our people in the area," Terrence said proudly. "As we have always been friends to them."

"One less thing for me to worry about then." I indicated the back door. "Shall we?"

Tensions eased as I led them down the dirt path to my spot by the river. The Eno was running high with the rain we'd had a few days ago and greeted us with its rushing voice. Sunlight filtered through beech, pine, and sweetgum trees to dapple the dirt floor of my miniature paradise. Chickadees and warblers called as they gleaned insects, and a heron took flight at our approach.

Vikki whistled. "Well, then. Ain't this a sweet setup."

"Please be seated." I indicated the chairs and inclined my head, hoping that I was striking the right balance of humility and leadership. This was my first time dealing with more than just one were in a situation that didn't include others from Otherside, so I was playing it by ear. Even with Terrence's advice, I wasn't certain how to properly welcome representatives from multiple clans.

When they'd all taken a chair—Terrence in the middle with his back to the slope, with Vikki on his left and Ximena on his right—I made sure everyone had a small serving of meat and mead. We did the usual greeting ceremony, in which I participated without question this time, given that a small amount of mead hadn't affected me the other night and not doing so might undo all the work I'd done up to this point.

Ceremony done, I offered them all another refreshment before settling in the chair with my back to the river. "I'm just here as facilitator and witness."

"Understood." Terrence paused as they all peered around the clearing then took deep, sniffing breaths. The cats' jaws dropped in a Flehmen response. Only when all three nodded did Terrence continue. "First, I swear that I am Terrence Little, obong of the leopards of the Carolinas, and I roar with leap's voice." He held up a hand—and started shifting. Spotted fur sprouted as his hand grew and transformed into a leopard's paw. He flexed it to extend long, wickedly curved claws, before shifting back. All of it was far smoother and less painful-looking than the partial shift I'd seen Roman make a few times.

Ximena did the same. Her paw was bigger, with rosettes rather than spots, and I wondered if she made a bigger cat than Terrence did despite her smaller human form, given that feline jaguars were bigger than leopards. "I swear that I am Ximena Kan, jefa of the jaguars of the Carolinas. I roar with the prowl's voice."

Vikki shifted her hand, bones and fur rippling to reveal a white paw tipped with long black claws. "I swear that I am Viktoria Volkov, beta female of the Blood Moon clan claiming the Blue Ridge Mountains. I howl with the pack's voice. But I also speak with my own."

I kept myself very still, not wanting to show approval or disapproval with any reaction.

Leaning back in his chair, Terrence steepled his fingers. "Well, then. We have an ambitious one."

Vikki didn't bother to deny it, only ducking her head with a small smile.

"Your brothers don't know, nor your father, or they wouldn't have sent the beta female," Ximena guessed. "Does Irina know?"

"No," Vikki said.

Ximena narrowed her eyes. "What could be so dangerous that even your mother doesn't know?"

"She wants to start her own clan," Terrence drawled, the sharpness of his attention belying the slow ease of his voice. "On land ceded from us."

Vikki slowly reached for a can of beer and cracked it open, toasting the two werecats.

"Rebellion." Ximena snarled to show teeth that were a little sharper than they were a minute ago. "We are fighting to *avoid* attention, and you propose bringing rebellion here, to the heart of our territory."

I started to step in then shut my mouth. If they wanted me to arbitrate something, they'd ask.

Vikki's eyes silvered, and the beer can dented slightly under her hand. "Only if something befalls Blood Moon. So long as the clan is strong, the agreements outlined by my brothers stand: territory ceded by Acacia Thorn and Jade Tooth in exchange for a voice in the alliance, held by me as representative. The only wolves who join me here are those I hand pick."

Something sly entered her tight smile, sending prickles up my arms, despite the warm day.

"So. Not rebellion. Revolution," Terrence said.

Chapter 17

A long silence stretched, filled only by the sound of the Eno crashing over rocks and the birds going about their business. I took a breath to speak then swallowed it at Terrence's sharp glance, reaching into the cooler for a Cheerwine.

"Explain to me why, when we are already oppressed and even hunted in both our forms, the werecats should accept this side agreement," Terrence said in a low, dangerous voice. "You may see yourself as a revolutionary, but this smells of exploitation. Using our bodies to shield your ambition. Besides, Old Niko has been looking east to the Piedmont for years—what's to say this isn't part of it?"

Ximena nodded, anger clouding her face.

Vikki stiffened, her expression tightening. If she'd been Roman or Sergei, I'd say shit was about to hit the fan, but she visibly gathered herself and bowed her head for a moment before looking Ximena and Terrence in the eye. "That's why I'm proposing to take the ceded land in name only. The members of your leap and prowl can stay where they are and continue using it as they always have. I'll make a show of claiming the land to satisfy my father. But we all know what happens when empires overstretch."

"They fall," Terrence said softly, finally relaxing enough to take another sip of mead.

Vikki nodded. "If Blood Moon should do the same, I don't need to stay here long term. I just need a springboard. The territory would be ceded back."

"What's your ask, then?" Ximena snapped. "Get to the point."

"Let me and Sergei, and whoever might join us, stretch our legs in the wilder patches from time to time. The collar binds him with silver, and even if he was fixing to burn himself getting it off, the price of shifting back before his sentence is completed is death. I'll play my role in front of him, just in case Callista makes him an offer that makes it worth the risk." Tension made Vikki's movement stiff as she pretended nonchalance in taking a sip of her drink before continuing. "All I ask is that, should anything unfortunate ever come to pass and Blood Moon scatters to the winds, you might look favorably upon my suit."

"And in the meantime?" Ximena said tersely. "We all know how well your kind keep agreements."

I understood then that Terrence's move to bring the leopards and the jaguars into the alliance had had two layers to it—not only a seat and a voice to keep themselves safe and out of the Reveal, but to secure them the help they might need should Blood Moon or the Volkovs overreach and the more numerous wolves seek to claim more than they'd bargained for. That land had been ceded in the first place spoke to how seriously the leopards and jaguars took the opportunity to have a say in a community that must have sidelined them almost as much as it had me. I felt sick, seeing once again how deeply I was in over my head and how much I had to learn.

Something in my scent must have shifted because Terrence narrowed his eyes at me before returning his attention to Vikki.

The werewolf slid from her chair to kneel, lifting her chin to expose her throat. "I run at your direction," she said. "My teeth guard your den."

My eyebrows shot up. Something about this moment felt pivotal, even as I wondered what Vikki's endgame was. She was smart, politically savvy, and had an agenda. Roman was naive enough to offer something at face value. But not Vikki.

"Why?" Terrence asked quietly, giving voice to my thought.

Vikki fisted her hands and looked at all of us. "Roman told us why you don't want to come out. We have to do better, or none of us will be safe when the wolves are eventually revealed to the humans. I know the role my people have historically played, pushing out the native wolf and coyote people while participating in atrocities against the rest of you in our human skins. My father might be content to say it's all in the past. Roman thinks reforming toxic masculinity in the clan will be enough. I think blaming the patriarchy is just a way to excuse all the other issues we know are there."

Ximena looked like she'd been slapped, jerking back with eyes wide, and looked at Terrence.

The wereleopard just smiled, lips closed and eyes slitted. "So you help us, and yet still help yourself."

Vikki slumped, seeming to deflate at the flatness in Terrence's voice as he refused to jump to welcome her as a savior. "In the end, yes. But I hope that it can be a start. If I'm in a better position, I can do more to help all of us."

Terrence looked at Ximena, whose lips tightened as she shrugged. "The opportunity to win back our land would be welcome," she said. "But we shouldn't have had to trade it to begin with."

That had the sound of a long, old argument, especially when Terrence sighed and closed his eyes in a long blink.

"We'll discuss it between ourselves," the wereleopard said. "Difficult choices were made to take advantage of an opportunity, but Ximena is right."

Vikki eased back into her chair and kicked a sweetgum hull. "I hear you. I—perhaps I should go do some consideration of my own. Perhaps I didn't fully understand or appreciate your perspective."

Terrence's brows shot up. "A wolf who can acknowledge room for growth. Ancestors take me now."

"I'm trying," Vikki said, irritation flashing into her voice and eyes.

Raising a placating hand, Terrence said, "I know. It's just there's a whole hell of a lot for y'all to try, and I need you to see that and do the work yourself."

Vikki's jaw clenched, and she looked sullen as hell. "Okay."

"Okay," Terrence echoed. "Let's table discussion of the side agreement and talk about what having wolves as allies in the Triangle means for the ongoing issues here: the hunt for a vampire sorcerer, Callista's continued control of the area—no offense, Miss Arden—and the Reveal."

"None taken," I said. It was true, after all. My phone buzzed in my pocket. Doc Mike's name came up on the caller ID when I checked. "Excuse me. Otherside calls."

Terrence waved a hand and leaned forward to dig into the cooler, handing out more drinks as I stood and wandered a little way off before answering.

"Hey Doc, what can I do for ya?"

"Arden." He sounded shaky and afraid—not good in a new Othersider.

Traffic sounded unusually loud in the background and I frowned. "What's wrong? Are you okay?"

"I don't—" he huffed. "I don't know how to explain this."

"One word at a time. Breathe," I said. "Do you need me to come to you? Did something happen at the morgue?"

"No, no, I'm fine, but something did happen."

I schooled myself to patience, pacing the riverbank as he found his words and reminding myself that until a week ago, Doc Mike had thought he was just a good medical examiner— not a latent necromancer. Something had happened with the lich lord, something he refused to talk about, and I wondered if this was part of it.

After another big breath, he said, "I—after what happened, I started paying more attention when something felt wrong. Arden, a body came in today. Open and shut case, gunshot wound to the heart, close-range shotgun blast that destroyed the chest cavity."

"Let me guess. Not open and shut," I said, unable to hold my tongue given the agitation quickening his usual Deep South drawl.

"No. I mean, that's what I filed, of course. I know my role in the community. But when I *listened*—you know what I mean— it felt like the morgue did a week and a half ago, when the bodies went missing. So I looked closer, I found signs that the heart had been removed prior to the shotgun blast. Clean cuts from a sharp instrument like a scalpel, not the tearing destruction that you'd see from a bullet. And no evidence that the heart had been destroyed within the body cavity itself."

The hair on my arms and neck rose. According to Janae, some soul magic called for heart's blood or the heart itself, and there was only one known sorcerer in the Triangle: the lich's accomplice. He was kicking off again.

"So the shotgun was a coverup. Was he killed in Raleigh or just dumped there?" I asked, thinking fast.

"The police think dumped because there wasn't enough blood in the body or on the street."

"Any idea who he is or where he was from?"

"No, he had no wallet and no identifying marks or tattoos. But Arden…" He took a long, shaky breath. When he spoke again, his voice shook. "When I *listened*, it felt like I opened something in myself. I got a flash of a building. In Durham, from the skyline. A bar, maybe, but on its own lot. Brick. Wood door with glass in the center. The street number started with an eight but I didn't get the whole thing or the street name."

I stood in shock, feeling as though I'd taken a solid punch to the solar plexus. I knew exactly what place he was talking about.

Callista's bar.

For the body to feel wrong to a latent necromancer, with no blood and evidence of the removal of the heart, had to mean the vampire sorcerer was involved. No wonder we hadn't found him. We'd been searching in the Raleigh area. Callista's bar was the last place we'd look, especially with a body dumped near Raleigh. The only question was whether this was a feint to keep us looking in the wrong direction or a taunt to goad us.

Fuck.

"Arden?" Panic threaded Doc Mike's voice.

I scrambled to pull myself together. "Doc, you cannot ever speak of the place you think you saw, do you understand?"

"Oh no, oh Lord in heaven save me, what—"

"You will be fine," I said, "but you have to keep playing mundane. You did exactly right to call me. Is there any possibility someone could overhear you?"

"I'm out walking. After your friend who came for us, I don't trust the shadows anymore."

My friend, I thought ironically, wondering if Troy would be amused or offended to be categorized as such. "Good, that's good, very smart. If there's anything you can reasonably do to keep the focus on the Raleigh area and shotguns in your report, that will help all of us."

"You know what this is about," he said.

"I think I do. But I'm going to need you to pretend you don't and erase the record of calling me from your phone, okay?" It'd still be on his phone bill, but it was the best we could do for now. "I'm going to take care of this. Don't worry."

After a long pause, Doc Mike sighed. "Okay."

I frowned, concerned about the level of emotion coming through. Doc Mike had always been cool as a cucumber, no matter how weird the cases he called me in on were. "Are you sure you're going to be okay? You don't have to do this just because you've discovered under the worst possible circumstances that you're an Othersider."

"I'm sure," he said after another pause, sounding more steady. "I want to play my part."

A thought struck me. "Are you still in contact with Ms. Janae?"

"Yes," he said, more warmly. "She's been a blessing."

"Good. Perfect. See if she'll cleanse you and make sure you're all closed up. Good spiritual hygiene and all that."

"Oh. I didn't think of that. Thank you, Arden."

I breathed a quiet sigh of relief that he wasn't of the mindset that witches were evil. "Sure thing, Doc. I'm gonna go get started on this right now, okay? So don't hold onto worrying about it."

"Okay. Bye now."

I ended the call and scrubbed my fingers through my hair before loosing a frustrated whirlwind to make the branches overhead sway. All of the evidence was so circumstantial that I wouldn't dare bring it to mundane cops if this was a human investigation. But as I stood there, seeking the balance of my intuition and my logic, it felt right.

Callista was working with the witch-born vampire.

I didn't think she'd been working with the lich, though I suspected she'd known of him before I brought my information to her. She'd been focused on destabilizing Torsten's coterie before they could cement their alliance with me. Sergei had been the link there, taking her money and funneling it to the

Modernist vampires, with none of them aware that one of the Modernists had bitten and turned a sorcerer who'd been in league with the lich.

A headache threatened as I connected all the dots, missing my white board. This wasn't something I dared commit to writing though. Not with Callista directly involved.

Everyone was still human when I stormed back into the clearing, and the talk seemed to have shifted to lighter topics. They paused at whatever expression was on my face.

"Why do I have a feeling we're about to be called to arms?" Terrence said.

"Because I've just received a possible tip about where we can find the vampire sorcerer." I looked at the sky and prayed this wouldn't become a disaster. "He might be here in Durham, not in Raleigh. I went back to Gideon's lair last night and found no sign that anyone had been there since we destroyed him. The call I got now means that makes more sense."

Ximena shifted in her seat. "There are only a few places in Durham that could shield that kind of magic user from us. The witches stink of shame and anger every time we go out with them, so I don't believe they're hiding him. That leaves only one place."

We all knew where that was and what it meant. Grim anticipation lit each of their features, and Vikki's eyes silvered before she regained control of herself.

"If your business is satisfactorily concluded, I have some investigation to do," I said.

Chapter 18

Before charging in and throwing accusations, I needed to do some research. Callista wasn't my only problem—there was still Artemis's request to consider, and Neith's. Keeping all these plates spinning required something counterintuitive: taking a moment to pause. I couldn't help but feel like I'd missed something big and obvious, not just about our sorcerer vampire but about Callista. Why was she doing all of this? Even Gideon had had a reason for selling his heart and soul to a djinni.

The weres had cleared out, with the leopards and jaguars waiting for Vikki and Sergei to leave before heading out themselves. My house was my own again, though the cedar-and-musk scent of my guests remained, reminding me painfully of Roman even if the tang of cat was heavier. I lit some incense, opened the windows wider to let in fresh air, and got to work.

With a fresh cup of tea at my side, I settled in front of my computer to research the myths around Artemis. There had to be a clue to help me in the old tales. Maybe something that would tell me who she was looking for so I wasn't fighting both Callista and the gods.

I suspected that Callista might be a demigoddess or something. Her powers were beyond the rest of Otherside, if not quite those of the gods themselves. Duke had suggested that she was something close to a goddess, while advising me not to look too deeply. "That way lies madness," he'd said.

But why? I scowled as I checked for myths of demigods that might match Callista's description. Nothing. Tried again with local lore. Still nothing.

Changing gears, I ran a search for myths about Artemis. Shock froze me at what came up. One of the first results had the name Callisto attached to it, a nymph of Artemis, turned into a bear and hunted nearly to death when Artemis victim-blamed her for being raped by Zeus before being thrown into the sky as a constellation.

Callisto. Had she become Callist*a*?

Shit. I'd been right. I'd been so focused on a grand scheme that I'd missed something so obvious I wanted to kick myself into next week. Othersiders chose names from myth all the time, especially when they were hiding their real one or on their second or third lifetime among humans and had learned enough to dare being more obvious about themselves. I'd had a vague notion that Callista was probably one of those names but had never dreamed our local mob boss was the original holder.

My heart thudded as dizziness spun my head. That might put Callista at over five thousand years old. However powerful nymphs usually were, I had a feeling that being trapped in the lines of a constellation had supercharged her. If she'd escaped and spent the last however many hundred years building up her power, if she still carried a grudge against the gods...

I breathed shallowly to avoid vomiting.

"Fuck," I breathed, repeating it when just once wasn't enough to convey the full feeling. Had she known that I'd acquire other powers? And why had she shown me off to some of the gods? I thought back to my first visit to the Crossroads. Ogun had said, "You've drawn our attention, sylph."

So that meant she had to be working for the gods. But maybe not all of them?

"Even Artemis never saw so much," she'd said, right before dragging me there in the first place. I'd been too overwhelmed to comprehend it then and had forgotten it with everything else going on. But maybe that was why everything about me had been kept so secret. She needed me to take revenge against Artemis, Zeus, or both. Whether that was by denying them having me or using me against them or trading me to the other gods in exchange for something else, I didn't know. Either way, it didn't matter. She had to strip my allies away to get me back under her control now, even if doing so meant war in Otherside.

It might be waged quietly, but people would die nonetheless. If Callista was stronger than I'd thought, it'd be even worse.

I'd already lost Grimm to the fight against the lich lord. We hadn't been on great terms at the end, nor had we had a good history, but I hadn't wished her dead. The list of people I'd be willing to lose to Callista's power struggle with the gods or the vampire sorcerer and the rabisu started and ended with the remnants of House Sequoyah. Maybe Sergei for his betrayal, though I'd never admit it out loud.

I frowned when I realized that Troy wasn't on that list, wondering when I'd looked past the fucked-up shit he'd pulled and set him fully in the category of ally. Sipping my tea, I tried to work through the shift there. I didn't want a friend so badly I'd consider Troy, but somehow, he'd become someone I relied on. The internal conflict bugged me, and I stared at my screen without seeing it.

I was so lost in my thoughts that I missed Zanna coming into the house until she poked me. My nerves made themselves known in an embarrassing shriek.

"Sorry," I said when Zanna just stared at me. "Thinking. Do you want a beer? The weres brought tribute. Something in a paper bag as well."

Zanna's face lit up, and she went for the stacked cartons, sniffing the bag on top. "Honey taffy!" She tore it open and plunged a hand in, coming out with a fistful of candies wrapped in wax paper. "A most excellent tribute. They may return."

"I'm sure they'll be glad to hear it," I said as neutrally as possible. I didn't plan on inviting them back if I could help it, but who knew what would happen now?

Pulling my thoughts back again, I decided I needed to refocus on the problem at hand and map out what was going on with Callista. She wouldn't just wait for me to steal her thunder. Zanna watched with solemn eyes as I went for a notepad and a pen then shoved the laptop to the side to make space. The pen hovered over the paper as I tried to open my mind to the nudgings of what I suspected was a weakened form of the Sight some djinn had.

Callista, I scrawled, drawing a circle around it. *Sergei* went in another circle. I joined them with a solid line, knowing there was a connection there. The vamp sorcerer and the rabisu made another circle, off to the side. I made a tentative, dashed line between that cluster and Callista. She'd drawn Sergei into her machinations, and she'd known about the lich lord before I'd told her about Gideon. Doc's vision was weak evidence, given his lack of experience, but I had faith in him.

Pure antagonism made me write *Keithia* next, and I tapped the pen against the table as I thought through that one. She'd made threats, but it wasn't just that. The elven queen thought I'd been mindmazed. If she figured out that I hadn't, then she'd know who was behind House Sequoyah's downfall. Cold gripped me as I made another dashed line. Callista might have carried out the action, but that was expected. I'd been the one to carry the intel. Despite the fact that I'd been acting in my capacity as a Watcher, I'd be the culpable party, at least as far as the elves were concerned. Especially if Callista concocted some kind of lie elevating my involvement.

Evangeline, Troy's blood sister, was another concern. She had made it more than clear that she'd take the slightest excuse to break treaty and leave the alliance if it meant having the chance to kill me and avenge the boyfriend who'd died for House Sequoyah's sins.

Pausing, I studied my mindmap. Troy had said someone had called up the remaining Redcaps. Had it been one of the Monteagues? If so, had they been working with Callista or in spite of her?

"Don't like that picture," Zanna said gravely around a mouth full of sticky candy.

I glanced up and grimaced. "Neither do I. But something feels off."

Zanna slid from the chair, belching with the force of a much larger being as she hit the floor. "Dangerous game, tenant. Dangerous game. If you insist on involving us, I go to raise stronger magic. Protect this home."

Her fierceness made my heart swell. She could have left, found safer digs, gone somewhere where the other resident wasn't continually getting involved in shit that ended up shaking all of Otherside. "Thanks, Zanna. Let me know if I can get anything to help."

"More beer" was all she said before leaving via the sliding door to the backyard, making a big jump from the threshold to avoid the block of Air she knew would be somewhere but couldn't see.

More beer? The ten cases Troy had brought weren't enough?

I set that aside and buried my face in my hands, trying to push through all the feelings clashing in me. I needed a drink, even if it was a virgin one, and I needed to find out why the other elementals avoided Callista. There had to be a clue, and I really hoped Val had it.

* * *

Given that Val's kidnapping had scuttled our plans the last time we'd planned to meet at the bar on Mangum and Main, we decided to give it another shot. Defiance on Val's part, I assumed, to help her reclaim a sense of normalcy. I slumped in relief when I spotted her as soon as I walked in and smiled as she bounded up from the booth for a hug. The cheerful warmth of a sunbeam radiated from her, unusual only if you were expecting a human rather than a dea.

"Hey, girl," she said, showing her dimple as she grinned and sat back down. "Hanging in there?"

"I think so." I collapsed onto the bench across from Val.

She eyed me, frowning. "Sure about that?"

"No. But the winds of change are always blowing. I'd rather bend than break."

Her smile tightened, and she lowered her voice, glancing at the TV showing the news as she said, "Sometimes you gotta burn shit down and start fresh. It'll be okay, Arden. Fire cleanses."

"I really, really hope you're right."

"I am. Even if it hurts. Speaking of…" She grasped my hand and turned it over to inspect the palm. "Good. Taking a break or trying the blend?"

"A break," I said. "Busy. And, uh, let's just say my studies have expanded."

"Excuse me?"

I fidgeted, shielding hard to stop myself from letting a swirl of Air spin through the bar. "What happens if you add Earth to the mix?"

She blinked, going sallow in the low light as blood drained from her face. "You have got to be joking. That was you the other night? Laurel was shitting herself!"

"Sorry," I muttered.

Val glanced over my shoulder. "We're going to have to do something. This is getting too wild, Arden. But we'll talk about it later." She glared at me. "I don't even want to know what you've been up to not to call me about that!"

A quick glance over my shoulder stopped me from answering as a perky server approached. After we ordered—a whiskey sour for her, a virgin Cuba Libre for me—Val asked, "Any mundane cases? Or all stuff for the community?"

I winced and shook my head. "Nothing mundane. The community is eating up all my time, and frankly I'm too damn tired to keep juggling everything like I had been."

"You gonna be all right?"

"For now." The remainder of the cash that Leith, Torsten, and Maria had each paid me to investigate various Otherside matters over the last few months had been stashed at my house to avoid paying taxes on what normally amounted to at least a quarter of my yearly income for work I couldn't report. To change the subject, I asked, "Has the collective reconsidered joining the rest of us?"

"No," she said sadly. "I'm sorry, Arden. The older folks are still waiting for the—for you know who, to betray us. Again. *I* believe you. So do some of the younger generations. Sofi's been talking to people and Laurel too. But three against a collective…it'll take time."

I nodded, mouth twisting to match the sudden sourness in my gut. While it was nice to hear that Val's undine sister and the oread who had also been captured with all of them were on my side, it stung that the other elementals were still so reluctant to even speak to me. "And the first time one of them looks at us funny…"

She shrugged. "Exactly. They almost hunted us out of existence. You're an exception in more ways than one."

We paused as drinks were set in front of us.

"Can I get you anything else?" the chirpy server asked. When we shook our heads, she left us in peace.

Before I could pick up the thread of the conversation and ask why the collective avoided Callista, Val froze, looking at something over my shoulder as her expression flickered to apprehension. I tilted to look around the back of our booth and immediately spotted the concern.

Troy was making an appearance, which might explain the sudden rise in the sourness in my gut. The sense of paranoia I used to experience as he drew near was absent. I hadn't realized how much I'd come to rely on the itchy feeling in the back of my mind telling me when I was about to start having a bad day.

"Go," I said, turning back to Val before Troy spotted us. He probably wouldn't do anything to Val, but given his loyalty to his House, I didn't want to risk it.

Val's brow pinched in concern. "You sure you can handle a Monteague on your own?"

"This particular Monteague, yes."

"Shit, Arden. That's badass."

"I know. Take advantage of it."

Val didn't need to be told again. She grabbed her backpack and slipped out of the booth, angling for the bathrooms with her face averted. If I was her, I'd wait there and then head for the rear exit via the kitchens as soon as Troy was seated and had his back to that part of the bar.

After a few seconds of chat with the hostess Troy joined me, taking Val's seat.

"Finch," he said by way of greeting.

"Monteague." I sipped my drink, noting the tightness around his eyes. "Please don't tell me you're already walking back your promise not to treat me like an assignment." He might have come to the rescue the other night, but that was to complete one of his own missions, regardless of that little moment we might have shared afterward.

He scowled at the implication that he'd break his word. "Don't worry. I'm here on business. Who'd I miss?"

"Nobody. You couldn't have called rather than interrupting my outing?"

Troy slouched, spinning Val's abandoned whiskey sour with a liquid grace I'd never seen before, even in him. One that raised flags. If I'd had any control of the bond between us, I'd have checked it, but it was closed. Falling back on my observational skills and the scent on the air currents flowing from him to me told me he'd been drinking, but that was absurd. This was the prince of a high elven House, a member of the Darkwatch, and an individual particularly concerned with both doing and being seen to do his duty.

And yet, if it was anyone else, I'd say he was drunk or had been drinking with the intent to be in that state. Every hair on my body stood up.

"What are you doing here?" I asked.

"Did you manage to slip my grandmother's net? I know you slipped mine and Alli's."

I fought to keep my expression blank. There was no fucking way I was answering that question. "Did you have a reason to be here, looking drunk and asking awkward questions?"

That sobered him a bit. He frowned at the drink in front of him before taking a sip. "I have a choice to make."

Chapter 19

I didn't like the sound of that at all. "What choice?"

Troy looked at me for too long for it not to involve me. That pissed me off.

"What. Choice?" I repeated more harshly.

"Evangeline wants you dead. She's the one who sent the Redcaps the other night." He watched my reaction as he sipped the appropriated whiskey sour. Despite my efforts to keep my face neutral, he must have seen something he expected, because he nodded. "Keithia has backed her. I'm in the middle of it."

Chills ran over me as I looked for the exits. Troy had always, *always*, acted in the interest of his House. Without flinching and without failure. Helping me was incidental or a thing he did to advance some objective of his own.

My voice shook as I asked, "How long do I have?"

He frowned and glanced around the bar. "You really think I'd kill you now?"

"You just said your sister and your grandmother want my head. Yes, I think you're sizing me up for a fucking pike or a placard. How long?"

Troy leaned back in the booth, looking more than a little sick. "We shook on being allies. I thought I'd proved that I meant it."

"And?"

"You cleared the debts between us, so why else would I be here if not to keep my word to you and the alliance?"

It took everything in me not to stand up, get in his face, and yell. This mysterious bullshit was getting on my nerves when I was already worried about whether or not he'd recognized Val from the lich's lair and a dozen other things.

I leaned forward and firmed my voice. "So what is the fucking choice you have to make?"

Troy finished Val's drink in a single gulp before answering. "Whether I defy them in the name of progress or drag my feet to give you time to come up with something. Do I play courageous or smart? Daring or cautious? Satisfy my duty to my House and queen or, for once in my Goddess-forsaken life, do what I actually believe is right and not just what I'm told? Tell me, Finch. What's the right play here? What serves the greater good?"

I stared at him, utterly dumbfounded. *This* was why he'd been drinking. We had a tentative truce, but nothing I would have counted on for this.

Yet here he was, warning me. Asking me for guidance.

"What aren't you telling me?" I asked.

Slowly, he reached out and tipped my chin up with a single finger. The gold flecks in his eyes flared as they searched mine. Chills raced over me as Aether jumped from him. He was powerful even when he wasn't trying, and that scared the shit outta me almost as much as catching myself thinking his eyes were pretty. Even so, I went along with it, conscious of the humans drinking around us.

"Too clever," Troy said before dropping his hand. "Careful. That's dangerous. Especially when you're going toe-to-toe with us. With them."

"Well?" I snapped. "You gonna tell me, or are we just playing verbal footsie?"

"It's a Catch-22. If I don't get rid of you, Keithia will have what she needs to disown me." He lifted his dark brows, and I

151

nodded. His being disowned meant my protection from the caprices of House Monteague—maybe even my immunity—would be that much harder to enforce. Perhaps even impossible. I wasn't completely naive. Troy and I might have a rivalry, but he was the one who kept his House honest where their actions toward me were concerned.

"Evangeline agreed to the alliance though," I said. "The terms were no more species laws over the general law. She swore in blood."

Troy rolled his eyes and slouched again, lower than before. "Come on, Finch, you're smarter than that."

"Callista," I said, cold with certainty. I'd known she'd be making plans to move against me. She needed to take me back in hand and regain the power I'd stolen for myself, something to make sure that nobody else tried the shit I had. "Evangeline's got a side negotiation with Callista."

"There you go." He toasted me with the now-empty glass then frowned to find it in that state when he went for another sip.

Cold chills raced over me as he confirmed my earlier suspicions. "Shit."

Callista did not fuck around. If she allied with the strongest elven House in the Triangle, I didn't know how long the witches and weres would stay on my side. The djinn would always go wherever it was practical, and that would leave me with the vampires—good in a fight but significantly reduced in numbers and availability, given their recent internecine battles and dealing with the lead-up to the Reveal. Then I'd be alone again, easy pickings.

I don't want to be on my own again. I worked too fucking hard for this!

I pushed the thought aside to revisit later, when Troy fucking Monteague wasn't looking at me like I needed to make a smart decision right this second. "What does she want?" I asked.

Troy shrugged. "What she's always wanted. Power."

"So, what, she allies with Callista and leads the Wild Hunt? Subverts it?"

Troy's jaw muscles bunched, and he nodded.

"The gods appear in my *office*," I hissed, leaning forward and keeping my voice low enough that even an elf might have to strain to hear me. "In my *home*, and give me orders. She thinks she's just going to get rid of me?"

The look he gave me weighed and measured me down to my soul.

"There is that," he murmured, looking as though that settled something for him.

"What's that supposed to mean?"

"You're avoiding making a choice again. I have a week to decide what mine will be."

My heart pounded, and my mouth dried. "I thought you said—"

"Relax. The choice isn't about whether to kill you. It's about how far I'll go to uphold the oath I swore to the alliance. And to protect you as the embodiment of the greater good for the territory."

I slumped, exhaling heavily, and just barely kept a hold on my magic. The way Troy tensed told me my eyes must have flared for a second, but all the humans were occupied and weren't paying attention to two normal-looking people in a booth.

"Your word means that much to you?" I still didn't know if I could trust him. Nobody went from drowning people to saving them in a few months.

"It's all I have."

"Aside from the money and the title and the—"

"And nothing. It's all on my grandmother's sufferance." He tilted his head, studying me. "She can take everything with a few words, including my life, and Evie will help her. They don't want this new future, no matter how much it serves all of us. How much *you* serve all of us. I finally see that now, thanks to you."

What had Keithia threatened him with for him to be here now, talking like this? It clicked then that he was looking for a life raft, one that I didn't know if I could throw him. "Monteague…"

"Alli's waiting for me." He rose and pulled out his wallet to drop a twenty on the table. "Good talk, Finch."

I sat there, mind whirling as I tried to process what the hell was happening, then got up and chased after him. He ignored me when I caught up, keeping his hands in his pockets and his head down as he headed for the parking garage across the street.

"I don't like you," I said as I walked alongside him.

"I know."

"But we're allies."

He glanced at me sideways. "Glad to hear that got through."

"And frankly, I need you to keep the rest of your House honest."

"Is there a reason you're telling me things I already know?"

I huffed. "Just making sure we're on the same page."

"So?"

Catching his arm, I ignored the jump of magic between us. "So if you meant what you said about upholding the alliance and protecting me, I'll figure something out. Okay? Have faith."

He studied me, looking almost sober. "That's the problem," he said, leaning closer and lowering his voice. "I do, or I'd be waiting in your woods at the edge of your wards to hunt you down, not trying to find a better way."

As I stood there, bile rising into my throat, a muscle in his cheek twitched. He lifted his hand as though to squeeze my shoulder then thought better of it and walked backward a few steps. "Prove me right, Finch. Even if it's only because Evie will come for you if I fall. Only next time, she'll have Callista and our whole House behind her, not just a handful of discontents."

I watched him take the steps up into the parking garage two at a time. If I'd been conflicted before, I was completely lost now. Did I actually have a friend?

"Prove him right, Finch," a mocking, male voice sing-songed behind me before it deepened. "Because little Evangeline won't be the only one coming for your head."

I whirled. A thin, pale figure in a black hoodie stood behind me. His pupils bled into the rest of his eyes, and he smiled broadly to show small fangs. Around his neck was a stone similar to the one the lich lord had worn. When he had my attention, he must have dropped a shield because an evil that echoed Gideon's suddenly seeped from him. A passerby shied off the sidewalk and ran across the street in unseeing panic, and a car horn blared as the driver nearly struck him.

"You," I said, recognizing the vampire from the morgue. He'd attacked Doc Mike, back when he'd been more of a newborn undead.

"Me," the sorcerer agreed. "And thanks to *you*, I get to unleash hell. Oh—did our dear doctor like my gift? I left it especially for him."

My eyes darted as I counted the number of people who would be collateral damage if we fought here in the street. Too many, and I'd expose Otherside before we were ready.

The witch-born vamp smiled as he watched my calculations then looked over my shoulder at the sound of feet clattering down the stairs from the parking garage. "I'll be seeing you," he said, walking backward in exactly the same way Troy had. "Next time, I'll have my pet."

I fought down the hammer of fear pounding in my chest and lunged for him, but he was too fast, dancing away so casually that it was insulting before turning a corner. Air currents jittered in an unusual pattern, like he disturbed reality with his presence. The lich had been like that too.

As I took a step after him a hand closed around my arm, stopping me. I spun, fists up and ready to fight.

Troy released me as soon as I focused on him. "Not today, Finch."

"Next time," Allegra said from behind him, her attention on the street as she took a few deep lungfuls of air before looking at me. "Are you okay?"

"Why didn't you let me after him?" I snapped. "He was alone! I could have followed him."

"Think," Troy growled in an undertone, looking more sober than he had when we left the bar. "We're downtown. In the open. He wouldn't have shown himself if something hadn't triggered it."

Allegra said, "We need to regroup. Call the witches. Let them deal with this creature while we deal with the bigger threat."

Given her determination to protect Troy from himself, I figured the bigger threat was Callista and her deal with Keithia and Evangeline.

"Fine." The sickening combination of frustration and fear was going to give me an ulcer. We'd been looking for this asshole for over a week. He popped up literally right behind me, only to slip away like smoke in a breeze. That he'd claimed the rabisu as his pet only made matters worse. I shuddered at the memory of the demon slinking over the lintel of my bedroom door, oozing down from the ceiling to shred the bed Troy had just pulled me from to bits. I had really, really hoped that with the lich dead, it would be trapped on a different plane. Apparently not.

Troy's hands hovered like he was going to clasp my shoulders. He dropped them at my glare.

"You've seen our quarry now. You know he's close." He inhaled, much as Allegra had, then glanced back at her. At her sharp nod, he added, "We'll know him if we scent him again. Don't worry."

I scowled at him. "He's working with Callista. Probably staying at the bar. I just need to confirm it."

The elves looked dubious.

"Think about it. Callista targets Sergei and Keithia, knowing that they're the most likely to be swayed of the people surrounding me. She knew about the—the guy last week before I told her. She must be planning something to get me out of the way and regain control of the Reveal. Y'all have to be trying some kind of surveillance on her, right?"

The blank expressions on both their faces, combined with Troy's comment in January that they knew who her people were, confirmed it.

"Okay, so she's not going to arrange this shit on the phone. She has a computer, but she wouldn't risk your hackers with something big. If you know who some of her Watchers are, she can't use them either, not if she wants to run a side deal with Evangeline without Troy finding out." I spread my arms. "Who the hell else could have arranged all of it, other than the last person we would have suspected? The sorcerer is her go-between."

"It's a reach," Allegra said. "A big one. That's disgusting, even for Keithia."

Troy rested his hands on his hips and looked at his feet, agreeing without a word.

I slumped then straightened. "There's a quick way to test the theory."

The identically grim expressions on their faces made it easy to see them as the siblings they claimed to be.

Allegra shook her head. "No. I'm not going to the bar, and you shouldn't either. There are bigger fucking issues."

Troy crossed his arms, his lips pressing into a thin line.

She grabbed his shoulder. "*No*, Troy. Grandmother gave you her terms. You're already defying them as it is. I'll watch your ass, but I'm not finna join you on the chopping block for something this reckless."

Hazel eyes flicked to me, like he was asking for understanding. Or forgiveness. Maybe a consensus. Something I wasn't sure I could offer and didn't understand why he'd look for it from me. I wasn't his people. I wasn't anyone's people.

Allegra's hand tightened on his shoulder. "Troy…Arden, please. Let's be smart about this. I will help, but I won't throw my life away."

I pulled my hair out of its bun and retied it to give myself a few seconds to think. I hated it, but Allegra was right. "Okay. You're right. I just…"

"I know," she said, letting go of Troy. "I'm sorry. But if you're accusing Callista of something this big and we're in rebellion against our grandmother, we have to be smarter than this. Worse, we have to be smarter than *them*."

I nodded, ashamed at the relief that thundered through me as she gave me a reason not to risk facing Callista today. I'd have to figure out if she was truly Artemis's lost nymph and what to do about it sooner or later, but I didn't even know where to begin with that. "I'll call the witches."

"Keep us posted." Allegra tugged on Troy's arm to steer him back to the parking garage.

"Oh," I called after them. "Vikki and the cats came to an agreement, so fingers crossed she doesn't pull a Sergei on us."

From the look the Monteagues exchanged, they'd be making sure she didn't. I sighed and headed for my car, wondering if this alliance would ever be able to actually trust each other.

Chapter 20

After a sleepless night, I decided it was time to call in help on my powers. Janae had told me there was nothing I could do until they confirmed that their wayward coven member was in Durham. If we had to fight him, Callista, and the elves, I wanted to have as much to throw at them as I could.

The Redcap attack the other night had been a shitshow. There was absolutely no reason why an elemental who could control multiple elements should fear a handful of elves in the woods. I had it in me to be a force of nature, but I'd been making my usual mistake, thinking within the limits others had set. I didn't want to obey Neith but I also didn't want her coming to fuck with me for being disobedient while I was juggling everything else, so I called Val and asked if she, Sofia, and Laurel might be convinced to come over and give me a hand.

"Hallelujah," she said, sounding exasperated but relieved. "I thought you'd never fucking ask, girl! Make it lunch time. I'll get the others there."

I puttered around, equal parts annoyed and excited as I prepared to have guests over for the second time in as many days. After months of trying to give the elders and the Collective time and space to get used to the idea of both me and my work with the elves, I was finally going to meet with more than just Val. Which wasn't to say that Val wasn't great, just that I'd dreamed of belonging somewhere for so long. Quality was better than quantity with friends but still. What would it be like to have more friends?

Val texted me that they were on their way and would arrive a little after noon. There wasn't much to tidy, so I took care of routine tasks for my business while I waited. The boring work was exactly what I needed to calm down and focus my energy.

The other elementals had all agreed to come, but I was still surprised when they turned up. Val and Sofia arrived together. Val was a riot of energy while Sofia seemed to bury hers in uncertain depths. They brought a small package of maple candy for Zanna, which I left on the table where she'd see it the next time she came in.

Laurel arrived a short time later, betraying nothing, as solid as Occoneechee Mountain. With all of them present, I gathered the picnic I'd packed and led them down to the river, where all of our elements could be represented and expressed.

Sofia perked up as the rushing burble of the Eno reached our ears, surging ahead of us to sit cross-legged at the river's edge and dabble her fingers in the water. "I love this river," she said, eyes closed. "It always has so much to say."

Laurel's eyes lit up at the sight of the boulder I'd tumbled a couple of weeks back. She strode to it and rested a hand on a rough patch still caked with dried mud. "You shifted this? With Air?"

"Yeah." I dropped down on a log by the firepit I'd dug, ignoring the patio furniture I hadn't bothered to drag back up last night. Val settled in on the ground in front of the log, making the right-angle to the square surrounding the pit as Laurel scrambled up on my boulder to sit in half-lotus.

"Impressive," the oread said after closing her eyes and reaching deep. "It didn't want to move."

"I know," I said, unable to keep the grumble of frustration out. "Damn thing bloodied my nose with the amount of Air I had to use to wedge it out."

Val snorted. "So you handle everything like you handle Fire? Wrestling and forcing it?"

Grimacing, I shrugged. "I mean, it works, right?"

Laurel and Sofia opened their eyes to exchange knowing glances. They probably had the natural affinity that Val and I shared with complementary elements. Val just sighed.

"Do you breathe like this?" She gasped in and out, an exaggerated pant like a runner after a hard race.

I frowned. "I mean...no."

"Exactly. How do you handle Air?"

"I just do." Not knowing how to explain it, I showed them, opening myself to my magic and pulling one of the breezes winding through the valley to blow the leaves out of our small clearing.

They all stared at me goggle-eyed, and Laurel whistled. "Goddess. I suppose if you have that much raw strength, wrestling seems easy. Or maybe Air has to be captured like that. Hard to say, since there aren't any other sylphs around."

I shifted on my log, not sure whether I should feel embarrassed or annoyed because I already knew I lacked finesse. "Well, how is it for y'all?"

Val shifted into a seated position and extended a hand toward the sticks in the firepit. "I invite Fire and embrace it when it comes. Watch."

I dropped my shield completely, reading the energy as she opened herself to her element. Just as she'd said, her reach was less of a grab and more of a hand extended to a dance partner, inviting and anticipatory. The potential for the flames lived in the dry sticks, and she coaxed it forth.

My breath caught as Fire sparked in the pit, enticed by the fuel offered by the twigs, teasing into being as a dancing blaze.

"Did you catch it?" Val asked.

I nodded. It seemed so much easier when she did it, compared to my attempts to force it. I resisted the urge to catch the flames and wondered whether that method would work if the fuel had been damp.

"Earth needs to be encouraged." Laurel interrupted my thoughts. "It wants to help you, but you have to help it. Welcome it. Nurture it. It's reciprocal—when you're not bullying it with Air, anyway." She settled, sending herself deep into the rocky soil with the sense of a mother hen gathering chicks, or a tree extending roots. The idea was new to me. I thought of Earth in the sense of pulling weeds or shifting rocks. But I supposed that I could see where it would work. It was not at all what I'd done the other night.

"Water is a merging." Sofia dipped her fingers in the river again, opened herself, and to my mind's eye, fell.

I found myself on my feet, shaking and gasping for breath as I remembered Jordan Lake closing over my head, cold and airless as it poured down my throat. Tree branches whipped in a threatening breeze overhead as the other elementals sat frozen in place.

"You had a bad experience with water," Sofia said softly, releasing her magic and letting it ebb away with the river's flow.

Swallowing hard, I took one last deep inhale before I took myself in hand and forced myself to let go of Air. My throat closed around words that didn't want to be spoken. "The elves. I was thrown in Jordan Lake to die last winter."

Sofia gasped and covered her mouth, distress and pity pinching her face. Val snapped a stick in half and threw it into her little bonfire with an angry mutter. Only Laurel stayed as she was, though pain and understanding filled her eyes.

"You've experienced them at their worst but still work with them?" she said, her Scottish accent coming through stronger than usual.

I hugged myself and looked at the ground, kicking at a pinecone as I decided what to say. *Honesty*, I decided.

Looking at each of them in turn, I said, "I was raised to think elementals were some kind of freak form of djinn. That I was utterly alone in the world. Eventually, I discovered not only were there other elementals, but that the people who'd raised me did so with their own agendas, keeping me in the dark so that they could prosper." Gritting my teeth, I forced my hands to my sides, but couldn't stop them from clenching. "Then I found out that given my mother was a djinni, my father had to be an elf, since apparently none of the local wild elementals had any mysterious children."

Val looked away, regret painting her features.

"It's not your fault, Val," I said. "Callista kept me ignorant for reasons I'm only just discovering. But y'all are the only elementals who will acknowledge me. Do you know how that feels? To find your people but be rejected by most of them when all you've wanted your whole entire life is to belong somewhere?"

Tears threatened in all of our eyes. I blinked mine away.

"So yeah," I said. "I work with the elves. Callista wants to use me, probably for the Wild Hunt, and so do the gods. The djinn have turned their backs on me. The vampires and the wereclans want the power in my blood, but maybe they want me too. Hard to say. The elves? Most of them just want me dead, and you know what? At least that's honest."

Sofia pulled her knees up to her chin, tears flowing freely. "I had no idea," she said in a thick voice. "I thought you were just—I don't even know. But to be so alone…Goddess, how have you survived?"

"She didn't have a choice." Laurel's gaze weighed heavy on me, and I held it until she glanced down to the crack she traced absently. Then her eyes shot back up to mine. "You said, 'most elves.' That means not all are hunting you."

"For the moment, none are. I killed some and have an arrangement with others," I said.

She leaned forward. "Who?"

"House Monteague. But it's complicated. Unstable." Troy and Allegra would abide by it, but from what Troy had said, Evangeline or Keithia would break it the first chance they got.

"The elf who was at the bar? And the lich's lair?" Val asked. "The one throwing a fuckton of Aether around?"

I nodded. "That's him."

Laurel narrowed her eyes at me. "Arden, with that much Aether, he has to be powerful even among the high-bloods."

"He is," I admitted, wondering where this was going and if it was safe for either side for me to say more. I hissed a breath in and out. "What are y'all getting at?"

"I want to be out. Like you," Laurel said. "I want to grow my crops with all my gift can offer, not just the drabs I dare to feed our Mother when I pray nobody is paying attention. What do I have to do to make a deal? What was the price you paid?"

Sofia held her breath, watching me, and Val lifted her eyes from the flames.

"The drowning," I said bitterly. "The elf I'm allied with is the one who carried out their laws, then changed his mind. Thinks I'm useful, given that he's followed me into a dangerous situation and saved my ass a few times now."

That rocked them back. Their hope and fear weighed on me, their longing and disappointment stealing my words. I bowed my head, needing a minute to gather myself. Having to explain the evolution in my relationship with Troy made uncomfortable knots twist in my belly and a slimy feeling crawl over my skin.

Had I sacrificed too much? Was I still a doormat and letting him call it allyship?

No. Troy will be disowned for disobeying Keithia, and then he's as good as dead if Allegra can't save him. He's as invested as I am. I think. I took a mental look toward the bond, but it was still shut down harder than ever. Whatever Troy was up to, he wanted to be sure nobody knew. With a sigh of frustration for the elf, I looked at each of my fellow elementals.

"Will you help me understand the other elements or not?" I asked.

Val smiled lopsidedly. "You already have Fire. I don't want to be on the crew that responds to you burning your house down, if I can help it."

"I could use the favor," Laurel said bluntly. "I'll help, but I hope that if the opportunity arises you'll speak for me."

"Of course," I said.

Sofia stared into the Eno, tracing patterns on its surface with the hand missing a finger. "I don't want to be noticed again," she said in a quiet voice. "I want to be happy with Nazneen, ignored and unimportant. I'll help, but only if I get the opposite of Laurel's favor. If you speak of me, let it be that I don't exist, at least not as anything more than a mundane."

I looked away, into the trees. "I can only promise to try. The Darkwatch knows more—sees more—than I can account for on my own."

When I looked back at the group, Sofia was giving Val a long, solemn look.

"Fine," the undine said. "I'm in. But at the first scent of meringue, I'm outta here."

"Fair enough." I took my place on the log again, choking up as I said, "Thank you all for your support."

"Thanks for finding us a way to freedom," Laurel said.

I nodded. Maybe that was the key to not becoming a doormat—remembering that I had something valuable to offer too. Not just something to give but something others valued.

We spent the next hour and a half working through Fire, Earth, and—to my dismay—Water. Fire was easier to grasp with Val around, and even when it slipped away from me, lightning was simple. The more times I caught Fire, the easier it was to have crackles of electricity skipping across my fingertips.

Earth was harder. I wasn't used to welcoming anything or extending outward in growth rather than defensive violence. Still, I gritted my teeth and tried. Almost an hour passed before I was able to get the sense of it like I had the other night. Then, there it was, solid and heavy, so different from Air that I resisted it even as I tried to welcome it.

Water, I couldn't even begin to use.

Every time I tried to mimic Sofia's release, her merging with the element, I panicked, gasping for breath and convinced I was drowning again. Each failure wound me tighter, and I fled back to Air for refuge.

"We're getting nowhere," Sofia said at last.

I didn't disagree, having just shorn every tree in the clearing of all their new leaves, sending them bursting away in shreds of varicolored green. Dropping to my log seat, I buried my face in my hands, trembling as the memory of the lake closing over my head wrapped me in cold and dark.

My phone rang, and I answered without looking to see who it was.

"Finch, what the hell are you doing?" Troy said, sounding pained. "One minute I'm on fire, the next I'm buried alive, and now it feels like you're trying to drown us both."

I sat bolt upright, glanced around the clearing at my friends, and froze. "Uh…"

The other elementals exchanged glances. Whatever Troy had promised me about not invading my space, I couldn't risk that he wouldn't again. My life, sure. But not Sofia's. I covered the receiver, looked at Sofia, and hissed, "Get out of here. Now."

She didn't ask questions as she rose. Val tossed her the car keys and said, "I'll get an Uber."

When she was out of the clearing, I went back to my conversation. "I'm practicing," I said. "Sorry, I thought it was muted."

Silence.

"You still there?" I asked, grimacing. The elements weren't the only part of my magic that I needed practice with, apparently. *Does that mean he can sense when I practice with Air? Why hasn't he called about Fire before now?*

"Are you trying to tell me that you're practicing with multiple elements? All of them?"

"Does it matter? I mean, come on, you were there when Fire and Earth manifested. You saw me call lightning more than once."

Prayers to the Goddess bordering on blasphemy rattled down the line before he said, "Be very careful, Finch, and very clear. Are you actively, consciously practicing with elements other than Air?"

Sudden fear made my heart trip and my blood cool despite the warm afternoon. "What if I was?"

A long, tired sigh. "Then the Fire and the Earth weren't a fluke because you were in danger. If you have all four and can manipulate them at will, that means you'd be a primordial elemental, not a sylph, and we would all be in a lot more trouble than anyone thought with the gods sniffing for a Wild Hunt."

Somehow it was worse for him to say it than Neith.

"Oh," was all I could manage, swaying on my log, stomach churning as I looked at Val and Laurel with the expression of a kid being busted by her parents. If the elves knew about primordial elementals when it had surprised my fellow elementals, that couldn't be a good thing.

"I need to do some research. I'll call when I'm done. Pray that this means we have something to use against Evie," he said. Without waiting for an answer from me, he hung up.

"Well, fuck," I said to dead air.

Chapter 21

Laurel was giving me a weighing look when I looked up from tucking my phone away. "Someone else knows you have multiple elements?"

I winced. "He usually happens to be around when I get into the kinds of situations that inspire their appearance."

Val frowned. "The same Darkwatch agent? The Monteague? Just how much time are you spending with him, Arden? How does he know you were practicing?"

"More than I'd like and like I said, it's complicated." I hoped they'd accept the evasive answer given that I couldn't talk about the Redcaps the other night, or the bond. I shrugged. "He keeps Keithia and Evangeline off my ass, so better to keep him close than turn up dead, right?"

Both elementals looked at me as though they weren't certain of my mental faculties before Val combed a hand through her choppy bangs. "If you say so. Is he coming here?"

"I don't know," I admitted. "His track record on boundaries hasn't been great so far, but he's made me a promise."

Laurel frowned. "What, and you believe him?"

"Yes?" Oddly, I found it true. He had said his word was all he had, and I'd relied on it before.

To my surprise, her face cleared. "Good. Then I want to come along."

It was my turn to frown. "Come where?"

"You're not practicing for shits and giggles. There's something happening. Something big." Stubbornness and determination flashed in Laurel's blue eyes. "I want in."

I took a deep breath, staring at the embers smoldering down to ash in the fire pit. My desire to protect my fellow elementals warred with my desire for help. Troy had said the elves knew of other elementals in the Triangle but had ignored them because they were too weak to bother with. Did that mean they'd be more at risk of harm, whether from enemies or allies?

More importantly, was it my job to decide for her?

"Okay," I said, releasing a snap of Air in my frustration. The tree branches overhead shook, startling a few birds. I'd bargained for elementals to have individual says in the alliance. I didn't get to take that away from them because I didn't want the responsibility of feeling guilty if something happened later. That was on me to work on. I couldn't keep them away to make myself feel better or worry less.

Laurel straightened, a resolute look crossing her face as she pulled out her phone. As we exchanged numbers, she said, "What are you hunting, anyway?"

I gritted my teeth. "The lich's accomplice. Possibly a demon."

Val hissed, and the embers sparked anew as she fisted her hands on her hips. "Fuck. That means I need in too."

I started to ask why or tell her that she didn't have to do it, but then I realized why she'd want to.

"Sofia?" I asked softly.

Nodding, Val kicked a stone. "Yeah. You killed the guy that took her finger, but not the one that kidnapped her—us—in the first place." She leveled a hard look at me, and the muscles in her jaw bunched. "I would do *anything* for her to have a sound night's sleep again. She's all I have left of my family, Arden. All she wants is a quiet life with Naz. I can give her that. Your

Monteague didn't have a problem fighting with us before. I'll take the risk for Sofi and Naz."

As with Laurel, it wasn't my place to deny her this. "Okay. Then let's do this in a way that ensures we can leverage our powers. I'm tired of having this fucker get the drop on us."

"How is he finding us, anyway?" Laurel asked. "It shouldn't be possible for anyone to sense elemental magic except other elementals. I mean, I can't sense Aether or whatever the lich was using."

"I can kind of use Chaos and sense Aether, life, and soul magic." I touched my pendant through my shirt but left it where it was. It hadn't occurred to me before that that would be odd even among elementals, but both Val and Laurel looked at me as though I'd grown another head. Shrugging, I added, "I mean, I can't see the magic like I see ours, but I can feel the shape of it. Which means it's possible he's doing the same. Probably some spell lost to everyone except the djinn after Atlantis."

"Were you using your power when the sorcerer found you in Durham?" Val asked after digesting that bit of information.

I shook my head. "No, and you know I keep it locked down."

Val wrinkled her nose. "You used to."

My heart skipped a beat. "Huh?"

"There's…seepage," Laurel said cautiously, as though she wasn't sure how I'd take it. "Power leaking out, the way the ground feels right before a mudslide. Saturated and unstable."

"Or right before a fire finds a new fuel source and explodes," Val added.

Blinking, I sat down and stared at them. "I have a power signature? Like Torsten?"

Every time I went to Claret, I could feel Torsten's presence as a pulsing weight of power, thudding like a slow heartbeat and as warm as blood. The idea that I might be developing something similar was mildly terrifying.

"I mean, I've never met any of the power players in town." Val frowned. "But yeah. You had it locked down the first time we met. Remember when I said I'd have thought you were human? In the week between the lich and now, that changed. I wouldn't necessarily know what you were, but I'd know you were Otherside."

"And not to be messed with," Laurel said softly.

My mind whirled. I'd wanted the power to carve out a space for myself in the community, but I hadn't dared to dream that I could develop it myself. I'd been so focused on building the alliance that I hadn't stopped to consider what practicing with my magic might mean for me on an individual level.

"Well, shit." I didn't know what to make of that and wondered if it was part of Troy's recent attitude adjustment. "What does it feel like?"

The other two elementals frowned as they exchanged a glance.

"A jet engine just coming online," Val said after studying me a moment. "Not at full force yet, but kind of that hum in your bones, ya know?"

"Yeah." I rubbed the back of my neck. That gave me a whole new reason to practice. If I couldn't hide anymore, fight or flight were my only options—and I was tired of running. I also had to wonder how much longer I could continue working so closely with the mundanes. There was a reason the old and powerful tended to find a lair and stick to it. Was it normal to have a power signature at twenty-six? Maybe Hawkeye Investigations was closer to shutting down than I'd thought.

The question I'd never gotten to ask Val at the bar popped into my head. "Why do the other elementals avoid Callista?"

Laurel's face hardened as she crossed her arms. "About thirty years ago, those of us who'd been known to Callista started going missing."

"A few each year. It stopped when the shit with House Solari went down." Val stiffened as soon as the words were out of her mouth, her tan skin turning sallow as she stared at me.

Laurel didn't notice. "She let us think it was the elves, but we're not fools. We connected the dots, and the only link that all of the missing shared was that they were known to Callista." She saw Val's expression then and looked from her to me. "What?"

"I've never heard of House Solari," I said around the lump in my throat and the bad feeling in my stomach.

Val avoided my eye and started pitching twigs into the fire then reached out to it with her power to make the tiny flames dance. "That's because they were destroyed. Four years after the first of us started disappearing."

The math made me grimace. "The year I was born."

"The year the disappearances stopped," Val whispered.

Laurel's eyes bugged, and her jaw dropped. "You? They stopped because of you?"

I didn't like the conclusions we were coming to one bit. "Seems that way, doesn't it? If it was Callista, why would she need to keep kidnapping wild elementals when she could have a trueborn? When she could *own* one?"

Feeling sick, I looked toward the river. Horrific as it was, it would partially explain why my parents had broken every law held by both djinn and elves to conceive me. I might never know whether Callista pushed them into it, but Duke and Grimm had to have been involved somehow. My big questions now were: who had my parents been, to their people and each other, and had they been acting for or against Callista?

Either way, my life had been part of a plan.

Fuck that. I'm nobody's chess piece.

I was finally closing in on answers I'd been seeking my whole life, but a pang twinged through my heart as I realized now

173

wasn't the time. I could find out more about House Solari and who my father might have been later. For now, I needed to level the playing field. That meant stripping Callista of allies, as she was trying to do to me—starting with the lich's accomplice.

"We need to set a trap with me as the bait," I said, seeking calm and trying to keep the anger out of my voice. None of this was their fault. "If Callista's goal is to reacquire me and the witch-vamp can either sense or trace my power signature, then he has to go first. If he found the three of you once, he could do it again, but it looks like history's repeating itself. He wants me, not you, and now I'm easier to find. First question: where?"

"Somewhere near Falls Lake," Laurel said after some thought. "Close enough to Callista's that he should feel confident, far enough from major human centers that we should have room to move. Plus, the Eno empties into it. If you manage to use Water, Arden, it'll be easier with a body you're familiar with nearby."

Val pursed her lips and nodded. "Who can we pull in for this?"

"Everyone but the vampires and the fae," I said grimly. "The weres are expecting a call, so we'll have wolves, leopards, and jags. I think I can get at least two of the elves in on it. The witches will come as well, since he was one of theirs before the Modernists turned him."

"No djinn?" Val asked. "I thought they'd agreed to the alliance."

I grimaced, feeling the pain of my sundered relationships all over again. "I only ever knew how to reach two of them directly. One is dead. The other blames me for it and threatened to hang me by my intestines if I called on him again." No need to mention that both were my cousins.

Val mirrored my expression. "Oh."

"Yeah." I pulled a few stray curls off my face. They bounced straight back, and I shook my head irritably to clear them away. "Okay. If I can get everyone to move on this today, are you both still in?"

They nodded, expressions turning grim.

"Great. Let's head back up to the house and see what I can sort out."

Calling everyone sequentially would have meant spending the rest of the afternoon on calls and questions, so I sent a group text while Val and Laurel chatted over iced sweet tea. If the whole alliance wanted me to fix things, then they could damn well organize themselves to answer when I sent for them to help me. We'd meet in my yard, make a plan, and get to Falls Lake. Part of me felt like we were moving too fast, but it had already been over a week with our quarry on the loose and Callista orchestrating whatever she was planning to scupper our Reveal or bring me back under her control.

Responses came back in record time. Janae said she'd be there and would spread the word to her coven. Ximena and Terrence agreed to show up with their clans. I got a terse acknowledgement from Troy, not saying whether he was coming. Vikki responded with a voice recording that was just a big, exultant whoop with more than a little of a wolf's howl in it, making Laurel and Val jump when I played it without warning.

Which was how I ended up having people in my house for a second day in a row. This was getting to be a thing, one that I hadn't anticipated when I'd let Duke talk everyone into making me arbiter. It struck me that if the sorcerer could find me in town, he could probably find me here too, despite the wardings that kept people from looking too closely and suggested that those meaning me harm should turn away. Maybe that would have scared me a week ago. Now it just solidified my resolve to end him. I was getting harder and didn't know if that was a good thing. Only that it felt necessary.

While we waited for everyone to arrive, I filled Val and Laurel in on the alliance—the whos and whats of what they wanted to be a part of. Cautious excitement pulled them tight. Me too. Shit I'd been working toward for months was finally happening.

Vikki was closest, so it was no surprise when she arrived first. I hollered to the woods that we had company, not sure where Zanna was or what was needed for her to raise stronger magic but not wanting her to be surprised when our front yard filled up with allies. I winced as I directed Vikki to pull off into the yard. Parking vehicles off the gravel drive would tear up what little grass I had and make a mess of the wildflowers, but there was nothing for it. We needed to be organized before we went to battle.

Sergei glowered from where he was chained to the bed of the truck. As Vikki hopped out, I asked, "Will those chains hold him?"

"Silver-plated steel," she said. "I told him if he fights with us, I'd talk to Pops about reducing his sentence for good behavior. Until then, he'll be my good boy, won't you Sergy-wergy?"

The wolf snarled and showed his teeth but didn't snap as she patted him on the head.

I couldn't help but wonder what the hell the sibling dynamics were like in the Volkov household, but a ripple in the air currents and the pop of gravel announced another car.

"Janae." I spotted the older model silver Mercedes crawling through the trees. Four others were in it with her.

The witches spilled out of the car almost before Janae had put it in park, chattering amongst themselves. Energy danced around them, giving me the same goosebumps I always got when I visited Janae, but in more of a full-body shudder given that there were five of them and four weren't being particularly careful to shield.

They sobered at the sight of Sergei—obviously no dog, if you knew to look for a wolf—and stared at me with wide eyes as Janae made introductions. The middle-aged woman with the same strong features as Janae was her daughter, Hope. The athletic young redhead decked out in Lululemon was Sarah. A guy in cargo shorts and a T-shirt with the same red hair but brown eyes instead of green was Sarah's brother, Will. The last member of the party was Will's boyfriend, Cam, a big, dark-skinned man with the gentlest aura I'd ever sensed.

"So this is an elemental." Hope sounded equal parts impressed and wary.

"One of us, anyway," I said. "Two more have decided they want to join the alliance and will be helping out today." I whistled and waved at the house.

As I introduced Laurel and Val, three more cars rolled up the drive: Ximena's red Mustang, Terrence's black Charger, and Troy's black MDX. I frowned, wondering how close Troy had been to arrive at the same time as the Durhamites. We repeated all the introductions with the weres and their seconds, plus Troy, Allegra, and a small, dark-haired elf who looked an awful lot like Javier Luna. I swallowed past the lump in my throat as the man was introduced as Iago Luna—Javier's half-brother.

Troy had saved me from Jordan Lake, leaving Javier when he couldn't save both of us and complete his mission to stop Leith Sequoyah without breaking his cover. Guilt for Troy's choice weighed on me for the first time. I gave him a long look, wondering what was going on, and was met with the blank face that said he'd boxed up his feels and put them aside for the day. The bond gave me nothing.

Iago and Allegra held themselves stiffly at the introduction of Val and Laurel, who were visibly shaking even after I eased up behind them and rested my arms across their shoulders for reassurance. The little clearing that was my yard fell silent as thousands of years of history bore down on us all, and nervous eyes darted between the three elementals on one side and the three elves on the other. Knowing that there were elementals in the Triangle was different from seeing three of us together and being forced to reckon with the fact that I wasn't a fluke. Troy was the only one who didn't react, but he'd fought beside us last week.

Allegra shook herself and extended a hand first, a tentative smile on her face.

"I hope this can be a new chapter," she said. It didn't exactly break the tension, but more than a few sighs of relief stirred the air when Val and Laurel tentatively shook it.

"I guess that's everyone then," I said past the lump in my throat as I looked over my posse of Othersiders. "Who's ready to kick some ass?"

Chapter 22

The uproar I'd expected to accompany my plan didn't come. I think everyone had had enough of the uncertainty. The idea was simple enough: drive over to land Acacia Thorn owned via a mundane shell company at Falls Lake, goad Callista with a call, and see who she sent. If she was working with Evangeline or Keithia, they were out of Redcaps to send after me and would have to send House allies that we could whittle down. There were other Watchers, but I was gambling that they'd sit this one out unless Callista had something big on them and could compel their obedience. I had enough of Otherside behind me now that Callista wasn't the default power anymore. Ironically, that made her more dangerous, which was why I was ninety percent sure she'd send the vampire sorcerer. That asshole had his sights set on me anyway, and this would be the perfect chance for him.

There were a lot of shifty looks, both between the groups clustered by faction and among factions. This would be our first time fighting all together. The weres seemed easy with it, but they'd joined up with the vampires to fight the Modernists last week. For everyone else, this was a brave new world. Add in the fact that witches rarely, if ever, went into combat situations as anything other than medics or faith leaders, and we were blazing all kinds of new trails.

When nobody objected, we shifted to getting the roles nailed down. Zanna wandered out of the woods in the middle of that.

She snarled to look like Gollum protecting the ring at the assembly on "her" land until Janae popped the trunk of her car to reveal a huge Styrofoam cooler full of beer and cider and extended an offer to help beef up the wards on the house and lands. From Zanna's goggle-eyed look, the offer was more than acceptable, so the witches gathered around her to arrange that while the rest of us figured out the last details.

"Okay." I heaved a big sigh when no more adjustments were offered. "The witches take point on downing the sorcerer, since he was one of theirs and their magic is likely the closest and most effective. The weres split into thirds, and each group pairs up with an elf to patrol and hold the perimeter against interlopers."

Their heightened senses would hopefully let them spot a wayward camper or elven sneak attack. The weres would be the muscle while the elves could mindmaze any mundanes and send them on their way none the wiser. Iago would also be sensing for the rabisu given that his House's talents leaned toward the spiritual, as Sequoyah's leaned toward healing the body and Monteague's toward affecting the mind. I didn't know what the hell he could do about it, but I hoped that three elves plus me and a handful of witches could get rid of the demon if it did get summoned in.

"I call Callista," I continued, "talk some shit, and wait with the witches and elementals to kill the fucker who kidnapped my friends and helped trash Claret."

"And we all pray that there won't be any zombies this time," Troy muttered.

The concerned look Allegra shot him before blanking her expression made me wonder if the last few months were getting to Troy or if zombies in particular bothered him. Did the Darkwatch get an on-off rotation?

I resolved to keep an eye on him. The last thing we needed was an elf of Troy's power in a bad headspace.

Power rose behind me, and I jumped and spun, thoughts scattering. Moments later, the witches started chanting. They were holding hands with Zanna to form a circle, heads down. I couldn't make out what they were muttering, but prickles raced over me as life magic blended with Zanna's fae power. I hadn't even known the kobold had power like that—most of the fae relied on illusion—and I clamped down hard on myself as Chaos twisted in me and tried to join it.

"All good, Finch?" Troy asked quietly from behind me.

I swallowed and nodded as I unfisted my hands. "Yep. Good to get a practice run. Chaos is a bitch sometimes."

"Speaking of, we need to talk. Later," he said. The bond was still locked down tight, and I couldn't get a sense of his mood. His voice gave me nothing.

I glanced around. Everyone's attention was on either the witches or the perimeter. "About Chaos?"

"About your parentage."

Shit. I looked over my shoulder to find him as close as he could be without touching me. "What makes you think I want to have that conversation with you?"

"I might have a few pieces to explain the last week."

Gritting my teeth, I nodded before turning back to the witches. Given what I'd just learned from my friends, I ached to know more about this House Solari and whether my father really had been one of them. If that meant getting over my reticence to discuss the topic with Troy, so be it. Knowledge was power, and I'd need all I could get to face Callista—and then the gods.

* * *

Falls Lake reminded me enough of Jordan Lake that I had to run through some breathing exercises to calm down when we got there. It was a similarly undeveloped reservoir, edged in a sandy beach and ringed by loblolly pine and mixed oaks. With evening falling, a barred owl hooted tentatively. The waxing moon overhead offered a little light. The weres insisted it not being full didn't make a difference in their ability to shift, and that it actually made it easier to resist being pulled into it.

"The full moon is just a little more…fun," Terrence had said with a cat's grin.

When we were all in our places, I took one more deep breath. Nerves rattled me, and I pushed them away. This sorcerer wasn't a full-blown lich yet. With Grimm dead, I didn't know if there was even another djinni who'd be willing to do the work. The lich had had some fucked up spells though, and this asshole might have glamour on top of sorcery. A dangerous combo, if we weren't careful, and that wasn't counting the rabisu.

I pulled out the handheld radio the weres had given me. A member of each group had one so that we could coordinate ourselves.

"Everyone ready?" I asked.

When I had affirmatives, I reached for the elements—not just Air but also Fire and Water. Water skittered away, and I let it. I'd worry about it, and the gods, when I'd survived this.

"Time to get their attention," I muttered.

Zanna had given me the idea for this when she'd once suggested that I'd called a storm closer by practicing. There was a chance of rain in the forecast, and the day's heat spike meant a little lightning would be odd but not unheard of. I focused, taking note of the wind's direction and reaching big, then bigger and higher. The breeze cutting through the pines strengthened as I suggested it could do more, until the trees swayed, creaking, and all the birds went silent.

"Goddess," Laurel muttered.

I didn't reply, trying to find the shape of Air and Fire in the atmosphere, a spark that I could coax beyond a few crackles in my hand to become—

A blinding, ear-splitting crash split the sky as lightning exploded overhead, followed almost immediately by a bone-shaking roll of thunder. Gasps and a yelp burst from where the witches had hidden themselves behind the high log of a fallen red oak.

With the storm already encouraged, Water was more obliging. Unheeding of Sofia's instruction, I wrestled it, unwilling to surrender, twisting it from the sky like wrenching water from a towel. The atmosphere obliged; the humidity tipped over from a muggy blanket and into rain.

Rain, I could deal with. It wasn't the same as being underwater. I turned my face up, unable to help my grin of pride. This was the biggest working I'd ever attempted, and I'd made a storm from a hint and a suggestion. It'd be all over the news tomorrow, but unless they could read elemental residue, they'd be stumped.

Val and Laurel were looking at me with something resembling awe when I brought my head down and opened my eyes.

Using my power like this felt like a good stretch after a nap and I smiled wider. "Ready for part two?"

They nodded, and I took cover under a hickory tree to make my call.

Callista's voice was hard and dangerous when she answered. "I hope, for your sake, that you're calling in your capacity as a Watcher to explain the sudden storm over Falls Lake."

"Now that we both know what I'm capable of, I'm calling in my capacity as a primordial elemental," I said, the rage boiling in my heart making my voice as soft as hers as I caressed the hilt of the knife Neith had gifted me. It balanced my fae blade on the other hip. "I know what you did, Callista. I know why you kept me as a pet for twenty-five years."

Laughter that managed to chime like bells and rumble like the storm overhead pulled all the hairs on my neck up as it dragged a fingernail down my spine. "Is that so? Is that so, indeed? Well then. That means you know I can no longer afford to play the little game we've been playing since January, my dear."

The last two words were delivered sharply enough that I flinched at the feeling of a cut. I'd always hated when she called me that, but especially now. "Come out to Falls Lake so we can finish this like adults. Or I'll bring it to the bar."

"You wouldn't dare break the Détente. Not and risk your precious Maria. She needs your little Reveal too much."

It was my turn to laugh, and lightning crackled with it overhead. "If the bar is blown down with you in it, there's nobody to say that I've broken anything."

"You couldn't."

Her tone was ugly, but I pounced on a hint of doubt. "Maybe the foundations would go. Have you seen what I did with Iich's old place? Wasteful of you to throw away all those elves."

The silence told me she had seen or had sent someone. As usual when she wanted me to think she was backed against a wall, her tone became cloying and too sweet, like honey hiding the taste of poison. "What do you want, Arden?"

"I told you. I want you here at Falls Lake. Right now. And I want some fucking answers. I want the reason for the geas you put on Duke." I didn't know that she was the one who'd laid the geas on him, but it was a reasonable assumption. She wouldn't let anyone else with that kind of power in the area, not unless it was to serve her purposes.

"When you say finish this—how do you mean?"

I fumed. She was treating this like a game. "I had a visit from Artemis," I said nastily. "I'm sure if I prayed hard enough she'd take care of you for me, but I want my answers first."

The roar that echoed down the phone then had everything of an enraged bear in it, and nothing of the petite form she wore now. I'd been right. My heart fluttered as I wondered if I'd just made a terrible mistake.

"Stay where you are, if you're so eager to be thrashed to within an inch of your life and be left begging for the rest of it for the next century," Callista snapped before the line went dead.

My hand shook as I tucked the phone away and pulled out the radio. "Incoming, ETA unknown. She can travel the Crossroads and pull other people through the veil so—"

A slice of light split the night upslope of where we were, rotating to open like an elevator door. I caught a glimpse of the huge-ass silver sword that hung on the wall of Callista's office at the bar.

"Fuck it, she's here," I said around a suddenly dry mouth.

The figure that stepped through wasn't Callista's wispy frame though. It was the tall, gaunt form of the vampire sorcerer. Just as I'd anticipated.

A thrill ran through me, chasing the shivers of fear as I said, "Scratch that, it's the target. Get ready."

I suited action to words, pulling the god-forged blade and hefting it. I didn't like the way it hummed in my grip, but my other knife was meant to put down elves. It wouldn't do much against a sorcerer.

The portal snapped shut as suddenly as it had opened and the sorcerer's head swiveled to find me.

"I can sense you, little sylph. Your presence tastes like raw power now that you're not hiding. Delicious." His next words were in an ancient tongue.

"Rabisu!" I shouted as I recognized the overwhelming sense of evil seeping into the woods. He must have prepped the spell before leaving Callista's, which meant our situation had just gone from bad to fucked. We'd planned for it and had stopped to buy sacks of salt on the way, but all of us had hoped it wouldn't be needed.

The lich had been overconfident. His accomplice wasn't going to make that mistake.

"Surrender, Finch. It'll only hurt a little," the sorcerer rasped as he approached. "I could even make you like it."

Vegetation withered and died as he approached, and the spike in death magic sent my stomach plummeting.

I shook it off and set my feet. "I'd make you the same offer, but I'm not interested in surrender."

This jerkoff may have learned from our battle with the lich, but so had I. I set a wall of Air around him as the prickles of life magic from the witches spread out, circling us to create five points. He walked into the wall and snarled then clutched his pendant as he said a word I didn't recognize.

My wall shattered.

The backlash sent me reeling, head throbbing. I looked at him from where I'd caught myself against the hickory tree, disbelieving. Elementals were the only ones who could manipulate elemental magic like that...or so I'd thought.

I gathered myself, brandishing my knife.

The sorcerer grinned savagely. "Master Gideon had given himself entirely to death," he said as he stalked toward me. "The vampires were kind enough to help me balance death with life, opening so many opportunities."

To my left, Earth swelled.

"Balance this!" Laurel shouted. The ground exploded under the sorcerer's feet.

He staggered, and I fumbled for Earth, trying to forget the feeling of being buried alive to embrace its solidness. I followed the sense of what Laurel was doing and lent my greater strength to her effort.

The ground opened. The sorcerer dropped into a pit as Val sprang forward to throw fire on him. I switched from Earth to Fire, and my palms blistered as I sent a torrent of flame to join Val's. Earth and Fire melded in my mind, and I forced it outward before it could burn me from within. The sorcerer scrabbled at the edge of the pit, screeching like metal on slate as the bottom of it became lava. Witch chanting crested among his screams as the rabisu roared, manifesting fully on this plane with the ripping sound of wet canvas.

I left them to it, turning my attention to the demon as I pulled out the radio.

"Get Iago here, now!" I didn't even bother tucking the radio back, letting it fall as I dug for a handful of salt in the bag hanging alongside my elf-killer. My burnt hands stung so badly that I almost dropped the salt, but I forced myself to hold it, gritting my teeth as tears pricked in my eyes.

The rabisu flowed toward me. Eagerness rolled off of it in sickening waves. It remembered me as its prey.

"Come and get me, you ugly fuck," I growled around a dry mouth. I didn't bother throwing elemental power at it. When I'd tried that in my bedroom, it had only worked when I'd hit the damn thing with a good amount of salt first. I'd have to let it get close.

The problem was, if it was close, so were its claws.

Chapter 23

I threw the first handful of salt too early. The storm still raging overhead blew the white granules away, giving the rabisu an opening. Razor claws bit into the tree above my head as I tripped and stumbled to get away, fighting my own terror as much as anything else.

I backed my next throw with Air, forcing the wind to work for me as I hurled a heavy fistful of salt. The tree creaked, leaning precariously as the rabisu tore its claws free, howling.

Just have to keep it busy echoed through my terror-wracked brain. The witches had to put down the sorcerer. That was the priority. That, and staying alive.

The staying alive bit turned into an undignified scramble as I tried to draw the demon away from the rest of the group. It seemed to want me above all, so if I could give the others time to kill the damn sorcerer, then that'd be my job for the night. The heavy rain made the ground slick though, and I was covered in a mixture of sweat, mud, and dead leaves by the time I found a place to take a stand and pulled myself together enough to do so.

Another Air-backed handful of salt.

The rabisu lunged, intent on spearing me with claws and teeth like steak knives. This time, I dared a slash with the godblade when the salt made it solid on this plane.

The sound the rabisu made when it connected was nearly enough to strip me of my soul.

It was all I could do to hang onto the knife as I stumbled away, my heart pounding as though it would burst, my aura shredding. I dropped to a knee and gagged, tasting rotting meat and gasoline. Burnt marshmallow filled my nose when I inhaled, bringing my head up with a snap.

Iago had arrived.

Aether crested as he chanted in counterpoint to the witches and the thundering storm, and my head pounded with all the discordant magic. The rabisu took another swipe at me. I barely rolled away in time. The next swipe was aborted with an enraged screech as Iago finished his spell. Aether settled over me, and the rabisu's scream of outrage blended with mine as it slipped through my open shields and squeezed tight over my aura.

Had this been a trap all along?

No. Iago slid between me and the rabisu, still chanting with both hands raised in the gesture to stop. Life magic prickled and stung as the witches drew closer, shouting a spell of binding.

With a last infuriated cry, the planes rippled, and the rabisu fled before it could be caught.

"Damn!" Sarah hollered into a silence broken only by the sound of rain hitting the leaves above and the surface of the lake nearby.

"We got what we came for, child." Janae sounded weary. "Arden, are you all right?"

I could still feel Aether draping me, so no, I wasn't fucking all right. Not this close to another Goddess-damned lake. I couldn't stop trying to brush the magic off with my hands. Chaos flickered in me as it refused to budge, and I brushed harder, panting like I'd run a race.

"Easy, Finch! Take it easy." Troy skidded to a halt and knelt in front of me, just barely stopping himself from grasping my shoulders. "Iago, dispel this, please, before she gains another element and relocates the lake onto our heads."

Eyes wide, Iago muttered a counterspell. The scent of Aether flew from me along with whatever spell he'd cast, and I whipped Air in a tight spiral around me to help send the scent and the magic on its way. Everyone stumbled back, catching themselves on a tree where they could. Troy braced himself against the ground, looking pained when he dropped the arm he'd raised to shield his eyes.

"Is it done?" Ximena called. I hadn't heard her approach, but she was at the edge of the clearing with Lola keeping an eye on the path behind them.

"See for yourself." Hope indicated the pit. Smoke rose from it, bringing the stomach-turning scent of rotten barbeque on the damp air.

I pushed myself to my feet, gripping the godblade tightly as I made my way to the pit and looked over the edge. The rain had gentled, and embers hissed as it fell on them. The charred outlines of a twisted body rested at the bottom of the pit.

"The gem?" I asked. I wasn't about to leave that behind.

"I'll get it," Val said grimly. She dropped into the pit, not reacting as the embers cracked open and flared to set her damp clothes to steaming. Her grimace as she reached around the sorcerer's neck looked more like disgust than pain. Laurel and I gave her a hand back out, and Val dropped the bauble in my palm.

I hissed as the hot stone landed on my burnt flesh, barely hearing Val's apology as I dug for the memory of what I'd done to destroy the lich's amulet.

It resisted me.

Earth didn't like how I handled it. Finally, it surrendered to my efforts to wrestle it and combined with Fire to make the stone glow. I added Air to call lightning and barely turned my face away in time as the stone shattered. As it did, magic scraped against my aura, and I retched at the sensation as it fled.

Shuddering, I tossed the fragments into the pit and wiped the trickle of blood that started from my nose with the back of my hand.

"Back up," I warned everyone.

When they'd all taken several hasty steps back, I added more fire to what Val had already laid down, grimacing as my hands blistered further. A dark flame exploded upward with a roar that could only be heard spiritually. When it died down, I reached for Earth again, trying to do it with Laurel's gentle coaxing as I asked the soil to fill in the hole it had been so rudely removed from.

With an obliging shudder, muddy earth poured over the sorcerer, burying him and the slagged fragments of his amulet.

I dropped to my ass on the dirt, panting and hanging my head between my upraised knees to fight off a swell of dizziness. The world spun around me as the witches drew close again, casting one final spell to keep any evil locked where it lay. I pulled myself together and lifted my head.

"Good fight, everybody. Thank you." I bit my tongue before I could add that this was so much better than doing it on my own, with just Troy as backup.

Will and Cam grinned, leaning on each other. Val and Laurel hugged, having a moment of shared relief as they processed the fact that they'd just killed their kidnapper and used their powers in front of Othersiders—and were still alive. Ximena called the other weres and elves in from the perimeter. As everyone filtered back and shook hands, I sat in the mud, trying to feel good about the triumphant atmosphere.

We'd won a battle, a big one…but not the war. Not by a long shot. Callista had to have known that I wouldn't be alone.

This had been a test. We'd passed. This time.

"Do I want to know why you're not in a better mood?" Troy muttered as he crouched beside me. The wind from the storm almost blew his words away.

"We still need to get Callista," I replied in a low voice, hoping he couldn't hear the tight, ugly fear bubbling up in me at the idea of facing my former guardian. Unease slithered over me as I realized that with the necromancer dead, the vampires were back in play as allies. They could help against Callista, but it would need to be a sure thing. Everyone would need to be at their strongest, especially if the sorcerer had left her a way to summon the rabisu back.

That meant making Maria an offer of blood. My blood.

"What's wrong now?" Troy's eyes tightened as he tried to read my face, rather than gleaning something from the bond.

I grimaced. "I have to go see Maria."

He frowned. Then his expression hardened. "You're going to feed her."

"I have to be sure we'll win the next fight. You saw how close this one came. We only won the one with the lich because killing Grimm disoriented him. This one took most of the key players in Otherside to keep it contained and finish the threat without either exposing us or losing someone. Callista won't have the lich's weakness or the sorcerer's arrogance. She's too smart, and she's lived too long. We either catch her by surprise or go in force."

Muscles bunched at the corners of his jaw. "I don't like it. Torsten's line is known for two things: instability and how deeply they can pull you under with glamour."

"Are you worried about me or yourself?" I snapped, letting my fear and agitation out on him. I didn't like my plan either, and I didn't like thinking about Maria becoming a rakshasa one day.

"If you're asking me that, you haven't been paying attention."

192

That stung, as I suspected was the intention. It was my job to pay attention. I was good at it. I missed a few things sometimes, but I saw or figured out more than most.

When all I did was glare at him, he said, "I'm coming with you. I helped you hold off Torsten. I can manage Maria."

"You don't need to be there. She won't hurt me," I said, more out of contrariness than conviction. She wouldn't *mean* to hurt me, that I believed. But intention and result were always two different things. Between that and the memory of Torsten nearly rolling me, my stomach turned over.

"Are you trying to convince me or yourself?" Troy threw back lightly.

I didn't have an answer for that, so I said, "Doesn't matter. You're not coming."

"How much blood can a vampire take in one sitting?" he asked, a little too casually. "How much can you lose before you can't drive without risking an accident? Are you willing to spend the night there, underground, if she takes too much?"

I opened my mouth to snap at him again then shut it. Troy didn't ask questions that he didn't already know or suspect the answers to. It was one of the most infuriating things about him. My panic during the cave-in the other night gave him the answer I refused to.

He eyed me. "You're a little bigger than she is, but she could still take enough in a sitting to kill you if she got carried away by the novelty of drinking from an elemental. That's not counting the aftereffects of glamour. You saw what Torsten taking a few sips did, even with me in the back of your head."

"I don't need a babysitter."

"Then call me a bodyguard, if it makes you feel better."

That left me with my mouth hanging open until I snapped it shut and watched everyone else comb the clearing for any hints of remaining supernatural activity. The storm boiling east was bad enough without leaving more evidence behind.

"That's right," I finally said, tasting bitterness at the back of my throat. "I'm your assignment."

Troy shrugged and shook damp hair off his forehead as he looked out over the lake. He seemed as unbothered by my mood as he was by kneeling next to me in the mud with the rain still coming down. The mention of zombies was the only time I'd seen him fazed, and even that was buried. For someone whose grandmother was looking for an excuse to disown him, he was awfully calm—or awfully good at hiding it.

I sighed. I had no idea how much blood Maria would need for it to have any effect in her strength. She'd taken enough from Leith that he'd been weakened, his skin clammy, when I'd fished my pendant from around his neck, taken it back, and finished him. Balancing trust with practicality meant it might be preferable to have a ride, rather than crashing at Claret. I wasn't keen on sleeping somewhere I wasn't familiar with, especially not underground, nor did I want to take a rideshare if I didn't have complete control of my faculties.

"Fine," I said grudgingly, reluctant to admit that I needed anyone's help but especially his. Tendrils of guilt crawled through me. Accepting his help meant that I was actively damning him.

It was his choice, just like it had been Val's and Laurel's to join us here tonight, but…shit. Part of me was developing sympathy for the man, even if I still felt like he owed me for last winter.

Troy rose without a word and went to talk to Allegra. They had a quick, terse discussion that ended with her looking at me like I was a puzzle and him handing over the keys to his Acura. Iago frowned at Troy's back as he returned to me.

I pushed to my feet, deciding that Troy was going to have to wait for me to take a shower before we headed to Raleigh. There was no way I was going to see Maria in this state, not when I was still thinking about that kiss.

Chapter 24

"You stay out of it unless absolutely necessary," I muttered tersely to Troy as we exited the parking garage and started the two-block walk to Claret. Maria had consented for him to come with me. I suspected it was more out of curiosity for why I'd insisted on delivering my update about the sorcerer in person than for anything else. "I mean it, Monteague."

"You always do." He sounded much calmer than I did despite the tension in his shoulders.

I was still trying to decide if I was more uncomfortable with what I was about to do or with the fact that I had agreed for Troy to accompany me as a "bodyguard." Hell, the fact that I had a bodyguard at all. Everything about this was well outside the realm of anything I would have considered a possibility six months ago. Add to that the late hour, the post-battle aches, pains, and tiredness, and the beginnings of a power hangover, and I was ten different kinds of discombobulated.

I'm taking a vacation. Soon, I promised myself. I'd never had one, and I'd more than earned it by now. Of course, it would have to come after Callista was settled and the Reveal and the gods...

"Focus, Finch," Troy muttered as we approached.

I didn't bother replying as I flashed the bouncer my membership card and slipped inside with Troy close on my heels. The vampire lounging by the curtains that hid the passageway to the back stairs lifted his eyebrows in surprise but didn't stop us. I forced myself to breathe past nerves brought on by both the impending visit underground and the fact that I was about to let a vampire bite me for the good of Otherside. If it didn't scare me so bad, I'd have started giggling.

Downstairs, Maria waited for us by the door that led to her quarters, holding herself more formally than she usually did when I visited. I don't know how she pulled off a maxi dress at her height, but the azure blue color made her emerald hair pop. Noah lounged against the wall on the other side of the door, dressed to impress in black slacks and shirt—and looking grouchy as hell. I suspected that vampires had a similar mental connection between master and fledgling as existed between Troy and I, so his mood made my own more uncertain.

"Maria." I came to an awkward halt at the bottom of the spiral stairs. "Noah. Thanks for seeing me in person."

Maria tilted her head. "It's not often you volunteer to make the trip, baby doll." Her glance shifted over my shoulder. "And to insist on testing my master by bringing our Prince of Monteague along...well, how could I resist?"

I winced. Troy was not a popular guest at Claret. Maybe that was Noah's problem. *Wishful thinking. You know he's probably picking up Maria's mood, however pleasant she seems.*

"Shall we?" I gestured to the door. "Just us, please."

Maria's brows lifted, and she raised a hand to forestall Noah, who had pushed away from the wall so quickly that it just looked like he was suddenly upright. "Of course, poppet."

I gave Troy one last warning look, holding it until he settled into a parade rest in the corner. *Good boy. Stay.*

As soon as the door had shut behind us, Maria said, "This should be interesting." Wariness tinged her tone.

"The sorcerer-vampire-necromancer is dead." I led with the good news as my heart pounded.

Tilting her head, Maria said, "Get to the interesting part."

I took a deep breath. Blew it out as I hesitated. Tried again.

"Maria, I can't…I can't agree to be your partner." I pushed the words out as fast as I could. "My power is growing. I need the air and trees more than ever. I can't live underground. I can't commit to that."

Her expression tightened, but she forced a small smile. "I understand. Thank you for such a considered response and for coming to tell me in person."

She turned away, taking a few steps toward the door at the back of the entry room.

"I'm not done."

She paused, not turning around.

Taking a shaky breath, I said, "What if I let you drink from me, this once, to make sure that you could take on any dominance battles or human attacks? And to help against Callista?"

Maria spun back to me. "You would do that? For me? Without a partnership?"

Hope flickered in the depths of her eyes, and the vampiric darkness widened, just a little.

"Yes." I hugged myself and swallowed as I looked at the ceiling, liking being underground even less than I had before I'd pulled the lich's lair down on my head. "You can take enough to get a boost. But I have to be able to walk out of here."

"That's why you brought Troy." Her face fell. "You don't trust me. You trust an *elf* but not me."

I shrugged, uncomfortable for more reasons than one. "If I didn't, I wouldn't be here. But I plan on sleeping in my own bed tonight so…designated driver. Just in case you need a little more than a pint. Or you know, I can't hold off the glamour. The fight took a lot outta me as it is, but I didn't want to leave you open to attack from Callista. She'll be getting desperate." *It's not you, it's me.*

Maria took a slow step closer as her pupils widened a little more. "You'd let me use glamour after what Torsten did?"

I frowned. "I thought it was just kind of an automatic thing."

"No, baby doll," she said softly. "I didn't glamour Leith when I drained him. He was dying painfully when you ended him. I wouldn't want our one night to be like that."

"Oh." I didn't want it to be like that, either. "Okay. Then yeah."

She took another step closer. "You're sure of this? I won't force you, Arden. I don't want it if you're not certain or don't understand what you're agreeing to. I won't have that between us. Better nothing than that particular regret."

I laughed then, unable to help it. Here I was, trying to make sure that I wasn't making anyone else's choices for them, feeling guilty about them making their own decisions that happened to benefit me and not expecting the same in return. It was nice to be shown that maybe some of my allies *were* my friends, after all. Or at least that they were decent people.

Maria froze at my laugh, cocking her head as her dark eyes hardened. "I'm being sincere. Why is that funny?"

"It's not you." I loosened my stance and opened my body language. I couldn't tell her that I was okay with this with words alone. "It's—I'm trying to get used to the idea that maybe I have friends and not just allies who want to use me. It's kind of a revelation."

"We're friends?" Her tentative smile chased away the last of my unease. "Truly? You'd call a vampire friend?"

I wasn't the hugging type but hell. Maybe we were both a little broken. I closed the remaining distance and embraced her, knowing it had been the right thing to do when tension flowed out of her like water.

"Thank you, Arden," she breathed. "You have no idea what this means to me. With or without blood."

We stood there, having a moment, getting comfortable with what was going to come next. I focused on the smell of her under the iron and ash scent that all vampires carried, finding a trace of something sweet, like berries.

"Give me a minute." She pulled away, squeezing my arm with a small but genuine smile. "Since we don't know how elementals react to glamour, I'll let Noah and Troy in as spotters. Safety first!" The light note in her voice made coming here worth it. As she opened the main door and spoke to the men in a low tone, I pulled my hair up into a bun and tried to calm my sudden jitters.

Noah entered and looked at me suspiciously. "You offer my mistress this? Freely?"

"I mean…yes?" I frowned.

"What's the catch?" he asked.

"Noah," Maria said in a warning tone. She rested a hand on his bicep.

He shook free. "No, Mistress. I want to know what's behind this sudden change of heart." When he looked down at her, worry and real affection flickered across his face. "We can't afford—"

"I know," she said, squeezing his arm. "It's okay, my lovely."

I glanced behind them at Troy, now standing with his back to the wall where he could watch both the main door and the one leading deeper into Maria's chambers. The corners of his eyes were pinched, but he was keeping his mouth shut.

"Noah," I said, "The last thing I want is to bring harm to Maria or this coterie. That's why I came. Fighting the sorcerer tonight took too many of us. Callista is only going to escalate, and I don't want y'all to be a target because she has a bone to pick with the gods. Besides…" I lowered my voice. "If something happens to Torsten, we can't have a power vacuum. There can't be any question of who will succeed him. We can't risk the Reveal, not again."

"So you're crowning her," Noah said.

I shrugged, trying to shake off my nerves at this interrogation. "If you want to see it that way."

Noah bared fangs at me. "Seems like something Callista would do."

My heart rate accelerated, and I kept myself very still, recognizing both the barb and the threat.

"That's enough," Maria hissed. "You have done your due diligence. Wait here until and unless I call for you."

Her fledgling gave me one last untrusting look before throwing himself on the sofa. "As you command, Mistress. What should I do if the Master calls?"

"Tell him I'm occupied with alliance business." Maria held Noah's gaze until he swallowed, averted his eyes, and nodded.

I glanced at Troy again and lifted one eyebrow. "Anything from you?" At his tight negative head shake, I turned back to Maria. "Shall we?"

She gestured me toward the far door, giving me space as we went through it and stepping aside when it closed behind us. This room was the size of an overlarge master bedroom and seemed to function as such given the king-size bed mounded with pillows. I wasn't gauche enough to ask whether she had a coffin somewhere. The concrete floor was softened by rugs in jewel tones, and the walls were painted in similarly bright colors, giving the effect of being surrounded by stained glass windows. It was like the enthusiastic shade of her hair had been extended to her entire living area, and I stared, open-mouthed.

"Like it?" She sounded nervous as she edged around me.

"Yeah," I breathed. "It's very...you."

She grinned, and we stood there, as awkward as two high schoolers on a first date.

"So, how does this work?" I asked, unable to keep a quaver out of my voice.

"That's up to you. I'd recommend the bed and the bend of the arm, if you don't want a hard fall and an obvious bite. I'm assuming it would heal without a trace, but…" She shrugged. "Who knows with elementals? Some of the low-blood elves take ages to heal."

And I'm half elven. I drifted toward the bed and ran my healing fingertips over the amethyst-colored coverlet. *Of course it's silk.* After kicking my shoes off, I hopped on and made myself comfortable.

Maria waited by the door until I'd stopped shifting around. "You're sure this is a yes? A solid, enthusiastic yes? Despite me not knowing how an elemental will be affected?"

I smiled. The humans were in for a surprise when vampires turned out to be proponents of affirmative consent. "Yes," I said. "I'm willing to take the risk to be sure the alliance stands."

When she joined me on the bed, she eased closer slowly, giving me time to get used to her being that near, watching to see if anything in my body language suggested that I was changing my mind.

I extended my arm. "It's okay. Really. Something between friends."

She snuggled in close to my side, clasping my arm above and below the elbow. "Thank you." She planted a light kiss on the vein at the bend before meeting my eyes. "Look at me and let your shields down as much as you're comfortable with."

I did what she said, dropping them almost completely as her pupils flooded the entirety of her eyes. Glamour slithered over me, blending with my aura to lull me into a clouded embrace. I slumped, easing into languor.

Maria inhaled—and I fell into a spiraling galaxy of pleasure as her teeth pierced my skin.

I didn't quite pass out, but I wasn't all there anymore either. I had no idea how long I lay there, riding a silken wave as glamour and blood loss mounted. I didn't fight it, and I didn't let Troy in when I felt the press of the bond. This wasn't like with Torsten; it wasn't an assault. I was enjoying it. It was a break from all the shit I'd been dealing with. A chance to feel good for the first time in ages. I was aware of everything, but none of it mattered. No wonder elves had risked Leith's displeasure to come here.

All of a sudden, Maria eased my arm down and slipped away.

"Shit," she muttered, checking my pulse, then sighing with relief and brushing a curl from my forehead. "Still with us. Good. Thank you, Arden," she said. "This was more of a gift than either of us realized. Your blood…"

The sound of the door slamming open and closed again almost pulled me from the glamour-induced reverie, but I couldn't seem to open my eyelids. Just kept slipping, spiraling, feeling better and more relaxed than I had since…ever. Was this the vacation I'd been looking for?

"What happened, Maria? What's wrong with her?" Troy sounded like he was down a long tunnel, not in the same room.

Maria giggled. "Don't worry. She's just high on glamour. Hits her like an elf."

"Are you blood-drunk?"

"More like power drunk. She's more than anyone suspected."

"Get up."

"She's fiiine," Maria drawled, her touch light as she smoothed my curls. "It just affected her more than I expected, given how hard she fought Torsten. I stopped as soon as I realized she wasn't holding a boundary."

"Get. Up."

The bed shifted as Maria's weight was replaced by Troy's.

"Arden?" he murmured.

Gentle fingers tilted my chin and felt for my pulse. Thicker and more calloused than Maria's. Troy's touch. If I hadn't already been glamoured to hell and back, that might have knocked me on my ass. He'd never called me by my first name, and he'd never touched me like that.

"You actually care for her." Maria slurred a little. "Imagine that."

I tried to stir. Troy cared? Beyond a mission? That couldn't be right.

"Goddess, Maria. She's completely out of it."

"She let me in. I told you, I stopped when I realized how hard she fell."

"Of course she let you in. That's how Callista conditioned her—to submit fully to anyone she genuinely thinks will protect or care for her." Fingers brushed my arm. "How is she already healed? This looks weeks old."

"A little of this, a little of that."

"Enough, Maria. How?"

I knew what Maria's face looked like from her annoyed huff. "I told you, princeling, she's more than any of us realized. I've never tasted elemental before, but I'd bet my ass she's trueborn."

Shit. I fought the glamour harder, managing to groan as my eyelids fluttered. I still wasn't quite ready for that conversation.

"What makes you say that?" Troy said sharply.

"She smells like ozone, but she tastes like lemon peel *and* rosemary and sage. I am drunker than I've been since before I died, and I am going to have a hangover worse than the one I had after I drank from Leith. Is she okay?"

Troy didn't answer her as he sent a little pulse down the bond to me. An odd note tightened his voice as he said, "Finch, if you want help with the glamour, I need you to signal somehow. I won't break my promise on boundaries if you're not dying."

What he'd said about Callista conditioning me had shaken me, and I wondered whether it was true or how it played into my now-broken relationship with Roman—or my decision to allow Troy to play bodyguard.

Rather than fighting the glamour, I looked for the root of the bond between me and Troy. He'd closed us off. I couldn't use Aether to do anything with it but maybe I could wrangle Chaos? My heart thudded as I wrestled with magic in the confines of my mind. Finally, I managed to send a small pulse of Chaos toward Troy.

He grunted and jumped. "I'll take that as a yes. Don't hate me if I'm wrong."

Maria clapped. "Awww, you care what she thinks of you!"

Another giggle accompanied the sound of her falling into a chair. A soft murmur told me Noah was in the room as well.

"This is easier with touch," Troy muttered. His hand slipped between my head and the pillow to cradle the base of my skull. Funny that we both had the sense of the bond living there.

When he undid whatever it was that was blocking us from sensing each other, I gasped as a torrent of emotion and Aether exploded into my mind like a sugar rush. The emotion was pulled back and walled away before I could get more than a glimpse. Anxiety was topmost, but the glimpse of something else tantalized my curious mind.

As it had with Torsten's attempt to roll me, the bond's Aetheric magic pushed against the glamour, melting it like fog in the sun and helping me shore up my own walls against it. I gave it a last mental shove and regained control of my body, coming back to myself with a heave.

Troy was looking down at me with worry that disappeared into his usual neutrality as I blinked my eyes open. A new intensity sharpened his attention on me though.

"Thanks," I rasped as he pulled his hand away and shifted to make some space between us. Tilting my head to look at the vampires, I tried to keep my voice gentle as I said, "Maria, was that enough?"

"Oh hell yes." She groaned as she slumped against Noah on the chaise longue along the other wall. "Thank you, poppet."

I tried sitting up. My arms were still shaky though, so it turned into propping myself up against the pillows.

Troy watched but kept his hands to himself. "Are you all right now?"

"I'm gonna need a few minutes."

Nodding, he closed the bond down again.

Something made me reach for his hand. He jumped when I squeezed it.

"Thank you. Maybe it's not such a bad thing." I let him go and felt at my arm, finding that the two neat punctures were indeed healed up, as were the burns on my hand from fighting the sorcerer. My healing powers didn't usually kick in that fast, so maybe it was to do with the power shunted into Maria with my blood coming back to me in her saliva. I wondered what impact it would have on my usual power hangover.

"You two are so damn cute." She curled an emerald lock around a perfectly manicured finger. "I still think you should hate fuck, but I don't know that it would be hate fucking anymore."

I closed my eyes, thinking about the emotion Troy had tried to hide in the bond and realizing with a sinking feeling that I didn't know either.

Chapter 25

As agreed, I walked out of Claret. Making it to the car was as much as I could manage though. I handed my keys to Troy without a word, and he accepted them in equal silence. He took one look at me in the passenger seat and grimaced as he adjusted the driver's seat to accommodate his longer legs. I thought about scolding him for fucking with my settings but let it be.

We were halfway back to my place, passing the off ramp for Briar Creek, when he said, "We still need to have that chat."

"If it's the one about my ancestry, I don't have the energy for it tonight," I said with a heavy sigh, not opening my eyes or turning my head from where it rested against the window. "Besides, I'd rather have a chat about why you're defying your grandmother like this. She'd have been pleased as punch if Maria had drained me completely."

"Finch—"

"Not. Tonight." I hadn't gotten a good night's sleep in days. My house was spelled with proper wards now, not just my "keep moving" boundary stones at the edges of the property, and all I wanted was to go to bed, alone, and not think about anything for a solid eight hours. Maybe ten. "Boundaries, Monteague."

Boundaries or not, he insisted on making sure I got into my house and had something to eat before calling an Uber. I wanted nothing more than to collapse into bed, but he went digging in my cupboards until he found the glasses and thunked a highball full of water on the table while I waited for a frozen pizza to cook.

"Drink at least three of these. Juice is better," he said, sounding hostile.

"Why do you care if I do?" I asked the table from where I was slumped on it with my forehead on my arms.

"Why do you insist on making it so difficult to keep you alive?"

I wondered how we'd gotten here. *First he throws me in a lake, then he fishes me back out and holds me captive for three days, then he decides we're allies, then he doesn't want to help me with Maria's ball, and now he's risking being disowned to play bodyguard.*

I was sure there was a reason for all of it—some duty or oath—but all I said was, "Keithia isn't going to approve."

"No," he agreed in a hard voice. "She isn't. Good night, Finch. Don't forget to lock up."

By the time I lifted my head, the front door was closing behind him. I watched him jog down the narrow drive to the main road with a detached sort of curiosity, wondering what game he was playing this time or where he'd given his word that would make all of this make sense.

The damn elf even haunted my dreams that night, after I'd finished my pizza, locked the door, taken another shower, and gone to bed. It was probably just eating so late on top of the blood loss, but it weirded me out all the same. Things were getting too complicated with Troy. Dreaming about finding him on a windswept beach, looking out over the waves with storm clouds rolling in, was better than having the gods pull me into the Crossroads, but they'd probably start doing that again soon.

As much as I wanted out of the dream, waking up was worse. The power hangover from working so heavily with the elements was worse than ever, probably compounded by dehydration and blood loss. My mood was not improved by the fact that I hadn't listened to Troy about the juice and knowing that I'd probably be feeling less bad if I had. I didn't feel as weak as I had last night—yay for accelerated healing—but my head pounded like an elephant was marching on it, my stomach felt inside-out, and my mouth was tacky with dried saliva.

I groaned, feeling miserable all over again when I reached for the water on the nightstand and realized it was still on the kitchen table. *I'm taking the day off.* I still had no mundane case, much to the regret of my bank account, and while we'd need to move on Callista sooner rather than later, I wasn't in any shape to do it right that second. Guilt sank its claws into me, and I shoved it away. *I can't help anyone in this state.*

Easing to the side of the bed closer to the bathroom, I slid from the covers and stumbled to catch myself on the wall before making it there. I knew better than to turn on the lights as I opened the faucet and hunched over the sink to drink straight from the tap. Water had never tasted so good. Gulping it too fast did uncomfortable things to my stomach though. I stopped and let myself slide to the floor, shaking and trying to breathe slowly in through my nose, out through my mouth. I'd never vomited from a power hangover, but I supposed there might be a first time for everything.

When I'd quelled my stomach's rebellion, I levered myself to my feet using the countertop and inched into the kitchen. Last night's pizza was gone, and I didn't have any leftovers. Cooking was beyond me. Hell, boiling water for tea was beyond me.

"Juice," I muttered as my stomach let it be known that food was not acceptable just now anyway. I collapsed into one of the dining chairs with the whole jug, sipping it straight from the container.

The tangy sweetness settled me, taking the edge off my headache. *That's better.* I watched the shadows shift across the yard as the sun rose, wondering what Zanna was up to and what exactly the new wards protected against. Probably should have asked yesterday, but I'd been a woman on a mission.

As much as I wanted to rest my mind, it shifted to the conversation with Callista yesterday. She'd underestimated me despite my creating the storm. Or had it been a test? A sacrifice of one chess piece to see what—or rather, who—I was playing with? Whichever it was, I'd called her out. If she was smart, she'd strike today somehow.

Unless she can't.

That was an interesting thought. Callista had never been one to get her hands dirty. She crouched at the center of the web and struck from the shadows, using her Watchers as surrogates. But how many did she actually have? How many of them did she have enough leverage with that they'd pit themselves against me now? I'd gathered allies and strengthened my power beyond that of any being I knew of in Durham, other than Callista herself and the heads of each faction. And the gods of course, but they, like her, wanted people doing their work for them.

I forgot about my hangover in the rush that accompanied that realization.

Am I that powerful now?

My head was pounding too badly to think on that for long. I went back to bed, taking the juice and some saltines with me. Sleep found me again after three crackers.

I wasn't asleep long before my ringing phone woke me up. I strongly considered ignoring it—the extra sleep was finally making me feel better. But people only called when it was urgent. The caller ID had an unknown number, and my stomach flipped. One of the last unknown callers I'd had to my private, unlisted number was the lich.

Nothing for it. I stabbed the answer button with my thumb. "Hello?"

"Arden?" A woman's voice. One I knew.

"Allegra?" I frowned. She'd always been content to work through Troy before. "Is everything okay?"

"No. Everything is most certainly not fucking okay." She sounded like the controlled fury of a building thunderstorm. "Keithia is out of patience with whatever the fuck is going through my brother's head. Troy has until tonight to either capture you, kill you, or turn himself over for trial."

My brain did that spacey thing brains do when they're hit with completely unexpected information and completely unexpected emotions at the same time. "What?"

"Trial. You're to be brought under elven control, or he gets chained up in her playroom and tortured until he either confesses to plotting against the House or says something to mitigate his actions and give Keithia an excuse to come for you openly herself."

I went hot then cold, unable to find words because I couldn't figure out what the hell I was feeling. This had to be Callista's play.

"Well?" Allegra snapped. "Got any ideas, *Arbiter*?"

"Why are you calling and not him?"

"Because he's too fucking proud to ask for help and feels guilty about whatever the hell he did to you to owe you a debt," she fumed. "I, on the other hand, will do whatever I have to do to protect him."

"Fine. We buy time." I wrenched my thoughts back into a semblance of working order as I tried to process the idea of Troy feeling guilty.

"How the hell do you suppose we'll manage that?"

"Send him here." My throat tried to close around the words, but I forced them out. Troy had proven himself. Whatever the hell was going on with him, I couldn't lose a solid ally. Maybe forestalling Keithia and Evangeline would give me space to work on Callista as well. "We make up a story. He tried to come for me, as ordered. I beat him. I take a picture of him looking messed up, send it to you, and tell the elves to back off or I tell everyone in the Triangle that House Monteague broke faith with the alliance."

"That only works if Callista is completely removed as a fallback. She summoned Evie to the bar last night. Then this happened."

"Then we take out Callista," I said harshly. "I'm done trying to maneuver around her. I'm done playing games, and I'm done with her thinking she owns me. We buy enough time to set up a strike with the weres and the vampires, and we end this. I'll burn down the fucking bar if I have to."

I was shaking with a rage whose source I couldn't really pinpoint.

The line practically hummed with Allegra's tense silence. "Let's do it," she said in the soft voice some people get when they're ready to fuck shit up. "But I need you to understand something, Arden. I like you, a lot, but my life is sworn to Troy. If something happens to him, let's just say you and I are gonna have a real bad time."

I grimaced. "I understand."

"Do you? Have you faced an elven knight?"

"No, but I put a knife through Leith Sequoyah's heart, and then Troy and I killed all his friends. I will handle this, Allegra. Tell him the setup. I'll be waiting by the river." We both knew that Keithia or Evangeline or both would have eyes on Troy, even if they wouldn't dare escalating the situation further by crossing onto my land just yet. Allegra couldn't just drop him off at my house like he was a damn pizza.

"Then may the Goddess shelter you both," she said.

I hung up, wondering how my one day off had turned into this shitshow.

The first point of order was to get my stomach under control and get some food into me. I went with rice heavily seasoned with ginger and chicken broth. A cup of spearmint and chamomile tea did the rest.

Zanna didn't appear when I shouted for her, so I assumed she was off in the woods. Figuring that was for the best, I made my way down to the river. I had no idea when Troy would get here, but spending some time out in nature would be as good for me as anything else.

I clambered up onto my rock and managed to find a comfortable way to lay on my back. The stone was warm with morning sun, and I let myself sink into a restful state, passively tasting the breeze and trying to get more comfortable with Water by settling into the flow of the Eno. My aches slowly ebbed away as my overtaxed body recovered and the day warmed as morning became early afternoon.

The sudden sense of Troy in the back of my mind made me stiffen. He'd opened the bond, letting me know he was on my land and headed my way. I sighed, easing up on my side of it as I sat up. I didn't turn around when I sensed him entering my clearing, not sure what I was feeling.

"How do you want to do this?" he said after looking at my back for a long minute, sounding completely emotionless.

This was all too weird. I scrubbed my hands over my face, wanting to say so but not wanting to drag it out more than necessary. "It has to look good."

"Blood and bruises."

I nodded.

"Might as well make it fun then."

That pulled me around, and I frowned at him.

Troy stood stiffly, hands in the pockets of black cargo pants. His hair was swept back off his face. The silver chain around his neck disappeared into a black crew-neck T-shirt that allowed the edge of his House tattoo to show under his collarbone. No-nonsense black boots laced to his ankles. He'd come dressed as though this really was a mission.

"Come again?" I said.

"You need to learn how to fight Othersiders hand-to-hand."

"I take hapkido classes," I said, not sure if I should be offended. Probably not, given my poor showing against the Redcaps when I'd had to fight for my life earlier in the year. Still, I wasn't *that* terrible. Anymore, at least.

"You train against mundanes. The biggest challenge there is hiding that you're faster and stronger than them."

He had a point. I'd gotten much better in the last few months, but I'd never sparred against an Othersider. Fought for my life, yeah, but never sparred.

"Magic or just hands?" I asked.

"No magic, unless you feel genuinely threatened. In that case, I've messed up."

I slid down from my rock.

He squared up and rolled his shoulders as I prowled closer. Despite the open bond, all I got from him was focus. He was on a mission and too fixated on what we had to do to sell this lie to allow anything else in.

Wishing I had his certainty and single-mindedness, I mirrored his stance. We'd never actually fought each other one-on-one before. Usually, it was either him ambushing me or us fighting alongside each other. I had an idea of his training and style—mostly krav maga, with a focus on stopping a threat rather than escaping—but I'd never faced it directly.

He countered my first moves easily, blocking or dodging away, and pulling his return attacks. "Stop holding yourself back, Finch. Come on."

"I'm *not*," I snapped, launching into another attack. When he dodged my jab, I followed it up with a hook. He cleared it, flowing into a low leg sweep that should have taken my feet out from under me. Improvising, I jumped over it and lashed out with a kick of my own. It set me stumbling off balance but caught Troy in the mouth as he rose from his sweep.

He grunted and fell back to recover his balance, holding up a hand for a pause and dabbing at the blood from his split lip. "Good. That shouldn't have worked, but you're fast when you're not getting in your own way."

Chapter 26

For some reason, that infuriated me. Sparring while angry was ill-advised for half a dozen reasons, but to hell with it. His eyes widened as I sprang forward, and he just managed to block a swing at his face.

"Finch—" He cut off to block the flurry of punches I aimed at his gut.

One got through, then another, and a third. With a snarl, he caught my wrist before I could land a fourth. The forest spun as he levered me around and locked my arm behind my back. When I tried to break free of it, he held me in place against him with an arm around my middle.

"Stop." His breath was hot against my ear. "Listen to me."

Struggling too hard would dislocate or break something, so I did.

"What?" I panted. My blood hummed, demanding freedom and vengeance.

"This isn't sparring anymore. You're angry." The bond carried patience but also a hint of fear.

I squirmed. Damn right I was angry. And if he was afraid, it was because he'd determined that I might be able to take him.

"You don't like the idea that you're getting in your own way, do you?" he said softly.

"No, because I'm not!"

"Right. So you're one hundred percent a victim."

I drew my head forward, getting ready to throw it back into his face. I'd show him a damn victim.

He let me go, dancing away fast enough to kick up dirt.

I poured all my rage into another attack, not even really aware of what I was doing. Only that I'd needed this outlet for far too long.

We ended up in the dirt, and that was what did me in. Troy's training had more ground fighting techniques. I'd gone with hapkido because the idea was to get free and get the fuck away. He had learned to subdue.

I found myself belly-down, spitting out dead leaves with his weight on my back and shoulders. Heat flared from him through the bond, chasing away the cool focus he'd maintained.

"Enough," Troy said in a frustrated growl. "I'm sure I deserved this, but if you really want me gone this badly I'll save you the trouble and turn myself in to my grandmother."

I froze and anger fled as I worked through that, trying not to let my mind wander to the elf on my back at Jordan Lake.

His grip eased a little. "Is that a yes or a no?"

"Get off me."

He hesitated then shifted to drop to the ground beside me. I'd managed to get a few blows in. His split lip had been joined by the beginnings of a black eye and a bloody nose. He was favoring his ribs; he'd broken a few in the fight against the lich last week. Elves healed fast, but they might still be tender. I winced as my hands suddenly hurt, reminding me of the impacts my brain had lost track of.

Dragging myself up to mirror his cross-legged seat, I said, "I cannot for the life of me figure you out."

"You could just ask."

"Could I?"

His sandstone-and-moss gaze rested heavily on me. "Yes."

"Fine. Then what the hell is all of this?" Frustration made me shout the words. "You keep—you move against me, then you help me, then you shut down, then you come to the rescue, then you need my help. What the fucking hell, Monteague?"

His eyes never left mine. "You've shown me a way out. A way to be better."

"Out of what? A life of luxury and privilege as an elven prince?"

"I don't want it."

"Excuse me?" How could he not want…everything? Everything I wanted—financial and personal security, connections, a family, influence, power—he had. And he didn't want it? That slow, simmering rage came back, bubbling under my skin as I forced myself to wait for him to explain himself.

"I don't want it!" He looked away then, jaw bunching as the bond roiled. "The price is too high. Dropping you and Javier in the lake was the last straw. Murdering an ally? To complete a mission? Following the law means killing an innocent woman who has spent her life hiding in fear and doing her best to mind her own business? A woman who then goes out of her way to help everyone else after she's discovered in the worst possible circumstances? That's not—That is wrong. It's not who I am. Who I thought I was."

Hunching forward, he buried his face in his hands, starting when he rubbed the injured spots.

After turning to spit blood, he took a few breaths. "I believe in order, Finch. I believe in giving my word. But I thought I was here to help people. Not murder them for doing nothing but existing. It was all abstract, until it wasn't. If being a prince means doing the things I've done, then I don't want it. I want to be able to face myself in the mirror again."

Something that felt icky and oily slithered through me, and I didn't know if it belonged to me or to him. "So all this is atonement?"

He shrugged and didn't answer, acting as though the river held his entire attention.

I wanted to mock him. *Poor fucking you.* But I didn't. Something in his posture wouldn't let me. I'd demanded that he do better—be better—and apparently he'd taken it to heart. I couldn't even feel more than a tiny spark of satisfaction at what it was costing him.

"You feel beat up enough to justify losing a fight?" I asked instead.

Troy prodded his bruises and winced. "This'll do."

He rose and limped back the way he'd come in, fetching a coil of rope from behind a tree before returning to where I sat and dropping it in front of me. As I frowned at it, he dug in his pocket and produced a slim bracelet of woven metal then grimaced as he slid it over his own wrist. The sense of him in the back of my mind cut off abruptly, as did all sense of him as an Aether-wielding elf. He'd neutralized himself.

"Lead?" I asked.

"Woven with silver. Nobody will believe that I just gave up." He lowered himself to rest on both knees. Bitterness thick enough to choke tainted his words and tension sang through every line of his body as he looked up at me.

Apparently I was supposed to tie him up before taking the picture.

"Shit," I muttered. The man always took things seriously, but this was unexpected. "You trust me to cut you loose when we're done?"

"If you don't, I doubt you have the stomach to do worse than my grandmother could."

The dead, lost tone in his voice made me snatch up the rope. He clasped his elbows behind his back and let me tie him up like a solstice present, arms together then strung to his ankles.

My pulse hammered as I stepped back and examined my handiwork. Lots of rope. Solid knots. The bracelet and the cuts and bruises. Shit, I'd believe he was a captive if I was just looking at a photo.

"Fall over and pretend you're knocked out," I said, not knowing or liking what was churning in my gut.

He obliged, dropping bonelessly to the ground and grunting as a stone or something caught him in the side.

I turned his face to my phone's camera, making sure my hand cupping his chin was in the frame. Then I shifted to get a photo of the bracelet and the ropes binding him. "I assume that thing is generic? Nobody is going to look at it and go, 'Oh, that's his and he's faking'?"

"Standard issue," Troy growled. "You could have picked up a few of them from the Redcaps, if you hadn't buried them all first."

"Great," I muttered. The elves must have had some messed-up politics if they carried cuffs that would neutralize their own kind.

I pulled up Allegra's number and composed a text with the photos attached. "He looks good like this. I might keep him," I read aloud as I wrote. "Tell Keithia to back the fuck off or the alliance will know that House Monteague are oathbreakers working with Callista. If she sends anyone else, I'll pull her ugly-ass mansion down and set the pieces on fire."

Send text.

There was a small chance they'd forward that message to the mundane police, but this was Otherside business. They'd have to explain what the hell Troy had been doing on my land to begin with, and there was no real way to do that without including

220

Otherside secrets. Besides, the elves were too proud to admit a failure like this. They'd do what they could to keep it quiet.

Troy jerked against the ropes binding him. His usual calm was fraying, if the tightness around his eyes and the tic in his cheek was any indication. "Done?"

"I guess so." I drew the godblade and cut him loose. There was no way I'd be able to undo the knots I'd made.

As soon as he was free, he clawed off the ropes and bracelet, letting them fall to the dirt as he caught my wrist and snarled at the knife. "Where the hell did you get that? It reeks of veilside power."

"A goddess." I broke his hold and wrenched my hand away, tucking the knife back in its improvised sheath at the small of my back. It was mine. I didn't like him looking at it.

"Finch…" He didn't continue his thought when I lifted his eyebrows at him. "Fine."

I scooped up the bracelet and pocketed it. He scowled but said nothing, though I caught a hint of frustration and a dash of fear through the bond, quickly suppressed. That left us sitting side-by-side again, looking at the Eno.

"What's your plan for Callista?" he finally asked.

I shrugged. I didn't really have one. "Burn the bar down, if I have to."

A smile flickered at the corner of his mouth. "Alli said as much, somewhere in all the swearing. You're really going to take her?"

"I have to." If he was going to pretend that our fight and his humiliation in front of his House hadn't just happened, then so would I. I wrestled with what to say before deciding to give him some truth. "She was kidnapping elementals. Then I was born. The kidnappings stopped. Whatever she wants, I have."

The weight of his gaze pinned me. "Valuable information."

"We're allies, right?"

"Does that mean we can have that other conversation now?" I pulled my knees up, hugging them. "If we have to."

Troy grabbed a fallen sycamore leaf, shredding pieces from it lobe by lobe. "For you to be a primordial, you have to be full-blooded on at least one side."

I nodded, gritting my teeth.

"More likely on both sides. One djinni parent, one elf."

Cold sweat broke out on my back, shoulders, and arms, defying the day's warmth.

"But you knew that."

"Yeah," I admitted, wishing I didn't sound quite so hoarse. I pulled more tightly into myself.

"Damn. I'd hoped Maria was wrong when she said you were a trueblood."

"No such luck."

"But you don't know who your parents were?"

"No," I said, my voice still rough. It wasn't a lie, but it wasn't the truth either. Not with what Val and Laurel had surmised the other day. I hoped the part that was truth would be enough for the part that wasn't to escape his notice.

"That's not all." He sounded a little too tense to believe me fully. "One or both parents would have been powerful. Definitely high-blood, if it was on the elven side. I don't know about the djinn equivalent."

"Oh." I thought of the lost House Solari and felt lightheaded as I recalled the pendants that Leith, Troy, and I each had.

In a flash, I remembered snippets of pain from my childhood. Djinn whispers that had pierced the veil and bitten me in my sleep. The djinn had always come to me when I was trapped in the space between falling asleep and waking up. They spoke to me of the drowning ones and the dancing of the Lost People.

Something clicked. The lost elven House. Was it the same as the Lost People?

Then something else. High-blood. Pendants. The two elves that I knew for sure had pendants were princes. I hadn't noticed necklaces or chains around the necks of the other Redcaps. *Was my father a prince too?* I took a deep, shuddering breath and held tight to my power before a gust of Air could escape in my agitation.

After a long pause, during which he was obviously trying to read my mood, Troy said, "I know it's a lot to take in."

"Yeah," I said. "I mean, shit. Twenty-six years, wondering...everything. Now this?"

He eyed me, as though he suspected it was more than that.

I let him look without reaction, finding myself in the unprecedented situation of not being sure that I wanted to know the whole story. I'd been looking for years for information about my family. Now, I was too scared to be honest and grasp it. What would it mean to be descended from elven royalty? Would that make it better for me with the local Houses or worse? I didn't know enough yet. Knowledge was power, and I needed more before I could feel safe enough to ask.

"You can talk to me, you know," Troy said when I didn't add more.

That made me deeply anxious and uncertain. "Can I?"

He shut down abruptly. "Fine. Don't. Has Alli written back yet?"

I checked my phone. "No."

"Then we're on our own for the rest of the day."

Sighing, I scrubbed my hands over my face, wondering what the hell I was going to do with the grouchy elven prince I'd basically claimed as a prisoner.

Chapter 27

If I'd thought it was weird having a house full of weres, having Troy around was a trip into the Twilight Zone.

After helping me get all my deck furniture back up where it belonged, he fetched a black duffel from somewhere out in the woods and dropped into one of the outdoor chairs. "I'll try to stay out of your way," he said. Digging into the bag, he pulled out a small box of Chapel Hill toffee and held it up before tossing it to me. "For the kobold."

I caught it. "You're just gonna stay out here? Not try to come in?"

He winced, giving his left shoulder a roll as he leaned his head back and closed his eyes. "You set boundaries. The house is one of them. Right?"

Unsure how to respond to his decision to actually respect what I wanted, I took the toffee inside and left it on the table. Conflict grew in me as I stood there, hands on my hips, looking out the sliding door to the deck at the elf prince taking in the sun like he was on vacation. Maybe he was. He was in limbo now, lying to his House and probably to this Captain because he didn't want to kill little ol' me in exchange for…well, everything.

Goddess. Was I worth that much? Or did he feel that guilty?

Then there were the other questions. What had they asked him to do over the years, that a man who was so married to keeping his oaths would break them like this? If drowning Javier

Luna and I to maintain his cover was the *last* straw, that meant there had been others. How many ugly choices had he made? How many bodies were there?

I sighed. I didn't want to think about his problems, and I didn't want him here. But I'd invited him, and that made him a guest. In Otherside and in the South, that had implications. I pulled out a pitcher and started a batch of sweet tea, my movements sharp with annoyance for myself, for him, and for the entire damned situation. While the tea cooled in the freezer, I filled a bowl with warm water, grabbed the first aid kit and a washcloth, and took them out to Troy, leaving everything on the table without a word.

"Thank you." He looked surprised.

I started back in to finish making lunch, stumped for a minute as to what elves ate. *Just ask.*

"I'm cooking. Anything you don't eat?"

"We're omnivores." His tone was guarded.

I turned back around and lifted my eyebrows. "With those teeth?"

He flushed. "Some animal protein would be appreciated, if you have it."

Nodding, I went back inside.

"Tacos," I muttered, digging in the back of the fridge for the ground beef. Quick and easy. As I sauteed meat and chopped vegetables, I wondered how the hell I had come to a point where I was not only hiding Troy Monteague but cooking lunch for him.

You need him. Right?

I'd told Val and Laurel that I kept him around because he kept Keithia and Evangeline off my back. If he couldn't do that, did I really still need him? Or was I just engaging in a habit?

He could bring other elves around. I stirred the ground beef in the pan, adding spices from my cabinet and not the pre-mixed shit from the grocery store. Troy had smoothed the introduction to Allegra then brought Iago in. Elves might not listen to me, but surely some would listen to a prince of their own people. What if, together, we could really make a difference?

The knife tucked behind my waist band dug into my back as I leaned against the counter to think, and I snorted. None of that mattered for now because I definitely did not want to find out what would happen if I let Keithia have Troy and the gods took exception to losing their Hunter. *Deal with Callista and the Hunt. Then worry about what to do with Troy fucking Monteague. Don't throw away a tool before you're sure you won't need it.*

The tea was cold by the time the food was ready. I loaded everything up with some paper plates, cups, and napkins on the tray I'd bought to have breakfast in bed with Roman and never used, kicking the door lightly for Troy's attention. He looked surprised all over again then jumped up and slid the door open for me.

"Eat, drink, and be welcome. No harm will come to guests under this roof." I tried not to sound surly as I set everything down. I had no idea how elves welcomed guests, but this was my house and I'd use the generic Otherside welcome.

Troy blinked as he sat back down, looking confused enough that I suspected he made the standard reply by rote. "I come with peaceful intent and will honor my host."

I looked off into the woods, waiting for him to serve himself first, as guests did, and wondering how awkward this was going to be.

"I told Alli not to call," he said.

Apparently, it was going to be very awkward.

I put my own taco together and had a bite before distilling my earlier thoughts into an answer. "Far be it from me to stand in the way of someone trying to do better for himself and others. Especially when one of those others is me."

"Still...I know it's a big ask."

"You said we'd be allies. So here we are," I said, grudgingly.

"Well, thanks."

I shrugged and poured myself some iced tea. "How are we taking down Callista?"

The sooner we managed that, the sooner we'd all be safer—and maybe I could have my house to myself again. *At least until the next crisis.* I had a feeling that this was the beginning of the end of the way I'd been accustomed to living.

"I've been thinking on that. We can adapt an old Darkwatch plan."

That caught my attention, and I stopped mid-bite. "Excuse you?"

He shifted in his chair, picking at taco fixings that had fallen out and dropping them onto the top of his next one. "The Captain started worrying about Callista's overreach around the time I was born. Unfortunately for us, she's either exceedingly cautious or frustratingly old-fashioned. Old tech—Nokia phones or landlines instead of a smartphone, desktop not connected to the internet. The wards on the bar are too strong for us to take down fast enough to storm it before she can mount a counterattack."

"It's a bit of both," I muttered. "Old-fashioned for the tech, cautious with the magic."

"Which is why we figured we'd have to bring the bar itself down."

I stared at him. "Y'all have a plan to collapse the bar. In downtown Durham."

Troy shrugged and poured himself some more tea. "That was going to be your plan, wasn't it? It was going to have to be an inside job. Something that would look like an accident when the mundanes investigated. We've been collecting intel on the building layout and architecture for the last decade."

There had to be a better way than pulling the whole building down. Yeah, it was what I'd threatened to do, but that was a last resort. Remembering the battle against the lich gave me an idea. "Monteague, can any of you sense elemental magic?"

"No." Sudden wariness pinched his face. "We can only see its effects when you use it, although the bond lets me sense you using it if it's a big enough working."

"So, what if her wards can't sense it either? If they're attuned to Aether or witch magic, would she notice if, say, a little elemental mole tunneled into her dungeon?"

Troy went very still. "First, could you manage that? Second, what dungeon?"

Having information the Darkwatch didn't was enough to override my reflexive shudder at the idea of being underground again, and I grinned. "She has a punishment space in the basement. I've only seen it once, but it's dank and nasty. Stereotypical as fuck."

"Which likely means that it was dug into soil not conducive to maintaining it," Troy mused, leaning back in his chair.

"And you know that she's not going to limit herself to escaping from the upstairs alone," I said. "Or that she'd only allow for the possibility of bringing victims in through the front or back doors."

The gold flecks in his eyes seemed to spark as he refocused on me. "Where's the other door?"

"Beats me." I shrugged. "But if anyone could find an unmapped underground space…"

"It'll be an elemental." Troy's sudden grin made him look roguishly attractive, and I made myself look away. He'd always been hot—sometimes it seemed like the elves bred for it—but this was pinging me a little too personally.

You're allies. Not friends. Definitely nothing else. No matter what he sounded like when he said your name the other night.

228

I cleared my throat. "So, ah…does that mean you'll go with me to find it?"

"If we can wait until nightfall. Easier to call shadows then."

The easy way he spoke of an ability that he'd once pretended not to have made me decide to test how deep our trust went. "Who's this Captain, anyway?"

Troy's mouth firmed into a thin line, and his good humor fled as he looked away, as though he knew what I was doing and was trying to decide whether to play along.

"He's Alli's birth father," he said after a long silence, one that I spent finishing another taco. "When mine left, he became like a father to me. When I earned my place as second, he shut down everyone who called it nepotism."

Shitting hell. "Wait, you're—"

"Being groomed to take over the Darkwatch, yes. Or I was. After this year…" That cheek muscle twitched. "Alli will have her hands full dealing with the assassins. I'll be lucky to make it to the winter solstice, and that assumes she isn't ordered to leave again to make it easier for them. She's very good at keeping me alive."

I studied him, half disbelieving. "You want out that much. You'd give up your House, your positions, *and* your adopted father?"

Sandstone was softer than his eyes as Troy looked at me. "Yes," he said, so softly I shivered. "As well as my properties, incomes, and titles."

I shivered. If that was true, it made him a man with nothing to lose because he'd already planned on losing everything. That made him even more dangerous than he'd been as a supernatural commando with a grudge and a hard-on for the law. I stared at him, the old fear returning as I realized that whatever the little moment had been at Claret, I still fit into a larger plan for him. One that might see me alive rather than dead but still a plan.

"Good. You get it now." From his tone, he was both pleased and bitter.

"What am I to you, Monteague?" I whispered.

He studied me, seeming to take in every curl in my hair then every line of my face. "I don't know anymore. Not prey. More than an ally. Beyond that?" He shrugged. "Now's not the time to figure it out."

"Okay," I said, appetite fled. "Fair enough. As long as you definitely don't want me dead as a way out."

"We've been over that."

I raised my hand placatingly and started cleaning up my lunch. "Forgive me a quarter-century of paranoia."

"Yeah." Tiredness slowed his words as he helped clean up his side of the table. "We both need to deal with our conditioning."

As I boxed up the leftover food, something occurred to me. Troy had reacted to the little pulse of Chaos I'd managed to send him as a sign while I was glamoured. What if he could help me with that? Asking seemed taboo somehow, enough that my heart pounded. But how silly would it be not to just…ask?

Roman's voice echoed in my mind: "You don't ask, you don't get."

Troy had already figured out that I was trueborn. How much harm could there be in trying to gain a little control over Chaos, when it could help us both manage the bond better?

Okay, so that last part was just an excuse. I wanted to ask because it was my birthright. If I didn't, I would always feel limited by what Val called "the curse"—being a maenad, a being who would warp people and maybe even reality, after a few too many glasses of wine. I wanted to be able to let loose and have fun, or at least to turn the power into a gift and use it to my advantage.

It's the least he can do if he's crashing at my house.

I finished putting food in the fridge and cleaning up the kitchen, going over the idea as I washed the pans, put the dishes in the dishwasher, and wiped down the counters. The only downside I could see was that there was some kind of elven taboo, but that wasn't really my problem.

Decided, I washed my hands and marched back outside. Troy was lounging in the same chair I'd left him in, eyes closed, bare feet stretched out long on the deck in front of him, hands folded on his stomach. His boots sat to the side, socks tucked neatly inside them.

"Is this the part where you tell me why you suddenly got very focused?" he asked. "Not that I was trying to listen in, but you've started projecting more in the last week. Easier to read when we're closer together as well."

I frowned, annoyed that the spillover Val had mentioned apparently extended to the bond with Troy. "I want to learn how to control Chaos."

That got his attention. He opened his eyes and looked at me, his dark brows lifting. "You hear the contradiction inherent in that statement, right?"

"Don't patronize me. I was able to signal you with Chaos before. I can't use either half of Aether, but I can sense both. There has to be a way to do something useful with Chaos."

I don't know what I expected Troy to do, but it wasn't easing gracefully to his feet and saying, "Okay."

"Okay?" I echoed.

He tilted his head and pursed his lips. "No promises. I learned Chaos as a theory for managing the fallout from a fight with a djinni, not as an ability."

"I guess I just expected to have to fight you more," I grumbled, uncomfortable with the continuing shift in our bizarre dynamic.

Troy snorted a laugh, offering one of his rare almost-smiles. "Because that always goes so well for me."

"You're learning," I said, somewhat mollified. It was probably as much because I was his walking life preserver as much as anything else, but why pick fights when I had one with Callista coming up?

Seeing that I wasn't going to go off, Troy leapt down all three steps down to the yard and landed soundlessly. "Come on." He turned to walk backwards a few steps to see if I was following. "I don't want to try working within this ward the witches set up."

I shook myself and jumped down after him, not liking at all how normal he seemed. *Is this another play? Force hasn't worked in months, so he's trying guile?* I realized that I was looking at his ass and flushed in equal parts embarrassment and frustration when he turned around again.

"If I promise that I'm not trying to mess with you, will you stop radiating suspicion?" he asked.

"I just don't get what you *want*," I snapped, taking my moodiness out on him.

"I told you—"

"No. You told me what you *don't* want. In January, I didn't want to be controlled by Callista anymore, but what I *wanted* was freedom to be myself. So, what are you running toward?"

A shuddering pull on my awareness made my eyes widen as Troy frowned. I spun, looking for the djinni that was about to make an appearance.

"What?" Troy drew a knife from somewhere and slid closer to me.

"Don't you see, little bird?" a deep, resonant voice said. "He wants you."

With a ripple, Duke materialized. I swore as my insides contracted. The last time I'd seen my djinni cousin, he'd threatened to hang me by my intestines. Yet here he was.

Chapter 28

I reached for Air so hard that Fire came with it. Lightning crackled over me, and Troy hissed as he took a step away, keeping himself between me and the tall, dark-skinned djinni who'd just appeared in my backyard.

"I didn't summon you, Duke," I said, barely able to form the words.

He regarded me with carnelian eyes, his gaze flicking to Troy and dismissing the elf. "I know," he said. "I'm here to collect my favor."

Blood drained from my face. I owed Duke for information he'd given me to find the lich the other week, but after our falling out, I'd gotten the silly idea that he wouldn't collect. Definitely not this fast anyway. Djinn had lifetimes to figure out how best to leverage a debt. I had no idea what the natural lifespan of a trueborn elemental was, but I had to assume I'd live past a hundred. For Duke to return after barely more than a week was bad. Real bad, like he wasn't expecting Earth to be around another century.

I let go of Air and Fire and rested a hand on Troy's arm to get him to stand down, ignoring the usual jump of magic when my palm touched his bare skin.

"Finch?" he said, voice tight, glancing to me as though for instruction. The scent of meringue grew thick.

"I acknowledge the debt," I said quickly, praying that I wasn't about to get a much more active lesson in managing Chaos than I'd been looking for. If Duke and Troy went head-to-head, we'd shatter the Détente. I took a shaky breath. "What do you want, Duke?"

The djinni looked casually at the claws that had sprouted from his fingers. "That was quite the show you put on yesterday." His usual laughing smile had an edge to it that I didn't like at all. "Calling out Callista that way? Showing off primordial powers? Hell of a show."

I thought fast. Callista wouldn't rely on House Monteague alone, not if she thought they'd hedge to save their prince. "She's sent you to kill me."

"Capture is preferred. Damaged or not wasn't specified." Duke glanced at Troy again. "Nor was an elven bodyguard part of the deal. Curious choice. And an ironic one, all Houses considered."

Duke had never expressed any particular bother about killing elves before, so this had to be part of the point. I set aside the burning question about why working with a Monteague in particular would be ironic and worked the spit back into my mouth. "That's inconvenient. How can I be of service?"

The djinni circled us, showing wickedly pointed teeth as he smiled his laughter at the sight of me trying to keep him in sight and Troy out of the way. "How good of you to ask. As much as I'd like to carry out my previous threat, it is true—you didn't call on me. That makes it a mite difficult to carry it out lawfully. More to the point, there is one person I find more infuriating than you just now."

"Callista," I breathed.

Smoke wreathed Duke. "Precisely."

"Get to the point. What do you want? I won't ask again."

"She has a bottle."

"Ah." So it had been Callista who'd bottled Duke before. "A bottle and perhaps a geas or two? Some other items?"

Duke's smile was ugly. "I see you understand the nature of the situation. Get me my items. Or kill her, I don't care which."

He's desperate, putting such loose terms on an agreement. Or trying to give me options? I didn't dare ask which. "So the debt is called, and so it shall be paid, with the life of the being known as Callista *or* the bottle and any other items recognizable by me as belonging to the djinni commonly known as Duke."

"And so it is," he snapped, eyes flaring. "Get it to me by the full moon, or I start taking pieces off of your friends."

Four days. I blanched then took a breath. I was already going after Callista. The extra days were actually a reasonable buffer for me to find his items if I didn't kill her the first time.

An idea came to me. "I can get it faster if you can get me into the dungeon."

"It's warded against unsummoned djinn, and it's not up to me to do your dirty work for you. Figure it out."

Before I could protest further, reality shimmered, and he shifted planes.

When I was sure he was gone, I bowed my head, shaking as I focused on my breathing and the feeling of the air around me. "Fuck."

Concern floated through the open bond, followed by a slithery feeling that I could only call plotting.

"What?" I said.

"Are there any other djinn you can call on?"

I gritted my teeth. *Not since you killed the other one.* "No."

Another idea sparked.

Troy stood with arms crossed, watching me warily when I brought my head up.

I offered him a tight smile. "But the djinn aren't the only ones who can use the Crossroads."

"Who—" The blood drained from his face, leaving him a sickly shade of yellow-brown. He swallowed, hard, in possibly the first show of fear I'd ever seen from him. "Oh."

"Artemis wants Callista." Offering up my former guardian felt icky, given what I suspected of the circumstances of the situation between her, Zeus, and Artemis.

But somebody's past trauma didn't excuse them from acting it out on others. It certainly didn't excuse the shit Callista had done to me personally, or anything she was planning for me by sending a djinni—my own cousin, no less—to collect me dead or alive. Nor did it excuse her past actions, if indeed it had been her kidnapping elementals. I couldn't take the risk that she'd tire of trying for me and go after Val, Laurel, or Sofia instead, now that they were known.

Wary admiration replaced concern in Troy's voice. "I would have thought you too principled to do that."

"If that's a polite way of saying naive, then yeah, I used to be."

"Noted," Troy said gravely. "What do you need from me?"

I lifted my eyebrows at him, still just not quite sure what he was getting out of all this.

He sighed. "If you won't trust good intentions, will you trust the fact that I need Callista gone so that she stops using my House against me? Not wanting the obligations isn't the same as being okay with Grandmother and Evie wanting to torture me to death for drawing a line."

I thought about that then offered a not-bad-Obama face. "Funny how that works."

Maybe he finally had an inkling of how I'd felt for years.

He scowled but didn't take the bait. "Well?"

"Artemis gave me a ring." I chewed on the cuticle of my thumbnail, wondering if this qualified for using it. "I was supposed to call her when Callista was gone, but fuck it."

This was becoming the lich situation all over again—there was a problem that everyone else wanted me to solve for them. The only thing stopping me from getting bitchy was the fact that I had a personal grievance this time.

"Wait here." I ran for the house, dug the ring out of my nightstand, and rushed back out.

Heart pounding, I looked up at Troy. He wasn't the ally I would have chosen, but he was the ally I had. Could I trust him?

He stared down at me, eyes pinching at the corners as he put his hands on his hips. "Finch, whatever it is, if it gets me breathing room to deal with my family and try to get them to do the right thing, I'll do it."

"I don't even know if *I* want to do it," I said. "But I'll tell you my thinking, and you tell me if I'm crazy."

"This should be good." Wariness like barbed wire prickled through the bond.

"Callista is going to know from Duke that the alliance stands with me and that we all fought together against the sorcerer. She'll know that with him out of play, the vampires can join the standoff on my side. Right?"

"With you so far."

I nodded and started pacing, unable to stand still. "Okay. So, we have to assume that she still has other Watchers. They're not going to bother watching Monteagues, but after yesterday they might have an eye on the Lunas and are probably watching each of the were leaders in the area, Torsten's coterie, and the coven. But between Zanna and the wards, nobody is going to try coming here."

Troy winced. "What, and risk a kobold's curse? No. If we hadn't planned today, I'd wait until you headed for your office or try luring you out."

And how would you do that? He almost certainly had a plan for it in his back pocket. That was a question for another day though. "Fine. Then all of that means it's likely nobody knows you're here except your family, who think you're my prisoner and are waiting to see if I have other demands. So, our best shot is to go in right now. Just us. No phone calls, no warnings, no backup."

With a sigh, Troy looked skyward and scrubbed his hands over his face. I traced the ring in my palm with my thumb, waiting impatiently for him to think through the angles and find another way.

"What are we doing with Callista?" he asked when he met my eyes again.

I swallowed at the deadened look in his. He was already shifting into whoever he became when it was time to go on a mission. I looked away as the memory of Leith's burning corpse flashed through my mind. "Kill her if we can. Chase her off and let Artemis have her if we can't."

Bile rose to my throat at what I was saying. Otherside justice was clear-cut, and I was within my rights. That didn't mean that I had to like being pushed to kill. Confusion made it worse as Troy's comment about Callista conditioning me flashed through my mind. Was that where my reluctance came from? I didn't recall being so reticent about killing Leith.

"Don't overthink it," Troy said. "Callista is no innocent, and you have just cause."

"I know," I whispered. "I just...I wasn't a killer until six months ago."

I waited for him to tell me that I'd get used to it or brush it off, but all he said was, "Don't use that ring until you're properly dressed and ready to go."

I looked down at my jogging shorts and red T-shirt. "What's wrong with my clothes? I can move in these."

"You'll lose skin if you hit the ground. At the very least, get more weapons."

Fair point. The problem was my idea of what to wear or gear up with came from action flicks and what he wore to missions.

He read my hesitation. "I'm not coming in to help unless you explicitly ask for it."

I almost shut him down. Almost.

But there was something in the way he looked at me. Uncertainty, maybe. Crossing my arms, I evaluated him and tried to find a reason not to invite him into my house. I tried telling myself that it was a security risk, that a Darkwatch agent and elven prince in my house was a death sentence. But he'd already broken in once—to save my life. Then he'd made sure I'd eaten the other night.

I couldn't keep testing him. I had to either get over past actions and move on or cut him loose. Just like I had with Roman.

"I need help. Please," I said between gritted teeth as I glared at him. Asking for help so nakedly galled me. I'd managed on my own up till now.

I managed as a private investigator solving mundane cases. Not as Arbiter to the most powerful people in Otherside. Not as a damn assassin. The decision I'd been mulling over a few days ago came back to me. Was my time as a mundane PI over? Was I ready for that? If I wasn't, what the hell was I really going to do about it? Sometimes the Universe didn't give you options, it gave you directions.

The almost-smile was nearly a whole one this time. "Since you're asking so nicely…"

Scoffing, I strode back up to the house.

While I dug through my closet and drawers for something more like Troy's outfit, he stalked around my house like a shadow. By the time I emerged from my bedroom wearing black cargo pants I'd bought on a whim, a black T-shirt to match his, and a pair of hiking boots, he'd found the shotgun I kept for home protection and laid out a bunch of other supplies on the dining table. The first aid kit I'd left outside sat incongruously next to the gun, alongside empty water bottles, protein bars, and a silver protection charm that I'd had tucked away in the back of my bookcase.

He looked up from where he was mixing salt and sugar with water and flicked his gaze over me. The boots got a slight frown, but I wasn't a damn commando and I wasn't going to mess up my nice leather boots for this. "Better. Where's the Ruger?"

Sighing, I spun and went back for it.

"And spare ammo!"

I dug that out as well.

"She's a nymph, not a human, and all I have are lead bullets that I don't even know will work," I snarled as I stalked back out and slapped the box of bullets down on the table.

"Better than your fists," he murmured, surveying the rest. "Knives?"

I turned and lifted my shirt to show him the godblade nestled at my back, crossed with a silver-edged blade I'd bought after killing the lich in an excess of paranoia about Sergei.

"Where's the other one?"

"That's for elves." I gave him a pointed look.

"It's enchanted. Do you really want to have just two little knives? Especially if my grandmother makes a play to get me back?"

Pressing my lips together, I went back for the eight-inch elf-killer, strapping the fancy tooled leather sheath to the thigh opposite the Ruger LCP. I felt a little silly as I went back into the kitchen, like a kid playing at soldier.

"What are you making?" I asked as he ignored me and carefully poured the water-salt-sugar mixture into the empty water bottles.

"ORS. For dehydration. You didn't have an electrolyte drink."

"Booze would do me better if I'm using my powers," I muttered.

After a quick look to gauge my seriousness, he got up and fetched the small bottle of brandy I kept hidden in the back of the pantry.

"Hey!" I felt more than a little violated. "Did you go through my entire fucking house while I was getting dressed?"

"You asked for help."

Yes, I had, but... *Dammit.* I fumed as he calmly packed everything into the duffel bag he'd brought with him.

Troy slung the duffel bag over his shoulder and lifted his eyebrows. "Shall we?"

"Fuck," I said. "I guess we'd better."

The ring weighed heavy in my hand. Troy and I went to the woods, where I figured Artemis would be more amenable to being called. I realized I had no fucking clue what I was doing as I traced my thumb around the edge and then slid it onto my middle finger. *Nothing to it but to do it.*

"My lady Artemis, I beg your attention." I tried to tamp down my annoyance at the phrasing. She'd demanded that kind of cringey shit before. No use pissing her off before asking a favor. I waited, shifting from foot to foot while Troy stood unmoving, stretching my senses for some confirmation that my call had been heard. "My lady—"

My second attempt faltered as a white tear in reality preceded the pressing rush of power that I'd come to associate with the gods. In a bizarre mirror of my last visit to House Monteague, I grabbed Troy's arm and tugged him down as I knelt. The bond tightened with a frightening intensity as he went to a knee beside me, and I'd never heard his breathing so short.

"First time meeting a facet of the Goddess in the flesh?" I muttered.

Troy didn't answer. Probably for the best, given that Artemis stepped through the tear right then.

I glanced up while keeping my head tilted down. Artemis appeared much as she had the last time: tall and muscled, armed with a bow and a quiver of arrows, wearing a long tunic belted in leather tooled with a conifer pattern alternating with leaping stags and hunting dogs. The blood moon was as bright as ever in her eyes, though her auburn hair was in long braids this time.

"My lady," I said.

"The nymph is dead?"

"I—no, my lady but—" I found myself on my back and struggling to breathe before I had the thought to shape my next words. Artemis's sandaled foot landed lightly between my breasts, and all I could do was try to focus on surviving this moment. "I know—where—"

"Lady, please," Troy said in a voice that was so devoid of breath and feeling that I barely recognized it.

Pressure eased as she turned to him, her expression delighted. "The Hunter!"

Troy bent closer to the ground and spoke words I never imagined I'd hear from the proud elven prince. "I live to serve."

I gasped for air as Artemis gave him her full attention. The bond filled with sharp splinters as Troy lost his sense of self, spiraling into fog and mist. I scrabbled for Chaos and pushed against the intrusion, as I'd felt him do against Torsten, and he dragged a gasp of breath in, still lost in her gaze.

Artemis's lips curved in a dangerous smile.

"Already defending one another." The weight of her power lifted, and she took a neutral stance.

Troy collapsed, and I resisted the urge to check his pulse, focusing on the goddess's sandals.

Chapter 29

"Goddess," I said, "I've found your nymph. I ask—I beg—your indulgence."

"You found her?" The weight of Artemis's eyes was almost too much for a mortal to bear. If I hadn't had so much practice in the Crossroads first, I'd probably be taking it like Troy was.

I risked drawing on Air to maintain my equilibrium, but the goddess didn't seem to notice. Or care. "I did. My Hunter and I seek to pursue her. We—" *Own it, he has nothing to do with this plan.* "*I* beg your indulgence."

"Speak."

"Passage through the Crossroads. We will either drive her to you or kill her ourselves."

Laughter like a stag's mating roar split the woods, making the leaves tremble on the trees. "Bold. I like you, sylph." Artemis tilted her head, and the blood moon in her eyes flashed in the light of the lowering sun. "Or no. Primordial, now. Neith had the right of it, as ever, the bitch."

The stag's mating cry echoed through the trees again. "A primordial and an elf, and the tension…" She hissed. "Even my father would be tempted by you, but this Hunter resists. How delicious."

I quivered, not daring to distract myself with considering the implications of her words.

"I grant your request. Hold tight to your Hunter, Mistress, or you may lose him in the veil. Elves are beings of shadow. They don't travel well in the realms of light."

Without question, I launched myself at Troy.

As reality shivered and he trembled beneath me, Artemis dove into my mind, seeking the knowledge of her lost nymph. I screamed, burying my face against Troy's back. Artemis plucked the idea of Callista's bar and the dungeon beneath it from my brain. The universe compressed, and I held onto Troy for dear life.

* * *

The musty scent caught my attention first. I gasped as though I was coming back from the dead, flopping onto my back and reaching for my element out of reflex. I was underground again, and Air didn't come easily. Earth was there though, quiet and solid, waiting for me to get over my unease about being underground and acknowledge it.

A tug at the back of my mind reminded me that I wasn't alone. It was weak, faltering.

"Troy," I gasped, forcing myself to my hands and knees as I sought him.

There. He was face-down halfway across the room, the duffel bag full of supplies between us. I gathered it as I scooched his way. He didn't react when I flipped him onto his back.

"Troy!"

Nothing but a white-rimmed fluttering of his eyes.

"Fuck."

The hint of an interplanar portal hovered in the corner. Small and sparking but still present. More of a threat than a beacon. I searched the dungeon as I shook Troy again. It was the same space I remembered from my one brief visit. Most important, there was no Callista.

That state of affairs likely wouldn't last. There was no way she wouldn't sense a goddess powering through her wards to dump a primordial elemental and an elven prince on her doorstep.

I tried to remember what he'd done to pull me out of Maria's glamour and prayed that I wouldn't kill him attempting it myself. Gritting my teeth, I knelt and pulled his head into my lap. With closed eyes, I rested one hand at the base of his skull and one on his forehead, seeking through the bond with Chaos. The power slithered through me before striking to him like a chameleon's tongue and sticking to the point in his aura where the bond connected.

I started to push...then froze. This wasn't like with Maria. I'd still had a sense of myself; it had just been fogged and rolled under. Troy was splintered.

"Come on, dammit," I whispered, wondering how long I had to pull the pieces together before Callista appeared. My heart hammered as I imagined a sphere instead, one that slowly compressed inward. Sweat dripped down my forehead and trailed down my back as I wrestled with Chaos. The sphere tightened. Splinters of Troy's essence quivered like iron seeking a lodestone.

With a jolt, they snapped into place. Troy arched with a gasp and scrabbled for his longknife, eyes wide and panic roiling in the bond. I held back a gag as burnt marshmallow assaulted my nose with how deeply he'd drawn on Aether.

"Shh, dammit Troy, stop!" I hissed, eyes darting to the door at the top of the stairs. "Hey! Asshole! It's me! Be still!"

He froze, his eyes searching my face. His training must have started asserting itself because he gathered his wits faster than I probably would have. "Finch?"

"Yeah. You good?"

"You saved me?"

I frowned down at him in consternation, pulling my hands away and easing him to the floor. "We came in as partners. We go down as partners. Right?"

"Glad you see it that way," he rasped.

A trickle of rising power overhead drew my head up, and I figured out why Callista hadn't confronted us yet. "Shit. She's summoning the rabisu."

Troy dragged himself to his feet. "Where?"

"Her office, I think. My question is whether she emptied the bar first. Come on."

Drawing the godblade from the small of my back with my off hand and hefting the Ruger in the other, I led him to the bottom of the stairs.

"Wait. Can you mask your presence or something?" He'd managed to sneak into Claret completely unnoticed by the vampires' superior hunting senses.

"Yes, but I can't keep it up for very long."

"Do it."

With a few whispered words, Troy became invisible to every one of my senses except for the bond.

"Okay, that is fucking creepy." I shuddered as the elven prince became nothing more than a shadow in the dark.

Then I dashed up the stairs and tried to open the door as quietly as possible, just enough to peek through the crack. The bar appeared empty. I couldn't see or sense anyone or anything other than Callista in her office and a growing sense of evil. Pushing the door open, I abandoned stealth in favor of speed and shot out the lock on the office door.

"Stop, Callista. Right now," I said as I burst in, leveling the pistol at her.

My former guardian had cleared her computer and keyboard off her desk and filled the surface with the items one apparently needed for demon summoning: carved bones, a small, open-topped pot with a fire burning in it, and a few bloody lumps of flesh. My stomach roiled as I recognized an eye in the mess. A white line split the ceiling at an angle and started twisting open.

Callista glared with hatred even as she kept chanting, her voice rising in volume, and I swept everything off the desk at her with Air as I fired at her chest.

Reality shattered, and she screamed as both the fire from the pot and the bullet hit her. I stumbled backward into the wall, trying to force my brain to make sense of what was happening. It was like the moment after I'd fallen into Jordan Lake, that horrifying disorientation of hovering at the line between air and water, trying to decide if it was safe to breathe while the sky was distorted by the water's surface and finding myself in well over my head.

Before I could recover, Callista stepped back onto this plane from a portal to my right. I barely dodged away from a grasping hand, holding her at bay with the godblade.

"How delightfully unexpected to find you here, my dear," she said. "All alone? Have you gotten arrogant, or did you take a few knocks to the head yesterday?"

"Artemis wants a word," I snarled.

Callista's green eyes widened, and I saw something in them I'd never seen before: fear.

"You bitch!" She roared with the fury of a bear as she struck with the speed of a viper.

She swatted the Ruger out of my hand as I tried for another shot, sending the bullet into the wall. There was no flare of pain in the bond from Troy so if it had gone through the wall, it had missed him. I switched the godblade to my right hand and drew the silver blade from the small of my back.

"You will regret this, Arden." Venom dripped from her words as her eyes glowed with power. "I will break you into so many tiny pieces that you won't remember who you were when I put you back together. You will grovel!"

I wrenched my mind away from the mental image of all the things she might do as my heart hammered. That's what she wanted, to distract me with fear. Not bothering to answer, I called Fire, blending it with Air to throw a bolt of lightning at her.

She dodged out the door, and the bolt hit the desk instead. The wood exploded and started smoldering as I swore and covered my face with my arm against the splinters. When I chased her out into the hallway, Troy was fighting her, keeping himself between her and the front door. Not that it mattered; if she really wanted to leave, she'd use the Crossroads.

"Oh, this is rich," she said darkly. "Keithia thinks her little prince is tied up in your crawlspace. All you've done in bringing him here is give me another tool."

She slashed at Troy with hands that transformed into a bear's paws, and he stumbled back with a cry as he wasn't quite fast enough.

Callista advanced, taking another swipe. "Do you want to watch me torture her, little prince? Do you want to help? The Monteagues are sooo good at torture that breaks the mind while leaving the body whole." She leered at me, still speaking to Troy. "Call it your reward. Your family are the reason she's mine to begin with."

What? I darted in, stabbing with the godblade.

She sidestepped into another plane again, and Troy and I put our backs together, panting.

The bond went funny as he tried to hide the sudden doubt that had filtered into him with her words. Doubt about me? Or his family?

"Where did she go?" he asked tersely.

"Veilside." I tried to catch my breath and slow the wild beating of my heart. My eyes darted as I tried to anticipate where she'd come through. She knew this bar better than anyone and could come from literally any direction.

Unless...

"Jump," I said.

Troy did so without question, and I created a thick cube of Air around us. He stumbled and grunted at finding the floor higher than he'd expected. We wouldn't have air to breathe for very long if I kept it solid enough to repel her, but I had to do something.

We waited, the bond taut between us and our backs tight against each other as I tried to focus on the moment, not on Callista's taunts.

"North!" I shouted, sensing a disturbance in that direction.

Troy whirled to face it, but as soon as the word left my mouth, I sensed one below us. A bear's frustrated roar echoed as something thumped against the bottom of my cube, and the disturbance to the north widened as Callista stepped through it.

"A standoff." She tapped her lips. "One that ends when you run out of air. How ironic."

My mind raced as I tried to figure something out. How the hell were we going to kill a being that could use the planes to escape and attack at will? And where the hell was Artemis?

Callista's lips curled in a cruel smile as she paced the exterior of the box I'd put Troy and myself in. "You're as stupid as your mother was, Arden. It took me years to lead Ninlil to the road that ended with you."

My heart clenched, and I wavered. Callista had rarely spoken of my mother growing up, usually only to dig at me. Knowing that's what she was doing now didn't stop the pain.

"Does he know?" she continued, nodding at Troy. "What you are? *Who* you are?"

Something inside me snapped. "*I* don't even know, you fucking bitch!"

At my back, Troy muttered, "Steady, Finch. Focus."

"What do you get out of helping her, little prince?" Callista's eyes glittered with savage amusement as she circled to the side. "Oh! Or is it a betrayal? That would be delicious. I taught her better than to trust elves. Will you prove me right? She'll never believe in your good intentions, no matter what you do. Give her to me. I'll smooth things over with Keithia. Or not. You could go far away. Live your own life. What's your price? Tell me. It's already yours."

Focus. With an effort, I shook off Callista's barrage of words and ignored the waver in Troy's mind. It was the same shit she'd done when I was a kid. I knew that. It was a distraction. What was she doing? What was real?

Then it hit me. *Reality. To fight unreality.*

I was a fucking primordial elemental. If I could blend Air and Fire, what could I do if I blended all of them?

"This is gonna hurt," I said, thinking of the epic power hangover I was going to have if I managed this.

"Finch?" Troy muttered, the bond solidifying as he pushed away his inner conflict and rocked on his toes in a ready stance.

As Callista paced another circle around us, testing the walls of my cube with pricks and stabs of Chaos, I dove deep inside myself. Air came easily, tugging at our clothes. Fire next, allowing itself to be coaxed to join Air, and the temperature inside the cube rose.

"What are you doing?" Callista snapped.

Earth was still waiting from my time downstairs. I forced myself to embrace rather than to grab and hissed as pressure grew from holding three elements at once. I wavered, locking my knees as they suddenly felt like rubber.

Troy swore, and after a breath of hesitation, his feet shuffled as he turned around. He tugged me back against him. "Whatever you're doing, make it fast."

I leaned back, letting him take my weight while I panted and tried to bring myself to surrender to Water. Jordan Lake flashed through my mind. Bubbles containing my life fleeing to the surface while I was stuck at the bottom, floating at the end of a rope amidst so many other corpses.

Troy had done that. Callista had been right. How could I trust him? How stupid was I?

I stiffened, and Water flowed right past me.

Callista sneered, showing bear's teeth. "You're making a mistake. You know you are. He's already hurt you. Made you his, one false choice at a time. Just like I did."

I trembled as I gritted my teeth. Was she right? Troy's advice had always seemed good. But had he just been manipulating me?

Troy's arms tightened around me. "Don't listen to her. Focus."

He would say that. He needed me. And then it clicked: that meant I had the power.

But it only mattered if I could claim Water before we ran out of air or died of heat exhaustion in the rapidly warming box I'd trapped us in. Squeezing my eyes shut, I held my breath, trying to trust us both enough to fall in.

"That's enough, Arden." Callista hammered a fist against the wall of Air. It gave slightly, my hold on Air weakening as I fought to hold multiple elements. "Stop this, and I'll let your pet elf and your elemental friends live."

But she wouldn't, and I knew it. She'd say anything, do anything, to keep her power. She'd already proven that. Her actions screamed where her words slithered. Still I fought Water, feeling the freefall. The splash. The tug of the concrete block at the end of the rope.

The scent of burning meringue flooded me, and I screamed as a soothing wash of Aether flooded me.

"Let it go," Troy whispered in my ear, sounding ragged. "Don't let her be right. Don't let her keep you in a box. Whatever you're trying to do, you have to let go."

And with a sob, I did. My mind's eye played the movie of my drowning in reverse as I surrendered. Water flooded me, and I screamed my throat raw at the sensation of drowning in the heartbeat it took for it to join Air, Fire, and Earth.

"No!" Callista shouted. Power rose. She was escaping, again.

Not this time, bitch. I dropped the walls of my cube, stumbling against Troy as I threw a mass of blended primordial power.

It struck the opening portal into the Crossroads and collapsed it with a boom that shook the bar and shredded our auras. All of us staggered and fell as cracks split the walls, dust fell from the ceiling, the lights went out, and the sprinklers kicked on.

A stag's braying stabbed through the sudden silence, resolving itself into laughter as Artemis finally deigned to make her appearance.

"Delightful!" she called, clapping. Silver light like a full moon shone from behind her.

I couldn't answer. I was too busy shuddering in a heap on the floor. Troy lay still beside me, barely breathing, the bond quiet, maybe broken. Maybe he was dead.

Callista stirred. "No," she rasped. "No! I won't go back to the sky. I won't!"

Artemis's smile was cruel. "That's up to my father. Personally, I'd prefer a practice hunt before the real one begins. Bear is always such a delightful challenge."

Her hand closed on Callista's throat, and the last thing I heard before they disappeared to another plane and I passed out was screaming.

Chapter 30

Consciousness brought the first throbs of a power hangover, and I breathed shallowly as I sensed through myself for injuries. *Scrapes, bruises. Weak aura, shielding is gonna be shit.* Hopefully I wouldn't need to hide myself anytime soon. Groaning, I started to sit up then fell back when the world spun so fast I thought I might vomit. The sprinklers had cut off, leaving me lying in a shallow puddle of water in the pitch dark.

"Thank the Goddess," came a ragged whisper.

"Monteague?"

"Yes."

I had the sense of hands hovering and reached for where I thought one was. He grabbed it and followed my arm down to my neck, checking my pulse before pulling away again.

Swallowing past the nausea, I asked, "Are you okay?"

"I should be asking you that. What do you need?"

"Water." My mouth was so dry I was surprised it wasn't cemented shut. "Booze, if I need to get up and do something sooner rather than later."

It was probably a little late for that, but I'd never tried ameliorating the power hangover after the fact. Something told me I wasn't going to have the rest of the day to recover though, and the speed with which the headache and nausea were mounting into cramps and shakes started to frighten me.

"Fast," I amended.

The sound of the basement door was the only clue I had that Troy had moved. His step was as soundless as ever, even on the wet debris of the floor. *Damn elf magic.*

I focused on breathing slowly, in and out, trying to figure out what to do about my aura and the tattered feeling to the bond between Troy and me. Could I tear it free? Did I want to, or was this even a good time?

Leave it. The sudden doubt around wanting to be rid of it threw me for a loop, but I'd look at it later. This was not the time to mess around with Chaos-warped Aether. If there was any lingering evil from Callista's attempt to summon the rabisu, something might try to fill the gap it left.

"Here," Troy said. A rustling noise told me he was digging in the bag. He pressed the water bottle to my chest before reaching back in for the flashlight and clicking it on.

The cold light showed an utterly trashed hallway. What the lightning and primordial explosion hadn't ruined was waterlogged. There wasn't a single light working. Callista must have shut the security shades after kicking everyone out because no natural light made it through the little window in the door to the main bar.

I gritted my teeth and forced myself to push into a seated position, scooching until my back was against the wall. My arm shook as I opened the steel water bottle and lifted it to my lips.

Troy watched, the pinch at the corner of his eyes suggesting he was concerned and trying not to be annoying about it. Four long, ragged cuts ran over his left arm and shoulder.

"She got you pretty good," I said when I'd gulped down half the bottle. I grimaced as my stomach decided it didn't much appreciate the ORS and accepted the bottle of brandy from Troy next. "You gonna need a doctor?"

He glanced at his shoulder and tentatively rolled his arm, wincing as the torn skin pulled. "No. It's shallower than it looks, and we heal fast."

Nodding, I cracked the seal on the brandy and downed two good-sized gulps of it. My stomach roiled, and I tasted bile as I held back a heave and breathed through it. The first hints of relief curled through me a few breaths later.

"Oh, thank fuck," I muttered, drinking a little more.

"You didn't know if that would work?"

"Usually I do my drinking before I play with my powers, not after." An uncomfortable thought struck me. I'd need to be real careful to find the line between enough not to be debilitated and not so much that I flipped into maenad mode. Enough people had dropped hints or insinuations about why Troy stuck around that I didn't want to be the one crossing a boundary. Maybe an elf could resist the call, maybe not. I didn't plan to find out.

Troy just grunted, pulling out the first aid kit and then tearing through the rest of his shirt to get a better look at his wounds. Callista's claws had just missed the House tattoo under his collarbone and curved over the well-defined muscle of his upper arm. Fortunately for him, they were, as he'd said, shallower than they first looked. Still, another fight with me, another shoulder wound. Bad pattern starting for him.

I extended the brandy, and he took a swig before splashing some on the wounds with a silent hiss and passing it back. After three more swallows, the hangover started to recede to a dull roar, and I closed the little bottle up. I'd be tipsy but not so much that the maenad powers would waken. Troy, with his good looks and bleeding wound, would be a little too much temptation for that side of me if I lost control.

While he tended himself, I dug around in the now-wet duffel bag, trying to find my phone. "Shit," I said when I found it and

257

checked the calls. "Word's gotten out. Half of Otherside has called me."

I didn't feel up to returning calls individually. *Group text it is.* Unprofessional but hell, I'd just unlocked my strength as a primordial for the first time, and I was drained.

"Callista's gone," I read aloud as I swiped the message out. "The bar is mine."

As the implications of that statement weighed on me, I froze and looked at Troy.

He met my eyes with a blend of fear, anticipation, and respect. "Claim it," he said when I hesitated. "Call the leaders in, make them re-swear to the alliance. Put the pressure on Keithia."

Still I hesitated. Not just because of the seeds of doubt Callista had planted. The magnitude of such a play would shatter Otherside, where all I'd done before was shake it. Callista had maintained the balance of power with cruelty and an iron fist for centuries.

Could I do better? Did I deserve this?

Doubt crept deeper, and fear. This wasn't what I'd set out to do. All I'd wanted was enough power to stand alone, minding my business and living my life. I hadn't set out to topple Callista. I'd been pushed into it.

While I battled the clutches of impostor syndrome, Troy sat quiet and tense, his shoulder forgotten.

"I need a minute," I rasped, using the wall to slide to my feet and stumbling toward the main bar. I punched the buttons for the security shutters, allowing them to open a crack before hitting them again to stop them. How long did we have before someone got brave enough to come down or the magic warding the bar wore off and exposed us to the humans? I had to decide, right now, but my brain kept telling me, *You can't do this. You're not enough.*

I leaned on the bar, propping my elbows on the surface and burying my face in my hands. *Even if you can do this, you'll have to give up Hawkeye. All your work for your own business will be wasted,* the voice in my head continued. *You'll be known, and seen, by everyone. You'll have to fix everything, for everyone. Let someone else take this.*

But I'd still be pulled into fixing all the problems. I just wouldn't have control over how it was done. And I'd already been thinking of giving up Hawkeye Investigations for something bigger and more challenging. Why not this?

Because it's too much. With all the experienced leaders in the Triangle, who the fuck are you to take control?

"Finch," Troy said softly from behind me. "Look at me."

I wanted to ignore him, but I could feel him standing there. He had more patience than I did. I made him wait another minute before I turned and looked up into his face.

"Do you know why I saved you and not Javier?"

The words hit me like a slap. Troy had always avoided talking about Jordan Lake before, accepting responsibility more out of a grudging sense of duty than decency, or so I'd thought. Coming on the heels of what I'd had to push through to reach Water, it was almost too much. I shook my head no, unable to answer.

"Your air was gone. I had to film until there were enough bubbles that Leith would be convinced you were both dead. Between the hypoxia and the hypothermia, I could only save one of you. I had to choose the person who would be most useful to what I was trying to accomplish. Javier would have been the better short-term choice. But you had more potential." His eyes searched mine, the color washed from them in the low light but the intensity stronger than ever. "Callista was right. I thought that I could make you my tool. But in the end, I think I'm yours."

I took a deep, shuddering breath, trying to think past the memories of that event and understand what he was saying without saying. Callista had picked at a deep fear of mine when she'd tempted Troy. Could I really trust an elf? Could I really trust *him*?

"You don't need permission, Finch," Troy said intently. "You just need a plan."

A plan. I can make a plan. I'm good at that.

My heart hammered, and dizziness joined the fog and the hangover headache still throbbing in a band around my head. This would change everything. Not just for me but for the Triangle. Hell, for Otherside at large. Nobody did shit like this. Nobody revolted against the established order that kept everyone in balance.

That kept everyone in their place.

The thought hit me like one of my lightning bolts. Yeah, this would change everything. It would be a pain in the ass. I would struggle, and I would get shit wrong.

But Laurel and Val could live freely. I could protect Terrence and Ximena, and their people.

I could do so much to adjust the balance of power so that it was more equitable. But only if I embraced the fear, stepped up, and claimed it.

Troy relaxed, exhaling slowly at whatever he saw in my face then stiffening as I let exhaustion, confusion, tension, and hell, maybe even the brandy drive me to seek comfort in the unlikeliest place: leaning forward and hiding my face against his chest. His heart was pounding, and I started to pull away, flushing in embarrassment.

His arms came around me, quickly yet carefully, tentatively, keeping me there and sending my heart to race along with his.

What the hell am I doing? The memory of how he'd said my name and the gentle touch of his fingers against my jaw at Claret kept distracting me from the thought that I should pull away.

"You can do this, Finch." His voice rumbled through his chest, against my ear. "You don't need me or anyone else. But you do have to believe in yourself."

Banging on the front door pulled us both upright before I could form a response past the tightness in my throat. Troy sprang back, guilt flashing across his face for the half second it took for him to find neutrality.

"Hello?" Vikki sounded muffled. "Is this place open today?"

I looked at Troy, trying to figure out what the hell to say.

He shook his head. *Now isn't the time.*

I nodded then hit the switch for the security shutters and jogged to the door as they rattled up. Early evening light streamed in, making me squint.

Vikki's eyes widened when I unlocked the door and pulled it open. She turned back to the parking lot, whistled, and waved.

"We figured a white woman banging on the door would be less likely to be taken as trouble than Terrence or Ximena," she said in a low voice when I frowned at the wereleopard obong and the werejaguar jefa belatedly sliding out of their cars. "What the hell happened? Where's Callista? You look like shit."

"I was just about to text everyone." I stepped back and fished my phone out of my pocket. I was out of time to decide. Everything in me felt too tight as I hit send on the text with a resolute thumb then added a second: *Get to the bar by midnight.*

Vikki frowned at the buzz from her own pocket then read the text with wide eyes. "Lupa's teats. You staged a coup?" she said breathily, glancing over my shoulder. "With the backing of House Monteague?"

"The Monteagues don't know he's here, and it needs to stay that way," I said as Terrence and Ximena slipped into the bar behind Vikki. "Are the spells holding outside?"

"They're holding," Terrence said, his usual drawl sharper than usual. The musky scent of agitated big cat filled the bar as he and Ximena took everything in, eyes darting, nostrils flaring, and jaws slightly dropped as their inner cats tasted the air. "Blood, smoke, water, ozone, magic…a stag and a bear? What the fuck happened? 'Scusing my French, ma'am."

"There was a god here." Ximena's eyes shifted to the red-gold of a jaguar. "Arden, what is this? What's going on?"

"I'll explain when everyone is here," I said.

Troy leaned against the bar, probably looking neutral and unbothered to everyone except me. The bond was slowly ebbing back as our auras replenished, and tautly held worry rested behind his cool hazel eyes.

I took a seat at the bar. "What are y'all doing here?"

Terrence crossed his arms, still taking in the damage. "One of my people was here when Callista shut the bar. Said she suddenly got scary as all get-out, shut off the music, and ordered everyone inside to leave. He called me. I called Ximena and Vikki. Then Maria. Nobody could reach you or Mr. Prince there. I guess we see why now."

Suspicion flickered across Ximena's face and hardened as she looked at Troy. "Why didn't you call on us?"

"A djinni called in a debt," I said, striving to keep my voice even. Callista wasn't dead yet, so I'd need to find Duke's items. Something for later. "Given yesterday, I had to assume Callista was having you all Watched."

"Everyone except him?" she said.

Troy cleared his throat, catching me with words on my lips.

"My House and the Darkwatch think the Arbiter is holding me captive," he said, sounding strained at the admission.

Vikki's eyebrows lifted as she connected the dots. "Callista is using Monteague like she tried to use Sergei and Blood Moon?"

The weres' faces closed down as they studied Troy and I with the wary intensity of predators.

I forced myself to meet each of their eyes solidly, in turn. "Yes. Callista is gone, and I'm dealing with the Monteagues. Is that going to be a problem?"

After a taut three heartbeats, Terrence shifted his feet and propped his hands on his hips. "Do the elves want to be part of this alliance or not? It doesn't seem like they're speaking with one voice or that they have the greater good in mind."

I glanced at Troy.

He looked pained. "You're not wrong, about either observation. Sequoyah is mad about Callista pulling most of the House down after Leith's betrayal. They're refusing to work with anyone. Monteague is split. The Lunas will follow Monteague, and the Darkwatch will follow the Conclave. Which largely follows Keithia."

Shit. I wished he'd said something about that sooner and gave him a hard look to let him know. He returned it impassively, although a curl of guilt tickled through the bond.

"Callista was the fulcrum," Troy added. "With her gone and Finch claiming ascendancy, they should fall in line."

"Should," Vikki said softly. "That isn't will. Double when it's elves and elementals."

I massaged my temples, wishing the Goddess-damned power hangover would go away. "One thing at a time. Sequoyah is weakened. Monteague will bide until they decide it's more politically expedient to get with the program or gain enough consensus to go to war. The Lunas won't move on their own."

I glanced at Troy for confirmation, and he nodded.

"With the sorcerer dead and Callista gone, we can move forward with the Reveal," I continued. "That cuts another leg from elven power. If Otherside isn't relying on them to keep us hidden, they'll have to come down off their high horses and deal with the rest of us."

Vikki's eyes glittered, and she smiled savagely. "I like it."

Terrence looked at Ximena, who shrugged. "Okay," the wereleopard said. "Works for us. For now."

I nodded, trying not to slump as relief suffused me. I felt like I'd passed my first big test, and I hadn't had to bully or threaten anyone. Just be smart and make a plan. "Y'all can look around while we wait for everyone else, if it'll make you feel better."

The weres exchanged a look then followed their noses. I avoided Troy's eye, trying to figure out what the hell I was going to say when the rest of the Triangle's Otherside leadership got here.

Chapter 31

In the time it took for the other key players to get to the bar, I found Duke's items in the rubble of Callista's shattered desk: a blue glass bottle with an eight-pointed star etched into the bottom and fixed in silver, a rune-carved bone that carried his Aetheric signature, and a dull iron knife with worn cuneiform on the blade.

I gathered everything up and wrapped it in one of the clean cloths from under the bar before heading to the parking garage under construction around the corner and summoning Duke.

He appeared in his true form of fire and smoke, eyes blazing and lip curled back over sharp teeth. "This had better be good."

Wordlessly, I extended the parcel. He snatched it, growing more solid and assuming his favorite human form as he looked at everything. Avarice and joy transformed his features.

"That's everything I could find with your signature," I said. "If there's more, I will hand it over if and when I find it. Call it a gift."

Suspicion made Duke stand taller. There were no gifts among djinn. "And in exchange for this gift?"

"I ask a warning should any djinn decide to move against me."

"How do I know you haven't found more and are holding something back?"

"The bar is half-destroyed, and Callista is gone," I said. "Artemis took her. I don't need to lie to you. The gods favor me." The hard look I gave Duke made him pause and look at me as though he was seeing me for the first time.

"She's not dead yet. I can still feel the weight of the geasa," he said after a long silence.

I shrugged. "Artemis won't be letting her go voluntarily. You said Callista dead or those of your items I could recover returned, the bottle chief among them. You hold three items, including the bottle. Debt was owed, and debt is paid. Once offered, once taken. And so it is."

Duke studied me, a hint of smoke curling from his shoulders. He wasn't happy, but that was the deal he'd made. "The debt is paid. And so it is."

Relief made me stand taller. "We're moving forward with the Reveal. Are the djinn going to be involved?"

"No. The Council deems we will wait and see what happens."

"Fine. Just make sure you're not a pain in my ass."

With a salute, Duke created a portal and stepped backward into it. "See you around."

Everyone was there when I got back to the bar. Maria had brought Noah. They were looking at everything with more than a hint of hunger, but maybe that was Troy's now-bandaged wound, spotted with drying blood. Allegra had a stoic-looking Troy trapped in a corner, her finger jabbing into his chest as she whispered intently. The three weres were lounging in a booth, drinking beers as they spoke quietly amongst themselves. Janae had brought Hope, and they stood grim-faced near the door. I was surprised to see Laurel and Val in another booth, keeping a wary eye on the Monteagues. I'd texted them but hadn't expected them to turn up.

All conversation stopped as I re-entered the bar. Tension ratcheted up a notch. My shoulders tightened to have so many eyes on me, all with varying degrees of uncertainty, expectation, or wariness.

Taking a deep breath, I closed and locked the door behind me, pulling the curtains before moving to stand in front of the bar. "Thank you all for coming. I'm glad you could make it on such short notice. The djinn will not be joining us, but they won't interfere either."

"What is this about 'Callista is gone'?" Allegra said. "What the hell does 'gone' mean?"

"It means I fulfilled a charge laid upon me by Artemis to return one of her wayward nymphs." I hoped my voice didn't come out as shaky as I felt.

Shocked silence met me, and I pushed on after reading each of their faces. Uncertainty was topmost now.

"The Old Ones are awake and moving between the planes. The Wild Hunt is coming. And I..." I took a deep breath as I prepared to say the words that would either secure my position or make me Otherside's most wanted among more than just the elves. "As it turns out, I'm not a sylph. I'm a full primordial. Today I gained Water. I control all four elements, plus Chaos. That's how I stopped Callista. That's why the bar is trashed."

I'd thought it was silent before, but I'd been wrong. No one so much as breathed now.

"I'm claiming the bar, Callista's rents and incomes, and her positions," I said into the dead quiet. "By right of combat and as reparation for wrongs done to me. However, I dissolve any and all obligations owed to her and to me. If you want to leave the alliance, now's your chance to do it without prejudice. But if you stay..." I fixed all of them with a look I hoped was stern without being overtly threatening. "If you stay, you are in this. Your people are in this. And in return, I will do what it takes to ensure equitable treatment for everyone in Otherside and keep us safe. From the mundanes and from ourselves."

"How the hell do you propose to do that?" Vikki sounded breathier than usual but uncowed.

"A parliament," I said. It was what I had originally proposed, back when Leith's body lay cooling on the floor of his murdered grandmother's house. "When we need to make a decision that impacts all of Otherside, representatives from all of Otherside get a say."

Noah stepped forward and spoke in a low, dangerous voice. "What's to stop us from overthrowing *you*?"

"Noah!" Maria hissed, teeth bared.

He ignored her, crossing his arms and lifting his chin while she seethed.

I slid off my stool and stood with my head bowed, breathing slowly, as I reached for the elements.

Air came immediately. Fire danced after it. The ground shook as Earth allowed me to embrace it, and I couldn't stop a gasp and an unbalanced step as I forced myself into the trust fall that let me grasp Water. With a twist of my mind, I gathered all of them together and formed a small ball that floated in my palm—a planet the size of my fist.

"This," I said.

When I released the elements, the ball collapsed in on itself with enough power to rattle the windows and make those standing reach for something to hold onto.

"I mean no harm." I tried to hide the strain that had put on me and swallowed past renewed nausea, wiping away the trickle of a nosebleed. "But I will take. No. Shit. Are we clear?"

Noah shivered, grimaced, and said nothing. Nor did anyone else.

I took the lack of answer for agreement. "Fan-fucking-tastic. Take the news back to your people and let me know what you want to do by the end of the week. The same terms we agreed to for the original alliance stand. I'm just trying to make sure that everyone continues to have a voice and a seat at the table."

"What about the bar?" Hope sounded unsure. "It's been the heart of the community for decades. Centuries, even."

I looked around at the place. I'd never felt particularly attached to it, but then again, it hadn't been a gathering place for me. It had been the lion's den, a place of evaluation and possible punishment. I was tempted just to burn it down. But Hope was right, and this wasn't just about me. Besides, how would it look for me to claim power and then immediately destroy something that had meaning for the local Othersiders?

"It'll need to be refurbished," I said grudgingly.

Terrence raised a hand and flicked it in a wave. "Some of our folks are in construction."

I pressed my lips together then nodded. "The spells will need to be removed and reset after a thorough sweep."

"I'll do it," Hope said. Janae looked worried at her side but firmed her jaw and sighed when I looked at them.

"And we'll need a bartender," I said.

"Your kobold likes beer," Troy said softly from behind me. "Plus, it would give the fae a place of honor that they haven't really had outside their realm in ages."

I wanted to glare at him, but he was right. I looked at the floor and let the idea ruminate. I could always run Hawkeye on the side, but this might solve my cashflow problem until I could figure out what to do about taking new human cases or charging for Othersiders.

"Okay," I said. Goosebumps rippled over me, and I swallowed as my stomach twisted. "The bar is under new management. Who wants a drink?"

I went behind the bar and ran my hand over the counter. Callista had stood here my entire life, molding and shaping

Otherside as much as she had me. Now, here I was, with the opportunity to lead better. *Be the change.*

Val and Laurel made their way over, looking like they were just trying to make it through the day.

"We'll talk to the collective," Val said. "We're in for ourselves but..." She shrugged.

I nodded and hugged them both before they left.

A rapid-fire conversation in Spanish erupted as Ximena and Terrence rose and approached the bar with their empty bottles. Vikki trailed after them, frowning.

"Okay." Terrence raised his hands to Ximena with a small, cat-like smile before turning to me. His face fell into more respectful lines. "Acacia Thorn and Jade Tooth are in, on the same terms as before. We also want the bid for the construction job on this place."

"Done." I slid the two of them cold bottles. It was nice to have allies I felt pretty secure in trusting.

Vikki edged in on Terrence's other side. "If the terms are the same and we keep the new territory, I see no reason for Blood Moon to back out. Besides, you're less of a bitch than Callista."

"You think." I slid her another beer and grinned at her sudden doubt.

"Roman will want to come back." She watched me warily.

I shrugged to hide the pang in my heart and forced nonchalance into my tone. "He's a grown-ass man. He can do what he wants, so long as y'all abide by your agreements and play nice with others."

"I've been granted emergency powers to make the decision in the best interest of the coven," Janae called, tucking away her cell phone. "The witches will renew the agreement. We don't want to go back to the way things were, and we want the contract to do the ward reset and renewal."

"Glad to hear it," I said.

They waved off my offer of a drink and stayed where they were, chatting silently.

Two factions down, one abstaining, two unknown. I counted the weres, witches, djinn, elementals, fae, elves, and vampires. *Two to go.*

Troy approached from the side and leaned his hip against the bar. He looked a little silly with his shirt half torn off, but it was negated when he put his business face on.

"We can't speak for House Monteague, let alone the rest of the elves," he said in a low voice, glancing at the weres.

I ground my teeth as Terrence and Ximena focused on Troy with predatorial intensity. "Excuse us, please?" I said to them. "I'll make sure anything pertinent gets communicated, but everyone still has the right to share things privately."

When they'd moved back to their booth, Troy said, "Evangeline made the agreement in bad faith. Keithia backs her. I will abide by agreements I made. Allegra will follow me. But that means the House royals are split. Keithia will have the deciding say."

Allegra stepped to Troy's side. "I'll work on Keithia, but I'm not gonna lie. It's going to take some doing. Especially with Evie a lost cause."

I looked up into Troy's sandstone-and-moss eyes, wondering where the hell shit was going with us. "What if I release him to your custody as a sweetener?"

Troy frowned, and Allegra lifted her brows. "Yeah, that might help. Keithia could save some face, and it might defuse whatever countermove she's planning. The Captain was pissed that Troy was sent after you without Darkwatch approval, so that'll give us room to maneuver."

I nodded, hoping that room would extend to the Reveal. "Then you're free to go," I said to Troy. "Thanks. Y'know, for…everything."

"Don't mention it." He gathered up his duffel.

"Wait," Maria said as the elves made their way to the door.

The low conversation in the room lulled then picked up again as I lifted my eyebrows at everyone as a reminder to at least pretend to mind their business. We all had excellent hearing and the room was mostly empty, but it was harder to listen in when you were talking yourself.

"The Raleigh coterie will stay," she said in a low voice when she, Noah, and the elves had gathered at the bar. "But we still have the same problem. Torsten is deteriorating, fast. We'll be lucky if we get through the rest of the month before we have to put him down, but if we do, the Modernists will stage a coup."

I had really been hoping for at least a day or two of rest. So much for that. "Sounds to me like we need to move up the Reveal to throw them a bone before they get impatient. If Torsten is falling apart, we don't have more than a few days, right?"

Maria nodded.

"Plus, Callista is only gone, not dead. We need to do this before she escapes Artemis again and figures out a way to either scuttle it or get me back under her control."

Troy sighed, looking grim. "Not to mention I probably don't have much time left before my grandmother convinces the Conclave to have me arrested. If you want me and Allegra on security, it has to be sooner rather than later."

Maria found the pleasant mask she wore when she was pissed. "Of course. So, what, are you proposing I execute an entire bloody ball in the next twenty-four hours? How the fuck would I do that?"

"My calendar is free." I hated the words leaving my mouth. "I can help with something. If nothing else, we can do a live social media stream."

"Social media," Maria scoffed. "How low-brow."

"It's *democratic*," I said. "It also ensures that your message is the first one on each platform. You control what goes out and what the angle is, rather than allowing a reporter or journalist to translate and misinterpret or twist your words. Because believe me, they will. They can barely coexist with other humans."

Her face twisted like she'd drunk pickle juice. "I see your point, though I'm not keen on it."

"Sleep on it," I said.

"And the ball?"

I rubbed my temples, already tired of this ball. "Find some local influencers."

"Politicians," she said. "Their calendars take weeks to coordinate."

"No. *Influencers*. Big names from social media. Show off vampire glitz and glam, make it look like the ultimate lifestyle. Fly them in from out of state, if you have to. Tell them the event is so exclusive that it could only be shared the day of. You'll have dozens of beautiful people with hundreds of thousands of followers each, all sharing a carefully curated vampire experience."

Maria looked dubious.

I gritted my teeth and schooled myself to patience. "Trust me, it'll go further with the parts of the general public that are more inclined to accept vampirism than some stuffy politicians. You might even get a crop of willing donors out of it. The internet trolls will be out in force either way, so play offense instead of defense. Put your Modernists on finding them. Call it an olive branch to focus them on something other than removing Torsten and then you."

Noah's expression was carefully blank. Troy was looking at me like he'd never seen me before.

"What?" I snapped, crossing my arms with a scowl. "You have a better idea?"

273

"I think the Darkwatch and the queens dramatically underestimated you, your political aptitude, and your level of integration with mundane society," Troy said. From his expression, that might not be a good thing for me.

"Yeah well, y'all wanted an arbiter. That means I'm gonna be one, not some damn puppet waiting for one of you to stick your hand up my ass. I had enough of that from Callista."

"Lucky us," Maria said in a tone that left no doubt that she, at least, saw it as a good thing. Possibly as a sexy thing.

"Is that a yes?" I knew it wasn't wise to push a vampire but was unable to help it.

"Fine. Yes. We'll do it the night after next, although Hekate only knows how the hell I'll get out-of-state guests here in time."

"Thank you, Maria." I grasped her hands and kissed her lightly on the cheek. "I know this is a shitshow, but we'll get it done. All of us, together. For Otherside."

"Oh. Well then." She blushed. "Meet me at The Umstead at noon in two days and don't forget your evening wear." Her mood shifted to something almost celebratory. "Find something nice."

With Maria and the elves flanking me, I waved everyone else in to tell them the new plan for the Reveal.

They looked at me with varying degrees of shock, awe, or green-gilled anxiety as I laid out our next steps as a community. They bitched. They moaned. They argued and cajoled. Magic and tempers flared. But they all agreed. This was the only way forward for Otherside in the Triangle, and we were out of time. Callista might be gone but the gods were waiting behind the Veil, their sights on me and anyone connected to me. There was no more hiding for any of us, not if we wanted to have a chance to establish ourselves as the safe bet before the Wild Hunt.

In the end, that's what it'd come down to for the humans: survival via the lesser evil. Othersiders might prey on humans or rely on them to grow our numbers, but the gods would ravage everything in their Wild Hunt before washing the world clean in a second Great Flood. The humans would die. A few might survive, like the chosen ones in their myths.

And Otherside? We'd be stuck in the middle. Neither fully part of this world nor fully able to exist without it. Apex predators with our down-chain food supply at risk, forced either to prey on each other in the absence of the far more plentiful humans or die out.

As an elemental, I could probably make it regardless. Hell, I could create my own little island paradise after the end of the world, troubled by nothing and nobody, living off coconuts and fish, enjoying the sunshine and unpolluted air. But it wasn't about me anymore. I'd wanted the strength to stand alone and the power to fight off my enemies—but I was learning that there was a price, and that the price was belonging. It was taking action.

It was leadership.

We needed to convince the mundanes that we were not only the lesser evil, but that we could be their partners in surviving the end of the world if we worked together. So I stood shoulder-to-shoulder with two elves and Maria, and I told the alliance that the Reveal was happening in two days whether they liked it or not.

Because hell, if our alliance couldn't make it, I didn't know who would.

Part II

Chapter 32

Two days passed in a whirlwind.

I ended up with what I was pretty sure was a bridesmaid's dress. I'd be underdressed for a vampire gala, but I hadn't had a century or two to grow my wealth. Needing a dress that would leave me free to move in case of emergency had limited my options, and I'd been forced to go for something beaded above the waist and meshy tulle from waist to knee. The only good thing was that it was a rich, forest green that reminded me of the woods. Otherwise, the whole thing had itched when I tried it on, but there was nothing else in my size, budget, and deadline, making me even grumpier than I already was about the whole affair. I glared at the dress bag out of the corner of my eye as I made my way down to Raleigh.

If I was honest with myself, I was also cross about Roman not being there and, just to be contrary, with the fact that he might come back to the Triangle. I may have been reluctant to make our relationship as formal as it became and even more reluctant to let him maintain that connection after he'd broken it, but I'd enjoyed our time together. It would have been nice to go to a fancy party with him on my arm. He cleaned up nice. Going with his sister and the elves didn't have anywhere near the same appeal, even with whatever weird moments Troy and I kept having.

Make the most of this evening. I couldn't afford pettiness or grudges anymore. Every time I tried to charge ahead or go it alone, I ended up regretting it. That didn't mean I needed to wait around for everyone or to be a doormat for whatever the hell came into their heads, but it did mean it was time for me to start learning to be a team player. I couldn't change a system built to exclude me on my own, even if I was somehow nominally in charge.

Allegra seemed cool, and having an elf as a friend could come in handy—if I could convince her that I wasn't trying to get Troy killed. Her good feeling toward me had cooled somewhat as Troy dug in deeper and Keithia lost patience.

Fair, but it still sucked. At least it wasn't about me being an elemental.

I pulled onto SAS Campus Drive and found it lined with news vans. Tonight's event might be even more of a circus than I'd anticipated. I had to show my ID when I turned into the parking lot for the hotel. A hotel staffer checked it against a list before waving me in to a packed lot. I could only imagine what a pain in the ass security was going to be with the hotel's paying guests mixing with whatever influencers the Modernists had managed to rustle up.

Troy and Allegra were waiting outside the hotel with garment bags of their own, somehow managing to look more alike than Troy ever had next to Evangeline. It wasn't just that they were both dressed head-to-toe in black that screamed "security." There was something in their stance and twin expressions of bemusement as they watched the goings-on. That and the inexplicable yet certain sense of readiness oozing from them. Troy also held the duffel bag he'd had before or one exactly like it.

"Where's Vikki, and what the hell is all this?" I shifted the garment bag on my shoulder to wave at the police and idling reporters.

"Your girl Maria's pulled out all the stops." Allegra glanced at me. "I dunno who she glamoured to get them to shut down the street, but this is a legit red-carpet affair now. Vikki is taking wide perimeter." She gestured vaguely toward the trees surrounding the property.

As she spoke, a couple more hotel staffers rolled out the carpet in question, blazoned with the hotel's stylized U logo. Maria followed them out, somehow managing to look glamorous rather than dramatic in flowing linen with a wide sun hat, long gloves, and shades. She grinned when she spotted us, somehow keeping the tips of her fangs covered with her lower lip.

"There you are!" She practically bounced over with far more enthusiasm than I would have expected from a vampire at midday, hours before she exposed her entire species to the humans. Maybe it was my blood in her, giving her extra confidence. The scent of heavy sunscreen wafted from her. "Allegra! I didn't get to tell you the other day, but it's good to see you again, now that you've decided to come home. How's Darius?"

Allegra's brow pinched in a frown, as though she hadn't been aware of the vampires tracking her movements.

Troy huffed a sigh. "Maria. Leave it."

The vampire lowered her sunglasses and winked before spinning back to the hotel. "Come along, ladies and gent. We've only got a few hours."

As we all trailed behind Maria, Allegra leaned close to Troy, who shook his head and squeezed her shoulder at whatever she hissed into his ear.

"Later," he murmured.

I darted around them and trotted to keep up with the shorter woman. "Maria, is this all signed off at the national level at least? Like, am I going to have to fight off others of us on top of watching out for mundanes?"

She flipped her hand. "Of course it's signed off. Nobody's happy about it, but Giuliano and Luz talked their masters around. With the whole East Coast on board, the West Coast followed, then South America. Where the New World goes, the Old is dragged along."

"Why would they help?"

Maria tugged the sunglasses off her face and tucked them into her neckline before giving me a steady look. "Because they're hoping I'll fuck this up."

She was off again before I could comment. The elves and I followed her through the art gallery and into a small conference room that was apparently the base of operations, if the easels holding maps of the event spaces was any indication. "Will this do for you to organize everything?"

Troy and Allegra glanced around, their eyes falling on the same points in different order. One or both of them drew on Aether, and I shivered as it rippled over me.

"Yes," they said together. Before we could say anything else, Troy held a finger to his lips and pulled a wand out of his duffel bag.

"All clear," he said after sweeping every part of the room, twice.

"Is it just us three and Vikki running security?" I asked when he was finished. My stomach knotted as it crashed down how out of my depth I was.

"No," Maria said. "There will be others. Our people. You four are my wild cards."

I crossed my arms and studied the carpet. Something didn't feel right, but I couldn't say what.

Troy turned to Allegra. "Viktoria has perimeter. Two on Maria, one on Noah?"

"Yep." She pursed her lips. "I'll take Noah."

Maria tilted her head. "You're not his type, if that's what you're after."

"He's not mine either, and we're here to work." Allegra nodded to me. "Unless I'm mistaken, Arden doesn't have security training. Troy already knows how she fights. If shit hits the fan, I won't have to worry about protecting Noah and figuring out a new partner."

"Fine. You handle the wards. I'll scout the interior." Troy frowned at the room one last time before turning back to Maria. "This room stays locked at all times. Nobody else comes in for any reason. Got it?"

"Other than the briefing I need to have in here, you mean." Maria tipped her head, looking torn between baiting the elf prince and not being a pain in the ass.

The uneasy feeling grew, but I kept my mouth shut and let Troy handle the security. That's what he was here for, right?

He frowned, eyes scanning the room. "They get searched before they come in."

"Yes, sir." Maria pulled two cards from her pocket, ignoring Troy's glare at her saucy tone. "Two rooms, for changing or in case this turns into an all-nighter. I'll let you three decide who stays where."

Troy glanced at me with an odd expression and took one of the cards. "Let's go."

I took the other card. As Allegra and I moved to follow Troy, Maria caught my arm, letting it go when I turned. "A moment, Arden?"

The elves exchanged a look and left, already discussing the floor plans.

When the door closed, Maria's face became as serious as I'd ever seen it. "Why do I get the feeling you're not quite on board with this?"

I winced, uncrossing and recrossing my arms as I looked at my feet. "I am. We've got to do it. I mean shit, half of it was my idea."

"But?"

"But I never thought I'd see the day when Otherside's power players looked to me to help get us through something this big, and something's off." The words I'd been stewing on since chasing Callista off leapt from my heart and out of my mouth before I could stop them. I flushed and bit my tongue.

"Ah. Yes, I suppose you have had quite the year, poppet." She squeezed my arm, offering sympathetic support and letting me go. "Look at it this way. If it goes badly this evening, you won't have to worry about the gods anymore."

I winced. "I should be so lucky."

"With which outcome?"

"I don't even know. Let's just get through tonight." I checked the number on the back of the fancy little envelope the room card was tucked into. "Can I get the final guest list? I want to do a little snooping of my own." People intelligence would be just as important as the grounds reconnaissance. Callista might be gone, but there were plenty of other folks in Otherside who might want to fuck this up.

"Of course. I'll send Noah with hard copies."

My room was one floor down, a spa-level suite that rivaled the size of some studio apartments. A short foyer opened into a combo bedroom-living room area, complete with a sofa, armchairs, a small table with two more chairs, and a massive bed. I hung my dress in the walk-in closet, wondering what the hell a tourist needed a walk-in closet for. I didn't even have one of those in my house. The bathroom was bigger than mine too, and I shook my head in wonder at the extravagance. The furnished patio looking out over the garden was a nice touch though.

I'd barely gotten my computer set up at the desk when a knock at the door announced Noah.

"The guest list," he said with the distant voice and gaze of a man with a million things on his mind.

"Thanks." I accepted the embossed folder he extended. "Everything going okay?"

"It will be. It has to be."

With that less-than-comforting comment, he strode off. Noah might have played Modernist to get Maria the intel she'd needed, but he didn't seem to share their excitement. Why would he volunteer to be front and center? I didn't need to know everyone's reasons for being involved, but it helped when I did. Or maybe I was just nosy. Either way, I had a list of names to review and no time to devote to vampire moods.

I set up my computer and started digging. It wasn't long before I came across a name I thought I recognized: Dominique Bordeaux. A Google search turned up nothing useful. Not good. Not good at all.

Another knock interrupted.

"What?" I hollered in the general direction of the door.

"It's me, Finch."

Before I could get up, he knocked again.

"Goddess burn that man," I muttered, jotting a quick note before trotting to the door. When I opened it, I repeated, "*What?*"

Allegra peeked from behind Troy and grinned. "Hey, Arden. Got a minute?"

I started to tell them that no, I didn't, because I was certain the name I was checking was an Othersider. Then I remembered that both elves were Darkwatch. The elven security branch had connections of their own. Maybe they'd know. I left the door open as I stalked back to the desk, trusting that they'd make themselves at home.

Allegra did, dropping onto the sofa and leaning forward to rest her arms on her knees, apparently content to let Troy take lead. The prince stood in front of my desk like a kid waiting for the teacher's attention.

"Whatever it is, spit it out." I spared half my attention for whatever he was going to say and typed in another search that I hoped would lead me to why this one guest seemed so friggin' familiar.

"There's a fae here," Troy said. "Of sorts."

"Not some basic bitch either," Allegra chipped in. "We would have missed her, but I've just come off a case that required—well, I know what I sensed."

I looked up and gave each of them a measure of my "I don't have time for this" face. "And?"

"It's a succubus."

I tensed, suddenly reminded of why that name had stood out to me. "A succubus. You're sure?" Succubae and incubi were rare, more demon than fae. There was only one on the Eastern seaboard, as far as I knew.

"Like I said, I know what I sensed." Allegra scrubbed her hands over her face, then looked more closely at me. "You look like that means something."

"I recognized a name on the guest list but couldn't remember how I knew her or knew of her. Given what you've just said, I think I know who she is. I'm almost certain she's a Watcher."

Chapter 33

Maria, dressed in an impossibly white one-shouldered dress with a diamond rabbit brooch pinned to it, was giving terse orders to a few of her people when we were admitted to the room. "Our Master will be fine. We *will* get through this. When we do, our coterie will be a shining example to all of Otherside. We will have honor. We will have prestige. And we will be fed as humans line up to realize all of their darkest, most sensual dreams. Know it. Believe it. Live it."

She nodded to acknowledge us as I shut the door, then returned her attention to the vampires packed into the small space and paused to meet the eye of everyone in the room.

"Mingle. No glamour, not even when we're Revealed, unless it is to save a life or protect the coterie. No feeding except on existing pets and partners in a private room. Nothing sordid. I'm counting on all of you in particular to sell our lifestyle as something for the best and most worthy of humanity to aspire to. Now go."

"Yes, Mistress," a dozen vampires said in unison. They gave us curious glances as they filed out. I didn't recognize any of them from my past visits to Claret.

"Modernists," Maria said softly in response to my lifted eyebrows when the door closed again behind them. "A handful willing to call me mistress in exchange for positions of influence after the Reveal."

"Divide and conquer," Troy said. "I like it."

"You would." She frowned.

I gritted my teeth. "There's another Watcher here. A succubus."

She hissed, showing fang, and her pupils dilated fully. "Who?"

"Dominique Bordeaux is the name she's using today. Any idea how she would have gotten on the list?"

"One of the children, I'm sure." Maria's face darkened. "Not all of the Modernists were willing to follow me. Some wanted simply to mass together and get rid of Torsten as a group. That is *not* how we do things. It would be anarchy. They don't understand what—Never mind. It doesn't matter."

Troy crossed his arms. "You're telling me that not only is Torsten a rakshasa, but you also don't have full control of the coterie?"

"Yes. I am," Maria snapped. "Any other bright questions?"

"What would be the worst thing to happen tonight?" he asked. When Maria narrowed her eyes at him, Troy added, "That will be why Callista arranged for a Watcher to be here. It's a test. She sent someone Finch would spot. She wanted us to know that whatever happens, it's her doing."

Maria's coffee-brown irises bled back as she focused on strategy rather than reaction. "I see. In that case, that someone dies. Publicly and violently. That our carefully constructed story of civility is shattered as or soon after we spin it, and we're painted to look like animals."

My stomach clenched. "She's going after Torsten. Or maybe Noah."

Troy's face blanked as he considered that. "Finch is right. It's what I'd do. Torsten is unstable, Maria's power base is weak and insecure, and there's a splinter group already coordinating with Callista. With her gone, there's nobody holding the reins. Take out Torsten with public violence, and the coterie might shatter. Take out Noah, and Maria will fall soon after, regardless of how much power she gained from you, Finch."

Maria glared but didn't disagree. Troy nodded as though that was all the confirmation he needed.

Something about that didn't fit for me though. "Why would Callista have done that, only for the Reveal to end in bloodshed and the deaths of everyone she would have drawn power from? You two are thinking maximum damage. There's another side to it."

"And what's that, sugarplum?" Despite the nickname, Maria's voice was as hard as her expression.

"If she removed Torsten or you, Maria, she could've stepped in as a savior to the rest of the coterie," I pointed out. "You're more valuable, being both sane and better adapted to the modern world, so my bet is Torsten. With the Modernists half hers already, you'd have to fall in line."

"What would that have gained her?" Troy asked, sounding doubtful. "What would it gain Bordeaux, now that Callista is gone? There has to be a reason she still came."

"Leverage," I said, a sour taste growing on the back of my tongue. "Y'all are forgetting that it's not just us in play anymore. The gods are back as well. For Dominique, there might be an oath involved. I mean, Callista used geasa on the djinn. Until she's dead, all oaths, geasa, and vows are still in force. Duke said as much the other day."

"Burning hell," Maria spat. "The Hunt. Of course." She pressed her hands to the table and leaned into them. "Of all the worst possible times."

"Does that change anything in the plan?" I asked.

Looking to the floor, Troy shook his head. "I don't know yet. We have to write Torsten off as a loss either way, so shoring up Maria and Noah are probably still our best plays. Maria, can Torsten be put under lockdown?"

"No," she said. "He's permitted me to stand as spokesperson, but he'll want to see this through and claim the credit." Old bitterness dripped from her words.

"Of course." Troy frowned as he thought. "Fine. You or Noah stick to Torsten all night. He doesn't go anywhere without one or both of you. That lets Alli, Finch, and me stay close to the three of you while Viktoria holds the perimeter. We'll prioritize you and Noah if this goes sideways."

"If that's our best option, then that's what we'll do." Maria shook her head. "Let's go. I want Bordeaux found before the announcement."

"One thing I don't get. Why would Callista have assigned someone you were bound to recognize?" Troy asked me. "We need to know what she's likely to try."

I was glad the bond was muted. The intensity in his face would be overwhelming if it was also in my head. Looking away, I tapped my fingers on the conference room's oval-shaped table and thought back to the conversation I'd been caught overhearing as a teenager. Now that I had a few more pieces of the puzzle, some details came back. "Dominique is…from what I remember, she's an interrogator and sometime assassin. The original femme fatale."

"Of course she is," Allegra grumbled. "Anything else?"

I shrugged. "I was like, fifteen, when I last heard anything about her. Callista beat the shit outta me for eavesdropping. I kind of blanked out anything else."

Allegra looked troubled.

Troy's expression was unreadable as he said, "So we assume her primary objective is information, secondary is a target."

"Probably," I agreed.

The elves exchanged a look. Maria just sighed and pinched the bridge of her nose.

"I was Callista's *ward*, not her confidante," I said. Something in their expressions made me feel defensive and snappish. Or maybe it was just their presence or the weird feeling in my gut that wouldn't go away. "Most of what I learned from her was to stay the fuck away from elves, for all the good *that* did me."

Troy winced. "What does this Dominique look like?"

I tensed all over again. "I don't know. Like I said, I was a teenager and listening where I'd been told not to." My voice caught as I shared the only thing I did recall. "All I know is that the voice was feminine and smoky. Sexy. She sounds exactly like this." I said the last few words in the voice I remembered.

Maria straightened and looked at me like I'd done something threatening.

I shrugged. "What? I was a sylph before all the primordial shit. Vocal mimicry is a passive power."

"Smoky voice," Allegra said, eyebrows lifting. "Anything else, any other sensory details?"

I tried to think back to the air patterns. That was easier for me than physical senses, sometimes. It helped trigger sensory inputs.

"Jasmine," I said. "I smelled jasmine coming from the room. More like the flower itself and not so much the synthetic perfumey kind. You know what I mean?"

The elves nodded, their focus going distant.

"There was a trace of jasmine on the walking path around the lake," Troy said. "Viktoria called it in when she didn't see any growing, and I scented it as well. Faint and fading fast. I didn't see any either and assumed it was a guest's perfume."

Allegra wrinkled her nose as she refocused on the room. "Hard to tell indoors. They have some kind of artificial fresh scent being piped in, something meant to soothe and dull the senses. I'd have to be close to pick her out."

We hashed over a plan for the next hour. Or more accurately, Troy and Allegra argued over how to identify a succubus in a crowd of vamps and human social media influencers, and I did my best to ignore them as I scanned the guest list for more surprises and grilled Maria about anyone who seemed off. They agreed on a few other points but hadn't settled on anything related to Dominique by the time we needed to change for the ball, and I hadn't uncovered anything else of interest. They were still bickering, like siblings, as they left to get dressed.

I headed back to my own room, annoyed at their back-and-forth yet, deep down, jealous that they had each other. I had built this damn alliance out of an aching need to have people of my own to rely on and hell, be friends with. But even if I could call Maria, Val, Janae, and Zanna my friends, sometimes it was hard to fight the feeling that everyone else had someone else first. I was always the third wheel at best.

My chest tightened. I was half djinn, half elf. Only the djinn knew that, and they'd never acted like I was really one of them. The elves had condemned me out of hand, to start. Allegra's acceptance was an outlier. Roman had accepted me, but he was gone. For all my efforts, I still didn't quite fit anywhere.

Be depressed later. Focus on the job now. None of my personal issues would matter if tonight went badly or if Dominique was here to do anything more than report back to Callista. I kept reminding myself of that as I changed into my bridesmaid's dress and did my makeup, but that just meant my thoughts snarled on worries about what Artemis was doing with Callista and whether the nymph would be back.

I sighed as I twisted my hair in rows from the front of my head to the crown, pinning each one in place and letting the rest fall in tight, natural curls. My plate was going to get a lot fuller before I could clear it and sooner or later, some of this work needed to generate more income than Troy's pocket change. Taking over the bar wouldn't pay out for a while, not with the refits it needed.

With a last check in the mirror, I forced my face into a smooth mask of unconcern.

"We've got this," I told my reflection.

Weapons were trickier. Hiding my all my knives and my Ruger LCP wasn't quite possible—not for all of them anyway. The enchanted fae-made knife wouldn't do much good against vampires or a succubus, but it would put a human down quietly if it came to it. I wasn't naive enough to think that the vampires or Dominique were the only Othersiders that might make trouble. Keithia and Evangeline would still be gunning for me until they had no other choice. Probably why Troy was acting so weird. He was likely waiting for his loyalties to be tested again.

I settled on my slim silver stiletto dagger, tucking it into my clutch purse. It wouldn't do much, but it was better than relying on my powers alone. I was oddly reluctant to leave the godblade behind, so that went in a thigh sheathe under the dress.

Bang. Ready for the world to change.

Chapter 34

My heart raced as I left my suite, mentally running over everything I did and didn't know about the evening's events and its guests. Troy and Allegra were waiting by the elevators, alone in the hallway next to a classy vase.

"I wish I'd thought of that," I said when I saw Allegra's suit, tailored to look feminine but allow her freedom of movement and, presumably, more options for hiding a weapon. Her locs were up in a bun, and she looked confident and ready. Troy looked like a James Bond stand-in, tall and lean in a classic tux.

"Come on, you look lovely!" Allegra replied, elbowing Troy. "Doesn't she?"

"Sure," he said with an uncomfortable shift and a cursory flick of his eyes. "Can we go up now? I don't want to leave Torsten alone for too long."

I pressed my lips together and pushed the button to call the elevator, resolving not to care about his response. *We're allies, not friends—or anything else.* Roman would have told me I looked nice. But that didn't matter because Roman had said he loved me and then left.

"You are the *worst* date," Allegra hissed behind me.

"We're not dating," Troy muttered back. "I don't—"

"Stop it, T. We can't stick out as security. If you can't sell this, go home and let us girls do our job."

The elevator doors slid open, and I stepped in, crossing my arms and keeping my face neutral as I waited for them to join me.

Troy's jaw tightened then relaxed as he ended the staring contest with Allegra. His face transformed into a pleasant expression so fast that I blinked.

"Better," Allegra said as they stepped in after me.

We rode up in silence. Fortunately, it was just a floor, and we were out before it got awkward.

"Here we go," I murmured as the doors slid open. My heart skipped at the pulsing air patterns. Seeing the guest list was one thing. Feeling the presence of dozens of humans, knowing we were about to lift a veil several millennia old, was another. *Where did Maria find this many influencers so quickly?*

Allegra stepped out first.

"Noah said he'd be on the patio. See you on the other side," she said before easing through the crowd.

Troy offered his arm. After a heartbeat of hesitation, I took it. He wasn't the only one who had to sell this. Going in as each other's dates was completely different than going into battle together. It was awkward as hell. We slapped on matching vacant smiles and made our way to the ballroom.

Sound and airwaves assaulted me as we drew close, and I gripped Troy's arm tighter for a moment. I might be comfortable around humans, but I didn't usually have to worry about managing around them as the new leader of the Triangle's Otherside community while on the arm of an elf and with a coterie of vampires in the same space.

It wasn't just the noise and the air movements. It was the magnitude of what was going to happen. I had to be more human than ever when I'd never felt less so, while part of Otherside revealed itself in a room that could explode at the slightest misstep—and likely would, if that's what Dominique wanted to happen.

That's why you have allies, I reminded myself. Of course, if someone had ever told me I'd be escorted to a vampire ball by Troy Monteague, prince of a high elven House and all-around tightass, I'd have laughed myself silly.

"Monteague, what is going on with us?" Tension tightened my words. This was not the time, but if I was going to be relying on him this closely for this big of an evening, I had to know.

"Who says there's anything going on?" His words were delivered with a fresh grin that had to be an act, given the sudden tension in his arm. He looked as though I'd made an amusing complaint about my outfit, especially when his eyes darted down to my neckline.

I forced a smile of my own as I backed him out of the line queuing to pass the guard ropes and into a doorway. He stiffened as I tilted my head and brushed by his mouth to whisper in his ear. "Don't fuck with me. People have been making insinuations for weeks. Something shifted the other day. I know it did because now you're acting weird instead of just grumpy. I need to know what's going on. I cannot afford to fuck this night up because I'm distracted with wondering what the hell is going on in your head."

Hands roughened with swordsman's calluses enfolded my jaw when I pulled back, and I froze.

Lips pressed to mine, soft at first, then more demanding when I didn't push away. Shock switched my brain off, and my hands tightened on the front of his tux. Goosebumps raced down my arms, and for once, I was glad my back was to the room.

"That's what," he said.

The pain behind his sandstone-and-moss eyes didn't match the passion that had been in his kiss.

Head spinning, I took his proffered arm automatically, wondering what the fuck had just happened. My brain was as useful as scrambled eggs, and I blinked as I tried to recover my thoughts.

"Was that fucking necessary?" I hissed, my face on fire, not sure whether I was more upset that he'd broken his promise on boundaries or that I thought I might have liked it.

No. You're just missing Roman. That's all this is. That…and an elf just kissed you instead of killing you. I shivered.

Troy leaned in close to murmur against my ear. "Given that aggressive little push, in this venue, for this event? It was either a fight or a kiss, and if it was a kiss, you needed to look *exactly* the way you did when you turned back around." When I took a breath to tell him off, he added, "I'm sorry, and it won't happen again."

I looked anywhere but at him, and flushed deeper when I caught Allegra's astonished expression as we approached where she waited at the guard rope with Noah and Maria.

"Everything okay?" Allegra asked when we made our way to the front and were close enough to speak quietly. A note of shock pitched her voice higher than usual, and I flushed all over again.

"Peachy," I said, my voice rougher than I meant it to be. "Noah, good to see you again."

"And you, Ms. Finch." He leaned in for a quick cheek kiss. "I wanted to thank you personally for your gift to Maria the other night and for securing me such admirable protection."

Noah rested a gentle hand on Allegra's shoulder for a moment. "I wasn't sure about you, but let's just say I heartily wish you success now."

I inclined my head. "Of course."

"Excellent," Maria said. "Shall we? Torsten is inside."

She gave Troy an unblinking look that might have been a warning then turned and made her way into the ballroom without waiting for an answer. I nodded farewell to Allegra and Noah and let Troy lead me in her wake.

I would have expected the kiss to make things more awkward, but it seemed to have broken some of the tension that had been flowing between Troy and me. I knew what his problem was, and now we could both relax into our roles. We hovered close enough to Maria and Torsten that we could act if needed, casually circling them, staying in their orbit while trying to look like we were doing nothing of the sort.

The humans were having the time of their life, all wide smiles and selfie sticks, posing in groups and in pairs and alone with champagne and caviar against the backdrop of the room's art and the outdoor terrace.

I elbowed Troy. "We should take a selfie."

He glanced around the room and, for once, didn't argue. We turned to keep Maria and Torsten in view as he snapped a few photos on his phone before tucking it back into his pocket.

An enthusiastic male voice with a California Bay Area accent pulled my attention. "Hey, I'm Blake. I don't think I recognize you guys. New to the scene?"

I smiled and pulled out my human act. "Hey! No, we're actually locals."

"Cool, cool. I guess that means you guys know the hostess then?"

"Oh, yeah. My boyfriend's family goes way back with hers, right, hun?" I leaned into Troy's arm and willed him to play along.

He wrapped the arm around my shoulder, reminding me so much of nights in with Roman that I ached.

"Business relationships." Troy flashed a winning smile as natural as any politician's.

"Lucrative." Blake returned the smile with perfect, too-white teeth as he offered his card and told us how many followers he had, in case we wanted to do some influencer marketing on the West Coast. Then he flitted off, one butterfly in a room full of them.

"This is going to be a long night," I muttered.

With a snorted laugh that seemed to surprise even him, Troy slid his hand to the small of my back and steered me toward Maria and Torsten. They'd drifted closer to the massive projector screen at the front of the room. I let him do it, reminding myself that we were playing a role and doing my best to suppress the shiver it drew. The longer we were in such close proximity, the easier it was to play the part, and I bit my tongue before I could ask if he was using Aether on me somehow. He only smelled of rosemary, sage, and man; there wasn't a hint of the toasted meringue scent that would suggest he was using magic.

Maybe it's a passive ability. Goddess knew I had several of those. Maybe the elves did as well. There had to be a reason why their roles in hiding Otherside from the mundanes always involved persuasion. I resolved to keep my wits about me.

A hint of jasmine cut through as I took one last sniff for Aether.

Troy leaned in close. "What's wrong? You locked up."

"Jasmine," I whispered, gaze skipping over the crowd. Useless, given that I didn't know who I was looking for. I strained my ears, trying to hear the voice I'd mimicked earlier. I knew Troy had scented it when his hand tightened at my waist.

"Good nose." He pulled out his phone and swiped out a text message. "Telling Alli and Viktoria to keep their eyes peeled."

"Great. I'll warn Maria if you grab us drinks—nonalcoholic for me, please." That should get him away from me long enough to get my head on straight. Passive magic or not, it was starting to bug me how comfortable I suddenly was with him.

Troy melted into the crowd, and I eased closer to Maria, smiling as though I hadn't seen her in ages as she spotted me.

"Hi, darling!" I said in the big, fake tones that everyone in the room seemed to be using. When she leaned in for a hug, I whispered, "Dominique is here. We need to get this show on the road."

"I thought I scented jasmine." Maria leaned back, and we made bullshit small talk until Troy came back with two glasses of what I hoped was just sparkling water.

"All they had was lemon." He wrinkled his nose as he passed me the glass.

I arched an eyebrow. "The best kind."

"If you like the scent of—never mind. Cheers." We clinked glasses, all of us pretending we weren't keeping an eye on Torsten and everyone he was speaking to. The master vampire seemed more put together than he had the last time I'd seen him. I wondered if it would be rude to ask how much of that was due to my blood and how much was due to someone else's.

"He seems all right," I said instead.

"For now." Maria reached for Troy's wrist and checked his fancy watch. Troy allowed it, sipping his water to cover a grimace as Maria said, "We have an hour before the announcement."

I glanced outside. "Before sunset?"

"Exactly. Let them get used to the idea while we're all in the light together."

An hour to find and stop a succubus that none of us knows by sight before she can make a move. Then the whole world changes.

Chapter 35

The hour passed in a strange combination of dread and boredom. Troy and I got better at our couple act, managing to avoid selfies with the influencers while playing off each other to gather information and search for the succubus. If anyone noticed that we also followed Maria and Torsten around the room, they didn't comment. Most of them were probably too busy getting drunk on free champagne and fancy cocktails or doing the latest TikTok challenge whenever the DJ played the right song.

Dominique hadn't struck—as far as we could tell—by the time Maria stood at the front of the room, tapping delicately on her microphone with a demure smile.

"Good evening, folks." She leaned on just enough glamour to send a ripple through the crowd and draw their attention. Phones popped up, hovering above the heads of those in front of them, recording everything.

"Here we go," I breathed. Troy and I had found places on the side closer to the door out to the rest of the hotel, keeping an eye on Torsten. Noah and Allegra were near the door leading to the patio in case she needed to whisk him away. Easier for an elf to hide herself and her charge on the twilit grounds than in a crowded hotel, especially one of the Darkwatch.

"You must all be wondering what the big secret is, the reason for this grand event." Maria leaned forward with a conspiratorial eye. One of the Modernists was in the front row, recording it all on her phone for display on the big projector screen, and Maria looked straight into it as she continued. "I imagine this will be a difficult thing for you to take in. Many of you won't believe that it's real. But I stand before you to share a truth long held secret."

She paused and let the room settle into dead silence.

I tensed, heart hammering, searching faces.

"Humans have imagined vampires for centuries. Yes, that's what I said: vampires." Another long pause, as the humans frowned and exchanged glances, snickered behind their hands, or rolled their eyes. I played along, looking at Troy. He glanced at me then returned his attention to the room.

Maria spread her arms wide and smiled to show fangs longer than I remembered them being when she'd sunk them into my arm. "Well. Here we are. Alive—or rather, undead—and in the flesh."

Shocked silence fell over the room before a nervous laugh broke out.

"Come on, lady," a tall, gym-muscled man with an orange-looking fake tan said. "You can get fake teeth like that online. What's the real announcement?"

With impossibly slow, clockwork-jerky steps, Maria walked toward him. The crowd parted, tension rising as she stopped pretending to be human. The Modernist with the phone followed her, shifting to keep them both in frame as Maria stopped in front of the man who'd spoken.

She tilted her head and ran a finger down his chest. He shuddered, inhaled, and jumped back, wide-eyed.

"That is the real announcement," Maria said. "Vampires exist and have done for centuries. We are not the animalistic villains of Stoker's imagining. In this modern age, we can no longer hide from humanity, nor do we wish to. We want to join you. We're people too, after all."

"But it's daytime!" someone called out.

I scanned the crowd, trying to gauge the mood. It didn't feel like glamour was in play, but the older ones could be quite subtle with it. For all I knew, the relative lack of response was down to having a roomful of vamps, all exuding a subtle pressure rather than an overt charm. I swallowed, hard, waiting for this to go sideways.

Maria turned, which put her face in full sun. "So it is," she agreed. "There are so many hurtful rumors about my people. I hope that all of you might help us dispel some of those here, tonight."

Muttering rose in the room, a confused undercurrent. Some people sounded pissed off, like this was a big hoax wasting their time. Others had an expression like the Rapture was here and they'd been chosen.

I shifted. The crowd was turning, and we still didn't know whether it would turn our way, let alone when or how Dominique would play her hand to tip it. I scanned the crowd and read the air molecules as they were agitated by fidgeting, shifting humans. My heart hammered, and it was all I could do to lock down my shields and control Air, to not allow a nervous gust to whistle through the room or the seepage of my power signature. A hint of burnt marshmallow flared and was smothered. I wasn't the only one on edge.

Maria turned back to the Modernist with the phone.

"Bear witness," she said to the camera.

As we all watched, she shed her personal glamour. Her cheeks grew gaunt, her skin sallow. Her fangs stood out sharply against thinned lips. The faint beginnings of a power signature ebbed out, a slower, softer echo of Torsten's.

Then, as smoothly as she'd revealed herself, she reverted her appearance to what it had been when she started, before pushing past it to an impossible, angelic perfection. Those near enough to see it gasped and edged away, pushing against people in the back trying to get a better view.

I winced, hoping we weren't about to have a mosh pit.

Ignoring them, Maria said, "We are cousins to humanity, the victims of a virus that separate us from you even as we rely upon you. We know that we may be hunted now, by those who fear what they don't understand. All I can say is: think of the knowledge that would be lost from decades or centuries past. Think of all that you could learn and all that we could become—together. Think of being chosen to live forever."

Glamour rippled as she reverted her appearance to what I'd come to think of as her normal face. She clasped her hands at her waist.

"Thank you for your time and attention. We know that this is a great deal to take in, so a number of our coterie are available for questions and perhaps, for a lucky, consenting few, demonstrations. Follow the white rabbit." She winked and tapped her brooch.

The low arguments in the room erupted at the suggestion that vampirism could be demonstrated. People looked around, spotting rabbit brooches, jewelry, and prints on others in the crowd. Small pockets opened up around those individuals, all of whom smiled to show sharp fangs. As far as I could tell, it was only Maria and a few of the Modernists wearing white rabbits. If something happened, most of what remained of the coterie after the recent house-cleaning could bounce back or relocate.

Tension ratcheted up. Voices rose along with it, confused, angry, maybe a few awed. I couldn't tell whether people believed us or whether there had been so much "fake news" fed to the mundane populace that this was just another conspiracy video in the making. As a community, we'd been so certain for so long that the existence of Othersiders would be earth-shattering. It was what the Détente and half the side-agreements between factions had been based on: the humans couldn't know about us.

We hadn't counted on the Reveal being just one more weird hoax.

Sweat made my dress stick to me as I tried to recalibrate my mind. Our existence was so real to us that we'd never considered that we might be fake news, that our lived experience and concerns might just be brushed aside. At my side, Troy looked equal parts sick and confused. We'd pushed forward with this grand plan to force Otherside out into the open. Risked our lives to get ahead of Callista. To get rid of her, even. Yet all the mundanes I could overhear were talking about deepfakes and special effects and spiked drinks.

We—Otherside as a whole—had thought that we knew humans from living alongside them in secret for thousands upon thousands of years. Yet we'd miscalculated the effects of the modern era. Badly. They might believe us. But they might also shrug off our controlled Reveal until a bloody accident forced us to the front page in the worst light and brought out the pitchforks.

Either way, we had maybe a few minutes before they processed what they'd just heard and fight-or-flight responses kicked in as they either fought each other over belief or pushed the vampires for more proof.

Given the angry faces and fisted hands, I didn't like the way it was going. Blood in the room, on top of this much emotional tension, could push a younger vamp to bite. "Monteague—"

"Where's Torsten?" he asked.

Shit. He'd been at the front of the room, next to where Maria had started out—until he wasn't.

"I don't know," I admitted, fighting a rising panic as I searched the room. "We can't leave Maria."

"Agreed," Troy said tersely. He leaned in, keeping his attention on the shifting, uncertain mass of humans. "One way or another, this is going to end badly. For me to have missed him leaving means either glamour or fae illusions. Are you up for this?"

"I'm gonna have to be," I snapped. We couldn't afford for the first stage of the Reveal to end badly and convince the humans it was real in the worst way. "Stay with Maria. I'll see if I can track down Torsten."

"How?"

"I'm a PI, remember? I find people for a living."

"Finch—"

"Just give Vikki a heads-up and protect Maria, okay?"

Troy scowled, tracking a shaken-looking man in the hotel's uniform as he made his way through the crowd, heading for Maria. "Damn it. Go."

I drifted over to where we'd last seen Torsten. A handful of people whispered to each other, eyes a little too wide and reeking of fear.

"Hey," I said.

They all jumped or flinched.

I made my expression match theirs. "I'm trying to find someone. Did you see a shorter guy, kind of thin, long dark hair in a braid? He had, like, a gold necklace thing."

"The creeper," one of the women said, shuddering. "What? You can't tell me he didn't weird you out." She lowered her voice. "Ohmigod, do you think he was a *vampire*?"

"Do you seriously believe that shit?" one of the guys asked. "This whole thing has Fyre Fest written all over it. It's a hoax. Fake news. Publicity stunt. Probably for all-night energy drinks or something."

"Sorry, y'all, I'm just trying to find my friends," I said before they could return to their argument over the veracity of vampires. "I think they might have gone with—uh, the creeper. Can you help me?"

"Creepy McCreeperson went that way," the other woman said. She looked like she was taking the revelation that vampires were A Thing a little better than the others or like maybe she hadn't believed it. "Maybe the bathroom? The guy he was with had mentioned needing to pee right before the 'announcement.'"

I gave her a shaky smile. "Thank you so much! I'll check there."

Maria's morphing face was on all of the TV screens in the bar when I passed it. The patrons watched with stark disbelief, their drinks forgotten as the ticker rolled across the screen: VAMPIRES IN RALEIGH—ELABORATE INFLUENCER HOAX? NEWS AT 9.

I hurried past, trying to read the air currents as I went. As I neared the men's room, I scented an undercurrent of iron and ash, chased by jasmine. After a quick glance to make sure I was alone, I slipped in. Another scent slapped me. Blood—rich, coppery, and fresh.

"Shit," I whispered, locking the door before edging along the wall and peering around the corner.

A limp hand curled from under a bathroom stall. I hesitated long enough to read the air currents. They were far too still for anything living. There wasn't so much as a breath to stir them.

"Double shit." I darted to the stall, pushing it open to confirm what I'd already known I'd find: a dead human, with two sloppy, torn punctures alongside his carotid. Blood pooled under his head. The kill was a mess but clearly vampire, if one pushed to savagery. It would offer the proof people were looking for in the way I feared most.

Hoping against hope, I pressed two fingers to the clean side of this neck. No pulse and cooling. Rocking back on my heels, I inhaled deeply, trying to get a sense for which vamp might be responsible. My nose wasn't that good though.

It had to be Torsten. I just couldn't prove it.

Cleaning this up had to take priority over finding the master vampire for now, but what the hell was I supposed to do? My heart thudded, and my mind raced over the options. Everyone had called Callista for cleanup for decades. It was on me now.

The scent of jasmine said that the succubus was involved somehow. This was probably her doing, so the kill was meant to be found. The bathroom door couldn't stay locked forever. Mundanes always had to piss, especially when the booze was flowing. News of the Reveal would only keep them at their screens or in their rooms for so long.

We had to get this human out and hidden before he was noticed. Come up with a cover story. Erase any video footage of Torsten entering or leaving the bathroom, if it'd been him. Find and glamour or mindmaze any human witnesses. The to-do list lengthened in my mind, and I embraced Air to capture the faint gusts whirling in from the air conditioning vent. The comforting familiarity of my power helped me get a grip.

"Focus. You can do this. You fucking have to," I whispered to myself as I pulled out my phone.

The first text went to Maria. The second to Troy and Allegra. The third to Vikki. In the time it took me to wrap my fingers in toilet paper and dig out the victim's wallet, there was a rattle as someone tried to open the door, then a knock.

"Arden?" Noah called.

I dropped the wallet and darted to the door, unlocking it and opening it a crack before swinging it wide to admit him and Troy.

"Was it Torsten?" I asked as I locked it again behind them.

Noah's nostrils flared. "Yes. No other *moroi* scent here." His eyes darted to the corpse, and he stiffened. "Damn it. I'd hoped we had more time." Kneeling by the body, he tilted the man's head, grimacing at the puncture marks. "There's no denying this was a vampire." He dragged a finger across the wounds and licked the blood from it. "Definitely Torsten."

"Can you, I dunno, heal it? Conceal the marks somehow and make it look like something else?" I asked. We were running out of time. Someone was bound to notice one of us missing, especially if Dead Dude had come with friends.

"Maybe if he was alive. Bites only heal over in living humans." Noah frowned, glancing at Troy. "You any good with healing?"

Troy shook his head. "That's more of a Sequoyah thing. Allegra and I could maze any witnesses, but we can't do much for the body. We could cut the marks out, but we'd still need to get the body out and hide it."

"You couldn't use your special trick?" He'd made himself invisible at Claret and Callista's. Why not here?

"Not for long enough to get a body out of a venue this size packed with this many people," Troy said with a pained look. "And before you ask, it takes more power to cover a shock the size of, say, the sight of a man carrying a corpse out. I can handle the security systems and maze witnesses, or I can drain myself trying to carry him out. Not both."

An idea struck.

Chapter 36

"We don't need to hide the body. If we call it in, it'll go to the Raleigh morgue. I'll contact Doc Mike, tell him what to expect."

Noah frowned. "Will he be up for this? He didn't seem comfortable with Otherside when we were there last."

"He'd just learned vampires were a thing after being attacked by a vampiric sorcerer, and then had you heal him," I snapped. "Of course he wasn't okay. But he held it together when we went after the lich, and he wants to help. Giving him this shows him we trust him. He's already dealt with vampire cases before. He'll know what to put in the report and what not to." I caught Troy's eye. "I know the elves have EMTs and at least one CSI on the payroll. Call them in. Now, before Keithia gets wind of this and finds a way to twist it."

He started to answer then caught himself, his expression shifting oddly. "Of course. But Finch, if we do it this way, there will have to be a police investigation. A mundane one."

"Then let them investigate," I said, despite the fact that this would turn everything about how Otherside operated on its head.

New day, new process, right fucking now.

"The body wasn't drained. There's enough blood on the floor that he could have died here, even if some of it is probably in Torsten." I frowned, realizing that meant he must have been pulled away. The succubus? Something to deal with later. "How better to convince the humans that this wasn't vampiric? You and Allegra can fuddle the witnesses enough that there's nothing reliable. We have elves in critical placements and a medical examiner who's a latent necromancer. Whatever the hell Keithia's problem is, y'all have to see that this is not the time for it. Are you trying to tell me we can't handle this?"

After a long pause of consideration, Troy said, "We can."

"Okay then. Let's do it."

The easiest way to hide the puncture wounds was to stick a knife through them. I hated giving up my new silver one, but I was the only one carrying.

"I think I'm disappointed in you," I said to Troy as Noah lined up the knife and stabbed then wiggled the blade around to tear up the imprint of teeth. "No weapons? Nothing?"

"I think I'm disappointed that you think I need a weapon," Troy countered.

There wasn't much to say to that.

"The mundanes will be looking for Torsten," I said instead, trying to cover all the loose ends while we waited. "There were at least four witnesses who saw the vic leave the ballroom with him."

"We can maze them," Troy replied.

"Them, yeah. But everyone they might have passed? All the video surveillance?"

"We've managed up to now. We'll manage again." Troy grimaced. "Somehow."

"'Somehow' isn't going to cut it," I hissed. "Will we manage, or do I need to call the rest of the alliance and tell them to prepare for damage control?"

"Stop bickering," Noah cut in. "You two are worse than djinn. There are enough vampires here to do a group glamour. If the elves can manage the video, we'll handle the mundanes.

You just need to find Torsten and make him disappear so there's no vampire suspect for the humans to prod at or jog memories. We might be Revealed now, but we can still manage a cover-up."

"Okay." I tried to keep the overwhelming relief from showing in my face or voice. I should have asked Noah how they'd deal with it to begin with. "Sounds like a plan."

Troy ran both hands through his hair as he looked at the ceiling, his expression suggesting that he was trying to think of any other way out of this. Finally he said, "I'll go check on the security footage."

I scowled at his back as the door swung shut behind him then jumped when Noah put a hand on my arm.

"Don't worry about Monteague," he said. "You're doing fine."

That nearly made me crumple in relief, but I gritted my teeth and locked my knees. "Thank you. I appreciate that."

Nodding, Noah cleaned the knife as best he could and handed it back, the hilt wrapped in one of the tiny hand towels rolled up on the sink. "I tore the wound up enough that this shouldn't be a match, but probably best you find a new knife," he said.

I accepted it then dropped it in the hamper and covered it with the towel. "This is supposed to be a murder investigation. Finding a knife means they won't be looking for fangs."

"Good point."

Noah's calm was starting to rub off on me. Maybe it was a passive effect of glamour. My mind was still running at a hundred miles per hour, but I was focused rather than freaked out. Considering angles, looking at the scene like the private investigator I was trained to be, thinking of the questions. "His ribcage," I said, stomach turning. "If we're saying I found him, it needs to look like I tried CPR."

"What does that have to do with his ribcage?"

311

I knelt next to the body and steeled my courage. There was no going back from this. "Done properly, CPR will crack the sternum or at least a few ribs. It needs to look like I tried to save him. A human with my training would."

Leaning forward, I tilted the corpse's head back, pinched the nose, and breathed into its mouth to make sure my DNA was present. Then, gagging, I did chest compressions, pushing the heel of my palm down hard until there was a crack.

"There." I rose, wiping my mouth with another one of the fancy towels and leaving it on the counter. Better the mundanes looked to me for answers than anyone else who might have left evidence in this bathroom today. I grabbed another and pressed it hard against the dead man's neck to make it look like I'd tried to stop the bleeding as well. "Now for means, motive, and opportunity. Opportunity is clear. Means is covered." I indicated the hamper. "We have witnesses that saw this guy leave with Torsten. What's the motive?"

"If Torsten's dead, does it matter?"

I blinked at Noah's pragmatism. "You're really okay with the fact that we have to put your master down like a rabid dog?"

"All things come to an end, and his has been a long time coming. The coterie is fragile because of his lack of leadership." He fixed me with a hard stare. "Maria holds us together. If something happens to her, that's when we'll have a problem."

"Understood." The statement left me chilled but understanding what his attitude problem had been at the bar the other night. "You should probably get out of here. Best not to have any vampires present when the cops arrive."

Noah nodded slowly. "Callista would never have offered herself up like this. I'm glad we have you."

He ghosted out as I choked up in gratitude.

My phone buzzed in my purse, and I pulled it out.

Video and security staff handled. Call the cops, Troy had texted.

I did so after making sure that everything about the corpse was as it had been when I found him—the angle of his head, the wallet in his pocket. Given that there were police units stationed outside the hotel for crowd control, it didn't take them long to arrive. I'd deleted my messages to and from my co-conspirators, exited the bathroom, and was leaning against the wall with both hands visible when they hustled forward. My jaw was tight as I prayed to the Goddess that the vampires and elves had had time to do their mind tricks.

I recognized the man at the front of the pack of humans. "Detective Rice. I'd say it was good to see you again, but…" I grimaced.

"Ms. Finch. I'm not sure I like you calling in a body right after the last odd case, with some bullshit about vampires playing all over the news." The big, buff cop stopped in front of me, looming, as a pair of EMTs darted past us into the men's room. A hint of meringue followed them, and I calmed enough to answer the detective.

"I don't love it either." I bit my tongue to keep from babbling. I might have grown accustomed to dealing with mundane police, but we were at a turning point in history. Now was not the time to give something away.

"You wanna tell me what happened?" He asked after a moment of waiting for me to elaborate, pulling out a notepad and a pen. "On the record, of course."

"Of course."

"Start with what you're even doing here at all. I wouldn't have thought a local PI would have much overlap with what I've seen of the attendees."

"Sure. I'm on a case. Tailing a stalker for the hostess." I described Torsten, hoping I wasn't digging a grave for myself or the vampires. "He slipped out in the uproar."

"So you thought it was appropriate to go into the men's room looking for him?"

I shrugged, heart pounding. "I mean, he is a man. If he wasn't there, I needed to find him fast, not wait around to see if he came out."

"I see," Detective Rice frowned. "And the dead guy?"

"I saw a hand when I peeked. Went in. Found the vic. My guy was nowhere in sight. Tried administering CPR, but the vic was already past saving. Called y'all."

I shut my mouth again, tried to figure out what to do with my face, and settled on a rueful grimace. Maybe he'd commiserate. Over Rice's shoulder, Troy slipped around a corner, halting when he saw me cornered by the detective. I could smell the Aether rolling off him from here; he'd just done some heavy work. When he saw me looking, he nodded. I hoped that meant we were as covered as we could be.

The EMTs came out of the bathroom.

"He's deceased, although it looks like someone attempted CPR," the first one said. He had dark hair and blue eyes and seemed weak in Aether to me. A low-blood branch of House Sequoyah or Monteague, maybe.

"Thoughts on how he died?" Rice asked.

The second EMT, a small woman who looked like a high-blood Luna, said, "The stab wound in his neck probably did it."

Detective Rice glared at me. "You didn't mention that, Ms. Finch."

"You didn't get there in your questioning, Detective."

Both elves stiffened on hearing my name, glancing at Troy. Rice followed their attention, and Troy strode forward so quickly it seemed he'd already been in motion by the time the detective had spotted him.

"Stop, sir, this is an active police investigation." Rice held up a hand to forestall him.

"Just checking on my date." Troy smiled warmly and extended his hand. "Troy Monteague. Everything okay here?"

It was a good thing the detective was looking the other way because the elven EMTs looked almost as startled as I did. *Goddess save me. When he commits to something, he really commits.* I glanced at the EMTs, giving a quick shake of negation upon finding their eyes hard on me. *Not real. I'm not trying to steal your precious prince.*

"Your date." Rice's tone was flat, and he stepped back so that he could see me and Troy both. "You failed to mention a date, Ms. Finch. I don't like the number of surprises I'm already encountering with you."

I shrugged. "It was a cover. Not pertinent to the investigation." Glancing at Troy, I added, "It's okay. He knows I'm here looking for someone."

A muscle twitched in Troy's cheek. "Got it."

"And what do you do, Mr. Monteague? How do you really know Ms. Finch, here?" asked Detective Rice.

"Private security." Troy fell into the blank face and parade rest stance that was more normal for him. "Contracted for the event. I was assigned to Finch and asked to keep a low profile while she investigated a potential problem."

Detective Rice eyed him warily, not looking at all happy about his transformation from amiable date to possible threat. "That, I believe." Turning halfway back to me, he said, "You said you were here for the hostess. Did you know anything about this announcement?"

"Nope." I widened my eyes and lifted my eyebrows, going for innocently shocked. "Helluva thing to say to a packed room of people with several million social media followers between them, huh?"

My mouth dried as silence stretched between us.

The EMTs shifted to make space for another elfess in a CSI jacket and, to my surprise, Doc Mike.

"Hey, Doc," I said with a genuine smile. "They called you out personally for this one?"

He smiled back as we shook hands. "Lots of hullabaloo given what's on the news, so yes. What are you doing here?"

"You know me...being nosy." I grinned wider in spite of myself.

Doc Mike had wanted to play his part for Otherside, and I'd doubted him the first time he'd said so. But here he was, coordinating with the rest of us as smoothly as though he'd always been an Othersider. He had, but he just hadn't known it. Knowledge made the difference, and he was handling it well now that he'd had time to settle into it.

Rice's attention sharpened. "You seem to know an awful lot of people around here, Ms. Finch."

Doc Mike flashed his eyebrows at me and followed the elven CSI into the bathroom. I relaxed despite the detective's suspicion. So far, everyone we needed was where they needed to be, except Torsten.

"I worked the body theft case, remember? I had to talk to Dr. Miller as part of my investigation." I tipped my head and pulled my face into a concerned look. "Sorry, Detective, but if you've got this under control, I need to go back to my case."

Rice tapped the pen against his notepad.

Troy's attention sharpened, and the scent of Aether grew cloying enough that even the mundane detective wrinkled his nose.

"Something isn't lining up here, Ms. Finch, but I have a feeling I'm gonna have a hell of a lot more to deal with if vampires capture the public imagination." The detective scoffed, rolling his eyes. "Vampires. Next I'll hear about werewolves. Fucking B-movie bullshit up in here."

I rubbed my neck to cover a shake of my head at Troy when he tensed and said, "Who knows. We good?"

"For now. Stay in town though. I have a funny feeling about this case." He gave me a hard look, like it was somehow my fault, then headed for the ballroom.

Chapter 37

I waited until he was out of sight to let myself slump and give in to the shallow breaths of panic. My hands shook so hard I thought they'd rattle off, and I clenched them into fists.

Troy stepped in close, more like he was trying to hide me from passersby than threaten me. "Can you handle this, Finch?"

Resisting the urge to embrace Air, I straightened and met his questioning gaze. "I can do whatever I have to do. Never forget that."

Rather than getting defensive, Troy's expression eased, and he nodded. "Good. Then I'll tell the Captain and the Conclave this was worth the risk when they haul me in for debriefing. Let's go find Torsten. I spotted him with a woman on the security feed. Might be our succubus."

That was a relief. Air currents were difficult enough to read in buildings as busy as hotels even under normal circumstances. People were always going from rooms to restaurants to amenities to bars, air conditioning was running on overtime, and staff were bouncing around between it all, doing their quiet, underappreciated work. With the additional movement and agitation generated by an earth-shattering revelation and a police investigation, it was impossible for me to figure out where Torsten or Dominique might have gone after our victim had been drained.

"That detective is going to be a pain in the ass," Troy grumbled as he led the way.

I trotted to keep up with his long, fast stride as we headed for the elevator. "We'll deal with him when we have to."

"What happens when we find him?"

"You're asking me?"

"You're in charge, whether my people like it or not." He pushed the down button with a little more force than necessary.

It took more effort than I'd ever admit not to straighten from my position or squirm where I stood. After a quick glance to make sure we were alone, I whispered, "We have to assume that he's either a rakshasa running from an unsanctioned human kill, under Dominique's influence, or both. In any case..."

My courage failed.

"If he's so far gone to reason that he's abandoning corpses in public venues, you know what that means," he said.

Writing Torsten off as a lost cause was one thing. Taking the action to remove him ourselves was another thing entirely, something that should have fallen to the vampires. My stomach churned, and I couldn't help looking down and picking at a fingernail.

"Finch."

Troy and I looked at each other. Even with the bond muted, we read each other's minds.

"I know," he said. "You don't want to do it, and I can't do it without breaking a separate treaty and nearly three decades of my queen's work."

"Is there any way to keep him rational, then?"

To his credit, Troy thought about it. His grimace said it all. "Not in time to keep a roomful of mundane influencers alive and not without sacrificing Maria or giving him enough of your blood that we'd be shooting ourselves in the foot after your donation to her."

"Fuck." I pinched the bridge of my nose, trying to stem the rising headache. I suddenly missed being just a simple private investigator, one that only dealt with humans and their mundane issues.

The elevator finally arrived, and we stood aside to allow some well-dressed folks pass.

When the doors were shut behind us, I said, "So, for Maria to stop Torsten, she'd have to fight him. She might be able to manage with my blood, but the alliance can't risk her being injured. We—"

"Have an option. One you're refusing to consider."

I frowned. "What the hell are you talking about? I don't—"

The look he gave me dove into my soul and froze it solid. "You do see. You know what has to be done."

Blood fled my face so fast I wavered on my feet, turning it into a step out of the elevator as we reached our floor and whirling on him. "You can't be serious."

Troy stepped close. His gaze deadened by degrees until it looked like there was nobody home, the same look he'd had when he'd trapped and tagged me in Chapel Hill, and later when he'd thrown me in Jordan Lake with a concrete block tied to my ankles.

"Goddess," I breathed. "Is that what you really are? An assassin?"

"I'm whatever I need to be." Emotion had washed from his voice.

"There has to be—"

"There isn't. Stop making this difficult for yourself. Make the choice and move on."

I stared at him. "Monteague…"

"What?" Troy took a step closer, so I had to crane my neck all the way back to look up at him, and spoke in a voice I could barely hear. "This is what power means, Finch. Difficult choices.

Ugly choices. Making those choices and deciding which tools to use."

"You would be a tool. For me." I couldn't keep the bemusement from my voice even as I wondered if this was part of why he wanted out so damn bad.

Troy tilted his head. "Haven't we already had this conversation? You know the answer to that."

"I don't—Will you stop looming like that?" I flushed at the outburst and fisted my hands, ready to fight him if he laughed outright.

A smirk broke the cold blankness of his face, and he took a half step back. "As you wish, Arbiter."

The title hit me like a slap, making his point all over again. "Don't call me that," I snapped. "Especially not here."

Chatter from down the hall alerted us to more hotel guests, and we stepped into the corner, playing the cute couple again. A disapproving throat-clear from the direction of the elevator suggested it was working.

"It's what you are," Troy said when the doors had shut again. "You don't get to claim the title when it suits you and abandon it when it's difficult. Every queen-in-waiting learns—"

"I'm *not* a fucking queen of anything, so don't you dare." Embarrassment at my own hypocrisy sharpened my response. That statement was exactly what I'd thought about him, back when he didn't want me throwing his princely title in his face: that it was a privilege to decide not to be what you were.

Troy's smirk twitched a degree wider.

"Stop laughing at me." My blood boiled. I clenched my fists as though I was physically holding onto my magic.

"As you wish." His face stilled as he buried his amusement, but I knew he was still enjoying this entirely too much. "The point stands. You have an option, and you have the necessary loopholes to execute it."

"To execute Torsten. Ugh." I crossed my arms and looked down at my feet, a cold nausea flaring in my neck and throat. Troy's nearness was necessary for us to talk privately, but I felt trapped. What would it say about me if I went through with this? Was there any other way? Did I know enough about Otherside to see it when an elven prince who'd been trained to intrigue didn't?

As a private investigator, I'd learned base human nature. Torsten had struck me as power-hungry and arrogant but not cruel. Vampires had been human once. Some adapted; some didn't. Torsten had lasted a millennia, suggesting that he'd adapted better than most.

While I wanted to believe that he hadn't intended to kill the influencer, my understanding was that becoming a rakshasa was like rabies. The longer we waited, the more dangerous he'd get. All of Otherside hung in the balance now that the vampires were known to humanity and the mundane cops were involved in a murder investigation—one that was ultimately down to Torsten's actions. Could we afford to find out whether rakshasas could be managed? Did any of us have the time or resources?

"Finch?"

"I'm *thinking*," I said.

"Think faster. We don't have time for this."

My head snapped up, and I went onto my toes to whisper in his ear. "There's always time not to be an asshole. Especially when *murder* is on the table. You can't reverse that."

Pain flickered behind his eyes when I leaned back to glare up at him, taking me aback with its depth. "I know. Trust me, of all people, *I know.*"

Tension quivered in every line of his body.

I started to say something rude then remembered what he'd said about letting Javier die when he chose to pull me out of Jordan Lake. Another elf had later died at Troy's hand as preemptive blood payment for the first. In a week's time, Troy had murdered an ally to fulfill the mission against Leith then his little sister's crush to avenge that ally. He'd also helped me against the remaining Redcaps when the odds were heavily against us. I was standing here because he'd made three hard choices rather than falling in line with prejudiced laws.

"I'm not just sending you off as a tool," I said, heart twisting as I made my decision. If I was going to order a thing done, I had to be willing to do it myself or at least to see it done. Having Torsten murdered for something that wasn't really in his control would kill a piece of me, but I could deal with that later, in the safety of the woods at the Eno River.

There really couldn't be any other way if neither Troy nor I could see it now. Maria might have the strength to finish Torsten since drinking from me, but the timing was such that we couldn't wait for the Reveal to be over and hope that there would be time for a dominance battle or hope that one of the Modernists wouldn't challenge her while she was weakened from the fight.

Troy scowled and took a step back. "You're not coming with me."

"Like hell I'm not."

"Finch…" He pinched the bridge of his nose like finding patience was an effort. "You've become a general in a growing army. The Wild Hunt is coming. You might become the single strongest entity in the Triangle with Callista gone and the only one who can really do anything about the Hunt. But only if you're alive."

"Nice try. If we're doing this, I'm coming."

Troy stared through me, thinking without seeing me. "That changes how I can approach this."

"You saying it wouldn't be easier with an elemental as bait?"

He focused on me so suddenly I had to fight not to take a step back into the wall. "You'd do that?"

323

"Would it help?"

"Immensely. But it means you risk getting bitten or taking a knick from me."

"Just a knick. Not killed?"

The smirk resurfaced then melted into seriousness. "I'll try my best."

My stomach flip-flopped at the note of something that sounded protective in his voice. "Fine. What's your plan?"

"I take you to Torsten and tell him I want to renegotiate the treaty between his coterie and House Monteague," he said slowly, as though he was expecting objections.

"And what, my blood is the sweetener?"

"Exactly."

"Okay." I inhaled hard and exhaled slow. "Let's do it."

"I need my knife first."

I shivered at the thought that I was really going to trust him to do this then nodded. Callista had lied to me my whole life. She'd tried for Troy when there was more for him to gain by betraying me, and he'd been steadfast. Still, he was who he was, and I was what I was. It was all I could do to swallow the words "Don't make me regret this" and follow him to his room, waiting outside as he got what he needed. My phone kept going off with texts from Noah, Allegra, and Vikki, updating me on what was happening—which was, so far, a whole lot of nothing as far as Otherside was concerned. Most of the humans still thought vampires were a silly hoax and were more intrigued by the murder investigation.

My earlier ease with Troy vanished as we approached the room he'd seen on the security footage. We exchanged a glance. At his lifted eyebrows, I gritted my teeth and jerked my head in a nod. His hand closing around the back of my neck made me shudder as our playacting became a little too real and triggered a memory from the boathouse at Jordan Lake.

"Don't," I whispered shakily when he let up. "Make it real."

Instead of answering, Troy tightened his grip again and pounded on the door twice.

After a pause, the door swung open to reveal a gorgeous woman with ivory skin and midnight hair, built like the Venus of Willendorf. She inhaled deeply, taking our scents as magic swirled around her.

I stiffened with shock, and Troy's hand on my neck tightened.

"Hello, Arden," she said in a voice as smoky-sweet as good barbeque sauce.

I recognized it and the scent of jasmine. "Dominique."

"You remember me!" She clapped, delighted, and eased away from the door with enviable grace. The lapis-blue gauze draping her flowed with her movement. "I wondered if Callista had beaten the memory out of you. I warned her she might have, but she has such faith in your abilities."

Troy propelled me in, letting the door shut behind us with the firm silence of doors in quality hotels everywhere.

More memories assaulted me, leaving me shuddering and breathless enough that I probably looked exactly as scared as I should be if I was Troy's captive for real. Callista had been furious. I'd been in pain for days afterward, given that that had been my first taste of her bronze nail punishment and I healed human-slow from the beating. Something about Dominque's voice and scent brought it all back from where I'd hidden it in a corner of my mind.

"Where is Torsten?" Troy said in a threatening growl as he drew his knife from a sheathe between his shoulder blades. "I saw him with you on the security cameras. I came to make a deal with him."

"No, I don't think you did." Dominique tilted her head and smiled. "Even if you're telling the truth, you're quite obviously too late."

Chapter 38

The scene awaiting us when we entered the main part of a suite that copied mine was not what I'd expected. Torsten sprawled on the bed, his head hanging off the foot, looking blissful.

"Doesn't look like it," Troy said.

Dominique smiled as though he was foolish as hell. "Then you know nothing of my kind. Torsten is dead. He just doesn't know it yet. But come, put the knife down, my prince. Your reputation precedes you, but we all know this whole thing is a farce. I have far more interesting business."

I hissed as the knife pressed closer to my throat. The threat of present danger brought me out of a past I'd conquered, and my brain cleared and focused.

"Torsten still looks alive to me," Troy said. "Save him. Or don't. But I could still give this bitch to the Conclave if you won't make a deal."

Rolling her eyes, Dominique focused on me. "Tell him."

The blade scraped under my chin as I swallowed. Could Torsten be saved? I didn't know. What I did know was that we didn't have the power here. My voice shook as I said, "Monteague, let's hear her out."

Instead of listening to me, he pulled the knife away, kicked my knees just hard enough to drop me, wrenched my head back by my hair, and repositioned the blade.

My pulse thudded under metal warmed by the heat of my body, and my mouth went dry. Had I miscalculated? I held myself very fucking still.

"I'm under oath, Bordeaux," Troy said.

"To her, I imagine, which is why you're playing this up so much." The twinkle in Dominique's eye suggested she appreciated the theatre, even as she dismissed it. "As intrigued as I am by the idea of the prince of House Monteague swearing himself to an elemental, I have larger concerns. You want something? I may be able to get it for you. Or something better."

I scarcely breathed as Troy considered that. On the bed, Torsten rattled a breath—unusual, given that vampires didn't need to breathe. We didn't have much time left if the idea was to save him. I still wasn't convinced that murder was the best option. We hadn't even asked Maria what she wanted.

Troy let me go so suddenly that I gasped. By the time I found my feet and summoned a furious glare, he'd sheathed his blade and was in a parade rest, hand clasped behind him, looking at me as though waiting for me to give an order.

Dressing him down in front of Dominique would weaken our already shaky position, so I resolved to bitch him out later and focused on the succubus.

"Why did Callista send you?" I crossed my arms to hide how badly I was shaking at what might have been a bad end to this night and avoided looking at Torsten.

Dominique's smirk suggested she saw through me, but she didn't comment on it. "To make sure Torsten became a full rakshasa, get him to kill a human, and be discovered."

She smiled broadly, looking pleased.

I blinked, not having expected that honest of an answer. "Which you did, minus the obvious discovery?"

She shrugged. "Even with Callista suddenly and inexplicably gone, I don't know that she's dead. I needed to satisfy the terms of my bondage while leaving you enough of an opening that you could pull a save out of your ass. If you didn't, I could leave with my mission accomplished. If you did, you'd be worthy of my request."

Sighing, I resisted the urge to close my eyes and scrub a hand over my face. Another Othersider with a request. That might be my job now, but could folks not ask me for shit all at the same time? "What's that then?"

"I want out."

"Out of where?" I flashed from hot to cold at the implications. "The Triangle?"

"The whole bloody plane," Dominique snapped, her expression darkening. "I've served Callista since the French Revolution. Two hundred and twenty years of bowing and scraping to that bitch. Doing her bidding. Spying and murdering for her. It's enough. I want to go home."

Troy shifted beside me. "You need a cover story."

Dominique shook her head, beautifully furious. "I need to be dead. An elemental was too much to pass up, especially one as powerful as our darling Arden here is rumored to be. An elemental and an elven prince together?" She batted her lashes and tilted her head, seduction incarnate. "Much too good a chance to pass up. What with you in my debt and all."

In her debt? It was outrageous, but I gritted my teeth and forced myself to acknowledge that if she'd been able to compel Torsten over a cliff even with my blood in him, she could have compelled him to lose his shit in a ballroom full of people, rather than just the bathroom. That raised a question. "How'd you get to a master vampire, anyway?"

"You'd ask a girl to give up her secrets?"

I scowled. "For what you're asking us to do? Yes. Spill."

Dominique's eyes glittered much like Callista's had when she was pissed. "I'm not sure I like your tone."

"I'm not sure I like your request." I kept my voice low and slow. I needed to be in charge here. "But you came to me for help. If you don't want it, then you can deal with the alternative."

The succubus gave me a long, slow look up and down. One that suggested that fighting or fucking were equally possible resolutions if she didn't get what she wanted.

Summoning a confident smile in the face of my racing heart, I added, "Callista may be gone, but if you're sworn to her, you're not free until Artemis tires of playing with her. Who knows how long a goddess's interest might last?"

The scent of jasmine rose in the room. Magic swirled, skating over my skin like silk and promising pleasures I could barely dream of if I would only let it in.

I pulled on Air until even I could smell the ozone scent of my magic in the room, afraid I'd miscalculated.

Troy's longknife was in his hand faster than my eye could follow him drawing it, and the scent of burnt marshmallow lodged in the back of my throat.

The three of us stared at each other. Only her eyes moved, shifting between Troy and me.

Tension grew as Dominique drew herself up and Troy twitched his blade. I drew Fire into the mix, letting lightning crackle across my knuckles like a coin.

Then the jasmine and silk retreated, and Dominique was all smiles and flirtation again, as though the moment hadn't happened.

"What can I say? Torsten's instability was already known to Callista, as was his preference for exotic blood." She rolled her eyes mockingly on the word "exotic" and tossed her hair. "He was more powerful than I was expecting for one as far gone as he was supposed to be, but glamour is no match for the old magic to be found in sex and wine. Especially when wielded by a demon."

Her demure smile didn't fool anyone, not with her eyes bled to full black and leathery, ethereal wings suddenly visible over her shoulders as shadow filled the room.

I shuddered. We'd all assumed that succubae and incubi were fae. If they were demonkin, we'd just gotten lucky. Very lucky. I glanced at Troy to find him looking at me, as though for orders. As much as I appreciated the confirmation that we were in fact still on the same side, it was weird. Having an elf look to me made me uncomfortable. Even if we were allies. Especially when that elf had come here prepared to commit murder on my say-so.

Refocusing on the situation at hand, I said, "There's no saving Torsten?"

"None." Dominque smiled like a crocodile, all teeth and no remorse.

I glanced at the master vampire. He'd gone rigid, no longer gasping for breath but now leaking blood from eyes and ears. It trailed down his face, too dark to be oxygenated. Goosebumps raced over my skin, and I jumped as the air conditioning clicked on, doing nothing to help the reek of dead, rotting blood.

The knowledge that it would take more of my own blood than I was willing to offer decided me. "You get rid of Torsten. Then you get the fuck outta town."

"It has to look like there was a fight. I won't risk Callista escaping and coming after me for breach of contract. Nobody can know about this. As far as anyone is concerned, I'm dead." Dominique squared her shoulders and offered her arm.

Troy and I exchanged another look. I sighed and drew the godblade from its thigh sheathe, ignoring Troy stiffening in disapproval and Dominique's interest.

The succubus didn't flinch as I slashed her arm with Neith's gift and flicked blood from the blade to the baseboard, where it could look like we'd missed a spot in a hurried cover-up. A strange little laugh echoed in my mind, and the blade sparked, much like my elf-killer did when I fed it elven blood.

Ignoring it to deal with another time, I drew even harder on Air. "Both of you, stand as close to me as you can."

When Troy was pressed against my back and Dominique to my front, I spun bursts of Air at random, toppling the lamps, shifting the nightstand, and generally making it look like a barroom brawl had taken place.

When the room was trashed, I let my power go, hoping I hadn't done so much that I'd need a drink to counter the power hangover. We had too much to do for me to be fighting brain-splitting headaches and gut-wrenching nausea. Torsten had slid from the bed and was half on the floor, neck broken, looking true-dead with silvered eyes, withered skin, and brittle hair. Dominique looked lovelier than ever, as though Torsten's death had completely renewed her. I shuddered.

"You're not even winded." Dominique stepped back, looking as though she imagined her pun clever. "Well done, lovely."

"You need to go," I snapped.

"One last thing, since you were so helpful. He had words, before he was past using them." She tilted her head toward the vampire. "Would you hear them? They might mean something to one of you."

Troy and I nodded in unison, and the succubus smiled mischievously. "He said, 'The House of Jade and the House of Onyx are the keys to Ragnarok.'"

I frowned and shook my head, not understanding. "Thank you, but—"

"That's impossible," Troy interrupted. When I glanced at him, he was as pale as I'd ever seen him. "The House of Onyx is gone."

Dominique looked at me and smiled, slow and sweet. A bone-deep chill settled in me as she said, "Is it now? Are you certain?"

"Quite," Troy said.

I pulled my shields in as tightly as I could, walling myself away from Troy just in case shock let the block on our bond dip. Troy had a green pendant in the same style as mine and the one I'd taken from Leith when I killed him. It could have been jade.

And mine, now nestled safely in my nightstand, was onyx.

"How unfortunate for all of us, then," Dominique said with a smile that suggested it was anything but. "I suppose we'll have to find another way to face the return of the gods. In any case, be careful, Arden. Very careful. Callista always feared you."

"Bullshit," I said before I could stop myself.

"Why else would she seek to control you, to use you so thoroughly?"

A pounding started on the door before I could think of an answer.

"Master?" Maria's voice called.

"Take Torsten and go," I hissed to Dominique. "I don't want him found. Ever. When it's done, be on the next flight out of RDU. I don't care where it goes. Troy, escort her. Please," I added as his chin lifted.

"Yes, Arbiter." He glanced at the door as Maria knocked again.

"Pleasure doing business," Dominique said. "But I won't need any mundane craft, or an escort, to leave this place."

Before I could ask why not, her hand flashed toward my face faster than I could track it. As I stumbled backward, she knicked my left cheek with a sharp fingernail and smeared blood from her arm on the other cheek then knelt as Maria's knocking became a pounding.

Sucking my blood from her finger, she said, "With this exchange of blood I forsake my bonds and pledge my services to thee, Arbiter Arden Finch of the Triangle, mistress mine." Rising, she gathered Torsten's remains before turning back to me. "Now banish me, work a little more magic to cover that of my exit, et voila."

We didn't have time for me to ask questions if we were going to get her gone before Maria broke the door down or someone else came to find out what was wrong.

"I banish this succubus to whatever place or plane she calls home, not to return to this place or plane whether by wish or by summons for a year and a day." I used the djinn form and prayed it worked on succubae. I prayed harder that nobody would try to summon her back.

With a blown kiss, she twisted into the white nothingness that was the Crossroads and was gone. Torsten's corpse disappeared along with her, though the stench of old blood and damp ash remained.

"Go," I said to Troy, mouth dry. Succubae really were demons, or demon-adjacent, if she could do that. "Wait. Hit me first. We're supposed to have had a fight in here. As far as Maria's concerned, you're getting rid of evidence."

"If you say so," he replied dispassionately.

Even knowing it was coming, I wasn't prepared for the blow. The suckerpunch to my gut winded me and folded me in half. The knee to the face that followed broke my nose and dumped me on my ass, eyes tearing. He'd pulled both moves, even if they did human-level damage and hurt like hell. Before I could get a swear out, the sliding glass door to the patio opened and shut, telling me he'd gone.

I pushed to my feet and went to let Maria in, pinching my nose to stop the blood.

"Arden! Where is my master?" she snarled as soon as the door was shut behind her, Noah, and Allegra. The scent of my blood hit all three of them hard, sending pupils dilating.

Maria shook herself. "I can't find him, it's like he's—"

"Dead? He is. The succubus killed him, and I killed her," I said, blood from my broken nose spilling over my lips and the lie burning like acid on my tongue. "She admitted that Callista assigned her to make a mess of the Reveal before I got rid of her. She was under oath."

Noah and Allegra stood with grim faces. The vampires' eyes bled to full black, and a whiff of burnt marshmallow scented the air.

This would be tied to me—taint me—for the rest of my days because I could never reveal the secret. My stomach twisted into a painful knot as I realized that meant it would always be between Troy and me, leverage he could use if and when it pleased him to shift to someone else rather than follow me.

Swallowing, I pushed past it and gritted my teeth to set my nose before my accelerated healing could kick in to leave it crooked, hissing from the pain as I did so. "She pushed Torsten over the edge. He drained a human and left the body where the public could find it. We can't have that. Definitely not now. But I also couldn't have anyone else interfering."

Maria froze with the utter, sudden abruptness of the undead. "Torsten is gone? True dead? You saw the corpse?"

I clenched my jaw and nodded as firmly as I could.

Noah and Allegra kept their attention on me, both in a fighting stance.

Maria looked me up and down. Took in the room. Inhaled to scent the air. A light filled her eyes. Hope. Possibility. Ambition. Emancipation. "Where's our Prince of Monteague? He was here. I smell Aether and herbs. Male sweat."

Allegra's attention sharpened at the question.

Her face blanked as I said, "Disposing of the evidence. As I told him to do."

"The elf answers to you then?" Maria took a clockwork step toward me.

"He does." The words came out raspier than I'd intended. It was true; I'd given an order, and Troy had obeyed without question. But this moment felt big, somehow. Like every word I said was one that would change the path forward.

Maria reached behind her. Noah gave her his hand, and she pulled him forward and stood as tall as her height would allow.

"I claim mastery of Torsten's coterie, with Noah as my second," she said with a fierceness that must have spilled from the depths of her soul.

"Thank the Goddess." I gave in to the tiredness dragging at me and released some of it with a heavy sigh as I sat down right there on the floor then flopped onto my back. "Because I sure as shit didn't want it."

Chapter 39

We agreed that, with all the big plays out of the way and the humans more inclined to drink than get out the pitchforks, we could hammer out terms in the morning. Going home felt premature, but Goddess knew I had enough other work to do now. Starting with a damn good night's sleep. Besides, I wasn't keen on Noah's overprotective glares becoming physical if I stuck around.

Troy was leaning against the driver's side door of my car when I got to it. I ignored him and popped the hatch, shoving the garment bag with the dress I'd changed out of into the back and dropping my laptop bag on top before slamming the hatch shut. It wasn't that I wanted to be rude. I just didn't know what the hell to do about him right now.

"How's your nose?" he asked as I came around, keeping himself in the shadows cast by the light overhead.

Tiredness and tension made me short. "Fine."

He didn't answer but stepped into the light to peer at me. "You set it. Good."

The echoes of a power hangover dragged at me. I pushed them aside, trying to get my attitude under control.

"Thanks for pulling the hit," I murmured, antsy and wishing he would move.

"We need you in one piece." He glanced over my shoulder.

I turned to see what had drawn his attention.

"Allegra," I said as she drew close. "The vamps are squared away? Vikki is settled?"

"As much as they can be, and yes, I sent Vikki home grumbling about missing all the action. Hovering will be seen as an overreach now that the threat is handled and there's a new Mistress in Raleigh," she said. "What the hell happened with the succubus?"

"We fought. She died," I said after a long silence. "Just like I told you."

Allegra looked at Troy but answered me. "Whenever someone says, 'Just like I told you' it usually means they're lying."

I didn't reply.

She took a step to the side so that she could see Troy better. "Is she lying, T?"

He didn't answer either.

"Is she?"

I stepped between them again. "Is that really the question you want to ask right now?"

Allegra's lips pressed together, and her eyes narrowed. "No. Mostly I wanted to see if Troy had finally found something—someone—worthy enough that he'd consider lying to me. From the look of things, he has."

I tensed, not daring to look at the elf prince making a thundercloud over my shoulder. "What would it mean for me if he had?"

"That you have me at your back as well, even if it's going to make both our lives hell. Package deal." Allegra's face smoothed, and she reached out to squeeze my arm, making it quick and pulling away before I could get uncomfortable. "Let's go, T. I want to do some more surveillance before we leave. The humans still haven't decided whether this is a hoax or not."

Guilt pulled me, playing tug-of-war with tiredness. "I can stay."

"You need to go home," Allegra said sternly. "Delegate, Arbiter. Troy and I were trained for this. You were trained for investigation. With the cops gone and Torsten dead, there's nothing to investigate. We'll handle this. You go plan where Otherside goes from here. I'd recommend starting with figuring out how to get the rest of the elves in line because Keithia won't let this slide."

I looked at the asphalt under my feet and ran a hand over my curls. "Yeah. Okay. Thanks, Allegra. Thank you both."

We stood there, all awkward as hell as I tried to find the words to ask the question that had plagued me since Dominique had spoken of it. "So, why did you say the House of Onyx was gone?"

Allegra's attention sharpened. "Where did you hear that phrase?"

"The succubus taunted us with it." Troy stiffened. "What do you know, Finch?"

I hugged myself. I'd been wanting for years to know the truth about my parents. Troy had known not only what the House of Onyx was but also that it was gone. Did he have more answers? My blood pounded, dizzying me.

"Finch." Troy tensed. "What do you know, and why does it scare you?"

"Stay out of my head." I turned to look the other way and tried to remember to breathe. When I had myself more under control, I half-turned so that I could see them both again. "What happened to the House of Onyx?"

Troy frowned. "I don't see what that has to do with—"

"Keithia destroyed them," Allegra said softly.

"Alli." Troy's tone held more than a hint of warning, heavy and dangerous.

Allegra ignored him. "Arden, the House of Onyx, the Solaris, were once the greatest in the Southeast. Maybe on the continent. They fell when their prince—" She froze, her gaze locking onto me with new intensity. "Oh Goddess. It can't be."

Troy tensed, looking for a threat. When he realized Allegra was looking at me, not past me, he frowned. "What, Alli?"

"Think. Why did House Solari fall?"

He started to answer, and then the same thought that had struck Allegra must have hit him too. I edged backward a step as he focused on me. "Arden, what did Leith take from your neck at the boathouse?"

I swallowed and clenched my fists to stop them from shaking.

"A pendant," I whispered.

Troy reached into the neck of his shirt and withdrew a silver chain, from which the silver-wrapped jade disk I'd seen before dangled. It looked just like the topaz disc wrapped in white gold that I'd taken from Leith—and the gold-wrapped onyx that usually hung around my neck.

"Does it look like this?" Troy asked, voice so tight it was strangled.

I nodded, once.

"But a black stone. Wrapped in gold?"

I nodded again, more sharply.

He scrubbed his hands over his face as Allegra started swearing in a soft but fervent voice.

"The djinn said it belonged to my father," I whispered.

Allegra's swearing increased in volume, and Troy stared at me, pale and shocked.

"You're supposed to be dead," he said in an empty voice. "The Darkwatch has the death certificate. The Solari heir was lost in the Cape Fear River."

I shook my head. "They found me in my mother's arms. I was put in foster care and raised by humans for the first seven years of my life until..." I frowned as a puzzle piece clicked into place, and I lowered my voice, checking to make sure the parking lot was empty. "Until Duke found me and brought me to Callista. But if the gods can't find a nymph, how did a djinni find a child in the mundane foster care system?"

A twinge of lemony, djinn-flavored Aether pulled me around with a hiss.

Troy followed my lead, and Allegra crouched as though to face an attack.

Duke half-materialized in the shadows, where he wouldn't be seen. "Because I knew where you were to begin with," he said. The pain in his carnelian eyes warred with the mocking laughter in his face. "And now, you know. Ironic that it's the Monteagues who free me from that particular geas, given that they were ultimately the cause of it."

The bottom fell out of my stomach, and my head spun. "What?"

"Congratulations on finding the truth," Duke said bitterly. "Your name was never Finch. We just picked a bird because Air was the first of your powers to manifest. But you were born Arden of House Solari, the only child of the elven prince Quinlan Solari, sired on the djinni known as Ninlil. May the knowledge bring you joy, cousin."

With a last, cruel smile, he vanished.

I stood there, shaking so hard that I had to sit on the rear bumper of my car. One thought clamored for attention.

"Keithia killed my parents?" I whispered to the asphalt between my feet.

When neither Troy nor Allegra answered, I looked up to find them looking almost as shocked and stricken as I felt. Troy looked absolutely sick.

"Was Duke telling the truth?" I asked, more forcefully. "Answer me!"

"Yes." Troy sounded like the word had been dragged from him. "The Solaris are referred to as the Lost Ones, but it's not that we lost track of them. It's that they lost their way, or at least that's how we tell the story. Their prince… A djinni came to him. She said she'd had a vision. The Wild Hunt was coming. The only way to see its end would be for Otherside to unite. Starting with them."

Hot tears burned as they filled my eyes. "I can't believe this."

"I don't know how long it took her to convince him," Troy continued, as though I hadn't spoken. "When my grandmother caught wind of it, the djinni—your mother?—was pregnant. Keithia gave the Solaris a week to kill her and her unborn child. They broke every law and all tradition. They protected them both. They'd bought into the djinni's tale."

I hunched in on myself, both wanting and not wanting to know more. I didn't want to think about the fact that the family of the only two elves I'd come to trust was responsible for so much of the pain and fear in my life.

He didn't stop, only sounding more hesitant as he lowered his voice to a whisper. "My grandmother allied with the Lunas to take on your father's House. It was a massacre. Your parents escaped, but they only made it to the Cape Fear River before the Monteague House Guard destroyed their car and sent the wreckage over a bridge. The river was in flood. Difficult to cross. Keithia proved herself worthy of taking the mantle of High Queen when she mortally wounded both your parents and left their bodies to the current."

Where humans found my dying mother and dead father. I swallowed past my gag reflex, breathing too shallowly to think straight, as I wondered if the meteoric iron blade that Troy carried was the same one that had killed my parents.

"When the last Solari was dead, the Lunas were elevated for their role in the hunt." Troy crossed his arms, looking anywhere but at me. "We all thought the heir was dead as well. There was a damn death certificate!"

Allegra hugged herself, her eyes full of pity as she looked at me. "If Keithia had realized who you were that first time you were at the Monteague family estate, you would never have walked out of there. Goddess have mercy, Troy, what the fuck do we do now? We can't—Keithia can't know."

I gathered my feelings and shoved them into a box to deal with later. I couldn't do this here or now. Not on the heels of the Reveal and not with these two. "Sounds like if you want the world not to end, you keep your mouths shut," I said harshly. "This stays between us until I figure out what the fuck to do about it. Understood?"

Both elves nodded, blank-faced as their natural inclination toward hierarchy kicked in and they followed my lead.

"I'll be in touch. Just…let's get through the Reveal. The humans are going to lose their shit sooner or later. We don't need more blood in the streets."

I forced myself to stand and backed away from them to the door of my car. They hadn't been responsible. Hell, they would have been small children at the time. But all I could think of just then was destroying their House. I was suddenly glad that Evangeline had decided to be such a pain in the ass. It gave me options that didn't require me to take a high road I was no longer sure I wanted to stay on. I fumbled for the car door handle, feeling numb all over.

"Finch…" Troy called.

I looked up at him, face stiff.

"Evie already sent people after you once before," he pointed out hesitantly. The muscle in his cheek twitched in the overhead light, and every line of him was tense.

I sighed and opened the car door. "I know. But I've already learned that if I live worried about that, I'll never have time for anything else. We're going to need a plan to get the best of Keithia and Evangeline without destroying Otherside as collateral damage. To do that, I need to go home and calm the fuck down before I do something we will all regret."

"I don't disagree."

"Then what are you saying?" My temper was fraying fast.

He crossed his arms again and glanced at Allegra, who was giving him a serious look, then met my eyes. "Let me re-open the bond. If she comes for you again, you might not have time to go for a phone."

I wondered if I looked as surprised as Allegra did just then. "You want to...what? Be able to come to the rescue? After what we just heard? What you just told me?"

"Yes," he said, jaw muscles bunching. "For what it's worth, I'm sorry for what happened, although that's nowhere near enough. My House owes you. If you're still willing to call us allies, then I will do what I can to start paying the debt."

Allegra whistled low and long then grimaced, looking guilty as hell.

"Me too, Arden, although sorry isn't nearly enough. Troy, find me when you're done," she called as she backed up and then jogged back toward the hotel, angling for the path that led around to the forested grounds.

Troy waved to acknowledge her but kept his attention on me. Six feet, two inches of lean, dangerous Darkwatch agent stared down at me, impassive in every way except for the pinch at the corners of his eyes.

The evening's bombshell aside, we'd only just come to an accommodation about boundaries, one that we'd both crossed in the last few days as needed. Could I trust him to stick to it? If I could, did I want him in my head again? The itch of paranoia every time he was within a half mile? Knowing that he could probably get a sense of not only where I was but what I was feeling?

No. Not really.

But I did want to survive.

Troy could have left the rabisu to tear me to shreds in my bed, but he'd come for me then. He'd come with me to fight Callista without question. He could have sided with Callista or betrayed me with Dominique just now, and he hadn't.

Keithia had killed my parents, not him.

I had to tell myself that twice more before I could breathe normally, but finally, it stuck. Being allies with him was getting harder and weirder, but it also kept me alive. Now that I understood how ugly my history with House Monteague was, I wanted one of them on my side as a safety measure. Why not take their prince? I liked the poetry of it. The vengeance.

"Fine," I said. "But you keep yourself to yourself. Our agreement about boundaries stands, or there's gonna be a freak wind event. Got it?"

"I'm a man of my word," Troy replied in a taut growl.

I gritted my teeth. "That's the only reason this is even open to discussion. Do it."

Before I could finish the sentence, Aether rippled off of him and the sense of his auratic signature echoed in the back of my mind again. He started to say something else, a pained expression tightening his face, but he pressed his lips together and strode off after Allegra without another word.

Shaking my head, I got into the car.

The drive home was both too long and too short with everything I'd accomplished in the last two weeks, all the ways I'd grown, and everything I'd learned.

I was the Arbiter now. The lich and his accomplice were both dead. I'd gained control of primordial powers unseen since Atlantis. Callista was gone, her power shattered, her base mine.

The vampires were Revealed, even if the humans weren't quite ready to believe it yet.

All the power players in the Triangle's Otherside community looked to me for action and answers—for now. That was terrifying, and I still wasn't sure that I was ready for it. But possibly most terrifying of all was the quiet rage burning in my heart and the knowledge that I now had enough power to right the wrongs committed against myself and anyone else.

The only question now was where to start.

Acknowledgments

Writing a book at any time can be difficult work. Writing a book during a pandemic, a contentious election year, and a time of social change is more so. I'm incredibly lucky to be in a position to keep writing and publishing, and appreciate the readers who have stuck with the series this far. Your investment in my stories, your time, your enthusiasm, and your reviews mean the world to me and help me keep going on the indie author journey. You have all played a role in my chasing a dream, and I'm forever grateful.

As I was wrapping up the last stages of the publishing process for this book, I received news that *Elemental* had won the Grand Prize for the Writer's Digest Self-Published E-book awards. It's wild to be recognized like that for a debut fantasy novel, and I will be forever grateful for those who took a chance on *Elemental* as an indie novel before it became an award-winner.

I can never understate how grateful I am for the support of my family, especially my parents and sister. You've always been my biggest cheerleaders and you've helped me introduce so many people to my stories. My extended family has also been incredibly supportive, and thanks go to them as well.

My editor, Jeni Chappelle, continues not only to help me deliver my stories in the best way possible, but also to be a spot of sunshine in the writing community.

More thanks also go to Stephanie, who has beta read all three books now and calls out so many things to make the story better.

All of my friends have been so supportive, but once again, I have to call out RSL. Whenever I am fortunate enough to have something to celebrate, she is the first one screaming her joy for my success to the heavens. We should all be so lucky to have friends like her to celebrate with us.

Also by Whitney Hill

The *Shadows of Otherside* series
Elemental
Eldritch Sparks
Ethereal Secrets
Ebon Rebellion (coming 2021)

The *Flesh and Blood* series (as Remy Harmon)
Bluebloods

Praise for *Elemental*

"Arden is a winning protagonist, pushing against PI stereotypes in small but telling ways, and the denizens of Otherside—particularly the vampires and djinn—have well-developed personalities. Hill also has a fine ear for dialogue and a good sense of timing, and the story builds steadily and believably, resulting in a genuine page-turner." —*Kirkus Reviews*

Praise for *Eldritch Sparks*

"...although Hill's worldbuilding will draw the reader in, it's the strong-willed, hard-boiled protagonist who will keep them engaged, as Arden's narration ties the speculative elements together and brings a sense of simmering urgency to the proceedings...A compelling book of Otherside that goes from strength to strength." —*Kirkus Reviews (starred review)*

About the Author

Whitney Hill writes award-winning adult fantasy with sizzle and soul from Durham, North Carolina. Her worlds feature the diversity she has lived as a biracial woman of color and former migrant to Europe. She draws on these life experiences to write characters drawing on inner strength to carve out a place for themselves.

Whitney also enjoys hiking in North Carolina's beautiful state parks and learning about world mythology.

Learn more or get in touch: www.whitneyhillwrites.com.
More books by Whitney: whitneyhillwrites.com/original-fiction/
Sign up to receive email updates: whwrites.com/newsletter

Join her on social media:
- Twitter: twitter.com/write_wherever
- Instagram: instagram.com/write_wherever
- Facebook: facebook.com/WhitneyHillWrites

Learn more about the publisher, Benu Media, at benumedia.com, or sign up to receive newsletters with the latest releases at go.benumedia.com/newsletter.

One Last Thing…

If you enjoyed this book, please consider posting a short review, recommending it on Goodreads or BookBub, or telling a friend who might also enjoy this story. As always, thank you for reading, and for your support!

CPSIA information can be obtained
at www.ICGtesting.com
Printed in the USA
LVHW092334150921
697901LV00002B/182

9 781734 422764